HANGDOG SOULS

Marc Joan

Deixis Press

First published in 2022 by Deixis Press
www.deixis.press
ISBN 978-1-7397081-0-8

Cover design by Libby Alderman
paperyfeelings.co.uk

Cover art based on an original mixed-media painting by Prasad Natarajan: 'Moon Cycle, Datura stramonium, Eucalyptus viminalis and Rose-ringed Parakeets', ©Prasad Natarajan 2022

Typeset using Garamond Premier Pro

☾

HANGDOG SOULS

Marc Joan

Deixis Press

❈

To my other, better and much longer-suffering half, Sue,
and our lovely children James and Sophie.

Thanks, all of you, for putting up with my long hours of writing.

ECHOES

SHAME'S ASPIC

"Tippoo ordered Ukalipt trees to be planted in great numbers, first in Nandy near Mysore, and later in the Nilgherries, those mountains which march almost to India's tip."
- An Eye-witness Account of the Kingdom of Tippoo Sahib
John Curry, 1803

Part I: The bloody sands

I call it a dream, but it is not. It is a memory that I remember when I am asleep.

When my sleeping self is taken by the dream, it is as though the recollection is more real than the reality in which my body sleeps. It is as though something says to me: Look – there you are, up to your fourteen-year-old shanks in the icy waters off St Cast, while the aide-major talks of *balance*. Just where you have always been, and shall be forever.

Yes, there I am: and the tide washes me bloody to the thighs with what it brings to shore.

While I dream, I hear the rumble of the Cauvery river, split by this island of Seringapatam; I smell the scents of Indian madder and moonflower, released by this Indian night; I feel the soft warmth of Usha's skin beneath my arm, the slow kiss of her breath against my cheek. The dream makes of these real things themselves only a dream. I sense that they are there, yet I cannot believe in them.

Look. He has developed a habit, the aide-major, in the thirty minutes since the British bomb-ketches have ceased firing on the shore; since the British fleet gave up the rescue of my stranded comrades. He wades through the Channel waters, searching for an Englishman too wounded to stand; such as he finds, he pulls back to the shallows where I kneel, the guard's musket barrel nuzzling my ear. Then he stops before me, holding some broken man-boy by the hair, so that my countryman must look at me. "*Allons,*" he says, wiping wet lips with thumb and finger. And then he pushes steel into the throat of his catch and saws away. He does it slow, and observes me all the while, mouth agape and eyes a-staring, as though I am an exquisite mirror for his cruelty; as though to see my comrades' last agonies reflected in my face makes his pleasure double. The sea's spume laps red.

Usha's breath catches; she turns to one side, and is all at once tense and quiet, as though listening. Perhaps our child has woken; perhaps he has called out in his sleep. Or perhaps Usha feels, through my lockjaw stillness, something of what I live through in the dream. Her hand rests on my shoulder. I feel it; but I do not believe it. And yet, in the dream I believe, I ask help from the dream I cannot believe. Usha! Bring me back ... My limbs cannot move; I cannot speak.

How many slow deaths does the aide-major show me, beneath that blue, blue sky? In some dreams it is five; in some, eighty-nine; in some it is incalculable.

Usha! Beware the Sultan's men and the brutality of Power; make not an enemy of that Mohan Lal who cannot die; keep my secret from those who would harm us; but, above all, my dear love, keep safe Kuruppan our child! Usha ...

It has come to this: that I ask my wife to protect my son and me. I do not know whether this is part of the dream that is real or part of the dream that is a memory; I am unmanned in both. But I know this: in the dream that is memory, the aide-major speaks to me, and I know what he says, though in those days I had no language but English. He says: *See, boy; the price of desertion, the price of cowardice, the price of running. You have your life, drummer boy; but now, for the rest of that life, you also have this.* The blade has caught on something, some sinew that resists, and the aide-major pushes and twists until it is released with a jerk. *It is a fair exchange, boy. A balanced transaction. Keep your worthless life, but keep too the memory of what you did for your fellow-soldiers of the 67th Regiment of Foot.*

I look up, away, anywhere: the sky is of a most profound blue, an uttermost blue, a blue that cannot, surely, know clouds; against it flaps the yellow standard of the aide-major's battalion. All yellow, that cloth, all yellow bar a central emblem: a black fleur-de-lys, like the heads of three cowled snakes fanning out from a common noose. It whips evilly in the sea's breeze. I am racked by a fearful spasm; musket to my ear or not, I turn double on myself; and my vomit too is yellow and black. The aide-major nods, and my guard pulls me upright by the shoulder. *Look.* Another throat to slit, another life to add to my tally of betrayal. No! Vauquelin, I beg you!

"Husband!" Usha is pulling at my upper arm. "Husband!"

I try to still my gasps; my throat is raw, as if from drinking bad arrack. I sit up; I run my hands through my hair; I rub my legs. Their flesh is cold, like a drowned man's.

"*Husband*, is it?" I pant. "An improvement over 'Kuruppan's father', indeed. I should be pleased." I say this in levity, to wash away the dream-memory's outrages, but there is some truth in my words. For whatever reason, I have never persuaded Usha to refer to me as Mr Saunders, still less Patrick; I am always identified indirectly. But I love her none the less for her strange habits, and she knows it. Anyway, perhaps it is for the best: if she does not call me Patrick Saunders in private, she will not do so in public, where I must be known as Patricio Sorondo, the Spaniard.

"You were shouting." Something about her tension, about the way she looks to the window – open to all the Kingdom of Mysore – chills me. "In another language."

I get up from the charpoy and walk to the window. It is past the darkest hour; the moon is full, and the sky clear. I see only what I know to be there. In one direction, the massy fort of Tippoo, Sultan of Mysore; it hunches its black angles upwards like an armoured beast born of earth. To the left of the fort, I see the curve of Mohan

Lal's rotunda, where, as always, a yellow light flickers. He is peering at the heavens, doubtless; does he never sleep? As little as the thing he keeps in his basket, by all accounts ... as little as the devils they say he conjures up by his dark machinery. Above the fort, the stars Lal covets wheel their mysterious courses, slow and fine. In another direction, closer by, I discern the white tumble of the Cauvery's flow; and closer still, extending from the river to our bungalow, in pots or buckets or heeled into loose soil in readiness for replanting – my trees, my Ukalypts, my future.

"There is nobody there," I say. "And in any case, it was probably Spanish that I spoke. Or Portuguese." And it probably was; I have not spoken English for many a year. But Usha has only Tamil; she would not distinguish my mother tongue from any other language.

"You said *Vauquelin*." She mispronounces the word, but I recognise it. And coming from her lips, the name is like a blow; it is as if the boss-eyed, blubber-lipped aide-major had stepped into the room and caught her by the hair. "When you were shouting, you said *Vauquelin*."

I shrug. "What of it? The speech of dreams. Go to sleep, my love." I feign a yawn. "Go to sleep."

"I will," she says. But she remains upright, watching me in the soft darkness.

"What is it, my dear?"

"You know what."

I take a deep breath, and turn again to the window. The moon bars the ground with silver. "A beautiful night," I say.

"And some beautiful night or beautiful day, when they find out you are English, they will kill you. But first they will kill Kuruppan and I, so that you may see it. Mohan Lal will make it so."

"After fourteen years, my dear, I think they are convinced that I am Spanish. As for Mohan Lal – I do believe, Usha, that he may be less ugly than the portrait given him by gossip, and in any case – "

"Less ugly? He of the black arts? He that has made it a labour of two lifetimes to defile all gods, and break the link between birth and death, and that delights in others' pain as others delight in cool water? No painting could make him foul enough! Please, husband, do not make of this family something that may interest him. Please." I open my mouth to speak, but she waves me into silence. "As for your fourteen years of hiding – you have said yourself that if one true Spaniard visits Tippoo Sultan's court, you are unmasked. And now that Tippoo begs aid from Britain's enemies – " Her voice fails; her hand moves to her mouth as if to offer assistance.

"Ah! There, I can offer encouraging news. It seems that Tippoo has not gone to the Spanish, but to Napoleon, who is sending a military advisor. That is, a Frenchman, not a Spaniard. His arrival is imminent." Usha merely looks at me. "Darshan told me," I add. And at this she nods, satisfied. For my part, I frown. It is true that scholarly Devadarshan knows more than this wandering planter, but even so – are my words of *no* value? But Usha, one hand a-twisting at her marriage necklace, has thought of another matter for argument.

"Suppose this person's advice provides no shield against British cannon – and you know how many now whisper of *defeat* – then what? If the British prevail, they will hang you, either as traitor or as deserter."

Indeed, the British advance is massive, and steady, albeit slow; few believe that Tippoo will withstand it. Hence all of Mysore is now like a pot slowly coming to boil. But I have an arrow to my bow; it is one I fletched myself, without Darshan's aid, and with only a little help from Benedito da Souza. It is time I show its point to Usha.

"Listen, my dear. Benedito told me news of a treaty between France and Spain. They join forces now, to fight the British. Thus, Tippoo's new advisor will be the natural ally of Patricio Sorondo. And I am convinced that, if I can only convey to him the value of my trees – and their unmatched qualities, which will be as new to him as they were to Mohan Lal – he will support my application to move sapling and seedling away from the coming battle. His advice will carry more weight among Tippoo's ministers than my oft-repeated words."

And who, surely, would disagree with such advice? All know of Mysore's appetite for timber. Fast-growing timber, that is: to power smithies and forges, to feed the cannon foundries of Kunnakapoor and fuel the gunpowder factories at Taramandalpet. And *straight-growing* timber, to construct factories for war-rockets and other cunning ordnance; to make, in short, the multifarious vehicles of death with which the Sultan goads the British and their Company. For the Kingdom of Mysore used what little straight timber it had many a year ago, during the wars fought by Tippoo and his father Hyder; in fact, the Mysore Sultans ravaged their own country, if indeed it is theirs; and hence they tolerate me in this land, for my Ukalypts grow faster and straighter than any other tree. And the trees make a wondrous oil for the physic, to boot ... To leave these fragile plants, the fuel of Mysore's future growth, between two opposing armies would be madness. Such will be the military attaché's advice; I am sure of it.

I continue. "Indeed, he will, I am sure, see the value of placing such a crop at the edge of Tippoo's kingdom. There, you see, as well as being far from battle, it would be available for supply to the French, regardless of the outcome of the British action. And once my investment is safe, my love – then, *then,* we can flee."

Usha shakes her head. But I forestall further argument: "Listen. The day grows, and I must attend to my trees now. Be patient, Usha – I am clearing a path down which we may run. You and I and Kuruppan. To a new life, a new world. I promise you."

She does not respond; I walk from the room. But before leaving the bungalow, and as I kiss Kuruppan's sleeping head, I hear her take a deep, shuddering breath, as if to prepare for some great trial: a race, perhaps, or a labour of pain.

❖

Later, after measuring a selection of Ukalypts, and seeing to their watering and weeding, I go to Devadarshan; partly for his civilised company, but partly also, I confess, in the continued hope that he might intercede with Mohan Lal regarding the protection of my crop – a favour which Darshan has so far refused to countenance. But I would rather argue with Darshan than with a Frenchman, so I shall try again. He is sitting in the day's early warmth, in front of the low, flat-roofed abode where he lives and works.

"What news?" I ask.

He says nothing, at first, but nods at the mat laid a short distance in front of him, below the step on which he sits – close enough for conversation, but far enough to maintain hierarchy. Lowly gardener or not, I flatter myself that this place is set for me; certainly Devadarshan seems to enjoy our little dialogues, and my Tamil, I believe, is quite passable. Sometimes Usha laughs into her hands when I speak, by which sign I know that I have made some error of language, but I care not; her gaiety enriches me (I dare say that some of my errors are deliberate, for this reason). But Devadarshan never laughs: he only unsmilingly corrects my pronunciation, all the while hunched over his figures. How can a man speak and calculate at the same time? He is a mystery to me; and the extent and origin of his learning confound me. I am not alone in this – they say even Purnaya, first minister to Tippoo, seeks Devadarshan's wisdom. Before addressing my question, Darshan shouts for his servant Nanjan.

"What news, you ask?" he says, after Nanjan has shouted back. "Only bad." His Tamil is soft: the accent of a gentleman. Cross-legged on a closely-woven grass mat, a tray of writing materials to one side of him, a pile of parchments to the other, and his calculations before him, he is every inch the bookish Hindoo. "The Sultan has ordered another day of executions and amputations. The beasts are being readied, and the rope fresh-made. They say he wishes to clear the dungeons of ..." He pauses. "... foreigners." I nod, po-faced. It seems that all except the British know that British prisoners, taken in previous battles, have endured Tippoo's dungeons for many a year. "So, yes, the only news is bad. Unless you can tell me differently."

A crow flies to the ground in front of our mats, sees us and flaps away again. Its wings strop, up and down, up and down, as though to razor the air. Nanjan appears, a sleepy old goutard as nimble as a tortoise, and sets down tin cups: warm milk, sweetened and spiced, half of which he has spilled in the dust. Devadarshan, I believe, employs him out of kindness, for as far as I can see the old man is as much use as an onion skin.

"Well," I say. "I can tell you that my Ukalypts turn Indian sun and Indian soil into fine timber faster than even I had thought possible. *That* is good news. A most valuable asset to the kingdom! Worthy of protection in this time of war, surely! Such good fortune for the Sultan, to have this resource ..."

Darshan says nothing; he is deep in calculations. "Such good fortune!" I repeat.

He looks at me askance, from beneath one raised eyebrow. "It does not surprise me that you believe in *fortune*," he says, in a voice as dry as cinders, "given the *fortunate* route by which you acquired your, ah, valuable asset."

I laugh, as if he makes a joke; but I think I know his meaning. How does a Spaniard – whose country is as much at war with the British as is Tippoo's kingdom – acquire the seeds of the remarkable Ukalypt tree, brought from Australia by the British ship *Endeavour*, less than thirty years ago? But I have answers to that, and my account, I believe, holds even more water than the *Endeavour* did when it yawed into Batavia, on its way back to England. For Batavia is Dutch owned, and the Dutch are great traders with Spain; all know that, even in India. So why then should a Spaniard *not* have been in Batavia; and why would a Spaniard *not* have taken his chance to steal from the *Endeavour's* rented warehouses, while his enemies the English remedied her wounded hull and shipworm in the dry-dock? If Devadarshan knew more of the world, he would accept this tale as easily as did the Sultan's ministers that he serves. But, before I can speak, he resumes.

"When Patricio Sorondo, the Spaniard, first came to Tippoo's court, few concerned themselves with his tale of *good fortune*. Few cared. But now the British come, and people mutter that Tippoo's reign may end, and with it the Kingdom of Mysore – and so all men look to protect themselves, and some will do so by casting suspicion on others. For example: how does one Spaniard gain entry to the *Endeavour's* stores? Do the English value their treasure so little that they leave it unlocked and unguarded, take it who may? And why did that Spaniard choose to take *seeds*, of all things; and why *those* seeds in particular? It is as if the Spaniard knew what would grow from them."

I blanche beneath my beard, and begin a stuttered protest. Darshan is a good man, and I think of him as a friend – yet would he tell them I was English, if he knew? I do not wish to test him with such knowledge ... But my discomfort is covered by an explosion from the fields beyond the fortified walls. Our heads turn. One of Tippoo's war-rockets shoots across the sky, trailing smoke and sparks. Behind it, the long pole to which the rocket's iron combustion chamber is affixed gyrates like a screw. I have been told that the greater part of the damage done by such machines is by virtue of this bamboo tail, which dreadfully lacerates man and horse alike as it whips through enemy regiments. The rocket disappears from view; the crack and echo of its impact follow. Perhaps Tippoo's intent is to threaten dissenters within Seringapatam; perhaps he seeks to bolster the morale of his kushoon brigades; perhaps he wishes to dismay the British spies who doubtless see what we see; whatever its purpose, we are silent as the demonstration of Tippoo's weaponry continues. When it is over, Devadarshan sighs and returns to his figures again: "As I was saying: in this time of war, you would do well to bide quietly, especially given your – *circumstances*. Do not draw attention to yourself and your trees."

"I have no choice! My crop can endure pots no more; movements of moon and stars tell me it is ready to be planted out; and I cannot leave it here, to be ploughed and churned by battle, and by the machines of battle." I nod towards the wisps of smoke left by the war-rocket.

"I advise you to forget your crop. Doubtless some will survive, maybe more than you think; start again with those."

"No! I must protect my trees, every one. They are all that I have ..."

"You also have your family. They are more valuable than trees, I think."

"You do not understand. It is not a matter of one or the other. And for moving the trees, Mohan Lal would agree, if only it were put to him judiciously – "

"Perhaps it is you that do not understand. A meeting of forces approaches. The British and their Hyderabadi allies on the one hand, and our Mysore masters on the other, yes. But there is more." He nods towards the curve of Mohan Lal's rotunda, round against the sky. "The old man hides in there night and day; he tells none what he does, maybe not even Absalom the giant; but hints and guesses say that he seeks some grand conjunction, some confluence of power. Whatever that may be, we can be sure it will benefit none but Mohan Lal; and whatever tools he uses in his endeavours, it would be better not to be one such. So do not walk into the tiger's cage; do not go talking to him of *trees* and *fortune*. That is my advice."

"I do not intend to, sir! Perhaps I have more wit than you know" – Devadarshan tries to hide a smile; but I see it, damn him! – "for my strategy is to have the new military advisor, the one we spoke of, intercede with Mohan Lal on behalf of my trees and I. As you know, I can persuade no other to do so. Perhaps he will even have Tippoo's ear ..."

Devadarshan shrugs. "For that, you will need far more of the good fortune you have so far enjoyed. But again, I counsel you to choose silence, and to hope that those in power forget your existence." He raises his head and, for once, looks at me directly. "Truly. For your wife and son, if for nothing else."

And such is the power of Darshan's gentle guidance that I am almost persuaded.

❖

The sight of my crop, however, brings me new resolve. Darshan means well, but he does not understand; he is a scholar, not a man of practical bent. I must do what I must do. And so I determine to start packing straw around the trees in their pots, to ready them for travel. As though it were the most innocent thing, the most natural thing, to prepare to run at such a time as this; as though none could deny the sense of it. Devadarshan spoke of *fortune* did he not? Well, they say it favours the brave.

Sometimes it requires courage to run away. I do believe this; I do.

The dried grass and coconut straw smells clean; it rustles and resists as I tie it in bundles against a terracotta pot, over the soil and around the stem of a Ukalypt. I pour water over the packed straw; its fibres hold it well, like a sponge. Good; this will do. I show my handiwork to the pair of helpers Mohan Lal has allocated to me (they change weekly, by order, perhaps so that none can become too close to any other; the Sultan always fears plots among his subjects), and ask them to help me do likewise to the other pots. It is likely to take us a week of long days.

We have worked thus for perhaps an hour, and the sun has become hot, when I look behind me, as if my head were drawn to another's surreptitious gaze. There, by the lean-to shelter that serves as potting-shed – no more than a thatched roof set against one mud wall – two men stand. At first, I think it is a man and a child, and a sudden fear for Kuruppan claws at me. But as they walk towards me, I see that the smaller is made small only by the size of the creature that walks with him. It is Mohan Lal and giant Absalom: Absalom, who is cousin to the eunuch Goolam Kadeer – that Goolam Kadeer who ten years before gouged the eyes from Shah Ullum II and thereby made Tippoo himself weep. Only Mohan Lal saved Absalom from a scapegoat's death; which is why Absalom now would die for Mohan Lal.

"Well." Lal's voice is thin, and dry, and cold; it is thus that a lizard would speak, I think. Or a snake. "Well, *mali*." I know that he knows my name – at least, he knows me as Sorondo – but to a minister of the Sultan such creatures as I are named by their occupation, and thus to him I am only *mali*, or gardener.

I smile broadly, and make a namaskar, but my heart jumps up and shakes the bars of its little cage.

"Welcome, Your Excellency. Let me send for food and drink from my bungalow – "

Lal waves this suggestion away. "I neither eat nor drink during daylight hours, *mali*. And good Absalom follows my example." The giant makes no sign of having heard; hands like hams, their fingers curled towards his palms, wait at his sides; his beard, dyed henna red, falls over his enormous belly. He looks down at me dully, slack jawed.

"Some water, then, Your Excellency, to wash your feet, if you would honour me thus ..." For Lal has Power; and I will, as always, abase myself before Power if I cannot run from it.

"Enough, *mali*." Something in his voice makes me wonder if such empty flatteries bore him. "I am here for an accounting, not to be pawed by a foreigner."

"An accounting, Your Excellency?"

But he says nothing more; he only looks at me with his black, black eyes. And I find I am compelled to talk, like a schoolboy before his master. I tell him of my trees; of the numbers at one stage or another;

of the rates of growth I have measured, season by season, and year by year; of how this crop will be the beginning of plantations that will end Mysore's hunger for timber, forever. But only if they can be protected in this time of war.

He nods all the while, as we walk among the trees, with Absalom two paces behind. He sees the straw-wrapped pots, and something glints in his eye, and he smiles. But still he says nothing. I talk on.

This is the first time that I have spoken to Lal for perhaps three months, and one of only a few times since he dictated the terms under which I might establish Ukalypt plantations in the Kingdom of Mysore. He was then old but vigorous; the interceding months, however, have somehow sapped him. His skin is thin and pale; it is blotched with darker patches as if some rot were working its way up from within. Only his eyes are unchanged: dark and fierce.

Eventually, my words run dry. I have told him everything, I believe, that I can.

"And your boy, Kurban?"

"Your Excellency?"

"Your boy. Is he well?"

"Oh, *Kuruppan*! Your Excellency, thank you, he is very well. He grows, I believe, even faster than my Ukalypts! Ha, ha!"

"That is good. He is the perfect child, *mali* – perfect. See that you look after him."

And then, after some additional questions which show me – perhaps they were designed so to do – that Lal has understood and remembered every single figure and calculation I gave him regarding the propagation and growth of Ukalypts, the old man makes as if to turn to go. But all of a sudden he stops, and speaks. "We expect another of your countrymen, the morrow." My heart flips over itself again, and something buzzes in my head, as if I am about to faint and fall. He looks at me, a half-grin on his face: "At least – tell me again, which country are you from, *mali*?"

"Spain, Your Excellency!"

"Ah! Then our new military advisor is only a cousin to you, not a brother. A Frenchman, *mali*, come to teach our sepoys how to fight the British. And that after the British have whipped the French like

old horses for twenty years now, in all parts of my world and yours."
He laughs, thin and cold, and I wish he had not, for something about
it makes me shudder.

Then, at last, he leaves, followed by his brutish servant.

Later, when day nears its end and my helpers have left, I repair to the
potting-shed lean-to. If only I had had the courage to directly ask Lal –
Your Excellency, permit me to save my trees – instead of pecking around
the subject like a chicken in its coop. Once again, I feel the guilt and
shame felt by those who quail before authority. What did Darshan
say, only yesterday? *Hope that those in power forget your existence!* But
I do not need Devadarshan's advice on such matters, for I suspect
I know more than Darshan of what Power does to those who have
none. Indeed, it was Power that made me first run; only to run again,
and again, and again.

I often wonder how it would have been had I run down a different
road, or not run at all. In what world would I now live? And I
sometimes think that always, whenever I come to a fork, I run down
the wrong road, and find myself where Shame lies in wait, and Guilt
sets its gin. But I can never retrace my steps and take a different way.
That is forever the agony of this life – that it could, so easily, have been
a different, better life.

And yet, had I taken a different road, I would not now have Usha
and Kuruppan. Surely, there is some path we can follow, all three, to
a *better* world?

I rub away some dirt from the potting table; something catches my
skin. A brad: loosened by the drying and splitting of the table's plank,
it pokes its head proud of the surface. I work at it until it comes out,
and pocket it for re-use. In India, everything must be used twice, and
used once more. Like my shame; like the guilt from which I run, from
which I have been running since I was a boy.

To be that boy again; to take a different road, a different bridge!
Memories gnaw at my poor, guilty soul ... Look: I am standing behind
my father as the Inclosure men take his small-holding; as they fell the
trees he'd coppiced for fence-wood and kindling. The trees where I'd
sheltered and climbed since I first walked; whose twiggy branches first
led my young eyes, in some far-off night, to the stars in their infinite

majesty. The boy that I was knows each oak, and holly, and hazel, and elm; he knows the feel of their manifold barks; he has by heart the stories they have slowly grown. And Father's shoulders tremble with each falling trunk ...

I knew then that he could never protect me from the rapacity of Power. And I determined to escape from a world where Power does what Power wants, and damn all gentle folk. So I turned on my heel, and I left my father there; I took my fourteen-year-old feet to the Army, and became a drummer boy for the 67th Regiment of Foot. The boy that I was blamed my father for the loss of our land, our trees, for weakness before Power; the man that I am is tortured by the memory of what that boy did. Yes, I left my father to find his pauper's grave, alone. Because he could not withstand Power.

And what next? My comrades in the 67th Regiment of Foot were kind to their drummer-boy; they looked out for me; they showed me the ways of canvas and mud. But when that boy saw how things were at St Cast – when he saw Power raise its head again, and bare its yellow teeth – he dropped his drum and ran from those who'd helped him. He ran to Power, to the massed French, to the Regiment Volontaires Étrangers, 1st Battalion, with its yellow and black standard. Let me beat a French drum now, I begged, as the aide-major pressed his boot to my neck. Beneath his moustache, his lips were wet, and grew a white froth in their corners; he slowly drew finger and thumb together across his mouth, as if to wipe away his drool. He dried his hand on his sleeve, and he spoke: "*Allons*," he said, and marched me to the headland, where we watched Admiral Lord Anson retreat while my countrymen were slaughtered. And then he took me down to the St Cast sands.

I tidy away the day's work in the lean-to; spare pots are stacked against the mud wall, all awry. Soon – God willing, if only Power will listen to this poor planter – I will have no more need of these terracotta buckets. My trees will grow in the sweet soil of the Nilgherrie Mountains, their roots unbound. Thus I try to set my eyes to the future.

Evening will soon be here, yet the sum of this day's labour is my hangdog soul. Perhaps Usha and the child will drag me from this swamp; none else may.

❖

What can compare with the South Indian dusk? It warms, but does not oppress; it cools, but does not chill. It dyes the sky violet to indigo, and uncovers stars like trembling drops of quicksilver. By its grace, flowers release fragrances too subtle for the brash day.

Somewhere, a jackal calls; its high note disappears into infinite time. Usha sits cross-legged on a mat, minding the oil-lamp; moths make shadows that dart and jump. I play with Kuruppan.

Kuruppan! When my boy smiles, it is as if it is the first smile of Man; as if it comes from a place where kindness is deemed more of a virtue than the collection of wealth, where there is no more pain than a bruised knee. And he smiles often. Through Kuruppan, I feel the cool air of my childhood caress my arms, and smell the smoke from apple-wood fires; I see the grand oaks and elms of the Surrey Hills, taller than fairy-tales; I hear again the nursery rhymes my mother sang. *Little boy blue* ... With the brad from my pocket, we scratch pictures on a palm-leaf: dogs and monkeys, elephants and people. The gift of children is to give one's own childhood back.

I wish this could never end. I wish I were not surrounded by the unending death and pain of this place and time. Darshan said that Tippoo has ordered another day of punishments; my stomach churns at the thought. But I draw a camel, all the same.

"It has two heads, Father!"

"Then it will talk even more than you, little parakeet."

Later, I hold Usha in the darkness. Neither of us, it seems, can sleep. She asks, not for the first time, for stories of Australia. And this saddens me, for I know she only does this when she wants escape from her own thoughts. But I tell her, just as I have told her before. The deer that jump like rabbits; the little bears in the branches; the birds that screech but do not sing; and the trees, the trees.

I'd seen the Ukalypts all round Botany Bay, I tell her, taller than oaks, straighter than a plumb-line; I'd walked among them, touching their ribboning bark with a wondering hand. And during the *Endeavour*'s stay, from April to July of the year 1770, I measured the growth of one sapling and found it likely ten feet in a year, and that in soil so poor that an English farmer would leave it forever fallow. I did not need Banks' education or Cooke's authority to see profit in the Ukalypt's wood. And so I clandestinely gathered their seed pods – each pod having many hundreds of their powdery seeds – vowing to run, run with this wooden gold. Once in England, I thought, I'd turn my feet to Holland, knowing the Dutch hunger for timber to feed their ship-building needs; I'd make a plantation there. But the cleft stick of circumstance forced me to jump from *Endeavour* far sooner than that; it was in Dutch Batavia, on Christmas Day, that I ran. And in Batavia that I met Benedito da Souza, who told me of Mysore's wealth and Mysore's wants, and persuaded me to sail with him to Goa as midshipman on a Portuguese two-decker.

"Where is Benedito?" asks Usha.

"He is packing cinnamon and cardamom. He will leave within the month. If they let him." Indeed, as Portugal and Britain are allies, da Souza has always been in danger of being denounced as a British spy; yet somehow he survives and trades on, with a shrug and a smile.

"If *he* can leave ..." says Usha.

In the other room, Kuruppan warbles in his sleep, so sweetly. Between Usha and I there is a silence, and it oppresses me.

"My dear. Let us not be sad."

"Then let us find a place where we can be happy."

"That is my intent, love. Have I not said so?"

"Indeed, you have said so now for months and years. Yet we are here still, flinching from the Sultan's whip."

I know her opinion of our rulers well, and why she holds it. Her mother's family, Malabar nobles, fled before Tippoo's army to Travancore. There her mother was adopted by the Attingal royals, as is their pretty custom, and thus Usha is, or should be, a Travancore princess. But poor Usha was taken when Tippoo attacked Travancore in yet another of his expeditionary rages. Indeed, I have great sympathy with her views regarding the Sultan and his kind; such people are endowed with the gentler virtues as a toad is with feathers. But she seems, I believe, to forget our situation.

"We will not always be here. Trust me, my dear."

"It is not *trust* that will save us from what comes. It is action."

"I know that well!" I pressed my balled fists to my head. The cleft stick of circumstance! Has my whole life been thus?

"And yet, you do nothing." The sadness in her voice near breaks me.

"*Waiting* is not the same as *doing nothing*, my love. To move and replant my trees – this can be done only once, and must be done right. And for the right time, I have to rely on the cycles of moon and stars. Even *I* cannot hurry the celestial bodies."

She does not smile. "Your trees will kill us, all three."

"No, Usha! They will make for us a new life!"

"Unless we die first."

"Some plans need a gestation before they can be delivered."

"If you will not hurry for me, think of Kuruppan. He does not deserve whatever fate Lal would give him."

"I have said before, you make of Lal too much a beast. The old man asks after Kuruppan always – "

She sits up in an instant, as if pulled by the neck, and thrusts away my arm. "Lal? You have spoken with Lal? About *Kuruppan?*"

"He came to inspect my trees, only today." I say it airily, as though this planter welcomed Tippoo's ministers to his fields weekly. "And that he takes an interest in Kuruppan – "

"No! You know nothing of Lal! Even after all these years – "

I sense a storm about to break, and I without shelter.

"Usha, my love, you did not let me finish. I merely – "

"He would feed the child to Absalom! Or worse!"

"I merely meant to say that Lal may ..." I lower my voice. "If used judiciously, he may be of assistance to us."

"You wish to use Lal? *You*? To *use* him? *Him*? Does the blinded buffalo use the oil-man?" Her fierce whisper near burns me.

"His interest in Kuruppan is a form of currency, my dear, that we may spend." She opens her mouth and throws up her hands, but I proceed apace. "You see, if the French military advisor – who, let me say, is arriving *tomorrow*, Usha – suggests to Lal, as I think he will, that such assets as can be moved from Seringapatam, *should* be so moved to protect them from the British, and if at the same time I ensure that I am seen with Kuruppan in front of Lal, wherever possible, why then his head may be persuaded at the same time as his heart is moved. For

I do believe old man Lal is fond of Kuruppan, my dear." I nod, firmly. "Yes. I do."

❖

Usha shows a cold side over the next week, and I find it easier to work longer days. But even sable clouds may be lined with silver: the packing of my Ukalypts in straw is now proceeding more quickly than I could have hoped. One morning, I allow myself some few minutes of contemplation; I walk the rank and file of my seedlings, inhaling their sweet scent, which is always strongest at dawn. Each green leaf, a promise of Mysore gold. Each sapling, a signal of the labour of years. We shall run, Usha, yes; but we shall not run without these. For if this crop is lost, I am a beggar till my death. I have nothing else, nothing but empty promises and shame.

Sometimes I think of what I have not told Usha. Of Antoinette, to whom I promised all and gave nothing; who gave her all in helping me escape from France, and received nothing. I took her love, I took her language; I left her. Some guilt cannot be expressed, still less escaped; run as you like, it follows tirelessly. Yet I had no choice but to flee France, when I could; they had made almost a slave of me, and would, I am sure, have killed me in the end. But Usha would not see it in such light; she has too much honour.

I pluck a leaf, crush it, and rub it between my palms; the fragrance invigorates. I breathe in, deeper and deeper, as if this sweet Ukalypt might clean my sullied soul.

A movement interrupts my self-scourging: someone approaches, stepping through my pots and seedlings. A man. At first, a small hope rises: is it Devadarshan? His unsmiling counsel is always welcome. But then I see the man is younger, broader; he wears a sepoy's uniform. One of the Mysore men-at-arms, from Tippoo's kushoon squadrons. I make a namaskar as he approaches; he does not respond, but looks me up and down as if repelled by the sight of this faithless foreigner.

"You are Sorondo?"

"Yes."

"I come from Mohan Lal." My heart leaps, as if through hope or fear. "You are informed that the forthcoming day of entertainments is to be in honour of the new military advisor. The Sultan desires the presence of all who are not engaged in duties essential to the kingdom."

A pretty invitation! Damned if you neglect your duties in order to attend; damned if you do not. Only the ministers can say which duties are deemed essential, and they will not say. That is the Sultan's way: to subject all to a cruel caprice.

The sepoy continues, as if he had seen my hidden reluctance: "Better to join the audience, Sorondo, than to join the entertainers."

I make another namaskar, and laugh heartily: join the entertainers, ha! "I thank you, brother. Is there – may I ask, might there be, any other message? Perhaps the Minister requires my presence, to discuss this fine crop?"

"And perhaps you believe the Minister is accustomed to bandy words with unclean foreigners who scrape in the dirt, like dogs." He sneers and saunters away.

The braggadocio of Power. Will it plague me always? Sometimes it seems that some devil's lens has focused all evil on this one place and time, as if to see how a universe might be when no good people rule. There is no help for it but to run, with Usha and the child; run, run, run.

But first, make safe the Ukalypts! Where *is* the new advisor, damn him? They tell me he has been in Seringapatam now several days; but I have not seen him. I heard that he went to Benedito's factory, which is near to the likely line of British advance, but none can say any more than that. I *must* speak to the advisor; Benedito might be able to tell me where he is, but my messages to him go unanswered.

I watch the sepoy walk towards the bridge over the Cauvery, and my gaze follows the road to the far shore. There, the kushoon brigades are mustered. Before them, their Mysore commanders, straddling fine horses. And with *them*, I see a man. A European, surely, for he wears a hat, not a turban, and I never saw any in India wear a hat but the Europeans. At such a distance, I cannot be certain, but I feel in my waters that there – at last! – is the Frenchman who, please God, will persuade the Sultan's men to let me move my Ukalypts from harm's way.

I leave my trees and walk to Tippoo's fort. It takes longer than it might; the passage of carts and people, carrying stores of weapons and food in readiness for the expected blockade, is continual. Once there, I loiter by the fort's entrances, moving from one to another, hoping to engineer an accidental meeting with my intended ally when he returns from inspecting the kushoons. I confess, I have little idea of how to open an exchange of words with this stranger, and it is possible that my overture will buy me no more than a taste of his boot. But I must try.

And then – good fortune, as Darshan would say, and brought by Darshan himself! For, as I push through crowds and past bundles of produce, I see my friend and confidante on the road ahead of me, walking towards the fort; and with him, a man in the uniform of the French in India! I set my pace faster; I scamper after them; I smooth dishevelled hair and endeavour to bring my breath under control.

"Devadarshan!" I pant. "Well met!"

He stops, my friend Darshan, and looks over his shoulder, his face unreadable as ever. He answers not in Tamil but in slow and simple Hindoostanee, doubtless for the benefit of his companion.

"Ah, Sorondo," says Darshan. Then he speaks to the one who walks with him. "Sir – may I introduce Sorondo, the Spaniard who plants trees for the kingdom's future needs."

Darshan's companion, I see, fills out his uniform; it stretches tight across his back, and his neck bulges from his collar, showing damp flesh below dark hair shot through with grey. He turns slowly. And as he does so, it is though a great hand takes me by my neck and pushes my head down, down through icy waters, and grinds my face into the St Cast sands. For I see lips slack and wet beneath an oiled moustache, and bullfrog eyes staring wide as if in perpetual threat; I see thumb and finger rise to mouth, and wipe at lips; I see him look at me oddly, as if trying to grasp something half-remembered. And I hear him say to himself, musingly: "*Allons ...*"

❖

"What is it, husband?" Usha's voice is low and urgent. This damned day is near over; I am sitting inside the bungalow, on the floor; back to the wall, head to my knees. I cannot speak; I can hardly breathe. She runs fingers through my hair. "What is it?" I raise my head a little, and look to my hands. They tremble as if with ague. She is silent for a small minute, then sits beside me, puts her arms around me and draws me to her sweet softness. "Is it over?" she says. "They have found out?"

"Not yet. But they will. They will, now."

"Tell me."

"The new advisor. The Frenchman. I know him. His name is Vauquelin."

She makes a little frown. "Vauquelin? You said that in the night – that night you dreamed ..."

So I tell her. I tell her of St Cast; of Vauquelin's butchery; of how it returns to me sometimes, in the deepest nights. She is as silent as a rock.

"When he remembers me, we are all dead."

"Listen." She has her hands on my cheeks; she makes me look at her. "He has *not* recognised you. That is the important matter. And why would he? You were then a boy. You are now, I guess, a head taller, a shoulder wider, with a beard as full as a Mussulman's. So there is *no* reason for him to recognise in you the boy of more than thirty years ago."

There is truth in this. I am also now browned and leathered by the tropics' sun; no longer a pale and delicate worm of a child. There is probably but six or seven years between Vauquelin and I; in mid-age that means nothing, but at fourteen it is the difference between man and boy. Yet still the old horror gnaws at me.

"But I knew him on sight. So he may remember, some day. He may. And if he does ... You know that poor Benedito has had to flee? Darshan told me, when we were alone. Vauquelin had let it be known that he sees the Portuguese as he sees the British. Fortunately, Darshan warned Benedito of this before Vauquelin could tell Benedito himself."

"All it means, husband, is that there is now *no* reason for us to stay in this citadel of brutes. Not even for your trees. Do you agree?"

I turn my gaze to the open doorway. Through it I see my plants, their leaves dark against the day's fading light. Their exquisite scent ...

"*Do you agree?*"

All the money I have ever owned; all the labour of my strongest years; all caught in root and branch. From Australia to India by way of Batavia.

"Yes. Yes, Usha. We must leave as soon as we can."

But even as I speak – yes, even as I give my dear wife this assurance, God help me – I am wondering; I cannot help it. For Usha is right; Vauquelin will not immediately see beneath my beard; he may not at all; why would he? I may have less time, but I have still *some* time, surely. I feel Usha's eyes on me.

"What now, my love?"

"You did not tell me of Vauquelin. What else do you keep locked away?"

"My dear – "

"Tell me *everything*."

So I tell her – and I cannot meet her eye in the telling – of Antoinette. And then I tell her the truth of why I had to run from the *Endeavour* before it returned to England. Of Magra the New York Irishman, an *Endeavour* midshipman like myself, who knew that I was an army deserter. Of how he held it over my head night and day; of how he made me thus his whipping boy for all manner of misdemeanours, the nature of which grew more vile as the voyage progressed.

"Listen, Usha: one night, Magra made the Captain's clerk Orton drunk almost to death, and while the clerk was thus insensible, cut away his clothes and, as if he were no more than a dog's pup, sliced off the tops of his ears, and then told all that it was *I*, to the point that even poor Orton – who was my friend, Usha, my *friend* – believed it."

All that is true; indeed, by the time the *Endeavour* left Australia, Magra had turned all against me.

"So Captain Cooke would have had me punished for Orton's assault as soon as we docked in England; yet had I denounced Magra, Magra would have told all that I was a deserter, and then I would have been manacled until Plymouth, and there given to the army."

The cleft stick of circumstance, as always. But whose fault was it that the Irishman knew me to be a deserter? Mine, only mine; for it was the consequence of my own injudicious, rum-soaked confidences; my own weak attempts to curry favour with fearsome Magra.

After I finish speaking, I am silent for a while. Outside the bungalow, geckos chirrup. Eventually, I must speak.

"Well? I am worthless – is it not so?"

She turns to me; she puts a hand to my face. "You were young. You made mistakes. And had you not made those mistakes, I would not have you now. Such is fate."

"You forgive me?"

"I will always forgive you, husband. Always. Because I love you." As we hug, her hair catches on the dampness of my cheek. "I ask only this: forget your trees, and make plans to flee."

"Trust me, my dear. Trust me."

And as I say this, my lips to her ear, I look through the open doorway again at my trees. Their leaves move slightly, and their fragrance washes over me like balm.

That night, while Usha sleeps, I lie in tormented wakefulness. What now can I do? In the next room, Kuruppan dreams; I hear him say, *Little boy blue ...* Perhaps that is what decides me; I must act, or Power will take us all, including my blameless child. I cannot, must not, simply follow this world's flow like a leaf in the river. I must change my life through my own efforts; and if that requires diverting a river, so be it!

The words come to me as easily as the wind; as if some spirit of earth or air whispered into my ear:

O Absalom, be so kind as to beg of Mohan Lal an audience for this poor gardener ... I implore the benefits of his wisdom in this uncertain time, for albeit that the kingdom's Ukalypt plantations have benefited from the Minister's generous endowments; nevertheless, the kingdom's enemies such as the British, and the Nizam's men of Hyderabad their allies, will doubtless cause much loss of the Sultan's crop before those enemies of the Sultan meet their just and inevitable defeat at the Sultan's hand. And therefore I beg the Minister's sage advice now that the constellations favour their planting, on the protection of the

Sultan's property his Ukalypts, and, in order to follow the times given by the stars, I do most humbly request the Minister's sage advice at his most early convenience ...

Yes: this message, if dull-witted Absalom relays it in proper form, must give me at least a brief audience with Mohan Lal. Moreover, if all goes well, I may also seek his leave to absent myself from the public executions, three days hence. My stomach clenches at the thought of the Sultan's *entertainments* ...

Indeed, this will work to my great advantage.

I am sure of it.

Part II: The infinite stars

There have been three today. This boy is the last. Around his bare feet, something stains the pale dust dark, and his face, congested with blood, swells under the Mysore sun. From shoulders to ankle he is wound with coil upon coil of rope. He cannot even bend to vomit.

I ask myself who he is. A Suffolk farmer's son, perhaps, his livelihood lost with the Enclosures. Or a cobbler's apprentice from Liverpool, who tired of nailing heels to boots. No matter; like the others, his dreams die today, in India.

Mohan Lal, hands atop his damned basket, shouts to the sepoys who hold the prisoner upright. A metal jug glares brassily as they throw more water over him. This to stay the boy's swooning (naturally! – else what sport would there be?), and also to ensure that his bindings are well-soaked. For this is *new* rope; and as it dries in the sun, it shrinks, crushing the captive by degrees, making each breath more difficult than the last.

Behind the boy, the elephant shifts its wrinkled weight, as though bored by man's cruelty to man, and the rope that links the beast's hind leg to the boy's ankles loses slack, threatening to upend this son of Albion. Not yet! shouts Mohan Lal, and the *pahan* calms his charge.

The boy's eyes meet mine. Perhaps he wonders who this European is that watches his last hour. Perhaps he will die believing I am as French as jowly Vauquelin over there, lounging next to Lal like a fat-greased ape. Perhaps he will die with no belief at all, as if the sun had sucked his faith from him, and the rope crushed all his soul's hopes.

I cannot hold his gaze, and drop my eyes. I pray he soon meets the mercy of death, and finds a greater mercy thereafter. And then I ask myself, to what God do I pray? I that have bargained with Mohan Lal – I am beyond the reach of God.

The boy's eyelids flutter, and his jaw bites at the stifling air. Lal gives the signal: it is time for this comedy's final act. The sepoys step back; the *pahan* presses his feet behind his great steed's ears and shouts; the elephant advances; the boy's ankles are pulled from under him. He lands face-down on the stamped ground. One might expect such a blow to bring sweet oblivion; but no, the ropes' girth cushions him just enough. Teeth may be snapped and nose broken, but he knows still each small agony.

The elephant moves on, gathering speed. The boy is dragged behind, stop-and-start wise. Too weak to keep his head from the ground, he leaves a bloody trail: here pieces of lip, and there pieces of brow; here a tooth, there a ribbon of scalp. Lord, let him be dead by the end! Lord, let not this faceless thing live when they throw him to the crows and dogs of Seringapatam, as they did to the others!

When the rope starts to unravel, they shout to the *pahan*: Enough! The game is over. They take off the boy's bindings, and drag him away. He does not move. I look at the gathered crowd, at the serried sneers, at men whose delight in suffering makes of them something which is not Man. Hawk-nosed Lal grins at me a demon's leer. Behind him, giant Absalom drools into his beard like a dog, and beside, ape-faced Vauquelin smirks into his oily moustachio and picks at his fingernails. Devadarshan, of course, is absent; that gentleman-scholar is too civilised by far for this charade. But I? I am here; and so I nod and smile a traitor's smile, every outside inch of me a Spanish neutral, a humble trader, a bystander in the endless wars between Britain and Tippoo Sultan.

A traitor, yes, and worse than that: since last night's black transaction, I am a devil's acolyte, a trader of souls. True, needs must where the devil drives; but why then does my hangdog soul set itself in shame's aspic?

❖

I embraced Usha, the night that Mohan Lal sent for me, as though it would be the last time we touched; maybe I held her too tightly, for she gasped, but fear makes love intemperate. Then I hugged dear Kuruppan, and made some play of words, as if such nights came weekly; but the child said, "Father, why are you scared?" Outside our bungalow, two sepoys waited in the warm night; the hilts of their talwars gleamed under the moon.

I went to them.

❖

After the executions, I jostle and weave among the slowly dispersing folk: one bobbing hat in a sea of turbans. The illusion that has dogged me since last night's exchange with Lal is suddenly very strong: either I am not real, or this world is not. But I find that Vauquelin has fallen into step with me, and he is real enough.

"Well, Spaniard? You are promenading?" He speaks in French, which is the language we most share; he has but little Tamil or Hindoostanee. And, thank God, less Spanish.

"Promenading. Yes." I do not want this monster's company. Whenever he is near, St Cast is nearer, and I feel close to discovery; but he seems to think that, as I am a Spaniard and thus an ally, I must be his natural companion. Against this is set his unhidden belief that, as a planter, I am not a *worthy* companion. And thus I find his conversation turns always from turdy-mouthed banter to contemptuous insult and back again. It is hard to bear, but I must not make of him an enemy – still less do or say anything to dig up the sands of St Cast.

We press our way onward, through the outermost defences of Tippoo's fort. From here, I can see how the split Cauvery joins again to make an island of Seringapatam. Its water churns white around the rocks that make the crossing so hazardous, the island so defensible. Closer, I see my bungalow, and beyond that, the old banyan, and then, between tree and river, the open slopes which hold my crop and my future.

Will Vauquelin never leave? It seems not. Today, he wishes to describe one of the Sultan's pretty toys, another of Lal's inventions: a wooden tiger that savages a prostrate British soldier. Both Indian beast and European man are large as life, operated by pipes and bellows hidden within the tiger. By winding a crank handle, it seems, the bellows cause sounds to be emitted and parts of beast and man to move. But I have heard of this curiosity before, and Vauquelin's imitations of the tiger's grunts and the soldier's wails – enlivened by his demonstration of the Britisher's weak movements, of the puppet arm waving as if to implore one's assistance – add nothing to the accounts previously given me. I do not know why he tells me of this plaything: to emphasise the fate of Tippoo's enemies, perhaps, or to draw attention to the mechanical genius of Mohan Lal. As if I were in need of such elaboration! As we draw closer to the bungalow, where Usha waits, I aim for disengagement.

"I will see to my seedlings, now; the rituals of growth must be followed. But such farm-boy affairs must be dull as mud to a military man – "

"Dull labour indeed! Nevertheless, crops of food comfort the soldier's stomach, and for that I am grateful to all mud-constikened root-grubbers and their beshitten beasts. But I admit to you, Spaniard, I see no point to *your* harvest. In any case, the British will soon be here, along with the Nizam's men, damn his treacherous eyes; what then for your crop? Think you that the British will water it?"

"I shall move the plants to the Nilgherries within the week. It is time." There is no benefit to keeping this from him; he will know soon enough. But his smile goes, and he turns his eyes on me, and raises his chin.

"Ah? Days before a battle, you wish to run to the furthest edge of the kingdom? How convenient! Doubtless Mohan Lal has approved your desire to exchange the Cauvery's warm banks for the cold, but *safe*, mountains?"

Vauquelin grins as though at harmless badinage; but his eyes simmer. I take the opportunity for dissimulation.

"Yes," I say. "Yes, the Minister is satisfied with the arrangement." And this is true.

We walk past my bungalow; I observe the doorway from the corner of my eye. Nobody; Usha must have seen my companion, and cloistered herself inside. Good.

"Remarkable that, in times of war, the Sultan's minister should discuss plants with a Spanish gardener." Vauquelin gives me a basilisk stare; I make myself small and humble as a worm. I knew already that this man is like a dog with the raby disease; now I know that he lives only for the chance to savage the British. For it seems that Vauquelin saw something of Napoleon's crushing loss to Nelson in Egypt last year, and the memory has stayed with him. I understand too that his recent visit to Goa was equally ill-starred: all know that Vauquelin met there with emissaries from Turkey and Arabia, from whom he hoped to enlist military support for Mysore, and all believe that he failed utterly in this endeavour.

"Mohan Lal wished certain aspects of the accounts to be balanced. Expenses, and so forth. It is of no consequence." Again, true enough; but Vauquelin brings his face close to mine. Perhaps he senses that I am not telling all.

"Expenses that are of *no consequence*? A roof over your Spanish head; food to fatten your Spanish belly; clothes to cover your Spanish skin; these are of no *consequence*, say you! Why, the Sultan even provided you with a wife, such was his kindness."

I let the lie fall. In fact, they first gave Usha to me as a servant-girl, not from consideration of my needs, but to insult the Travancore Hindoo dynasty that had resisted Tippoo's invasions. For as the grand-daughter of an Attingal queen, what lower position, what greater shame, than to cook and clean for some uncasted foreigner? Only later, when his enemies in the South continued to be rebellious, did the Sultan decree that all Travancore women captives should be forcibly shamed by marriage: the higher the family of the girl, the more lowly her husband. But Usha and I had by then such mutual affection as to welcome this outcome.

"There are costs to growing timber, and unlike my Ukalypts, I cannot live on water and the sun's warmth." I keep my voice friendly, but Vauquelin's hostility is unassuaged. My neat ranks of seedlings and saplings, stretching from bungalow to riverbank, inflame him.

"Well then, let me inspect this famous crop, this dull-as-mud harvest that so exercises the mind of Mohan Lal, favoured minister in the court of Tippoo Sultan – indeed, I feel I have it in me to water your damned plants, Spaniard, which will honour them greatly, and you still more!"

And this hog of a man opens his cod and unburdens himself over the plant-pot nearest my feet. He does not even turn his back to me.

"This tree, Spaniard, will grow finer and straighter than any other. It will be the most upstanding stem in your regiment of weeds ... For vigour can be catching, just as cowards – perhaps – can learn courage."

The spattering weakens and stops, and Vauquelin shakes himself dry. Drops of urine are hot on my instep; a rivulet pushes against one chappal. All the while, he stares at me, seeking a challenge. God's body, I do not know how I make a smile, but I do.

"And on this subject, that is, of cowards, what news of that fatherless Portuguese jolt-head, that looby-witted lickspittle of the British, who ran back to Margao?"

"I have no news of da Souza."

"I did not find him at his house in Goa, Sorondo, and that was unfortunate, because I desired a meeting. To kill him, of course. But as he was not there, I left a message with his little companion."

He buttons himself, and adjusts his clothing. Somewhere, a bird calls in five iterations: *Feeva, feeva, feeva, feeva, feeva.* Each successive note a little higher. Something shifts in my mind, as though this world blurs and another springs into focus. But Vauquelin is still there.

"Yes, a pretty thing, and as spirited as any filly I yet broke, but I saddled her in the end. Your friend may run to the British and back again, but he runs home to a well-ridden mare. Cowards deserve cuckoldry, do you not agree?" Vauquelin looks over my shoulder, back to the bungalow where Usha waits with our child; his meaning is clear. I am silent; in my pocket, I find something small, and thin, and sharp. The brad, pulled from the split plank on my potting-shed table; the brad with which Kuruppan and I scratched drawings on a palm-leaf. I grip it hard; it enters my palm.

"I will leave you, Spaniard, to your gentle family, assured as I am of your *complete* devotion to the Kingdom of Mysore." As Vauquelin walks away, he aims a savage kick at a yearling plant. The clay pot shatters, spraying terracotta shards over the ground. Roots, white and fragile, poke their fingers into the afternoon sun.

I pull the brad from my flesh. Nothing; neither blood nor pain. *What am I now?* Slowly and gently, I re-pot the Ukalypt, pressing soft earth around its feet. I water it carefully.

It will live. But Vauquelin will not: somehow, I know this.

❖

In the moonlight, all was silver or tar. "You need no swords, brothers," I said. "Am I not a loyal servant of the Sultan?" The sepoys looked at me as though to cut my throat would mean nothing. I wondered if I had been discovered to be English, and if death by rope and dragging – or worse – would be mine the next morning. This impression grew stronger as my companions – one walking before me, the other behind – took me to the heart of Tippoo's fort, and then down, down into dungeons cut from the red earth.

The stink was thick enough to taste. And the horrors that I saw! Each worse than the last. Another young boy, with kohled eyes puffed from weeping. Dressed in the ghagra choli of a nautch girl, he rested from his duties – that is to say, from dancing and otherwise pleasuring those of the Sultan's court whose tastes bend to boys. He called to me in the soft burr of Devon, but I feigned not understanding. In the neighbouring cell, torchlight showed me five Hindoos – Nayars from Kerala, I guessed – who had refused to travel the Mussulman road. Stripped naked, they bled still from forced circumcisions; in the corner of their cell a cow's leg bred maggots.

Further on, a smaller cell held a gentleman in pied garments which might once have been a Lancer's uniform. He was tied to a chair, his head fallen forward to display the dozen nails projecting from his skull. As I passed, he slowly looked up to show me such pain as turned my bowels to water. The sepoy behind me followed my gaze, and laughed: "You see, white monkey? Each day, a little tap; each day, a little deeper, perhaps by the width of a rice grain." He spat through the bars, and pushed at my back.

❖

I stand, looking over seedlings and saplings; I wait for the soft evening to soothe away the bruise left by Vauquelin's company. The sky turns plum dark, and the air is heavy with jasmine. The dying day's orchestra plays. I listen. The Cauvery's rush and tumble. The call of a koel – *Ko-el? Ko-el?* – which carries always notes of loss and bewilderment, as though the bird questions a tragic fate. The shriek and squabble of parakeets, tussling over roosting places in the old banyan.

I examine the hole left in my palm by the brad. Still there is no blood, no pain. What am I now? What am I? The groans of Lal's machine echo still.

I turn, setting my feet homeward. And there, standing beneath the banyan and among its props, as though the great tree had produced a stem in the form of a man, is Devadarshan. He falls into step with me as I pass the tree.

"You were at the executions?" he asks.

"Yes."

"A bad business."

I shrug. "We are at war. The Sultan's enemies must die." And my soul must become smaller and uglier still, it seems. "In Spain, we would treat them similarly," I add, but I feel that my voice is unconvincing.

My companion is silent. As always, he gives the uncomfortable impression that he hears my innermost thoughts. When he does speak, it is to change the subject with characteristic abruptness.

"What will you do with Usha and the child?"

"What do you mean?"

"The deciding battle draws closer. All know this. The British and the Nizam's men advance daily."

"Ha! Straight into the maw of our kushoons! Mohan Lal's cunning war-rockets will flay our enemies' skins from their bodies!"

Devadarshan sighs deeply and looks to the dark sky. Scorpio winks, as though its constellation were complicit in my reckless agreement with Lal. The night's stars tremble, as if under the weight of unimaginable energies. The gnawed moon mourns a new wane. Cycles turn.

"Doubtless the Sultan's victory will be famous. My point, which I am sure has not escaped you, is that your fields and home lie outside the fortified wall. Look to your family, before it is too late."

"I will always look to my family" – my heart impales itself on the words and flaps like a skewered fish – "but that does not mean I will look away from my Ukalypts. I cannot allow the labour of many years to be trampled by British and Hyderabadi feet. I will *not* allow it!"

"Indeed, you have said so often, and too loudly. Hence – and all the more so since da Souza ran to Goa – there are those who suspect you of planning to flee. In time of war, that is a dangerous charge. I have warned you of this before."

Now is not the time to argue with him about Mohan Lal's promissory; I need time to construct a plausible form of words, to dye last night's affair a more pleasing hue.

"It is my trees that shall flee, not I. May I discuss this with you tomorrow morning? The day's entertainments have tired me."

"There is nothing you can do without Mohan Lal's support. And once again, I counsel you to avoid any such partnership."

We have reached the bungalow; Usha's greeting saves me the embarrassment of stammering a jolt-headed response. As Devadarshan departs, he offers a final thought:

"No crop is worth a harvest of souls. In any world. Remember that."

❖

The sepoy pushed me again, and I stumbled on. Past more cells, all profoundly dark and silent; then along a tunnel cut through stone and soil; and finally, when I thought to faint from fear and want of clean air, up again on rough steps of stone, through a door and out into – what? A huge room? More like a roofed courtyard; ah, no – a rotunda! Its great dimensions were peculiarly shrunk by its contents: namely, a structure of iron and copper and brass; an open framework of chains and girders, wheels and cogs; an arrangement of mirrors and glass globes, of thin wires and other structures whose purpose would have perplexed Isaac Newton. All gleaming and winking in the yellow light cast by scores of oil-lamps affixed to the walls. My eyes followed the machine's metal skeleton up, up to the domed ceiling which vaulted high above us. The roof's centre was pierced by a circular aperture, like a single, giant eye. Through this oculus the fresh and blessed night air fell, and with it the incomparable perfumes of the Indian night: jasmine and madder and moonflower.

The rotunda's shape was unmistakable; I was in Mohan Lal's observatory, that odd building formed, one might think, by some god striking Rome's Pantheon, making it toll like a giant bell, and caging its echo among the stones of Seringapatam.

❖

Usha has made food, but I cannot eat. The executions have sickened me; Vauquelin has enraged me; Devadarshan has troubled me; Lal's promissory gnaws at me; and men's barbarity drags at my soul. Pervading all is a growing sense of irreality: even my flesh does not seem my own.

"What did Devadarshan say?" asks Usha. "*No crop is worth a harvest of souls.* What did he mean?"

"Does anyone ever know what Devadarshan means? Not I."

"There was a time when you would not lie to me."

"Trust me, my dear. Please. We will talk later." I call for the boy, and Kuruppan runs to me. Usha looks at me darkly, but keeps her peace.

I ruffle the child's hair; his is a magical time of life. What did Devadarshan assert, hardly a month ago? "*Life's vigour is never stronger than at the age of five. From that point, all are slowly dying.*" As morose as any of his odd statements, but, as ever, with a kernel of uncomfortable truth.

"Let's sing, Father." I am teaching my son nursery rhymes, dimly remembered from my Surrey childhood. He loves music. It cannot do any harm – Mysore is a Babel of languages, and who would discern one foreign language or another in a child's sing-song nonsense?

"Very well. I shall do one line, and you the next. Agreed?"

"Yes!"

"Little Boy Blue, come blow your horn – "

"The sheep's in the meadow, the cow's in the corn – "

"But where is the boy who looks after the sheep – "

"He's under a haystack, he's fast asleep – "

"Will you wake him? No, not I – "

"For if I do, he's sure to cry!"

We laugh and clap; he does not know the meaning of these foreign words, but enjoys their cadence. As do I: it is good to hear English spoken in accents free of fear and pain. Indeed, these are the only times I hear my language from any other than one of Tippoo's prisoners; and that for fourteen years now. If not for the child, I believe I might have lost my mother tongue altogether.

It cannot do any harm.

Usha holds out her hand. "Come, Kuruppan. You must sleep."

Once she has put the child to bed, we talk. Telling Usha of the day's events is like a salve, but the wound still throbs beneath her sweet physic. And of course, I cannot discuss the actuality of last night's exchange; she would not grasp its meaning. Not because of any deficit in her ability to comprehend (I admit, her mind is to mine as a razor is to soap) but because, unless she had sat in Lal's machine, with the black powder in her eyes, and watched the whirl of the Infinite, comprehension would not be possible. That truth is mine to bear, and that burden mine to weighten with lies. Nevertheless, I feel the baleful power of Mohan Lal fade somewhat; this world seems real again.

"I do not understand," I say. "I do not understand why they so love others' suffering."

Usha is silent; one elegant hand rises to her throat. She must play with her necklace in order to think, it seems; I have teased her on this matter before. I watch her fingers twine and tangle the thread of black and gold; I follow their slow liberation as she reverses the process. And when her fingers are free, she speaks.

"Indeed," she says. "You still do not understand our rulers' ways; that is true. Had you more understanding, you would not have sought an audience with Mohan Lal."

She is about to continue, but I know to what end, and therefore I interject. "Without my trees, I am a beggar. Every coin I have ever possessed is trapped in their stems. And therefore, I am as caught as a coney in a gin. I have *no choice* but to move them, and therefore *no choice* but to discuss this with the minister." My logic, I believe, is unassailable; but Usha looks at me as though I am an idiot child.

"You English – " I hush her, incensed; this must *never* be said aloud, even when we are alone. " – think to negotiate with Sultans? You are absurd. They smile at you through their beards, they mouth words such as *Peace* and *Treaty* and you believe them! For them, deception and subjugation of others is an ancestral right. And you wish to make agreements with such people!" She waves her hand away, as though to jettison my foolishness.

"My dear," I say. Her stare is stony-cold, but I continue. "My dear, firstly, Mohan Lal is as Hindoo as any Attingal queen. So you see, I am not so absurd, as you put it, as to negotiate with Sultans. Only with their Hindoo employees. And secondly – "

"Mohan Lal is *no* Hindoo! And 'trustworthy'? Oh, doubtless! And doubtless his machines are only looms, and his basket holds only coiled thread!" Usha rolls her eyes.

"The proof of this pudding is in its eating, my dear – and as I have said to you, Lal now agrees that I may hide the Ukalypts. Which, with admirable foresight, I had already had packed with straw, ready for carting away."

Usha frowns. Necklace and fingers make a bird's-nest knot. Through the door, I hear Kuruppan heave a deep sigh, dreaming the dreams of a five-year-old, and my heart clutches itself. That this beautiful child should be born in such a place, in such times – the injustice of it! Jump, jump, to a *new* world!

"Even if Lal keeps his word," Usha says, "I see only this: that you are leaving with your trees – and your child and I must remain here, alone. Why can we not come with you, beyond Mysore's borders? And then *stay*?"

"Lal will not permit it. But also, consider this, my dear – what better proof of my allegiance to the kingdom than to leave – and then *return*? Any suspicions directed at me will be leavened – and *then* we can run, you and I and Kuruppan, while Mysore eyes are elsewhere. To the mountains, to the Nilgherries, to hide and prosper among the tall peaks. The coming battle marks a change, Usha. Even if Tippoo survives, he will be vastly weakened, and will have no means of projecting his diminished power to a part of India that was never really his. Whereas, if the British win – and remember, since the Sultan and his kushoons were trounced by Cornwallis at Seedaseer, all rumours say the redcoats shall indeed prevail – we shall be out of sight and mind among mountains that the British have never climbed." This is all true, or true enough; there is no need for her to know of the exact arrangement with Mohan Lal. Not yet.

"So my husband can divine the future. How fortunate I am."

"And the future I see is this: you and I, we will make an industry of my trees, of their wood and oil. We will grow old beneath their clean scent while our children grow tall in their shade. We will be happy." I nod at her, and stroke her shoulder. "We will be happy."

Usha releases her necklace. Perhaps I have mollified this Travancore royal. "You are determined to do this? Moving the plants, at *this* time?"

"Mohan Lal understands the sense in planting out the young trees now, somewhere far off, before the siege begins. Failing to do so would be to declare no faith in Tippoo's reach remaining long enough to grasp them in a new location, at Mysore's borders. And that would give sepoys another reason to mutter and look to their homes. Mohan Lal knows this." Yes, it is a good story; and again, it has nothing in it that is untrue. But it does not please Usha.

"You do not know what Lal knows. Still less do you know that which he keeps in his basket – it is more than it seems."

"And yet none have ever seen this famous *cobra de capello*! For myself, I believe the basket to be empty."

"You know what they say? That Mohan Lal cannot die? That he and the snake are one?"

"Stories watered by arrack and spouted by sepoys."

"Yet Lal outlived Tippoo's father Hyder. Take care that the old man and his machines do not outlive you – and us."

"Have faith in your poor husband, my dear."

I look for Usha's smile; but it does not come. "Remember Kuruppan," she says. "Do not steal his future to make your own."

And something twists in my very core, like as though I had the squinance or some precursor to a bloody flux. But it goes.

❖

Beneath the pyramidic struts of the machine, I saw a small, thin figure seated on a chair of European design: Mohan Lal. On the ground by his chair, the lidded basket. Behind him, a looming mass of flesh and beard: great Absalom. As I approached, I saw that the giant held a length of rope; at the end of it, like a dog on a lead, stood a billy. The goat's beard and curling horns were worthy of Old Nick himself.

Mohan Lal dismissed the two sepoys with a gesture; I was alone with the old man and his massive companion. The uncertain light obscured my interlocutors, but I knew what the shadows covered. Here, Mohan Lal, with skin as delicate and papery as the scum on boiled milk; with frail limbs that spoke of every year of his preternatural life; and with black, black eyes that set a chill wherever they rested. There, Absalom, with beard and turban; with dollipol-jolthead features; with the drop-mouthed cast that spoke always of one as witless and intemperate as any Tom o' Bedlam.

"So, *mali*," said Mohan Lal. "How goes it? Your sweet child, is he well?"

"Yes, thank you, Your Excellency – very well!"

"You are all happy beneath the illustrious aegis of our Sultan?"

"Of course, sir! The Sultan's generosity has provided us with every comfort. We are truly blessed, Your Excellency, and we thank God daily for this good fortune."

Mohan Lal nodded slowly. He looked up to the oculus, and his head moved, hardly perceptibly, from side to side, as though he sought to place something in the cosmos.

"Then why do you plan to traitorously abscond?"

The lamps' flames trembled, and Mohan Lal's eyes glittered. Absalom fondled his drool-wet beard with a hand like a bear's paw. The goat pulled at its rope and nosed the ground. The sweet night air fell from the oculus above. And I did not know how to answer.

❖

Usha sleeps, but I cannot. The shrieks of the machine and the smooth weight of what Lal gave me: they trouble me still. Some part of me remains in some place shown to me by Mohan Lal, a part that is *real* in a way that I am not, and it awaits my family and I in boundless peace and joy. How long until that blessed union? I am stretched, stretched; I wonder that my poor strings do not snap.

But my pain will be a bridge for my wife and child. Mohan Lal agreed it.

I leave Usha in blameless dreams on the charpoy, and walk outside. The moon silvers my plants; I swear I can see them growing. Row upon row upon potted row; each seedling a future tree, each leaf a promise of Tippoo's gold. I look up at the sphere that lights this night and each dark night; its pale hump signals movements of incomprehensible scale and magnitude, wonderful motions indicating – for those who can read these silvered scripts, these ciphers of light – favourable times for sewing, for planting, for harvesting. Such celestial progressions directed my first small crop of Ukalypts in the Nandi Hills, in Tippoo's pleasure garden there. And when my Ukalypts prospered in the soil of India, beyond even my greatest hopes, they brought Tippoo's mouthpiece Mohan Lal, shadowed as always by hulking, dull-eyed Absalom. The old man would pace among my trees, crushing the leaves in his hands and inhaling the scent, and question me on properties of Ukalypt oil ("... *a divine fragrance, Your Excellency, and of great benefit to the quinsy, pleurisy and similar ailments!*") and on patterns of Ukalypt growth ("... *ten feet per year, Your Excellency, and as straight as a mason's rule!*"). And finally, the message from the Sultan himself, relayed to me by Mohan Lal. I remember it well, for it was the day of Kuruppan's birth, and I was amazed that Mohan Lal knew of it. "*A most auspicious day to deliver a boy-child,*" he had said, smiling like a serpent. "*Truly, the calendar has favoured us – and the timing of the birth! Unique,* mali, *unique!*" As if seven-thirty on a Wednesday morning were a mighty auspice – but I knew that the Hindoos attach importance to these things, so I simply smiled and agreed. Then, the niceties complete, the minister transfixed me with his black eyes as he recounted Tippoo's wishes: "*You will establish a nursery in Seringapatam. There, you will grow Ukalypt seedlings, and establish plantations to remedy Mysore's want of wood. Your daily needs will be met by the kingdom; your payment will be given when you prove your crop."*

The arrangement pleased me little; it had no balance; the weight of risk was on my side alone; but some offers bear no refusal. All my wealth, my last and greatest hope, now sank roots in India's soil.

Perhaps the slow growth of the seedlings soaks up my soul-sickness; perhaps their delicate scent ameliorates it; perhaps the moon's clean light washes it away. I do not know; but this I know, that the burden of the day's horrors becomes less weighty.

Back in the house, Usha has turned in her sleep, and thrown out one arm, as though to catch shadow or light. I pause to watch her, and the moment holds a little eternity. In the other room, Kuruppan sleeps deeply and soundlessly. Between them, they hold my heart entire, though too they often make it fit to burst with love. Yes, I came to India to make my fortune; and as fortune had it, I have made a family without which I can neither live nor die. Gently, I lay myself down; sleep comes instantly, or something close to sleep, and takes me to other worlds.

❖

"Answer me, *mali.*"

I looked up, past the machine's bones; the oculus, all of a sudden, seemed to be not an eye for Man to peer at the stars, but a scope for the stars to observe Man. I felt the weight of their light; I heard the keening of their heavenly spectra. I tried to speak, but God's body, my tongue was as dry and crushed as a boot's heel. Mohan Lal held up a hand to make cease my stammering.

"Why is our Spanish gardener running from us, I asked myself, he and his dear son? What does he fear? What secret does he hide?"

I was close to throwing myself at his feet, to begging him unashamedly, to saying: Yes, I am English – kill me as you wish, but please, please, for all the merit of Heaven, touch not Usha and the boy.

"Your Excellency, I implore you – I have served the Sultan faithfully these fourteen years – I have birthed a timber industry the like of which this kingdom has never seen – "

"Ah! You wish to balance past labour against present betrayal? Let us weigh up the fruits of your labour, *mali*. Can you read this?" Lal held up a scroll: columns of Devanagari figures and glyphs.

"No, sir."

"Then I must explain it to you. Look, *mali* – you see the two columns? Two sets of figures; think of them as the pans of a set of scales. And just as with scales, one looks for balance, *mali* – balance. In the end, there must always be balance; for balance must precede profit. This is an eternal rule, *mali*. It applies to every world, in every universe. So why then should it not apply to you?"

"I do not understand, Your Excellency."

"This column here, *mali*; it is the accumulation of your costs over the last fourteen years. And the other column, *mali* – the much, much shorter column – this is the measure of your value to the kingdom." Mohan Lal made a show of squinting at the numbers, as though seeking to focus on something infinitesimally small. "Timber to the value of this; kindling to the value of that; aromatic oil for the physic, to the value of another." He rolled up the parchment and passed it over his shoulder to Absalom. "There is no balance, *mali*. None."

Above us, the machine's innards clanked hollowly; as though an iron giant slowly awoke, or a great key gradually turned in a greater lock. Mohan Lal glanced upwards, and then looked once more to me. "With unpayable debts behind, and enemies all around, small wonder you wish to flee, *mali*, to some little Spanish farm."

❖

In front of Devadarshan's dwelling, the sun draws exact shadows on the ground. We are alone; I take the opportunity to raise matters that I once would not.

"Darshan, what kind of ending comes, do you think?"

He raises one hand, palm towards me, as though to say, *Preserve me from such questions*. But then he breathes deeply, in through his nose and out through his mouth, and answers.

"You have heard the whispers as often as I. They have stirred the air in all parts of Mysore, ever since the British again began to knock at Tippoo's door. Since Seedaseer, they are louder still. And all say the one thing. With the French eclipsed in Africa and beleaguered in Europe, with Tippoo's hopes of Mussulman aid from Arabia dashed, and with the Nizam of Hyderabad allied with the Company, British power in the Deccan is now unassailable."

"Then Seringapatam is lost. The island and everything within will be harrowed by the British and the Hyderabadis."

Darshan is silent. Nanjan shuffles towards us from behind the house; he remains far enough away to be respectful, but not so far that he cannot listen, and now follows our conversation unashamedly. I decide to take a direct road to the object of my meeting.

"Darshan, I intend to move my crop of Ukalypts," I say. "They are to be planted atop the Western Ghats. Therefore I must ask you to requisition carts and beasts for the journey to the Nilgherrie foothills; bearers for the final ascent to Ootakamandalam; water to be provisioned for my trees as well as for man and beast throughout; and an escort for the journey." Devadarshan looks at me as if I am an imbecile. "I apologise for the precipitate nature of my request, but the star-shown time of my trees' planting is no less than five days from now, and no more than thirteen."

"And how do you think the Court of Mysore would receive your proposal? To run, with all your assets, at this juncture!" He turns away from me, back to his calculations, as if dismissing a child. "None would believe that you would return. Spanish or not" – he looks at me again – "you would be called a deserter, and you have seen Tippoo's treatment of such men." Indeed, I have: in the Mussulman way, the Sultan has these poor souls mutilated by the removal of nose, ears, both feet and one hand. But I have another die to roll.

"Ah, but if the journey were to be *sanctioned* by Mohan Lal – what then?"

Nanjan draws in his breath with a hiss, as though a thorn had entered his flesh. Devadarshan's fingers cease travelling over his parchment, and he becomes very still. His silence spreads forth like a banyan; if I stretch out a hand, I believe I could touch it. Indeed, for an instant I question my hearing, but the harsh call of a parakeet breaks my dream.

"What then? Why, then you could leave Seringapatam, you and your plants, and only Tippoo himself could stop you." He looks up, and for once he holds my eyes. The intensity of his gaze disturbs me. "The question is, at what cost?"

"None that I cannot pay, I assure you. The crop must be protected."

"And Usha? Kuruppan?"

"I hope you do not suggest that I mean to abandon them? You should know me better!"

"I know you better than you think, my *Spanish* friend, and I do not believe you intend to abandon them. Only that – "

"Well?"

As is his wont, Devadarshan's answer is elliptical. "The artifice of Mohan Lal extends far beyond constructing mechanical tigers that maul carved Englishmen for the entertainment of the Sultan. Even the rockets of war are no more than toys for him. I do not know the full capabilities of his machines, nor do I know precisely what he seeks and sees, hidden in his observatory. But I do know his broad intent." His eyes do not leave me.

I shrug. "If *you* do not comprehend his engines, how can I?"

He hesitates; something troubles him. "Let me ask you again – what kind of arrangement have you made with Mohan Lal?"

I expected the question, but still the answer sticks in my throat. "Nothing of substance. We spoke only in generalities." I cannot meet his eye.

He is silent for a long while. At last he speaks: "Promise me; promise that you make no transaction with Mohan Lal."

"I promise." The lie echoes between us, back and forth, and my ears burn hotter each time I hear it.

I leave Devadarshan shortly after; he can be very bad company when he wishes it.

❖

"Sir, I wish only to protect the Sultan's crop! The Ukalypts must be planted out soon, or die!"

"Indeed. The British are but days away, and only now must your trees be planted elsewhere. Doubtless your family would accompany you; and doubtless neither you nor they would return. They are cunning leeches, these foreigners, are they not, Absalom?"

Absalom remained silent. The goat strained at the rope, and shook its head.

"Your Excellency! For the times of sowing and planting, I follow only the moon and stars! They take no account of the movements of the British, still less of my own needs – "

"The moon and stars, *mali*! You who turn your gaze to the mud each day, you wish to speak of the moon and stars? With Mohan Lal?"

"Sir – "

"Enough!" Mohan Lal's voice was old, but carried still the force of an authority that could take or kill as it pleased. "The unbalanced must be balanced, *mali*. To be askew is blasphemy. You have sucked from Mysore like a sick foundling from a wetnurse; you have failed to meet your agreed obligations; and now you plan to run, run with your trees; with the boy."

"No, Your Excellency! Our agreement – "

"Is worth less than the piss of dogs. But have no fear, *mali* – we will make a better one. A transaction that takes account of weights and balances. A transaction that will endure. A promissory that cannot die." He looked at the stars again, and cocked his head as if to hear their pale echoes. "Come here, *mali*; let me show you where your true fates lie, in all their countless variety." His voice was soft with malice.

❖

The arrangements proceed apace. The trees in their pots have been packed onto carts, all cushioned with straw; water and food are stacked ready to be loaded. Devadarshan has ordered a sepoy escort, to guard our little caravan and assist as necessary. Twenty men to take us there, of whom sixteen will return immediately, leaving four to bring us back; we will travel lighter and faster on the return. Even better, Devadarshan – though his irritation with me is obvious still – has said that he will travel with us to Ootakamandalam. He is from the hills, and knows the Toda people in whose lands we are to plant, and understands their language, so his presence will be a great advantage. With the Court's authority that he brings, and the sepoy guard who will obey him, I believe that my white skin will be safe while it travels through these troubled lands. Usha too is relieved that this gentle, unsmiling man will accompany me.

"You see, Kuruppan? Father will not be on his own. Uncle Darshan also will go to the hills."

But his mother's words have little effect on the boy; something concerns him still.

"Father, when you come back – will you be like you were before?"

"Of course, silly one! I will only be there for five days. You will see no difference."

"No, I mean will you be like you used to be? Before you changed?"

We comfort the boy as best we can, Usha and I; we shoo away his frowns. I tell him to run and say goodbye to the trees.

"They will be taller next time you see them," I say. "Even the smallest will be taller than you."

Usha watches him weave his way among the carts. "He is right," she says. "He is right about the change." My wife turns to me; the intensity of her gaze raises gooseflesh. "What has happened, husband?" She puts out a hand and grasps my arm; her fingers dent my skin. "This is not you! This is not you!" Then she turns and runs; back to the bungalow, back to the dreams we built, as though to disinter the past and resurrect the world of two days and two lifetimes ago.

❖

The goat's blood spattered the earth; its feet still kicked as Absalom thrust his great hand into its slitted throat and tore out – what? A small thing, rounded and hard, maybe the size of a quail's egg. A bezoar, a madstone, like those that sometimes grow in the gullets of cattle; but yellow as a wasp. He pushed it into my hands; beslimed with blood and lung-snot it was, yet smooth as water, warm as a baby. Mohan Lal watched me, his eyes like black rivets. The scent of moonflower was strong.

"The eyes, Absalom." Lal's voice was scarce more than a whisper.

The giant shambled away and back again, bringing a box of pale brass, of the sort that Hindoos use to keep their paan, and Mussulmans their opium. He opened it very carefully. Even in the lamplight, I could see it contained a powder as black as sin. Into this, Absalom dipped his bloodied thumbs, and brought them out dark to the knuckle. He reached towards my face; I declare I near blubbered like a child as he thrust his thumbs into my eyes and rubbed; fine dust was pushed into and under the lids. But he did not gouge out my orbs; I saw still.

"Now, Absalom, clean your hands, very carefully, and then put him into the cradle."

'Cradle', indeed; it was an iron platform with chains by which a man could be fastened; greater chains ran from each corner into the topmost workings of Mohan Lal's machine, high above me, where the machine's apex was framed against the circle of sky. My eyes ran with inky tears, but I thought something winked at me from the infinite night beyond this world.

"And you, *mali*, see that you hold the bezoar tight, in both hands."

The air was warm, the chains cool against my skin, the iron cradle unyielding beneath my back. The machine groaned and wailed at my juddering ascent. Held not flat but at an inclination, I could still, at first, see Mohan Lal and Absalom. They were silent, and as I was raised aloft in sways and shudders, I wondered what hideous strength powered the machine.

"Look up, *mali*. All existence awaits you."

So I looked up, and, strange thing, the circle of sky above me took on what I then realised – and know now, with absolute conviction – to be its proper form. Not a disc of stars seen from afar, but a tunnel, a conduit, from which the flow and dance of unknown energies rushed past me and through me as though I were less substantial than air. Higher still I went, and the machine shrieked unbearably; I approached the oculus – or did it approach me? – and the great spin of the universe threatened to crush me. I wept like one devoid of reason. Higher still; and then – I do not know how it happened, but it was so – the machine's sounds retreated to an infinite distance, and I floated, free of chains, suspended in endless night, among endless stars. What rapture! The unfolding universe of universes, the wheels within cosmic wheels! The unimaginable momentum of their turning, the unnamed dimensions that link and leave, and link again, world after unknown, indescribable world! The joy; the joy!

❖

Our journey to the foothills of the Nilgherries is uneventful, though the motion of the oxcart threatens to shake bones from sockets, and my sun-baked head swims as though it has taken blows from James Figg. My plants, swaddled in damp straw as carefully as any mother's babes, are more comfortable than I; but that is as it should be.

Between Gundalpet and Goodaloor, we stop for the night. The sepoys sleep huddled under the carts, with thin cloth over their faces, that they might not breath dust. Devadarshan and I make our beds in a traveller's shelter: one of those ordered by Tippoo's father Hyder to be built at intervals along the roads of his kingdom. It is no more than a roof and three stone walls, but it suffices. I cannot sleep, so I lie looking at the stars. It seems that Devadarshan too is wakeful: he begins to talk of the constellations.

"Your European zodiac encompasses twelve signs, does it not? In our Jyotisha system, we recognise twenty-seven lunar mansions, the Nakshatra." He points out some. "Look – there is Kartika, the Cutters, the star group that makes Taurus in your system. And the bright one, bluish coloured – that is Chitra, which is part of what you call Scorpio."

"If you know the stars so well, can you not see in them your destiny and mine?"

"Destiny? As if we each have only one! We have every conceivable destiny, my friend – that is what I believe. And that is the pain of it."

"That we are obliged to make the right choices in life, you mean? I do not need the stars for this insight, sir!"

"I meant rather that our manifold destinies start in unitary form, but continually split. Like a rope unravelling into strings, and the strings into threads. In one destiny, your smallest Ukalypt unfurls a leaf; in another, it does not. And thus, a thread splits and separates. The pain is the knowledge that, in some unreachable world, we are each of us better, happier men."

I see again what I saw from the iron cradle; Mohan Lal's words echo at my ear; my heart hammers at its gaol. "Then why should we not jump from a frayed thread to a prettier, stronger one?"

"But what is it that would jump?"

"A soul; a thread of being! To exchange a life of misfortune for one in which the dice fall differently!" I bite my tongue; the promissory's unspoken weight sullies the air.

Devadarshan hesitates. "Perhaps in some places and times, the contiguity of threads may be such that two threads of one soul may intertwine again, may find union in some other destiny. But it would require special circumstances. For the different universes to be in ideal conjunction, to be closely apposed in some dimension we cannot see, and for forces and energies of which we know nothing to be perfectly harnessed and applied."

I smile in the darkness. For once, perhaps, I have more knowledge than Devadarshan. "Nevertheless, it may be possible to *break* this world's thread, and jump, jump to another universe – another life!"

"Perhaps. But surely then some share of that universe's energy would jump to this one, for the sake of balance. And where would it go?"

I remember Mohan Lal's unhealthy vigour. *They say that he cannot die.*

"Nevertheless, it is possible, no? To escape the injustice of circumstance, forever – it is *possible?*"

"All realities are possible." Devadarshan yawns, and turns over. "But *this* is your reality. Your thread is set in this pattern, my friend. The weave goes on."

I am silent; but in my head, I think: *for the moment.*

The stars glitter with cold laughter. Somewhere, a jackal bewails its outcast status: the loneliest of sounds.

I sleep, at some point; and at some point, I dream. At first, I am aware only of the motion of the stars – the great wheel of their movement, the dance of their manifold alignments. But then, I see that something does not balance; the pattern is awry. This troubles me profoundly; a dark fear grasps me, but I can neither speak nor move. I search the sky. There, where blue Chitra once was, I see a rogue constellation; I cannot look away. As I watch, a pale light issues from it, and makes a long, long path down to the dusty ground near my feet. From my left, something moves towards this trembling radiance, and walks into it. It is Usha, and she holds Kuruppan by the hand; they are embalmed in a blue effulgence. She hesitates, and looks up this path that leads into the stars. And then, with firm tread, she walks, my dear wife, up this pathway, and leads our child into the Infinite.

When I awake, I feel the irrevocability of change. My alignments are no longer of this world. Truly, I am out of place.

❖

What things I saw! Other worlds and other beings, yes, in unimaginable variety; but also our world in its true place – how tiny, how insignificant it was against the backdrop of the cosmos, and yet how wonderful, how manifestly necessary to the balance of existence, were its endless permutations. And when I looked closer, it was as if our world were a tree, and yet each branch and twig and leaf and bud held our world entire – the same and yet different – and the branches did continually grow together and apart and together again – forever and ever! And this tree like the countless others in the countless universes, ever and always nourished by and straining towards the pale ladders of gossamer force that streamed down from the stars, as sure as highways for those that can place their feet thereon. The arborisation of souls; no, the weaving and interweaving of the many forms of each soul, each form identical and yet different, each an interchangeable thread in a single pattern, a single cloth. I saw my many lives, in all their many possibilities; and in each of my uncountable lives, I saw one aspect of Usha, and one of Kuruppan, each of those aspects being taken from one of their own infinities of interchangeable existences.

Why is this existence, in this world, of any import, when it can be exchanged for any one of so many, many others? What value is there in any particular thread? Break this one, break that one; they continue elsewhere, and often in a more pleasing tapestry.

I do not know how long I stayed in that infinite dream, or fragment of a dream. I know part of me, perhaps the greater part of me, still walks there, in joy, in boundless love, holding a bezoar as heavy as gold and as hot as life. I know too that when the machine's grinding wail again came to my hearing, and the scents of night-blossoming flowers washed over me once more, and I felt the cold iron on my back and the chain's links biting my skin; when I saw the oculus retreat to its place in the heavens and smelt again the goat's blood; I felt like a soul entering Purgatory. I wanted nothing more than to return to those fields of paradise. And, yes, to bring Usha and Kuruppan with me, to walk with them in Elysium. To break our earthly threads. God forgive me, I wanted nothing more.

❖

The next morning, while the men make ready our carts, I look to the mountains above us, and then back over ground covered the previous day. A low mist collects: toddy palms raise their heads above this grey sea. They look black in the early morning light. Far off, a man shins up the trunk of a palm to collect the nuts. I watch him chop at a stem. The sound of the blow reaches me only on the following upswing.

Here, in the deep country, is the true India, I feel; as old as the moon, and like the moon its cycle of change brings it back always to what it has always been. The Mughal invaders, those barbarians from Persia and Irak; with their courtly rituals, effeminate intrigues and unmanly cruelties; with their foreign customs and opium-dulled dreams – they know nothing of this India, whose true inheritors are Usha and her like. Sometimes I ask myself why the Sultans came to this country, why they seek to be in it but not of it – but then I look at the Company, and I know the answer. Fear is the cause of most cruelty, maybe all; men seek safety from their fears in accumulation, whether it be accumulated power or accumulated wealth, which are the same thing. It has been thus since we collected sharp sticks into fences to keep at bay the dark forests and their denizens: the strongest have always had the most sticks, and the sharpest. As for this country – its warm heart has been impaled on a cold minaret for too long. Perhaps even the cycle of India can be broken.

Devadarshan calls me from my thoughts. It is time for the final ascent.

❖

Absalom loosened the chains and pulled me from the cradle; his hand under my shoulder almost tore my arm from its socket. I fell to the ground at Mohan Lal's feet, weak as a babe. The bezoar had gone; but Lal did not ask for it.

"Well, *mali*? Now that you have seen the stars on which you have called for so long, what think you?"

I can hardly answer him. "Sir, I thank you for this great gift. From all my heart, sir."

I do not know why it is – perhaps it is because I feel so weak – but Mohan Lal looks suddenly more well and youthful than before. Old, still, of course; but less frail and fragile.

"Did it please you, *mali*, the infinite world of worlds?"

"Oh, sir! Yes, most greatly! I have gazed upon Truth in all its myriad forms, and held it, and it will never leave me!"

"You are more right than you know. But then – truth, you say? There is no truth but the truth that is found in numbers, *mali*. Some say the stars give numbers to those who can read their trajectories. But I say the converse: that numbers do not emanate from the stars, but rule them." The old man's eyes were black windows onto an unknown future. "Now, what need have I, *mali*, to trade words with one such as you when I can calculate such numbers as rule the cosmos? Do you know?"

"No, sir."

"A little need, *mali*. A little thing. But only you can give it to me. Unitary, ternary, Yamagandam quinary. The cycles of five and thirteen, and their confluence in this the most unique of days. Your son, Kurban – you know the year of his birth?"

The question surprises me. "The Year of Our Lord 1794, Your Excellency." I do not address his mistake over Kuruppan's name.

"That is correct, *mali*: at half past seven of the clock. I have counted the years and hours more carefully than you can imagine. Now, let us agree a new exchange, you and I; a promissory that assures the future of your pretty family."

❖

The climb to Ootakamandalam is slow: the road beyond Goodaloor is too poor for carts, so my Ukalypts now bump and sway in panniers slung across the bony backs of oxen. The train of beasts trails wearily up rutted paths, and the sepoys lead their horses, grumbling that they are soldiers, not labourers. We pass deep valleys, filled with cascading growth – great trees hung with jackfruit, tangles of thorny vines – where the grinding call of insects is relentless. The day's warmth grows, but we reach higher elevations *pari passu*, and remain comfortable. Indeed, as we ascend, the cooler air invigorates me, and I feel my cares lift. In the furnace breath of the Indian plains, even on the cooler Deccan, I am oft-times out of sorts: the heat enfeebles me, sleep does not rest me, and small things provoke in me the most unreasonable rages. But amongst the thrilling zephyrs of the Nilgherries, I feel as though I am in the Surrey Hills again – more comfortable, more content, more English, more of a *man!*

Soon, in some sweet future, I will bring Usha and Kuruppan here, to the mountains; we will grow old among the clouds and cool breezes. We will be happy.

Devadarshan brings me back to this world of tribulation. He is walking next to me, a shawl wrapped around his shoulders as though this gentle air could chill him.

"Why so sad?" he asks. "This is what you wanted, no?"

"I miss my family. Even after one night and two days, I miss them so."

"Yet, being so far from your homeland, surely you are used to partings?"

"I had nothing there. So parting with it was no great pain." Indeed, I had had less than nothing: the balance was entirely negative. Only a sackful of deceits and betrayals, only dead loves and broken promises. But India has made a dim history of my guilt. In this world, everything is different.

"Certainly you have a beautiful family now."

"Yes! Kuruppan captures hearts wherever he sets foot. Why, even Mohan Lal cannot but stare at him and smile; I have seen it." Devadarshan looks at me oddly, as though perhaps he disbelieves me. "I have seen it," I repeat, and nod at him.

"Mohan Lal takes no pleasure in any living thing, except that which hides in his basket."

"And yet, he asks after my son each time we meet, and has offered – nay, commanded – that Mysore's best physicians attend him should he fall ill. So a sweet child may hold sway over even the most jaded of old men."

Devadarshan is silent for a little while. "May I ask, when did Mohan Lal first express an interest in your son, and what form did that interest take?"

"Indeed, from the very day of Kuruppan's birth. I remember it well, for I was touched that one in the court of Tippoo Sultan would note the birth of a gardener's son."

"And in your audience with Mohan Lal – the one where you made no transaction with him – did he speak then of your son?"

I keep my face averted, as though to carefully choose my footing on a path corrugated by the heavy Nilgherrie rains. "He spoke of him little; other than to confirm the year of Kuruppan's birth, there was nothing said." I look away from Devadarshan, to the great, jungled slopes and rocky falls, but I feel his eyes on me.

"Please remind me – Kuruppan was born when?"

"He is five, making the year of his birth 1794."

For the briefest time, I think that the subject is closed; but no. Devadarshan wishes to play his damned counting games.

"That is, 1794 by the European calendar. But Mohan Lal will measure years by the Kaliyuga system, which commenced 3,104 years before the European calendar. So Kuruppan, by that reckoning, was born in the year 4898. And he is five years old this year, which is the year 4903. And so ..." Devadarshan looks inward, to where he makes numbers dance. "And so, we have the beginnings of a pattern. Five and 4903 – these are unitary numbers. They are the product only of one and themselves. And 4898, the year of Kuruppan's birth – why, this is the product of three unitary numbers, namely 2, 31 and 79. And three itself is another unitary number." For once, he looks me in the eye. "Do you see?"

"I see a happy coincidence. What of it?"

"Coincidence, say you? What year did you come to India?"

"Why, 1785."

"Which is Kaliyuga 4889. And this too is a unitary number."

"Which proves only that there are many such numbers!"

Devadarshan's voice is soft. "Indeed, they are infinite in number; and yet they are rare and special things. Now, why would Mohan Lal – " But he hesitates, as though to swallow his own question and digest it, and does not speak again. I confess, I am not sorry.

❖

Mohan Lal sat in his chair. I kneeled at his feet. Above us, the machine shifted and groaned, and made its mechanical speech. The plaint of metal on metal, yes, but also a noise not heard but felt: an immense hum, as if one put one's hand to a great hive. It troubled each hair on each part of my skin; it made my very bones shudder. "You hear it, *mali*? The power of infinity, which is the power of Number. The machine showed you the endlessness of what-might-be. There you roamed, among all futures, dreaming of a pretty new home for your pretty family."

He bent over me more closely, his eyes like windows onto an unmeasurable night.

"In that dream, that state of infinite possibility, the you that still lives waits, anchored by the bezoar, for your wife and son – while here, the you that cannot truly die lingers on. It is as if your fingers hold the madstone in that state of possible becoming, while your feet tread this world's soil, in this state of slow ending ... as if you are a bridge between this world and all other future worlds. How may we resolve this, *mali*?"

"Sir –"

"Hush, *mali*. Understand what I am offering you. As you said – it is a great gift." He clutched my hair with one hand, and brought my face closer to his. "Yet even gifts may have a price. Here is mine."

High above, the oculus was black against the rotunda's pale ceiling; for an instant, I thought I saw a blue star, but it went of a sudden, as if covered by a cloud.

"I give you a fork in the road, *mali*. To one side, this world of pain. Yes, I can bring you back from what-might-be, so that you may live and die here, in some way, with your family. But to the other side, all future possibilities, *mali*. Imagine this world changing in whatever way you please – you can make it so, by walking that other road. For down that road lies whatever happiness you will."

He now had my hair by both hands, I felt his stinking breath, rapid and shallow, on my face.

"But in return, I demand two things. First: that you remain a bridge between this world and all future worlds, for all those who wish to cross, until you find, with a clear conscience, the happiness you must seek. Second: that your what-might-be world has, at first, no wife, no child; rather that they join you in that world by crossing the bridge at a time of my choosing. And of the two, the child will go first."

He released my hair, and sat back.

"What do you say, then, mud-fingered one? Do we have an agreement?"

"Your Excellency – such generosity! I cannot sufficiently express my unbounded gratitude – "

"Do you agree?"

"Sir, forgive my poor understanding – there is a little thing I must ask. If the what-might-be world is much like this world, but changed – from what point do the changes begin? When does the fork in the road occur?"

"Such forks occur in every instant of every day, *mali*. But as for when you choose your road, and make yourself irrevocably part of this other destiny that you so desire, that occurs when the first soul crosses the bridge you make. And that will be the child."

"Then, sir, I only beg your permission to first move my Ukalypts, sir, and plant them in the Nilgherries, so that they await me – and my wife and child – in my new home, my new world! I beg you, Your Excellency!"

Lal looked at me; his lip curled back to show teeth like a dog's; his eyes froze my soul.

"Oh, simple, simple gardener! The removal of your trees – I permit it." He turned to his servant. "Absalom! The agreement!"

The giant proffered a palm-leaf scratched with Sanskrit symbols. Lal held it up in the uncertain light. "I will read it to you, simple gardener, in simple Tamil."

And he did, and the syllables of that simple Tamil are cut now into my foolish, reckless heart. That souls would cross the bridge I'd made; I thought I had understood the meaning of these words, but I had not.

❖

The bulk of our sepoy escort has now returned to Seringapatam, leaving us but four men. The departees will collect the empty carts we left at Goodaloor, but Devadarshan has instructed them to let stay two mares and a horse-drawn gharry there for our return journey.

In Ootakamandalam, the land has been cleared of weedy growths, and the planting has proceeded more rapidly than I could have expected. The hill-people are intelligent and capable workers, and cheerful too, which makes the labour an altogether more pleasant experience than to cajole assistance from those sullen folk who live more directly under the Sultan's heel. How much of this is due to the sight of silver mohurs and how much is due to the influence of Devadarshan, I do not know; for he speaks to them in the Toda language, which to me has few similarities with Tamil, and I understand not a word. But what care I? My trees sleep in their new beds, safe from British, Hyderabadi and Mysorean clutches alike. I declare, if I do not firm the soil about every one of my Ukalypts myself, I come unreasonably close to it; and when the work is done, the sight of these young plants upstanding in the rich, moist soil gladdens my heart as nothing may beyond Usha and Kuruppan.

And then, a change: unprovoked, it seems, and odd. For a long, sweet moment, I see a gentle future: the trees have grown to immense heights, as tall as the tallest oaks of Kent, and stand like dark sentinels in the low mists. The scent of Ukalypt gum and Ukalypt oil, a fragrance like no other, pervades the very mountains. Usha, in a sari as blue as the pure sky, walks with me through the trees, older but no less beautiful. She smiles at me, and my heart flies and sings like a lark. All is peace; all is joy. Then the change is reversed, and the vision slips away. But it leaves something which is not a memory. What then? A promise? It was as if our world had twisted to one side, and shown me another, just as real, but somehow more harmonious, less soaked in fear and blood. For the thousandth time, I consider Lal's promissory; its hope sustains me just as its fear erodes me.

"Does the work please?" Devadarshan speaks softly, but his voice, so near, brings me to the present with a start.

"Very greatly. Yes, very greatly."

"They are planted well. Without doubt, your Ukalypts will span human generations. The soil is good, nothing eats their leaves, and the Todas do not bring their buffalo here to trample and churn the ground." He hesitates. "But – forgive me – I sense that something troubles you."

"These are troubled times," I say. I find that I am gnawing at my muddy fingernails; Nilgherrie soil is gritty on my tongue.

"The times have been so for forty years or more; but you have been thus for six days now." He does not say it, but I know his meaning: *You have been thus since your meeting with Mohan Lal.*

"Think you so? I had not noticed."

But Devadarshan, as is his wont when I say something that is doltish or a deceit, remains silent. And suddenly, as though his silence needs a weight of words to balance it, I can hold my tongue no longer. I tell him of that night.

Devadarshan listens, quiet as a rock, as I describe the harrowing passage through Tippoo's dungeons; Mohan Lal and Absalom; the goat and the bezoar; the machine and the cradle; and the stars, the stars, the stars. The worlds within and without. The lives without burden. The endless joy.

As I speak, I do not look at Devadarshan; it is as though I tell my tale to seedlings and saplings, as though I cut my story into their young, growing heartwood. When I am done, I stand still, and for a moment I feel that this mountain is an axis that is set by different perspectives, and that the ground itself has become a void that waits to swallow me up; I am about to fall down, down, down. Far away, a man shouts to his buffaloes, and I am the silence into which his cry falls: alone in this universe and every universe.

"What else?" says Devadarshan eventually. I look at him; he looks at his feet. Damn him; if he can read my mind, why then ask me questions? But I know that he means well. My hesitation speaks more clearly than I could have guessed, however, for he speaks again, with urgency, as he answers his own question.

"What! No, surely you did not make an exchange with Mohan Lal?"

"You do not understand! In this week, of this year, our reality nudges others more closely than ever before – Mohan Lal showed me! I have seen them! Worlds where rulers are benevolent, and men are peaceful. The best part of me stayed in that universe of possibilities, tethered by the bezoar, and I am now a bridge to better worlds, happier lives. *Guiltless* lives. Remember how we spoke of threads splitting and re-uniting? When I return to Seringapatam, Kuruppan and Usha will enter Lal's machine, and walk across that bridge to where part of me waits for them, and then I will pull my feet from this world, and unite with my happier self, and my family, across the divide."

"Dull-witted gardener! It is your understanding that is incomplete, if you believe that Mohan Lal is in the habit of dispensing gifts to any without a far greater benefit to himself!"

"It is an exchange! A commercial transaction! When my family and I trade this life for a better, then energy must flow from that world to this. To preserve the balance, as Mohan Lal would have it. And that energy the old man will harvest, to extend his life. It is fair."

"If that is the entirety of the trade, simpleton, why would not Mohan Lal have chosen any other in the Kingdom of Mysore? What is special about this Spanish gardener – or his family – and why did he require your *willing* agreement?"

I am angered by his tone. "Perhaps Lal is less black than you would colour him. Anyway, there is no harm in such star-gazy alchemy." My assertion is as much question as statement; I know it, and he knows it.

"No harm, say you? Kuruppan reaches the age of five in this year of Kaliyuga 4903; the year that, by Lal's calculations, as you say, other realities come closest to our own. The numbers mesh like cogs – and now I understand the nature of his interest in your son! To push your boy's life-energy into another world, to steal the balance as it flows back into this existence, and suck on it like a snake on a cow's teat – this is how the old man lives on. But your *son*!"

I feel cold, and small, and weighed down by something immense. I do not know how I am not crushed. Yet still I only say the lies that I wish were true. "It is but a commercial agreement. Am I not a trader, of a sort? I know how these things can be written and rewritten, and read in one way or another."

"So this gardener – forgive me, this *trader* – believes he can outwit Mohan Lal with words."

It is time for my last tarot draw. After this, the pack has only hanged men. "I was more artful than you know," I say. "I have not told you *this*: that Mohan Lal dictated the contract thus – that my 'heir and successor, the boy who is Kurban, must be the first to cross the bridge'. You see? Mohan Lal had the wrong name – he stipulated not Kuruppan, but Kurban. I have *no son* named Kurban." I nod at Devadarshan; but my cunning sounds hollow even to me, and he does not return my weak smile. Something about the way he shakes his head, slow and sad, clutches and twists the core of me.

"Your son is named Kuruppan, true," says Devadarshan. "But he is also Kurban, after the contract. Know you not? Kurban, in the Persian tongue favoured by the Sultan's ministers, means only this: *sacrifice*."

❖

The descent from Ootakamandalam is painfully slow; with but four sepoys to guard us, some of the villagers we pass become sufficiently bold to demand taxes in consideration of our feet pressing their land.

But we reach Goodaloor before darkness. There is a gharry, there, as instructed; thank God.

I do not sleep.

The morning brings a calm that I cannot trust. I breathe, long and slow, but feel that my lungs move only out of habit. Our sepoys are tense; they scan the horizon, and mutter to themselves. The British have moved faster than expected: their redcoats are close now, very close; everyone knows it. It is in the air; columns of smoke speak of it, crows gather and caw of it. And now the will to desert is in our escorts' eyes; if they decide for that route, they will doubtless murder us.

We set off as early as possible, at a pace likely to kill the horses; the gharry shudders as if to fall apart, but this gladdens me. I wish only to hold Usha and Kuruppan again and flee humanity's follies; to immerse myself in the lore of plants, in the quiet pleasures of their growth; to escape forever the barbarity of Man.

An eternity of dusty, bone-shaking hours passes in each tortured minute; late afternoon at last sees us close to our goal. We must go more slowly, however, as we approach Seringapatam, for fear of British or Hyderabadi troops, and each delay presses another skewer of ice through my heart. On one occasion, seeing my distress, Devadarshan attempts to give some solace through conversation, but in the way that he has, his words are less than comforting.

"That your son was born on a day and time such that his life force peaks exactly when the tangents of two realities touch – fortune smiled on Mohan Lal, it seems. Your only hope is to flee with your family before Lal starts the exchange."

"Would he not re-negotiate? I would do anything – I would serve him until death – "

"This agreement is of a form which cannot be easily reworked, still less undone. Mohan Lal's artifice has rewritten your very destiny. Did you not feel the shifting of worlds when you said *Yes, I agree* – said it, while the energies of every universe flowed through the machine? While the bezoar you held – and hold somewhere still – was warmed by another sun? Your life is now aligned with different stars. You would serve him until death, you say! It maybe that such service is already your destiny, my friend, and that you will now bridge souls for Mohan Lal until some other destiny annuls the contract."

I have no answer.

We reach the banks of the Cauvery barely before the British and the Hyderabadis; they are a mile distant, but it feels less than a hair's breadth. And we come perilously close to death from Tippoo's regiments: my pale skin invites a fusillade, and musket balls sing past our ears. One hits the cart, making the sepoy driver risk life to stand and show his uniform. Another ball hits me in the arm, and embeds itself in flesh. There is neither pain nor blood, and I squeeze it out as if it were naught but a splinter. Devadarshan sees this, and I read something in his eyes I have not seen before. Fear? No – it is pity. Pity.

The bridge to Tippoo's island fort has been barricaded; we abandon the cart and horses, and are admitted by men with faces full of the intents of war. I had thought to return to my house and collect Usha and Kuruppan, but Devadarshan pulls me with him.

"None are beyond the fort walls but soldiers now, and most of them Tippoo's enemies. Your family will be within."

I look towards my bungalow, my empty fields, the old banyan tree. They belong, now, to a different time, a different world.

Part III: Little boy blue

The sound and fury of this war horrifies; I had not thought it would be so hellish. From the British, the boom and echo of massed cannon; the whine and wallop of great ordnance. From Tippoo, the fusillades of rockets, bastinado after fiery bastinado breaking the very air. The crack and splinter of stone; the shouts and curses, the wails. The smoke stinging throat and eyes. The men grinning with the witless joy of battle. The stink of blood.

We race to the inner fort, Devadarshan and I. We seem safer here from missiles; yet the people are more tense and fearful. Perhaps it is because they are not sepoys, but women, children and old folk. They have not the release of action; they can only wait for their fate to be made known to them.

We search face after grim and tearful face, but I see no Usha, no Kuruppan. A massive explosion in the outer part of the fort makes us cover our heads. Burning hail pitter-patters around us, and lies smoking on the ground. Devadarshan grimaces and brushes hot metal from his arm; his skin blisters. My shirt is pock-marked with black-rimmed holes.

And then, another elision, at this time of all times: this day of May slips aside and I see a world ruled by blue gods, where colours shimmer like the purples of a peacock's tail, where there is peace and justice and all are brothers. I see an England in which the primroses and daffodils are putting up their pretty heads; where buds unfurl in Kent's orchards; where the snow's grip is but an unkind memory; where the Green Man winks from every bush. I see the mists of the Nilgherries, and a figure walking towards me through the swirling grey. A blue sari. I reach out my arms.

"Come back!" Someone speaks to me; it is Devadarshan. "You must find Usha and the child!" Yes, indeed I must. Not far off, there is a dull, continuous roar. A fire. The gunpowder magazine has caught.

"Look for them inside," says Devadarshan. "I will bring a weapon."

Someone calls to me; I turn, full of hope, but it is only Nanjan. He cowers at the foot of a wall, blinking at this world of noise.

"My family?" I bend and shout into his ear between explosions. He only gapes at me; I grasp him by the shoulders and shake him. "My family!" Something jolts his mind, and he grimaces with sorrow. "Below. They were taken below." He points with his chin.

I look around. From across the square, Vauquelin stares at me, head lowered like a bull. He is standing by the entrance to Tippoo's dungeons.

❖

"Well, *Spaniard*? The British make merry dancing partners, do they not?"

From the outer walls, the sound of musketry increases in intensity. The final assault has begun.

"I did not expect you to return, *Spaniard.*" His clumsy emphases do not escape me, but I no longer care. "Have you come to dance with Vauquelin, perhaps?"

"I have come for my family."

Vauquelin's blubbery lips are wet; one cheek bears scratches. His French officer's uniform is marked by sweat and dust. Something changes in his expression; it comes to his eyes, sees me, and sinks again, like a goonch taking a mouthful of air in a befouled river.

"Your family! They are beyond all harm, *Spaniard.* Follow me!"

Into the dungeons, then. As we descend, the sounds of war are modulated to bass grumbles that come up through ground and feet. Sudden tremors bring dust from the vaulted ceilings. Most cells are empty now; those that are not tell the expected tale. The Lancer is still bound to his chair, but it lies on its side, and the nails in his skull show only a little shank below their heads. The drummer boy's throat has been slit, and the top of his ghagra choli is stained dark. Their pain is done; their threads cut; they have found a gentler world.

"Here, *Spaniard.* Here." Vauquelin steps aside with mock courtesy, and gestures to the next cell. I walk in front of him to better see in the gloom.

Usha hangs, naked. Her blue sari is stretched taut between her throat and the iron hook set in the dungeon ceiling. Against the reddish ochre of the dungeon walls, the cloth sings out as though it were a slice of sky sent to collect her; to pull her up, up to realms of cerulean.

"Well, *Spaniard*? Will you not embrace your wife?"

Her body bears the signs of what Vauquelin did to her before death; I remember the scratches on his face. Behind me, he breathes fast and heavily; the tableau excites him.

"You were lucky to have such a pretty thing, Spaniard – life's dice favoured you in this, as they have in other matters before and since."

I am only half listening to him, if at all. The man-maggot's thoughts are of no consequence, now, for Usha is gone. As I look at her body, I feel a grief of infinite magnitude, a guilt that cannot die. I wonder how pain so great can be contained in all creation, let alone in this small world. None can forgive me but Usha, and Usha is dead.

"And yet you gambled her away, her and your son. Does that knowledge sit well with you, *Spaniard*?"

I feel the turn of the cosmos, and wonder that its momentum does not crush us all. What did Devadarshan once say? *There is no new thing in this world – only echoes of echoes, that echo forever.* From above, another terrible explosion makes the dungeon walls shudder, and sets Usha's feet a-trembling.

"When Mohan Lal asked for your brat child, *Spaniard*, after you fled to the mountains, your wife came too, to calm the child's bratty fears. They played little games, *Spaniard*. So sweet. Little songs, they sang. They did not know I listened. And I may not have your facility with languages, *Spaniard*, but even I know that *Little Boy Blue*" – he spits out the English – "is not the tongue of Spain!"

He is very close now; I can feel his breath.

"You have been lucky – but no gambler's run is endless – *Englishman!*"

The dagger's blade slices into my throat, passing through veins and arteries, driving down and across and lodging against my collarbone. It is a mere nothing, in itself, but the force of the blow unbalances me and takes me to the ground. Vauquelin has left the knife in my neck, and stands over me, triumphant, eyes full of a murderer's joy. Again, the ground shudders with British ordnance; dust falls from the vaulted stone of the dungeon roof, the motes like little stars in this black, black pit.

On my knees, I hold Vauquelin's eyes as I take the bloodless blade from my throat. His surprise is almost comical; he turns this way and that, he looks me up and down. It is as if he seeks to wake from a dream. But it is no dream; at least, no more of a dream than any other possible life or possible death. Yes, in this world, in this dream, it is now that I kill Vauquelin. In another world, I would take more time, and do it right, but here Kuruppan waits for me. So from my position on the floor I drive the blade up, up between Vauquelin's legs, through his ballock bag and into his bum-gut, and as he flails and screams I twist the blade, again and again, until my hand is fouled with what leaks from this hog of a man. "*St Cast,*" I say, and perhaps there is a glint of understanding in his eye, but I cannot really tell.

I leave Vauquelin bleeding his life away beneath Usha's gently swinging body. He will die beneath the soles of her feet, and that is an honour too great for him by far.

◈

I know where Kuruppan will be. God forgive me, I have always known it. I continue through the dungeon passage to Mohan Lal's observatory. The door is open; gloom seems to flow from it. The cries of battle are clearer than in the dungeons, yet seem further away. As though we are high, high above man's feeble disputes. I walk in. I still hold Vauquelin's dagger.

The tatties over the oculus are closed. In the half-light, I see black ashes on the cold flags. Mohan Lal's machine has grown: its girders and cogs, like the skeleton of an iron monster, now make a structure that fills the room's volume, a pagoda-shaped cage. But it is more alive than any skeleton or Chinese temple: it moves, this machine; it moves. And I swear, in its iron voice I hear words, ghastly syllables formed by the clank of chain and grind of cog. I look up. High above, suspended on a frame, I see a small figure, a splash of colour that almost glows in the half-light. It is Kuruppan; he has been painted blue, all blue, from head to toe. Each slow shift of the machine, each cog's roundwise step, raises his cradle higher, towards the machine's apex. And directly below the cradle, fixing me with the infinite night of his eyes, is Mohan Lal.

I call out to Kuruppan. His eyes are open, but they do not see me. The scent of moonflower overwhelms. The machine groans and shrieks, and Kuruppan's cage is winched yet higher. His feet twitch, and a hand reaches out to one that only he can see. To one that makes a bridge.

I start towards Mohan Lal; he has not moved. As I approach, he does not take his eyes from me; they are like pools of jet in a paper mask. Their hostility chills me. I fear him, this old man; yet I will kill him if I can. But as I start forward, I am lifted from my feet and hurled to the ground. Vauquelin's dagger skitters across the stones. Above me,

Absalom looms; eyes wide, he raises a talwar high above his head, two handed, ready to slice me in half.

"Stop!" Mohan Lal's voice is thin, but it pierces the air like a stiletto blade. "Sheath your talwar, Absalom; but hold him. The *mali* cannot die by such means. That part of him which lives, which truly lives, is no longer of this world. You feel it, do you not, *mali*? And if you are not of this world, if you are not truly alive in this here-and-now, why, how then can you die in it?"

Absalom pinions me with arms as thick as a strong man's legs. My feet dangle in the air as though I am a child; I feel Absalom's beard at the back of my neck. The machine groans again, and Kuruppan's cage judders. Outside the walls there is a fusillade of musketry, and someone shrieks with the pain of a mortal wound.

"All the universe requires balance, *mali* – remember? Balance between one world and another, one reality and another, one death and another. The gods dream of balance."

Something strikes a massive blow to the outside wall; one of the stones is pushed inwards, and plaster is thrown across the floor in shards and dust. The British have trained their cannon on the rotunda.

"But what now can balance a grief such as yours? It extends across all worlds; it troubles the dreams of each god, in every universe. It will contaminate all that it touches. You will search for its equivalent, yes, seeking forever a pain that matches yours and yet is healed, a forgiven guilt, but I do not think you will find it. Rather, all that you touch shall seek to exchange this world's grief for the promise of another world's joy – and you will bridge their worlds, *mali*, such that they annul their every self. To balance such a weight of zero – *mali*, it would be as if the force of every river's flow could find a single confluence, a single *I*."

The syllables of the machine have become more insistent; there is language there, but I cannot understand it. Kuruppan has reached the zenith; the machine reaches metal fingers towards him.

"There is more still; think you that you have reached the extreme of pain? You have not." Mohan Lal turns his gaze upwards, to Kuruppan. I struggle mightily, but Absalom is immoveable.

"This machine, where your son swings? Only a set of scales, *mali*. See how it moves, the machine? It is drawn by the very stars. Do you not feel their push and pull? Each five, thirteen and eighty-nine years, the pull waxes, and wanes the other years. And in this most unique year, where the cycles intersect, the pull is uniquely strong. Another reality, another world, close enough to touch, *mali.*"

Lal speaks to me, but his gaze remains upward: to my beloved son, to the invisible stars, to the uttermost Infinite.

"But this world is enough for me; I love it enough to never leave. How then to trade my death away? The accounts must be balanced, *mali.* To remain dreaming this dream, I must pull the thread from another god's dream; but what may I replace it with?"

The machine inclines its many talons towards Kuruppan, closer and closer still; its metal shriek rises in volume and pitch, and its chains shudder ever more violently.

"Not all souls are equivalent, *mali.* There are ripe mangoes, and there are grains of unsoaked rice. And to harvest the ripest of all fruit, not once but twice, in this reality and that – oh, *mali*! To send your own son to *two* deaths – what now can bound your guilt and grief?"

The tatties at the roof start to pull back, and Kuruppan raises his blue arms to the circle of bright sky, reaching up, up to where the smoke of war sublimes into a depthless azure. As though in parody, Mohan Lal raises his arms similarly, stretching up towards the machine's closing fist.

"Be gone, little mango."

I start to scream, but an explosion next to my ear drowns my voice, and Absalom takes me to the floor, his great weight landing across my legs and hips. He has fallen in such a way that his face is towards me; part of his temple and one eye have been blown away, and the blood runs freely over his face and into his beard. As I struggle from beneath him, I feel an arm under mine, helping me up.

"Hurry!" It is Devadarshan, appearing as though a gift from God. Fumes as blue as pyre's smoke still rise from the musket that he fired into Absalom's head. I look towards the roof, to where Kuruppan dangles in his cradle-cage, below the circle of sky. There is some trick of the light about him; the blue of his painted skin makes a harmony. It is a divine sound and I shudder with something akin to ecstasy. But Mohan Lal is bathed in the same glow, and the triumph on his face tells all. I run at him, but then the air becomes suddenly weighty, pulling itself from my lungs and hurling great lumps of stone through the air. The British: the wall has been breached. There is another mighty concussion, and the air is darkened by white dust.

❖

They pick their way over the rubble, these redcoats with wary faces; firearms at the ready, they look at me curiously, wondering perhaps how I still live. All is silent; at least, I hear nothing. Mohan Lal's machine is a tangled wreck of girders and chains, like an iron net that harvests shattered masonry and the choking dust of war. The cradle-cage which held Kuruppan swings gently, now only a few feet above the floor; it is intact still, but empty. Below it, Mohan Lal's European chair waits, strangely undamaged and upright, albeit covered in plaster dust; and next to that, his basket, overturned and open wide. One would think that Lal lies crushed beneath the fallen roof of his observatory, but I know that it is not so. And as I look towards the breached wall, I see a long thin shape – as grey and ungrippable as quicksilver, as intangible as a dream – slide over the ground and past a British soldier. The soldier stabs at it with his bayonet, and the whip and writhe of its body suggest a serious wound, towards its tail, where Lal's leg would be if the cobra were still Lal; but I know he will live, just as I know I cannot die. Now the soldier trains his musket on me, his face full of suspicion; his lips move, but I hear nothing.

Something shifts at my feet: Darshan. I bend down to raise his shoulders from the floor; his blood congeals in the powdered plaster. The wounds I see on his belly are such as cannot heal. A long gash in his scalp starts flowing freely, and a scarlet rivulet runs down his nose, making a droplet. As it falls, it catches the sun and winks at me merrily. My hearing is returning; there are soldiers shouting at me, but I do not mind them, for Darshan is speaking.

"Echoes of echoes," he says, "and more echoes of them, forever."

"I am sorry," I say. Indeed I am; infinitely and immeasurably so. Everything I touch, I destroy; all who love me die. Where is the balance? I wanted none of this. I wanted only to grow my trees and trade their harvest.

"Sorry," he repeats, but he says it in English. For some reason, he smiles as he dies.

The redcoats have lost patience and moved on; none impede me as I get to my feet and walk to the shattered wall. I look through the breach: the Hyderabadi regiments too have advanced, and now they run hot-foot up the slopes, towards me. Behind them, the Cauvery flows as it has for a thousand years or more. A few more deaths on its banks are as nothing to its unending march; tomorrow's pyres are less. I walk to its amber currents. The Hyderabadis assume, I guess, that I am one of their British colleagues; in any event, none challenge me. The water is cool on my feet; plaster dust ribbons away. Clash of cymbal, bellow of horn: war's music, the sound of men killing men, recedes as I follow the bank's gentle curve to my empty fields. My trees grow now in Ootakamandalam, yes, in this reality and in another, as that snake-souled devil promised; but my feet are rooted here while my fingertips claw another soil. The I that is *I* is suspended between, while Usha is dead in one world and Kuruppan gone, now, from both.

What does life hold when death is impossible? Perhaps I can subsume myself in the mountain mists – a ghost in the cold clouds – until there is nothing left of me but my loss. Perhaps I can become but the shape of a memory, missed by none, forgotten by all; a pale echo that sounds in other's lives, again and again, until one day it is answered by its own true echo and finds a sweet silence in that final union, that blessed confluence. Perhaps. Oh, Usha. Oh, Kuruppan.

A movement, from the higher ground above my fields, glimpsed from the corner of my eye; as if a red flag had flapped at the window of my bungalow. I drag my feet up the slope; here a terracotta shard, there a divot of red soil, there a dried Ukalypt leaf. The slurry of vaunted ambition.

When I push open the door, he does not hide. On the floor, his discarded redcoat; to one side, a gun that looks bigger than he. The boy's lips tremble; his trousers are stained with his fear. To send children into battle – what barbarity! Indeed, I know it well. But I can speak to this child, and weigh his guilt against mine. Desertion and cowardice? Yes, boy; I can speak of these. Come – let me show you another world, where you are braver, perhaps; maybe one where you slay Tippoo himself. Or, maybe, a world where you never left your mother's hug in Roseland, and you still run on the Cornish beaches with your young sister, and this land of heat and blood is but a half-heard rumour. Listen, boy. All worlds are real; they are just a stretch of hemp away, a well-placed blade away, a little bridge's span away. Choose this one, choose that one, boy; why not? Anything is better than this. So come, come; walk with me across the bridge, before its own weight, questing the water it straddles, makes it fall. For your grief and shame are tiny against mine: look, boy, look at what I have done. My own dear Usha hangs; my own son is unmade by my own thoughtless greed; my only friend is killed trying to help me, to reverse the mistakes I made. Such pain, boy! This world is full of it, now and forever. What can balance it but better lives in other worlds? It must be so. So come now; walk with me a little way. We will find balance, in this world or another.

Yes, there will be balance, boy; one day, there will be balance.

REDEMPTION THROUGH HER BLOOD

The Last Weeks of Edward Laseron,
Vicar of St Stephen's Church, Ootacamund, South India;
Incorporating Extracts from his Diary of 1861

We are expecting Sir William Denison, the new Governor of Madras, this week; it will be his first visit to Ootacamund. He will worship in St Stephen's, of course, so I must make it ready. But I have Monday for that.

Today, then, let the hassocks stay a-scattered and askew. Today, let me wait and beg, again, for an unreachable solace.

I unlock the church door: hinges grind into a counterfeit quiet. She is not here.

I wish I knew her name.

I sit towards the back of the church, on the chair furthest from the aisle, and close my eyes. The scent of last Sunday's worship: dead flowers, wood polish, old damp. The sounds of this high hill-station: crows, a horse and cart, and, far away, the angry lowing of a Toda buffalo. I lean to one side and rest my head against the wall.

Probably Denison will, like his predecessors, stay here in the mountains until the summer abates, and then return to a more comfortable Madras. Probably he will be as rigid and joyless and authoritarian as all those who England sends us in these times, with the

Mutiny less than five years dead – if dead it is. But those are matters for the Government; I can only make sermons, marriages and christenings.

And burials. I have done enough of them. Though some bodies, I believe, need no burial, and that is worse.

I shift in my chair, but find no comfort. St Stephen's is always so cold. The pillars, plastered and painted, resemble stone. Yet when you tap them, with a knuckle – *toc* – they sound hollowly, and with a hopeless note. As if their wood carries echoes from whence they came, as if the teak beams of Lal Bagh had been drenched in despair.

That St Stephen's roof sits on timber that once framed Lal Bagh's walls, Saunders once hinted, was reason enough for his aversion to St Stephen's doors. *Not because of Armytage, then?* I asked him. He gave me an empty stare and pulled at the dirty bandage on his neck. *Lal Bagh was more red than its name, more red than you can ever know,* he said. *As for Armytage, I offered only to make of his suffering a small and fleeting thing. Can you say as much, Laseron? Well?*

That was in the days I spoke to Saunders willingly, before they killed Emma and Kumar, and before I knew what Saunders was. Even so, I did not answer him.

Entry of Tues, 30th July 1861

Denison arrived today, with his entourage. He is staying at Lushington Hall; naturally.

Entry of Sat, 3rd August 1861

Today I made St Stephen's clean & neat in preparation for tomorrow's service. Such tasks tire me more week by week; my bones ache, my will bends. Only God – I suppose – keeps this man-shaped husk in motion. But since Armytage, I will not ask for human assistance. My small pains are atonement, & atonement may bring expiation, perhaps.

I would ask the woman in the blue sari of this, if I dared. If I were worthy.

After laying out the hassocks & hymn books, I add another verse to the Bible board at the back of the church: "As far as the East is from the West, so far has he removed our transgressions from us." Psalm 103:12. My sermon tomorrow shall focus again on forgiveness.

Forgiveness. Absolution. Redemption. Without such graces, life is inward agony. May God, or she who waits, grant me them.

❖

The service goes as such things go. Denison does as such men do, taking the front pew as if by divine right. He glances about St Stephen's, eyebrows up and mouth's corners down, as if our little church is a hovel that His Excellency graces, but reluctantly.

"Thank you, Laseron," he says to me afterwards.

"Thank you, Sir William," I reply. He looks at me askance, as if he expects more. I hold my peace, clam-like. But, being one of those who cannot abide silence, or who believes that the delivery of information is the same as good manners, Denison must speak, and above all (it seems), must speak of his own interests: of natural history, astronomy and the like; of his hopes that the life-filled sholas and clear skies of these mountains will support his amateur investigations, and perhaps even provide opportunity for planetary observations new to science. I gesture at the mists. "The skies are not always clear, Sir William," I say. He laughs and strides away: every inch the man who can do as he pleases, and always does, and always will.

I could have called after him: *And the sholas hold as much death as life.* But that would not have led to easy conversations.

Entry of Sun, 4th August 1861

When Denison left me, after the service, I locked St Stephen's door. As I turned away, I heard her. Behind me, in the empty church, weeping. Why? For all the unforgiven? For me? For Saunders?

"Their sins and lawless acts I will remember no more." Hebrews 10:17.

❖

The week before he killed himself, Armytage told me that Saunders came to him in the night, each night, and spoke to him endlessly. I did not ask him of what, and he did not offer to tell me; not then anyway.

Later he told all, but that day he had other concerns. Rather, a single concern: *How does one obtain forgiveness?* he asked. *True forgiveness?*

That was thirty years ago – I was hardly past twenty, and new to the church – and I gave him the answers the church gives to such questions. I did not then know what he meant by *shame* and *guilt*. But the others did, and they let him walk to the shola, the night he died. They let him walk there alone.

Their sins and lawless acts I will remember no more. But how can *we* forget, we poor men; how can we forget our sins: our acts, and the times we did not act? Making a tablet in his memory, and setting it in the wall of St Stephen's, in no way balances how they abandoned him and how they buried him.

How *we* abandoned him and buried him.

Entry of Sun, 11th August 1861

Each Sunday is more difficult for me; how can I preach of the forgiveness of sins when I am beyond forgiveness? I am dirty; the very soul of me is filth. There is no water that can clean me.

❖

After today's service, Denison lingers outside; I see him, by the church gates, holding forth to hangers-on. The false laughter of sycophants; the broad smiles of underlings; their over-friendly fare-thee-wells when he dismisses them. As I put my vestments away, he comes back into the church. Up the aisle he strides, grim-faced and cold-eyed, like a teacher who would whip a child.

"Laseron," he says.

"Sir William," I reply.

"I could not help noticing a native lady in the congregation," he says. "A woman in a blue sari. Standing at the back, in the shadows, head bent. As if to hide her face."

Or as if in prayer, I think. But I only say: "I did not see her."

"Since the Mutiny," he says, "the policy is to maintain distance between the British and the Indians. I hope to see you adhere to this more scrupulously. The Indians have their own churches."

I adjust the church plate and vestments on their shelves; I lock the cupboard. The pause grows longer than politeness allows. The silence becomes bloated. It is clear that Denison insists on some response, and will wait until he gets it. Should I feed him a semblance of polite acquiescence? Yes, I should; but I cannot. I turn and face him.

"Well?" he says.

"I take Napier's view," I say. And as I say it, I can almost hear Emma reading Napier's words to me, all those five violent, bloody years ago.

"I beg your pardon?" he says.

"Sir Charles Napier," I continue. "In his final book, he said this: '*The Eastern intellect is great, and supported by amiable feelings, and the Native officers have a full share of Eastern daring, genius and ambition; but to nourish these qualities they must be placed on a par with European officers*.' Had the Company and its army listened to old Napier," I say, "there may have been *no* Mutiny."

Denison is silent; I have the impression it is only my dog-collar that keeps him temperate. When he speaks, it is with the accent of a razor. "You do not understand," he says, "it is not a matter of amiable feelings, still less of recognising daring, et cetera, et cetera. It is a matter of ensuring the safety and security of Europeans in a land where we are vastly outnumbered. That requires attention to hierarchy. Perhaps you did not see the Mutiny's excesses. In any case, let me hear no more nonsense, either from Napier or you. Good day to you."

Perhaps I did not see the Mutiny's excesses! Oh Emma!

❖

Today being Thursday, the day I visit parishioners, I go to the Mackays' cottage, to minister to them and their infant boy, Arthur. We pray by the child's bed, all three, while the air rasps at his lungs.

On my return from this household of pain and worry, I see Denison. He is in fine fettle, as such men always are, untouched as ever by the trials of others.

"An evening promenade, Sir William?" I ask.

He waves a brass telescope at me: "I am going up to the ridge," he says. "The night is fine, and I dare say it was on just such a one that

Johann Galle discovered Neptune, only fifteen years past. Who knows what I may see from these equatorial peaks?"

Who knows indeed, I think, looking at the ridge and remembering what lies just beyond. "It is not safe," I say. And when he hides his sneer in such a way as to indicate contempt, I add, "There are leopards in these hills; sometimes tigers."

"There are no man-eaters here," he says.

"Even the jackals can be troublesome," I reply. (What else could I say? That there are more ways than one to eat a man?)

"Jacks be damned," he says. "I am a soldier, and I have a gun as well as a telescope."

And so he does. I watch him march up the slope, closer to the stars, closer to the endless reach of destiny.

Guns and soldiers; I have seen enough of them, from both sides.

❖

Entry of Sun, 18th August 1861

The service today was an agony; each word was dragged from me by habit alone, while my congregation shuffled & sighed. Outside, the mists were as heavy as I have ever seen, & the church's windows admitted only a thin, grey light. I struggled with the impression that those before me, who sat & stood & sung & prayed as I bade them, were only puppets, creatures of straw & string, & that beyond St Stephen's walls there was nothing but infinite void & that in all of creation there was nothing of substance beyond this church & these puppets, & that I was the only living thing in all places & times.

I do not count Saunders as a living thing. Nor her in the blue sari; but they are outside life in different ways. She is beyond it, while he is lost to it. He cannot even die.

I wonder if he himself made the unhealed wound in his throat.

❖

After Evensong, Denison again comes to me. He is characteristically abrupt, uncharacteristically subdued.

"I have some questions," he says. "Captain Morgan of your congregation indicated you might have answers. After all, you have been here thirty years, have you not?"

"Thirty years in India," I say.

"I understood that you had been here in Ootacamund throughout," he says.

"All except one year," I say.

"Which was?" he asks. I tell him when and where.

"Ah? You were in Meerut in '57? During the Mutiny?"

He speaks with a smile, as though it were a badge of honour. *Oh, Emma! Oh, you dear people who helped us so!*

"For my sins," I say. "But your questions, Sir William?"

He frowns at that, like one who is accustomed to direct the conversation, not to follow it; but accepts the change of course after a brief hesitation.

"You know I went to make astronomical observations, three nights ago, on the ridge," he says, "and an excellent night it was, clear as gin, quiet as the grave, even the jacks had hushed their howling. Well, I went over the ridge and down a little way to keep out of the wind. There I set up my telescope. I had hardly focused on the Pleiades when I noticed a scent, a familiar scent. One that I remembered from my time in Van Diemen's Land. The smell of blue gums. Such memories it brought!"

He stops briefly, as if listening to a whisper, then shakes his head and continues.

"With but one gun, and no dog, on a dark night, I did not wish to tramp around unknown countryside, and in any case I had sidereal observations to make. Also, I did not fully trust my sense for fragrance: I am not a hound. But I determined to return the next day, and did so, and – what do you think? There is a grove of blue gums over the ridge, Sir! More than a grove, a small wood! Damn my eyes if there is not!"

More than your eyes may be damned in that wood, I think.

"But how do Australian trees come to be planted in this remote corner of India?" Denison continues. "For planted they were, of that there is no doubt, and that several decades ago. Blue gums grow fast, it is true; but those trees are near two hundred feet, which needs a half century or more of growth."

"I know nothing of trees," I say.

He muses before resuming. "Yet the residents of Ootacamund are aware of that quiet, sweet-smelling place, are they not? They must be: I found a worked stone on the ground, in the middle of the wood. Perhaps two feet square, and I do not know how deep, but it was proud of the earth by six inches."

"If that is all, there will be another six inches below the earth," I say.

He looks at me askance. "So you do know it. Then what do the letters mean: *G.A.*?"

"Let me show you," I say. I take him to the back of the church. I push aside the Bible board to reveal what I prefer the board to hide. There it is, to one side of the church doors, set in the wall. The black tablet. The words chiselled into it are unpainted; in the church's gloom, one must squint to read them. But I know them by heart, and while Denison bends over the dark stone, I recite what I remember them to say:

In a wood near this place lie the remains of Lieut. George Armytage of the 6th Light Cavalry, who died at Ootacamund on 7th June 1830, aged 30.

Denison straightens and turns to me. "There is a British soldier, buried out there, among the blue gums? But why, when your St Stephen's graveyard is perfectly adequate?"

"Armytage shot himself, Sir William. Consecrated ground was deemed too pure for a suicide. We buried him where he died." (I do not add: In the hope that the pain that followed him would also be interred. We were disappointed in that, and more).

"You were there?" he asks.

"I had arrived in Ooty hardly a month before," I say.

"My understanding is that the church accepted suicides into its hallowed earth, even thirty years ago," he says.

"There had been a change in the law, about that time, yes," I say. "But changes in English law have always been slow to reach this part of India. We did what we thought was best, and buried him as suicides then were buried."

I hope Denison will ask me more of Armytage – I ache to unburden my conscience – but his mind moves on. The grief and guilt of thirty years past mean nothing to him. He starts speaking of blue gums, and of how well the Australian trees evidently grow in this climate, and of making more such plantations to remedy the paucity and cost of local firewood. He turns to leave, but something strikes him; he speaks to me over his shoulder.

"Odd," he says, "that people leave such fine fuel and kindling to lie there, on the ground. I dare say I tripped over enough to warm Lushington Hall for a month of Sundays."

"The wood is not theirs," I say. But he has already gone, fumbling at cigars and lucifers.

◈

Entry of Thurs, 22nd August 1861

Arthur Mackay has been taken by the Lord. The funeral is set for Saturday. In this death, at least, I had no guilty part. But it cut at the soul of me still, for once again I found myself powerless before an existence that has neither pity nor remorse, & to which all my prayers & entreaties are as smoke in the wind, & this only made me think again of Meerut. And Emma. And Kumar.

"In him we have redemption through his blood, the forgiveness of sins." Ephesians 1:7

◈

Yes, Meerut aches in me like an ulcer. Saunders knows it; he now salts this running sore daily.

And he is right. I could have stood between Johnson and Kumar; I doubt Johnson would have shot me, though truly he was like a man possessed. He had loved Emma, and he wanted blood to balance Emma's blood, and any blood would do as long as it was Indian blood. But I did not try to stop Johnson, and so Kumar – who had done nothing, nothing – died. Nor did I intercede for the others. Man, woman or child; I did not try.

My poor, dirty crucified soul! I know that the one in blue may forgive me if she wishes; Armytage told me that, just as he told me of Saunders (and I now know all that he said of Saunders to be true, so why not the rest?). But I have not seen her now for days, weeks.

I do not think she knows where or when she comes, nor even where 'here' is, if indeed she is ever *here* in any sense that we can understand.

I wonder if she looks for Saunders, or he for her.

❖

I do not know what to say in tomorrow's sermon that I have not already said, year in, year out. Innocents suffer, and we are all complicit in that, and who will forgive us? We ask God, of course, but his silence is an infinite enigma. Its pain has no ending.

I wish for peace and so I go walking among what Denison says are blue gums from Australia. It is true their fragrance is sweet; I remember it from the burying of Armytage. Indeed, the beauty of the setting – the clean perfume of the trees, the pure light of the mountains – sat uncomfortably with the ugliness of what Armytage's fellow soldiers did. Of what we all did.

They – we – had tied his body to a plank, to keep it rigid. His comrades, if that is what they should be called, laid it by the hole they had dug. An awkward grave, difficult to make; six feet deep, but only two feet by two feet broad. A well for the ill-starred. I remember the men cursed in an ungodly way as the digging proceeded, while Armytage's bound body waited patiently, a thing of sadness, of recrimination, of shame.

I said the words they wanted me to say. Then two men took hold of the foot-end of the plank, tipped it up and slid it – board and body together – down into the narrow hole, so that Armytage's crown was at the grave's dark base and his feet at the opening. As if he had dived into the earth.

I shall always remember the soles of his boots facing the sky, and the dirt collecting in the angle of their heels as the men filled in the grave. When they stamped the earth down afterwards, it had a hollow ring, as though Armytage were stamping back from below.

But I push those memories aside; I did not come here for them. I came for peace and, maybe, forgiveness.

The stone is still there, as Denison said it was. It is more mossed and buried than I remember, of course. For no reason, and not from disrespect, I stand on it. For a moment, I feel that Armytage and I tread on each other's soles, I head up and he, directly below me, head down. As if the stone were a mirror placed upon the ground, and Armytage's dead bones the reflection of my guilty life.

The woods bring me no peace, no absolution. Only whispers.

As I trudge away from the shola, back up to the ridge, something makes me look behind. There is a man, a European, watching me; I do not need to see the bandage on his throat to know who it is.

Sometimes I think Saunders may sleep there, among the blue gums; cold and weather mean nothing to such as he.

❖

Entry of Sun, 25th August 1861

I wish I had known more about forgiveness when Armytage came to me for help. And I wish I had known more of the one in the blue sari. But perhaps she would not have come to Armytage, because he had already started down the road travelled by Saunders. Perhaps she can never again walk the same paths as the vagabond Englishman with the torn throat, & that is the pain of it, & that is why she weeps. Or perhaps absolution would break down the wall of grief that stands between them. I do not know.

"You will again have compassion on us; you will tread our sins underfoot and hurl all our iniquities into the depths of the sea." Micah 7:19

Entry of Mon, 26th August, 1861

Today, in the evening, Saunders stood for hours outside my front door, which I refused to open. *I can tell you about the trees*, he said. *I can tell you what it cost to grow them, & what weight their branches bear.*

Once more, I stopped my ears to him & his litanies of shame. Have I not already enough for one man? He must leave me soon, & find another. He must.

"Blessed is the one whose transgressions are forgiven, whose sins are covered." Psalm 32:1

❖

Denison is preparing for his return to Madras. He pays a final visit to St Stephen's as I am laying out the hymn books. I hear him before I know he is there – *toc, toc* – and turn at the sound.

"Odd," he says, running his hands over a pillar, and then tapping it once more with his knuckles. "This is plastered as if it were stone; but it is not."

"Indeed, the pillars and beams of our church are of wood," I say. "The surface you see is a harmless deceit for the sake of appearance."

And now he looks more closely and says (again stroking the pale surface), "I notice the surface is irregular. But not by chance, I would say."

"You are correct, Sir William. The pillars were taken from Lal Bagh, in Srirangapatnam. The texture that you feel betrays old carvings on their surface. A skim of plaster could not completely hide them."

"Your church is built with beams that once held up Tippoo Sultan's palace?" Denison laughs. "Extraordinary!" he says. He laughs again, and again too loudly.

"Extraordinary," I rejoin, "that they could witness Tippoo's barbarous murders and cruelties, and yet find redemption in this house of peace."

Denison shrugs, but a shadow passes over his face. "Redemption," he repeats. "Someone spoke to me of that, only last night. Indeed, they spoke endlessly ..."

She is here! Over his shoulder, at the back of the church, I see the woman in blue. The end of her sari covers her head like a shawl made from the colour of heaven. Denison sees me looking, and turns, but she is gone. When he faces me again, he lets the silence swell; but this time, it is not to make *me* speak, but because *he* wishes to speak and cannot find the words.

"And who was it that spoke to you of redemption?" I ask, eventually.

He frowns: "A tramp," he says. "Anyway, it does not matter."

He looks about him; I wait. His hesitation is palpable; he hems and haws. Eventually, he comes out with it: "I understand," he says, "that you lost your sister in Meerut."

He does not say: *That you lost her to an unspeakably cruel death.*

I do not say: *Sweet tamarinds now stink of blood and cowardice.*

He continues: "My comment some weeks ago, suggesting you knew little of the Mutiny's horrors: it was ill-considered. Forgive me."

I nod: "Of course. Think nothing of it."

He leaves. And I wish that I could speak so simply and directly to Emma and Kumar and the others, and so easily receive the grace of forgiveness.

❖

Entry of Mon, 2nd Sep 1861

Denison has departed, him & his caravan. Ootacamund has sunk once more into a troubled calm.

❖

I find myself hoping that Saunders has also gone with the Governor, that he has perhaps followed one of Denison's people to Madras, there to find another audience for his stories of Shame and Guilt and his fleeting route to Redemption. To speak of that path that Saunders knows so well, and that he showed to Armytage.

God forgive me for wishing pain on others.

Perhaps this is what expiation means: to tell him stories that he already knows, and to listen in turn to the horrors that he carries. To bear the weight of what he has done, even for a little while.

❖

Saunders paces around my garden, in the night. From gate to front door to flower beds and back again. I close the windows each evening and draw the curtains and stoke the fire, but cannot shut out his murmurings.

Each whisper, a goad; each reminder, a crucifixion nail.

But how could I have absolved Armytage, I shout to my bedroom walls one black night. His failures are childish peccadilloes alongside my unequalled betrayals and broken trust. It is I, I, *I* that must be forgiven!

The walls echo with the infinite emptiness that lies between each shrieked word.

Sometimes, in the morning, I find marigolds on the doorstep, where Saunders has sat through the darkness. The flowers in a little heap, as if he had tried to make from them a golden, sweet-smelling dawn.

One night, my will breaks, and I open the door. "Come in, damn you," I say, "and we will discuss this once and for all."

"No; you come with me," he says, "come to the trees, and I will show you the price of their planting and of your climbing. The price of continued life in this world of pain and fear."

I shut the door again on him, and he is quiet a while. But when I am preparing for bed, I hear his voice, like a whisper through the window's closed casement.

"You know this has little to do with Armytage," he says. "You know that."

I wash my face, vigorously; I rub at my ears with soapy fingers. But still, I hear him.

"After all," he says, "it was not Armytage who ran, in Meerut; it was not him who ran like a jack before the dogs. Shall we talk of *running*, Laseron?"

He is silent a while, but that is worse, for the silence seethes with memory. I know what he wants: to balance my sins against his, to wallow in pain. And why not?

Why not admit what I and he already know?

Yes, Saunders, in '57 I could have stood fast the night the rebel sepoys came, but I did not. I ran, and I ran, and I climbed the tamarind behind our house, courageous as an ape. To see the tamarind's pods now, or smell their sweet flesh, is to hear what I listened to, hidden among the branches. *Oh Emma; sweet sister; how could they make you make such sounds!*

"Well? Does this satisfy you, Saunders?"

He is in the house, now; my admissions have drawn him in, like a crow to a carcase. I hold up an oil-lamp, to see him more clearly, and almost wish that I had not. He looks like a death that will not die. He stares at me without speaking.

"Yes, Saunders, the next day, Kumar helped me bury her, and then helped me run, *run* to safety. And you know how I paid back poor Kumar, don't you, Saunders? With Johnson's bullet and Johnson's bayonet. A cold, hard death, on that warm, soft night. This is the man I am, Saunders."

The oil-lamp hisses gently; on the wall, a moth rushes to meet its own shadow.

"So, Saunders; are you happy now?" I knuckle at an eye.

I have no more words. A jackal calls; there is no lonelier sound.

"You and I," says Saunders, "we understand pain. Let me tell you of mine."

And he does, and he does not stop, and oh, how can the world hold such injustice and agony! Surely it must burst with grief! Surely there is no absolution in all time that can accommodate man's cruelty!

They hanged her with her own blue sari in the dungeons near Lal Bagh; they killed the boy – her child and his. And such moments do not end: now, they kill the child in all times, forever. A murder that does not stop, caught in its own moment that cannot cease. Like Emma's, I will see it unendingly.

Perhaps all murders are one murder, from Lal Bagh to Meerut, to the ends of this benighted Earth.

Perhaps this Earth is another Earth's Hell.

How do we escape the globe's agony?

We are both quiet; I wonder if my trial is over. But no; Saunders speaks on. "There are other worlds, Laseron," he says. "Worlds where your courage saved Emma; or where there was no Mutiny, and all men are friends; worlds where you are a proud man, even in your most secret thoughts. Come, Laseron; let me show you these places, and the way to reach them."

He puts out a hand to me, a hand the colour of wax.

"Come," he says, "by the trees, by those blue gums I planted and heeled in with my own boot. I will show you. The pain is but a fleeting thing ..."

I push him aside: there is, must be, may be, one more door to knock at.

It is dark, but I run from my bungalow through Ootacamund's puddled streets, my lantern swinging and scattering drops of oil. The jackal calls again; I smell tamarind and eucalyptus. I unlock the church, and St Stephen's echoes with my gasping breath. Shadows jump and grow and shrink and hide.

She is standing at the front of the church, beyond the transept. Her back is to the altar, her head swathed in blue, her face in darkness. She waits. For me? For Saunders? For the world to cease its cycle of pain?

For the chance to forgive, to redeem?

I walk to the chancel, slowly, slowly. She does not move. I still cannot see her face, but that is a mercy; I know I could not meet her eyes.

I kneel; I put the lantern on the chancel floor and approach her, on my knees. I am saying something, but I do not know what.

I keep my eyes lowered. Beneath the celestial blue of her sari's hem, her feet are dusty and bare against the floor. I bend forward: if I were to put my head to her feet, oh, what expiation would follow? The dirt from the road she has travelled would clean me, clean me. Forever.

I lean forward. I incline my head.

The scent of tamarind.

My ears ring: Emma dies in this moment and every moment, forever.

My forehead touches cold, cold stone.

My last hope flies into the eternal void.

❖

I walk back down the aisle, knocking at the pillars as I go: *toc-toc,* the sound of an unforgiveable, irredeemable life. The sound of a cruelty that rings through all time. I leave the church.

What comes now? What next in a life charred by shame and consumed with guilt?

This: I must go to find Saunders among the blue gums, where Armytage dives into the black earth. Let that torn-throated wanderer guide me to better worlds, where Emma and Kumar still live and love, where my foul soul is not steeped in guilt.

There is no shame in absolution.

Come then, Saunders; show me your fleeting thing.

BLACK PAPILIO

"*The Magicicada spp. life cycles, with [their] prime periods [for example, 13 years] and highly synchronised emergence have defied reasonable scientific explanation since [their] discovery ... some 300 years ago.*"
- G Cardozo, et al., 'Periodical cicadas: a minimal automaton model', Physica A, 382, 439-444, 2007.

"*Who knows what curious hexapods, as yet unknown to entomology, seethe among roots or gestate unseen in rotting wood, waiting to erupt according to some periodicity beyond the normal human span of observation?*"
- Lepidoptera of the Nilgiri District: Revised edition, James Hampson, 1912

You should come along too," said Varma. "You might find it interesting."

Hugh Parry split the deck of cards into two piles and pressed them against the rosewood table. He bent each pile back with a thumb, brought the flexed cards together and released them gradually. The melding comforted him: the riffle and slap of the cards spoke of order and routine. A rhythm; everything in its place. Like tea-planting. He shuffled again, avoiding Varma's eye.

"And you've been working hard," Varma continued. "As a doctor, I recommend a short break. Look at Tyman."

"Exactly! Look at Tyman! That's *exactly* my point."

Varma rolled his eyes. "It's not contagious, you know."

Parry dealt seven cards apiece – *one,* one, *two,* two – placed the deck in the middle of the table, and turned over the top card. King of clubs. "There you are, Arthik," he said. "A king for a king."

Varma sighed, but smiled. Parry made a similar joke almost every time they played cards, and that was almost every Saturday evening. *King Arthik. The Rummy Nights at the Round Table.*

"So, what do you say? We could go on Monday, if that's convenient for you."

"I heard there's leprosy up there."

"You heard wrong."

"There's *something*. That's what broke Hampson. You said so yourself."

"Hampson was there twenty years ago. Epidemics run their course and disappear."

"But the mental aspect never disappeared, did it? The place still has a reputation."

"So?"

"Insanity scares the hell out of me. I've always had a bit of a phobia about it."

"You have a phobia about everything! Leopards! Mosquitoes! Steamships!"

Parry fanned out his cards, arranged them, and re-arranged them. For him, life was simple: one grew tea; one harvested it; one kept the workers happy with one hand and the Bombay-Burmah Tea Corporation happy with the other. And one did not mention Independence. Beyond that, one had the occasional glass of beer. If only Varma's philosophy were similarly relaxed.

"I blame Cambridge," said Parry, throwing down the Queen of Clubs.

"I beg your pardon?"

"Your eccentric interests. It's because you studied at Cambridge. The place sends everyone batty. It's well-known."

Varma's moustache twitched upwards at each end. He picked up from the deck, and discarded the six of hearts. He re-ordered his cards; as always, his movements were swift and precise.

"Guilty. At least, guilty of having interests. As for being *batty* – " As though on cue, a series of gunshots, remote enough to be muffled but close enough to be distinct, slapped the air. "*That,* my friend, is batty. That's what happens when you have *no* interests. Learn from Tyman."

"Why can't you get the people who *live* up there to catch the damn thing and *bring* it to you? You're a Travancore royal, after all."

"Which means as little to the hill-tribes as your British Raj. Anyway, my side of the family is much diminished. Tipu took everything, the barbarian, back in 1789. Including my great-great-aunt, actually. Hard to be royal when you live in grinding poverty." Varma waved a hand around the day-room of his sprawling bungalow. The gesture took in Tanjore plates and tiger skins; books and polished brasses; gleaming antiques of copper and ivory and silver.

"Poverty. Mm."

"Yes," said Varma, seriously. "But even if I were the Maharajah rather than the Maharajah's remotest cousin, I'd still need to visit the place in person."

"But *why?*"

"This is science. We can't rely on second-hand observations. We need to collect primary data. We need a specimen."

"*We* are not amused by the prospect." Parry discarded the ace of clubs.

Varma pounced, and laid down three aces and a run of low hearts. "Rummy," he said. "Ha ha!"

"Well done. Lucky as ever." Parry pushed his cards towards the discard pile for Varma to collect, leant back in his chair and looked through the open french windows. Delphiniums nudged the massed purple of bougainvillea; somewhere, the *chirrup-chirrup-cheep* of a mynah competed with the buzz of cicadas.

"Well?" Varma started Hindu-shuffling: *flip-flip-flip.* He observed Parry closely, like an amused teacher watching a slow pupil struggling with a sum. Parry's hands looked for something to do, but Varma had all the cards. Cut, slap, *flip-flip-flip.* He looked away from Varma, but only met the crazed stare and bared fangs of a leopard's head mounted above the french windows. Parry shuddered.

"Two days' hike to some benighted jungle village. Camping out in leopard country. For an *insect*. It's mad."

Varma dealt out the cards. His eyes crinkled at their corners.

"Four o'clock, Monday morning, on the Manimuthar road? You bring a sense of humour, and I'll provide tents and a guide. Agreed?"

Parry winced. "Five o'clock. Please." He slumped a little deeper in his chair.

It was all Tyman's fault: *"I know about Bedlam,"* he'd said. The maniac.

❖

"I know about Bedlam," said Tyman.

Parry nodded, focusing on his beer. Bubbles rose through amber. He didn't look at Tyman: at his staring, pale blue eyes; his untidy grey hair; his unevenly buttoned shirt. Most of all, Parry didn't look at Varma, who – he was sure – was smirking. *Mad Englishmen, midday sun, blah blah blah.*

"Fascinating!" said Varma. "If I show you the item that triggered my interest, perhaps you could tell us more? Please."

Parry risked a quick glance. Varma was serious. After all the ridiculous stories of the last hour – one-legged devils with Medusa eyes, black mists that rose from old wells, old soldiers who could not die – Varma wanted more.

Tyman lumbered to his feet. "Hurrah!" he bellowed. "All hail Babu! Hurrah!" He saluted the leopard's head trophy, as though in thrall to its dusty snarl. Parry carefully placed his beer on a coaster, and wiped a drip of condensation from its landing place on the polished rosewood. Tyman held his pose.

"Bedlam, then," said Varma. He pulled open a drawer under the card-table, and brought out the book. He oriented it so that Tyman could read the cover, and slid it towards the centre of the table. Tyman followed it with widening eyes; he opened his mouth to speak, but nothing came. He lowered his hand to point at the binding. Gold lettering gleamed in the afternoon sun: *Lepidoptera of the Nilgiri District: Revised edition.* James Hampson, 1912.

"Balderdash!" said Tyman. "Tripe!" He raised his eyes to the ceiling; his hands – palms up and fingers crooked – grasped at air; his lips pulled back to reveal clenched, stained teeth. Then he bent forward to reach for the book, leaning close to Parry. Parry fought the instinct to recoil.

"Where did you find this monstrosity?" asked Tyman. He opened the book with the tip of one thumb, fingers curled back, as though the smooth binding were contaminated.

"Read for yourself," said Varma.

Tyman frowned at the handwritten scrawl on the flyleaf; an educated cursive in dark ink, trembling as though with age or illness. He read it out. "*To Arthik Varma, with my very best regards. James Hampson Bt. July 25th, 1928.*" For a moment, the tremor in Tyman's hands stopped; he was very still. "What? He gave this to you?"

Varma nodded. "Yes."

Tyman raised a hand to his face. He wiped each eye in turn, as though to push away an irritant, and then examined his hand minutely. His tremor had returned. "Why?"

"A gift."

"A gift!" Tyman bent over as though in sudden pain, and fell back into his chair. "A gift!" Mouth agape, he fought for each wheezing breath, while his untidy grey hair fell over his face. His shoulders jerked in little spasms, and his face darkened with congestion. Parry looked at Varma, alarmed, but the doctor gave a minute shake of his head. *Not a heart attack,* realised Parry. *Tyman's laughing.*

"Better now?" asked Varma, once Tyman's contortions had ceased.

"God preserve us!" said Tyman.

"Indeed. And now – " Varma opened the book to the usual page, and took out the slip of paper.

"No you don't," said Tyman, getting up. "That's enough of that."

"I was just going to tell you how we'd heard of Bedlam – "

"No need. Not interested. *I* can tell *you* about the bloody place, if you want. And how to get there, more or less. You'll find *something* up there – no joking, chum – but I don't know if it'll be what you're looking for."

❖

Parry had become aware of Varma's over-riding obsession when they'd first met, about six months previously. Parry's habit was to walk the borders of his estate, each Saturday. On this occasion, he went past the track which led to the speckled idol, and on towards Tyman's plantation. At the fork, he turned away from the road to his neighbour's domain and followed the stamped dirt that led towards the over-sized new bungalow – still waiting, he thought, for the Travancore royal who'd commissioned it. Parry imagined a fat raja, bejewelled and beturbaned, issuing orders from a tented palanquin. *Bring me a tiger to shoot. Bring me nautch girls.* He left the track and walked up through the scrubby jungle to a point where the ground fell away and he could look down over his plants: clipped bushes pinned to the slopes by young shade trees. *All this beauty,* he thought, *and nobody to share it with. No wonder Tyman's mad.* And then, behind him, something moved in the lantana: something that trod cautiously on dead leaves. *Leopard!* Parry jerked around: but it was only a man. A lean, youthful man, with a butterfly net and a leather satchel. They looked at each other in silence. "Have you," asked the young man, "seen a black swallowtail, by any chance?" Dr Arthik Varma had seemed as eccentric to Parry then as he did now.

Nevertheless, Parry welcomed having a neighbour who was not Tyman; even one who would bend Parry's ear on the mathematical principles behind the growth of plants, insist on an audience for his translations of Sanskrit texts into English iambic tetrameters, or argue interminably about Tipu Sultan's mechanical tiger, endlessly eating a mechanical soldier in London's Victoria and Albert Museum: "It *couldn't* have been made by French engineers – the keyboard arrangement owes *nothing* to the standard European approach, can't you see?" And if Varma found Parry a little dull, he did not show it; so, over the following months, a Saturday routine of beer and cards developed naturally. "But why here?" Parry asked, on one such weekend. "I know you're taking a year off, but really, why here? Nobody here but hill-tribes, tea-planters and missionaries. Back of beyond."

"Precisely."

"You could have travelled around Europe."

"With France and Germany at loggerheads, and Stalin stamping over Russia with the boots of a peasant? No; Europe is less safe by the day. Anyway, I had particular reasons to build a little pied-a-terre right here. Two reasons, in fact. One was to be away from it all – away from Travancore, specifically."

"Ah! Escaping a shameful past."

"Escaping relatives seeking to marry me off, actually. Each woman they push at me is worse than the last."

"Poor you. The other reason?"

"This place is so remote as to be practically untouched – and because of that, there's still so much to learn here. The natural history, for example, remains largely unstudied in this part of India. Even the butterflies are incompletely catalogued."

"Why not collect stamps instead? You don't have to chase them through thorns and lantana."

Varma blew through his moustache. "Are you serious? This is not an exercise in amassing known items already catalogued by others. This is *discovery*."

"You hope. Maybe there's nothing new here at all."

"That, my friend, is where you are mistaken. Wait here one moment."

When Varma came back, he held Hampson's book. He offered it to Parry two-handedly, like a sommelier presenting a rare wine, and nodded as Parry read the handwritten scrawl on the front page.

"Last year, my final year at Cambridge, Sir James came up to Caius to give a talk on South Indian fauna. Homi Bhabha and I went along, expecting the usual stuff – you know, tigers, elephants, monkeys. But Hampson spent most of his time talking about moths and butterflies. And about one butterfly in particular."

Varma paused, and leaned forward; his eyes gleamed.

"Black Papilio."

Over the small valley, from Tyman's plantation, came the flat crack of rifle shots: each discharge followed by its own echo, each one a new report of the shooter's folly. *"Faces,"* Tyman would snarl. *"Lined up on the garden wall. Peering from the bloody bushes."* Or, on other occasions, more judiciously, and without meeting Parry's eye: *"Monkeys. Stealing mangoes, the little bastards."*

"I caught Hampson after the lecture. We got on pretty well, and he very kindly gave me a copy of his book. And I found something in it."

Varma held out a loose sheet of paper, marked with a brown strip where old glue had dried to a useless stain.

"Have a look," said Varma.

Parry took the paper. It was soft and greasy, like a rupee note. The handwriting was the same as that on the flyleaf, but younger, stronger. A set of naturalist's field notes: dates, places and a pencil sketch of a butterfly, with the distinctive shape – graceful fore-wings, hind-wings with tails at their trailing edges – of a swallowtail.

"That, my friend, is the Black Papilio."

"It doesn't look so different from any other butterfly."

"Look more closely. It has three tails on each hind-wing. Most butterflies have none. Even swallowtails usually have only one tail per wing. Some have double-tailed hind-wings, but I know of none with three. Also, most butterflies have patterned wings. Not this one. Every part of it, apparently, is the purest black. Even back in 1909, Hampson was convinced it was unique. Today, we can be certain of it. This is the *only* known record of the Black Papilio."

"He didn't catch it?"

"No. And he left the next day, in a hurry; for the health of his men, he claimed, but I'm sure that's when his own health began to fail. Something in the hills did not agree with him – or *vice versa*. He had to retire to England soon after. He never saw Black Papilio again. Nor has anyone else."

"So, once upon a time, an old man saw an odd butterfly." Parry shrugged. Varma regarded him with something close to pity.

"Don't you understand? Whoever finds a new species has the honour of naming it. That, my friend, is a kind of immortality."

"Papilio ego?"

"Ha ha. Close. In fact, I was thinking of something altogether more satisfying. *Papilio arthikvarma*. Obviously."

"Doesn't poor old Hampson get a say?"

Varma frowned, and gestured at the pencilled notes. "He suggested *Papilio ummattaka*, for some reason. But it's moot – he never got a specimen. And in any case, he's dead – Homi Bhabha wrote and told me. There was something distasteful there; suicide, maybe. Homi couldn't tell me much. But it wouldn't surprise me – I got the impression of a man with troubles. Not the sort to 'sleep a-nights'. You think Tyman has odd stories? Hampson had a few. For example, he said he met an old Englishman, in Ooty, with a slit throat that neither bled nor healed. He swore he saw the cut jugular, end-on, like an empty pipe, when the old man leant to one side ... Do all Europeans suffer from morbid imaginations, I wonder, or is it just you British? Anyway, Black Papilio is unencumbered."

Parry bent over Hampson's faded script. The lepidopterist's observations were concise: *"Date: June 5th [monsoon], 1909. Location: Cardamom Hills, Madras Presidency."*

"He doesn't give you much to go on, does he? 'Cardamom Hills' – only the best part of two thousand square miles to search."

"You appreciate my difficulty."

Parry continued reading, in his slow, patient way. Beneath the drawing of the swallowtail – each component of which was labelled with a single word, *black* – were some more notes. *"Habitat: Jungle glade (Datura). Species: Unknown. Not melanistic variant. Papilio ummattaka?"* And then, at the end of the document, separate from the other notes, like a scribbled afterthought: *"Bedlam."*

"Bedlam?"

"Yes. I don't know why he wrote that. Any ideas?"

"No," said Parry. "Tyman should know. Ha ha."

Something about Varma's silence made Parry turn sharply to look at him. "Oh no. *No*. Arthik, really. No."

"Didn't you say he'd been planting tea in the South for years and years? He must have heard something, at some point."

"Not *Tyman*."

"Beer and congenial company could resurrect all kinds of memories."

"I'm not having that man in my house."

"Here, then. Next Saturday, usual time?"

Parry sat back in his chair, and folded his arms. He glared at Varma, but Varma was flicking through Hampson's book.

"Excellent," said Varma. "I look forward to it. Have you seen this illustration of *Pachliopta hector*? Peerless. Absolutely peerless."

❖

After Tyman had disappeared down the unmade road, gesticulating and mumbling, rifle over his shoulder, Varma turned to Parry. His moustache twitched at each end, but he didn't say anything. As always, Parry felt compelled to offer excuses.

"Difficult to get people to come out here. It's easier for the corporation just to put up with him than to recruit someone else."

"Mm."

"The real business of running the estate is done by Somu. The overseer. Very capable, is Somu."

"For the sake of Bombay-Burmah, I'm pleased to hear it."

"Anyway, you asked me to bring him along. I hope you got what you wanted."

"In spades. Speaking of which, how about a hand of rummy?"

"Thanks, but no. I really ought be getting back. But listen, Arthik – I'd take Tyman's stories with a pinch of salt. You've seen him on a good day. He's often much worse. You don't know the half of it. Odd habits, apparently."

"Such as?"

"Well. For example, the story is – and this came from his bearer, by the way – the story is that he sleeps with a woman's stocking pulled over his head and face. Every night."

"Is that not the usual English custom?"

"No! And then there's the shooting at imaginary things. Thinks he's pursued by someone from his days in the Nilgiri plantations, someone trying to make him do something he doesn't want to do. He very nearly hit Somu once. There'd have been hell to pay if he'd done that."

"And yet, some of what he said had the ring of truth."

Varma was right, as usual. Amongst Tyman's wild assertions, one anecdote had seemed credible. The one when he'd actually looked at them as he spoke, rather than addressing the french windows or the leopard's head. *"You know how we've always recruited labourers from the hill-tribes? Well, the first planters found, now and then, that one of these men would go off home for a few days – and never come back. Or if they came back, they'd be unfit for work. Mentally unfit. Doolally."* (Parry had remained resolutely expressionless; Varma had nodded, straight-faced). *"When the estate managers asked what had happened, the other workers would always tap their heads and say, Badagamadalam. It's a village, up in the hills, well north of here. Badagamadalam. But that kind of name was a bit difficult for most Brits, and some joker shortened it to Bedlam."*

"Yes," said Parry. "It does sound plausible."

"Is it possible to double-check it?" asked Varma. "Bombay-Burmah must keep employment records. I imagine losing the odd employee to insanity would have been noted."

"I'll see what there is."

"And if it looks like Tyman's telling the truth, why, we can pay a little visit to the inmates of Bedlam."

"We? *We?*" Parry gritted his teeth. "Arthik – I'm sorry, but I will not be accompanying you on *any* such excursion. I hope I make myself clear."

"Perfectly." Varma's moustache twitched at each end.

❖

The first day's hiking was uneventful. From the Manimuthar road they took a dusty track to the river, and then followed the honey-brown waters upstream. Here, the jungle canopy kept the worst of the sun from them, and the air was cooled by the river, which made for pleasant travelling. Varma's employee, Mani, always ebullient, was even more cheerful than usual, especially after Parry had insisted on the three loads being of equal weight.

"But most of it's yours," said Varma.

"*Ours*," said Parry. "I've brought mosquito netting. Because I knew you wouldn't."

"Anyway, I'm *paying* him to carry my things!"

"Not enough," said Parry. Varma eventually acquiesced with the air of one who humours a child. As they proceeded, the routine of hiking took over; one foot in front of the other. The jungle's chirr ebbed and grew and ebbed: an orchestra of life.

"Something I meant to ask you," said Varma. "About Tyman."

"When it comes to Tyman, *nobody* has answers."

"He's been in India for the best part of half a century. Planting tea, man and boy. Yes?"

"That's right."

"But he wouldn't always have been round here, would he?"

"Oh no. These estates are relatively new. Back when Tyman started out, there were no plantations south of the Nilgiris."

"Aha! And I imagine that all the Nilgiri tea-planters would have known each other?"

"Yes. Very small community."

"Then Tyman would have known Hampson."

"What!"

"Didn't you know? Hampson ran the estates in Coonoor. In the Nilgiris, just below Ooty. He was there for about ten years. That day in Cambridge – the first part of his talk was all about Nilgiri wildlife." Varma paused to catch his breath, and turned to look at Parry. "So our eccentric Mr Tyman may not have been entirely open with us. Worth bearing in mind."

"Bloody typical," said Parry.

When evening drew close, they pitched the tents a short distance from the riverbank. Parry and Varma cooled their feet in the shallows while Mani cooked dahl. After they'd eaten, Mani sat back on his haunches and held forth as though at Hyde Park Corner. But the Tamil was mostly beyond Parry.

"Why's he so damn loquacious?" asked Parry, whose feet were still aching.

"He just likes talking."

"How about asking him what he can tell us about Badagamadalam?"

"Good idea." Varma put a brief question to Mani, and Mani took a deep breath, as if anticipating a lengthy answer. Parry listened to the flow of syllables, and watched Mani's emphatic gestures – his fists brought to his eyes, and then thrust away from his face, his fingers spreading and releasing nothingness to the empty air. As Mani ended, he waggled his head as though to say: 'That's the story; believe what you like.'

"Interesting," said Varma.

"Do tell."

"He said that a woman, one of the pickers who worked at Tyman's plantation, married someone from Badagamadalam. And she saw something happen in the village, several years ago. She told one of the other pickers, Mani's sister-in-law, and Mani's sister-in-law told her husband, Mani's brother, and Mani's brother told him."

"Chinese whispers. In Tamil, to boot."

"Maybe. But this is what the tea-picker is said to have said. Her father-in-law had been drinking toddy all day with some of the other men in Badagamadalam; towards evening there was an argument, or a fight maybe, and he stormed off. After a little while, since it was getting dark, she lit a torch and went looking for him, thinking maybe the drink had made him fall asleep somewhere outside. You don't do that in the jungle. A leopard might eat you." Varma smirked.

"Just get on with it."

"Well, when she found him, he was lying on the ground, on his back. She couldn't see too well in the torch-light – those things tend to smoulder rather than blaze – but it looked like he'd wrapped dark cloth around his face. She called out to him, and he started twitching; as though asleep but dreaming. As she got closer, the black cloth on his face rose up and dissolved into the night. Like smoke, she said; like the smoke from a burning soul. She woke him; but he was no longer her husband's father."

Varma paused; a nightjar grated the warm air, and geckos chip-chapped from their tree-trunk domains. Behind them, the river whispered to its sandy banks, and something splashed. But Mani had more to add; his voice was soft, and for once he was not smiling. After listening to him, Varma continued.

"There is a devil, they say, a devil who comes in the night and sucks the souls from those who sleep; he sucks it out through their eyes, leaving them mad, quite mad, and blind to this world."

Parry looked at Mani; Mani smiled, shrugged and gestured with one hand, an open-palmed wave that seemed to brush away such superstitions. But at the same time, he looked towards the dark bushes beyond the firelight, and then towards his own tent.

"So what happened to this chap?"

"Oh, he killed himself."

"Marvellous," said Parry.

❖

On the second day, the going became tougher as the warm, dry forests of the foothills gradually changed into rainforest. The tracks they followed became thinner and steeper; the thorn glades thicker; the mosquitoes more bothersome. Furthermore, a greyish bird had taken to following them, interrupting their thoughts with its infuriating five-fold call: *feeva, feeva, feeva, feeva, feeva!* – each repetition on a higher pitch until Parry's nerves wanted to shriek in sympathy.

"That's why they call it the brain-fever bird," said Varma, when Parry complained. "A kind of cuckoo. But you know, Black Papilio aside, this whole Bedlam thing is *very* interesting. Those instances of labourer discharge due to madness that you found in the Bombay-Burmah records – did you notice the pattern?"

"Most had some connection with Bedlam."

"Apart from the obvious, I mean."

"Then no," admitted Parry.

"The instances were not sporadic, my friend. They were *periodic*. Every five years. There may be an additional periodicity of thirteen years, but there aren't enough data to make a statistical case. The point is, the occurrences are cyclical. From a medical point of view, this is all rather intriguing."

Feeva, feeva, feeva, feeva, feeva!

"Damn that bird!"

"If mental aberrations really are over-represented in a population, there will be a reason for it. In-breeding perhaps; but then why does it manifest itself periodically? Maybe a seasonal toxin – but what kind of toxin would appear with a multi-year periodicity, rather than annually?"

Something occurred to Parry. "This periodicity. Five years, you said."

"Yes?"

"When was the last case?"

Varma grinned. "Five years ago."

"Oh, for Christ's sake!"

"Exciting, isn't it?"

They walked on, and Parry's mind turned to the horrors of mental illness: berserkers with knives, blank-faced dolts with drool-wet chins, cruel perversions cunningly hidden behind some civilised facade. But an exclamation from Mani interrupted his train of thought.

"Look," he said, using the simple Tamil that he knew Parry could follow. "Fishing." Mani pointed his chin at a man on a rocky overhang a hundred yards upstream; as Parry watched, the stranger went through the unmistakable movements of one throwing out a hand-held, baited line.

"Good," said Varma. "Hopefully he can tell us if we're on the right path for Bedlam."

The man remained squatting as they approached, one arm extended, elbow resting on knee, hand towards river, the crooked index finger waiting for a tell-tale tug on the line. The other hand held the spool: a piece of wood around which the line was wound. Several gutted fish lay on the rock next to him. He looked at the travellers incuriously, as one might observe crows scavenging food, but greeted them willingly enough. The ensuing three-way conversation between Mani, Varma and the fisherman was incomprehensible to Parry, but it ended with gestures that mean the same in any language in the world: the fisherman pointing emphatically up-river, and then to the right. *Up that way.* As Parry watched, the fisherman reeled in his line, took the bait from the hook and threw it into the water.

"Bit of luck!" said Varma. "He's actually from Bedlam. He says he'll take us there."

Feeva, feeva, feeva, feeva, feeva!

As the Bedlamite had indicated, they soon left the river's bank, taking a path through the jungle. And now the country changed again: years-old clearings – from slash and burn agriculture, said Varma – now being reclaimed by the forest. Some kind of weed had proliferated in these half-shady conditions: a bushy plant ranging from knee-height to shoulder height. It had untidy, ragged-edged leaves almost a foot in length and nearly as broad as they were long; its sparse, pale flowers were tightly shut, their white petals wrapped against each other. One of the plants overhung the pathway, and Parry struck at its leaves, intending to clear the way. From behind him, he heard an exclamation: Mani was telling him something, but Parry only could make out a few words. *Ummattaka. Vellum mattai.* Something white?

Parry called to Varma, who was walking ahead.

"Arthik? What's Mani saying?"

Varma paused, waiting for Parry to catch up. "That plant – it's the thorn-apple. Datura. Don't touch it."

"Poisonous?"

"Highly! In the old days, the Thuggi used it to dope their victims; even today, Rajput women smear its sap onto their breasts to dispose of baby girls. Some varieties are extraordinarily potent. Take care."

"It's everywhere."

"I must admit, I've never seen it in such abundance. Nor known it grow so large."

"What did Mani say about it? He sounded worried – am I about to expire?"

"Not immediately. Mani just wanted to warn you; he said *vellum mattai,* which is the usual Tamil name for the plant. It has many other names: in parts of the South they call it *kartika nakshatra.* Everywhere else, it's the fig tree that is associated with Kartika Nakshatra, but our southerners do things their own way."

"Kartika Nakshatra?"

"One of the holy stars in Hindu astrology. The same constellation that I was born under, in fact: Taurus in Western astrology, or the Pleiades, if you want to be exact. But my favourite name for the plant is one of your English ones – not thorn-apple, but *moonflower*. Isn't that a lovely name?"

"Because it has white flowers?"

"Because the flowers only open at night. At least, they start to open in the late evening, and they are still open in the early morning, but predominantly they are flowers of darkness. By the by, they have a five-fold symmetry – seen from directly above, their five petals form the shape of a pentagon – which nicely supports my theory that plant growth is dictated by Fibonacci primes."

"If you say so." Now that Parry looked, the moonflowers seemed to be everywhere: crowding against the narrow path, their dark, broad, curiously angular leaves reached towards the travellers; each of their closed flowers like a little white fist clutching a dangerous secret. Ahead, the Bedlamite turned to look back at them; the skewered fish dangled from his hand.

"Arthik?"

"Mm?"

"It occurs to me that we don't know this man. He could be leading us anywhere."

"You're worried about dacoits? This is not bandit country."

"Nevertheless, it'll be dark soon. And still no Bedlam."

Varma wasn't listening; but it was true – the jungle shade had grown deeper; the greens darker, the air cooler. And, just as Varma had predicted, the moonflowers had begun to open: soon, their pale pentagons dangled everywhere, the lack of pigment making them stand out in the gloom when more brightly coloured flowers were lost. *Corpse candles*, thought Parry. He paused near one that hung at head height, and inclined his head towards it. That scent: rich, heavy, almost nauseating. Something about it disturbed some deep, forgotten part of him. He inhaled again: tones of jasmine, of liguster and lily, of musk and hops. But elements of something else too.

"Hugh!" Varma was calling from a short distance ahead. "You can put your concerns to bed. Almost literally. We're here."

Feeva, feeva, feeva, feeva, feeva!

When Parry caught up with them, Mani was preparing to pitch camp in an area just outside the village. Badagamadalam itself caused Varma to go into transports: "Look at those huts! Domed thatch, reaching down to the ground – a single door, fitted into a raised threshold – no windows! What does that remind you of?"

"A Dutch barn?"

"No! No, no! This style of building is known only from one place in India – the Toda villages in the Nilgiris! There are some fine examples just outside Ooty ... To find something so similar, out *here*? Fascinating! Fascinating!"

Parry left Varma exploring his socio-anthropological interests with a gaggle of villagers; he was more interested in erecting the tents while there was still enough light to see. But, busy as he was, he couldn't help noticing something different about Bedlam, beyond the unusual huts. In most small Indian villages, visitors would be greeted, stared at, questioned and possibly teased by virtually the entire community. But the Bedlamites were cautious, almost subdued. Indeed, having engaged in the minimum interactions required by etiquette, including giving their visitors one of the fish from the river and some water to cook it in, the villagers – including the fisherman – disappeared into their homes. Parry could swear he heard the sound of doors being firmly shut throughout the village. And then silence.

"Something we said?"

Varma looked at the cluster of domed huts; not a soul to be seen. He frowned, shrugged, and said something to Mani. Mani's usual smile had disappeared; he was trying to light the fire while casting dark glances at the houses. He replied briefly to Varma's question, and then blew urgently on the kindling, piling brushwood on until he had a blaze far in excess of that required to cook some rice and one medium-sized fish.

"Mani says they're all scared of what the night brings," said Varma. "They'll be better tomorrow."

Parry looked over his shoulder, to the black jungle they had walked through; a moonflower nodded at him, like a pale face acknowledging an acquaintance. Just for a second, Parry thought he saw a dark eye open in the blossom and disappear again: a vulgar wink. The hairs on the nape of his neck responded to a primitive fear, and he turned back to the fire with a shudder. Varma was looking at him.

"Good thing *we're* not superstitious, eh, Hugh?" said Varma. He had a small smile.

"Leopards," muttered Parry. "There may be leopards."

Varma's smile broadened. "Maybe."

The food satisfied; their legs ached with healthy fatigue. But relaxation was impossible: the darkness amplified the jungle's rustle and hiss, and biting insects plagued them. These would fly in from the darkness, always from behind, and land lightly on hair or neck before moving onward to forehead or ears. Legs pressed on hair; antennae probed skin; proboscises dug at flesh. Once Parry slapped at his cheek and crushed a large, zebra-striped mosquito; in the firelight, its smeared blood-meal glistened darkly on his fingers, giving the impression that it heaved with parasites.

"I *told* you the mozzies would be nightmarish," Parry grumbled. And even Varma, for once, brushing at his hair in irritation, had no answer.

Sitting close to the dying fire brought some comfort, as the insects seemed to dislike smoke; but the fire soon fell into its own embers. Mani threw soil over the glowing remnants to keep them live until morning, and they fled to the shelter of canvas. But Parry made certain, that night – and made certain that Mani too would do likewise – that the tent-flaps were tied down tightly, and every tiny gap plugged with mosquito netting.

"That'll keep out the leopards," said Varma.

"Amusing. In fact, right now, malaria is my primary concern. Those mosquitoes were relentless."

Parry's efforts were effective; the insects were excluded, and all slept soundly. For the most part, at least: but Parry woke once in the night, thinking he'd heard the approach of rain. Thank God! The monsoon had been sporadic, so far, and his tea bushes would benefit from a shower. He held his breath, head cocked. No: not rain, but something else: something like the wind in the trees, perhaps. An odd susurration, almost like the furtive scrabbling of tiny feet on hard soil, or as though thousands and thousands of small dry leaves were falling to the ground. But fatigue – and, perhaps, some weakness of the spirit – prevented him from investigating, and he was soon asleep again.

❖

The first thing Parry noticed, when he exited the tent as dawn broke, was the heavy scent of moonflower. It had been discernible the previous evening, though smoke from the fire had mostly disguised it; but now, with the fire dead and the air fresh, it was powerful and unmistakable. He looked towards the surrounding jungle; the white blossoms were still open. The second thing he noticed was the dark powder lightly covering the tents.

"Odd," said Varma.

Parry remembered the sounds in the night. "The wind got up a bit, a few hours ago. You were asleep. Must have raised the ashes from the fire, blown them around a bit."

"Mm. Odd."

"Anyway, if you want to find your precious butterfly, you'd better get on with it, don't you think?"

"All in good time, my ever-hasty friend. In this kind of situation, a little local knowledge may work wonders. Let us talk to the Bedlamites, no? Perhaps they know where Black Papilio goes."

"You can talk to whoever you wish. I'm going to sit down with a cup of tea."

Parry's tea had hardly cooled before Varma, almost beside himself, came running back.

"Hugh! The most wonderful news! After twenty-odd years, there are still some here who remember Hampson and his butterflies – not only that, but the man Hampson hired to help him still lives here! He's still alive! Who'd have thought it?"

"Extraordinary! I'm delighted for you!" said Parry. And he meant it.

"Will you help me interview him? The sound of bad Tamil spoken with an English accent might, I don't know, jog his memory or something."

"Eh? Is that likely?"

"Who knows? Depends what state he's in. I can't tell until I've examined him. These conditions can be awkward to handle."

"*Conditions?* What do you mean, conditions?"

"Oh sorry, didn't I say? This man, Hampson's old employee – he's also a victim of the Bedlam syndrome. Mad as a coot."

"What!"

"A felicitous coincidence, wouldn't you say? We can investigate both symptomology and entomology in a single presentation."

"Arthik, I really don't think you need me for – "

"You *must* get over this absurd squeamishness, Hugh! It is unbecoming. People will start to question your moral fibre. Disease is as normal as health."

"Yes, but – "

"After all – a man who went blind and mad overnight? Don't you find that interesting?"

"No. And all you'll do is turn the poor man into a case study and paste him all over the Journal of Tropical Medicine or some such rag. You won't be able to help him."

"Maybe, maybe not. But a diagnosis might help others, don't you think? We can't guard against diseases if we don't know what they are and how they arise."

"My diagnosis is too much bad toddy."

"Really? My theory is some kind of parasite, no doubt of zoonotic origin. A nematode worm, perhaps, ingested in the egg stage via contaminated river water. After hatching in the gut and egressing through the intestinal wall, one can imagine some of the worms migrating through the viscera and ending up in the eyes."

"Arthik, *please!*"

"From there, one or two might track along the optical nerve and burrow into the visual cortex. That could explain the blindness and mental disturbance. Of course, direct entry of a viral or bacterial pathogen via the ocular mucosa is also possible. Anyway – they're waiting for us. Let's go."

"Arthik, I have *already* gone above and beyond – "

"Hugh. Listen. The sooner we find Black Papilio, the sooner we can go home, no?"

Parry swallowed, and closed his eyes as if to escape Varma's persistence; but instead of Varma he now saw the tea-picker's blind in-law, raving and drooling, with staring, sightless eyes that seeped worms and misery. And when he opened his eyes, Varma was still there, adamant, stubborn as a mule, flexible as a rock.

❖

"They keep him inside, apparently," said Varma. "Wherever possible."

The two men were outside the hut where the madman lived; the fisherman had gone in to check that the residents were ready to receive visitors.

"Out of shame?"

"No, I don't think so. I'm not sure why. Worried about what he might do? Possibly. Ah! We can go in now."

Inside the hut, the smoky air stung Parry's eyes. No windows: two small oil lanterns, with reflective tin backings, provided the only light. This revealed three people: their fisherman friend from the previous day, a middle-aged woman, and an old man. Again, Parry was struck by the difference between Bedlam and other villages he had visited. Where were the usual crowds of curious onlookers? It was as though the village lived in perpetual fear of contamination by the Other.

The old man was sitting on a charpoy in the classic pose of the blind – head raised and tilted back, eyes open, moving his head slightly with each sound as though to search for sights that would never come. And yet, he did seem to see; at least, from time to time, his head would move sharply in one direction or another, and he would point and exclaim as if the hut's walls displayed a horizon of delight.

"That's Jevana, and the woman, Nanji, is his niece," said Varma. "Let's get her side of the story."

There followed a reluctant dialogue with the unsmiling Nanji. "She'd obviously rather be somewhere else," said Varma, after a little while. "She has no interest in butterflies, and won't even address the question. Just another *puchi*, she says, who would even notice? As for her uncle, Jevana, she seems to blame Hampson. It was the Englishman who sent her uncle mad, she says."

"So that's why she's giving me dirty looks."

"Mm. They certainly don't like the English. The fisherman's had to take some abuse for bringing you here."

"Independence fever? Even out here?"

"No. Something else, I think. Some man who used to cause trouble. But that's incidental. Let's focus on Jevana. I've tried to get a better description of the form his madness takes, but Nanji just tells me to look for myself. She will only add two things. Firstly, she says that, in some years, during the monsoon season, her uncle becomes restless. His madness intensifies, she says, he becomes more excited and irritable, and during the night he will try to open the hut door. She says it is to let the devil in; the devil who comes with the rains, who walks the jungle at night. They have to tie Jevana to his charpoy each monsoon night to stop him doing this. I asked her if he had ever succeeded in opening the door in the night, at this time of year. Yes, she said; once, about a dozen years ago. He slipped his ropes, opened the door and ran out into the darkness. They were too frightened to follow him, so they made the door secure, and waited until the morning. Throughout the night, they heard him calling, calling, as though for a dear friend. And then in the darkest time of the night, he went quiet. They found him in the morning, just outside the village, his eyes streaming with tears, not of sorrow, but of the utmost joy. He said one thing when they helped him back to the hut, one thing only: *This is a very great gift that you have given me.*"

Parry looked at the woman, who returned his gaze unsmilingly; he looked at Jevana; he looked at the ropes attached to the charpoy frame. The man had gone quiet; his head was cocked towards Varma, as though straining to catch the words of a half-remembered song.

"And the other thing?" he asked.

"The other thing," said Varma, "I think is probably the main reason they keep him shut away. They say that most Bedlamites who become mentally afflicted are not joyful, like Jevana; or, at least, do not remain so. Rather the opposite: they are consumed with grief. Death follows soon after, most often by their own hand. Jevana is the exception, apparently, in surviving – and remaining happy, albeit deranged – for so long. But they have seen enough instances to be cautious; so they ensure they can keep an eye on him."

"I see," said Parry. He half-turned towards the door.

"Also, they say they don't want the babu to take him. Bit odd."

"The babu?"

"In this case, I think they're using the word as a respectful title, not to mean a minor bureaucrat: the Babu, not a babu. But I must admit, I don't completely understand what they're saying. It's all a bit confused. "

"Well," said Parry, "if you've seen enough – "

"Say something to him," said Varma. "In your execrably-accented Tamil, if you please."

Parry rolled his eyes, but complied. *"Ravile micham sattam keiten,"* he said, after some thought: *I heard much noise in the night.*

Jevana gripped the charpoy frame, and drew in his breath with a sudden hiss; in the half-light, his eyes roamed invisible territories.

"Hampson," he said, in a low voice. "Hampson."

Parry looked at Varma, who nodded triumphantly, as though to say: *You see?* Indeed, something had been released in Jevana; some memory had been tugged to the surface. He began speaking in slow, simple language, as one might use for a foreigner. Even Parry could largely follow him.

"Hampson. The sounds of the night. We search for *puchis*, do we not? Such foolish work! Such good money for the foolishness of children! But I show you the places to search, and the safe paths. You do not get lost in the jungle with Jevana. Ah, Hampson." He paused, his eyes questing the darkness for bright memories.

"We found many things, Hampson, yes? Many *puchis* for you to pin to boards. We were tireless, tireless. And when the black one came, I showed you ... Why did you not catch it, Hampson?"

Varma's fists were clenched; his eyes were fixed on Jevana, willing him to continue.

"We waited for its return, Hampson, you and I; you in your foolish hat with the netting that hangs down, and I with my flesh that is accustomed to the mosquito's bite. Night fell; the first night of all nights. *We must leave,* I told you. *This place is dangerous after dark.* So we turned back, you and I. And then the doors of heaven opened."

Jevana's eyes were half-closed, as though he were pained by the vision of some indescribable glory; tears ran from them, and he held out his hands to something that none but him could see.

"But *where*, Jevana? Where did you see the black *puchi*?" Varma could not contain himself.

"Such things! Such things I saw! I walked with gods, hand in hand. They kissed me on the eyes, as a mother would a baby. Everywhere I found brothers and sisters I had never known. I spoke with the neem and the owl; I heard the songs of the earth and drank down the black night sky. Such things!"

"Jevana! *Where was this?*" Varma was almost shouting, and for a second, Parry thought he would have to restrain his friend; the usually unflappable Varma looked ready to grasp Jevana by the shoulders and shake him.

"My brother the loris; the jasmine my sister. The movements of stars, the shrug of the rocks. Why should I cross the Englishman's bridge? There is no sorrow here. Such joy! Such rivers of bliss!"

"Damn it!" snapped Varma, in English. "Hugh – *you* ask him!"

"*Puchi – enge?*" asked Hugh, awkwardly. *Where insect?* But Jevana, seemingly lost in visions or memories of visions, only hugged himself, shuddering with pleasure.

"I swim in ecstasy, forever, forever. Ah, Englishman – what a great gift you have given me!"

Further questioning was futile; Jevana no longer acknowledged their presence, even for Parry's heavy accent. Varma's medical examination, in the gloomy light of the hut, was necessarily cursory, and told him nothing. He was frowning as they left the hut.

"Physically, he's robust, and there's no indication of any damage to the eyes; the pupil reflex is normal, but he's functionally blind, as far as I can tell. Must be some disturbance of the cortex."

"So, what now? Shall we go butterfly hunting?"

"Yes. But do try to sound more enthusiastic, old chap."

The two men circled the scrubby wasteland around the village in ever-widening circles, slowly penetrating deeper into mature jungle. The dark leaves and white fists of the moonflower were a constant threat at first, inhibiting progress beyond the paths, but further from the village became less abundant. Every so often Varma would freeze, like a dog pointing game; then Parry, following Varma's focus of attention, would see bright wings shuddering on a flower or flapping erratically through the warm air. Varma, silent and intent, would stalk the creature, moving more slowly the closer he got; once within range, he would net the insect with a rapid movement. Mostly, he released the creatures after a cursory examination; those that he wanted he would gently hold by the abdomen, between finger and thumb, so that their wings were folded back, and carefully insert them into waxed paper envelopes. The envelopes in turn were stored vertically in a compartmentalised cardboard box in Varma's large canvas satchel; which, of course, Parry was carrying.

Once, seeing Varma take a particular interest in a dark swallowtail he'd just caught, Parry found his hopes rising.

"Black Papilio?"

Varma shook his head emphatically. "No. But come here." He partially relaxed his grip on the butterfly, so that its wings could open: black fore-wings, with a white pattern that emphasised the venation; red and black hind-wings. "Look. You see those irregularities on the hind-wings? Like little pockets? Smell them."

Varma raised the butterfly to Parry's face; and as Parry inhaled, he found, not some insipid echo of a flower, but a rich and powerful perfume: roses and musk, lily and mignonette.

"Nobody really knows why some male butterflies have scented wings. My theory is that it has some function in attracting a mate. Pheromones, perhaps." Varma released the creature, and watched its panicked flight. "Beautiful – but not Black Papilio."

"Look – your hand," said Parry. Varma's finger and thumb were dusted with gold and black.

"Pollen. And wing scales. I'm as careful as I can be, but they always shed. Always." Varma wiped his hand on his shirt, leaving streaks of colour. He looked around, and blew through his moustache. "Well. I suppose we should be getting back. Damn it all."

"I'm sorry," said Parry.

"I don't understand it. We're in the exact place Hampson saw it, at the exact same time of year. There is no reason for us not to find it.

We've visited every flowering bush around the village – unless – aha! – ah, how stupid! Of course!"

"Now what?"

"What time did Hampson see Black Papilio? Do you remember? It was at *dusk*, Hugh! Dusk!"

"So?"

"So we've been hunting during the *day*; but suppose Black Papilio is *nocturnal!*"

"Arthik – we've been tramping around the jungle all day. I am *not* going to – "

"Therefore, we should be investigating night-flowering bushes! The moonflower, Hugh! That's why Hampson wrote *Datura* in his notes – he saw Black Papilio on a moonflower!"

"I am hot and tired, and – "

"And you will be fully recovered after supper and a short rest. Come on."

❖

Once again, the gathering dusk had sent the Bedlamites behind the tight-shut doors of their windowless huts; at the same time it had drawn forth the biting insects and the pervasive, disturbing scent of moonflower. Parry had improvised protection by draping mosquito netting over his head and face, tucking it into his shirt collar, and jamming a sun-hat on top to keep it in place. Varma treated such precautions with contemptuous amusement.

"The mosquitoes will still get to you somehow."

"They'll find it easier to get to *you*."

"At least I don't look like an English maiden aunt in mourning. Anyway, may I suggest that we circle around the village edge, visiting each moonflower in turn; if I go one way and you the other, we should meet back here, by the tents, in about half an hour. Going separately will increase our chances of finding something. Alright?"

The clouds, apologists for the poor monsoon, had rolled back, leaving a giant moon. Everything was painted in silver and black; everything either spot-lit with unsettling clarity or hidden in deepest

darkness. Parry, holding the net that Varma had given him, and trying
not to think about leopards, walked slowly through this monochrome
world; from moonflower to moonflower he paced, buffeted by a
powerful scent which seemed to grow stronger with each passing
minute. What *was* that smell? There was something in it of lilies, yes;
but lilies placed on a corpse to hide the odours of death.

When a mosquito found him, he would up his pace, but he soon
found himself tailed by squadrons of the creatures, seeking – and
finding – the exposed flesh of his arms and hands. But these small
torments were driven from his mind by a dark shadow hovering in
front of a silvered blossom. He crept towards it; either a butterfly
or a moth, but oddly blurred around its edges, as though it were
dissolving into mist. But wait: the creature was suddenly still, as
though listening, its shape and form suddenly focused. A butterfly all
in black; a butterfly with three dark tails on the trailing edge of each
hind wing; Black Papilio! Edging closer, Parry saw that the illusion
of blurring was caused by the wing-tails: the butterfly's trembling
pleasure made them shudder and vibrate, so that the creature looked
as though it were sublimating into the night. Parry, mimicking
Varma's technique, moved his net very slowly towards it; but the
butterfly, as though suddenly aware of his presence – indeed, as
though to greet an old friend – flipped away from the moonflower,
and into the mosquito netting over Parry's face. It moved over the
material with rapid, side-to-side movements, like a dog on a rabbit's
scent. Parry tried all manner of ways to catch it; first he put the
butterfly net over his face, and tried to scare the creature away from
his face into the trap; but that had no effect other than to press
the mosquito netting against his skin, such that he could feel the
scratching of Black Papilio's legs – oddly sharp and strong, for such
a fragile creature – against the delicate skin next to his eye. He
grabbed at it with his hands, but it was like trying to grasp smoke:
the insect would half-scuttle, half-fly out of his reach with peculiar,
jerky movements. Its speed and erratic changes of direction, together
with the way it would suddenly fly up and immediately return –
together with the optical illusion suggesting a creature without a
clear border – often gave the impression that there were several

butterflies around his face. But wait – there *were* several! Two or three – or was it six or seven?

Parry pinched at the mosquito netting and held it slightly away from his face so that insects' scratching feet were kept from his flesh. Now he could see that there were indeed a number of the creatures; they landed on the netting and moved rapidly across it. Sometimes, where the moonlight permitted, he could see a dark proboscis uncurl and probe through the holes in the netting, as though seeking nectar. Keeping the netting held away from his skin, Parry walked cautiously on towards the tents. He'd been away at least half an hour; Varma should be there by now. The group of Black Papilios on his face-net had grown to at least eight; sometimes he felt that he was looking out through a ragged black curtain pulled this way and that by an unfelt wind.

"Arthik!" he called out, softly. "Arthik?" He was by the tents, now, where they had agreed to meet. Where was the man? It would be a disaster if the Black Papilios left before Varma got here; Parry would never be forgiven. He made another lunge at the small cloud of butterflies, but the creatures' ability to avoid the butterfly net was almost supernatural. "Arthik!" Parry called more loudly, and stopped to listen; but no sounds came to him beyond a grumbling snore from Mani's tent. And now that he looked, Parry could see, on the tent itself, the odd movements of Black Papilios – their blurred flight as they hovered around the carefully-netted entrance, their curious scuttling movements when they alighted on the canvas.

Parry heard a small noise from the direction of the village – and then he saw him. Varma, on his knees, on the bare waste ground, facing away from Parry towards the domed huts of Badagamadalam. His hands were slightly raised, palms upwards, as though to receive the moon's blessings. *What the hell is he doing*, wondered Parry. *Praying?*

"Arthik," said Parry, as he approached. "Got something for you here. Look at *this*. Arthik?"

Arthik slowly lowered his hands; now that Parry was closer, he could see that they trembled slightly.

"Arthik. Look here." Parry moved forward very cautiously; was it his imagination, or were there fewer Black Papilios on his netting than before? "Arthik!", he said, urgency raising his voice. "Quickly!" But the last of the dark butterflies left his netting, disappearing into the silver-black night like smoke in the wind. "Damn!" said Parry. "Arthik, what the hell is the matter with you? Didn't you hear me?"

Certainly, Varma seemed to hear something; indeed, he cocked his head as though listening to some remote siren song.

"Arthik?"

Parry drew level with his friend, and bent down to shake him out of whatever sleepy trance he'd fallen into – but jerked his hand back as though he'd touched a corpse that moved. *Where was Arthik's face?* Between forehead and chin there were no features: only a shuddering black froth that trembled, and writhed, and remade itself continually, like black maggots in a bloodless corpse. "No!" shouted Parry, and lunged forward, sweeping the net towards Varma's head. The black froth boiled, rose into the night and dissolved away before returning, fragment by papery fragment, sometimes around Parry, but mainly around the weeping, staring eyes of Varma, seeking scleras clogged and darkened by the same black dust and golden pollen that powdered Varma's face. Parry pulled Varma to his feet, and half-dragged, half-carried him back to the tents, beating at the insects that crowded around their heads. He sat Varma down by the shallow mound of last night's fire, kicked away the insulating soil, and threw on brushwood from the pile that Mani had set aside for cooking breakfast, and blew until it blazed bright and hot. He pulled his friend as close to it as was safe; the heat and smoke largely drove the Black Papilios away.

"Arthik! Are you unwell? Speak to me!"

Varma turned unseeing eyes to Parry; he smiled beatifically, as one who possesses an eternal joy.

"Oh, Englishman," he said. "What a great gift you have given me."

❖

Smith looked at the note he had just read. Not at the words as such; at the paper, at the smudged ink, at the up-and-down letters which an ageing typewriter in Bombay just could not keep in line. He turned it over to look at the other side. Blank. He read the letter again. 'To:

Fraser Smith, Estate Manager,' etc. etc. 'From Andrew Trescothick, General Manager, Bombay-Burmah Tea Corporation,' etc. etc. 'Date: 18th July, 1949.' 'Dear Mr Smith, With regard to the individual' ... Etc., etc.

Smith shook his head. Who'd have thought it? The 'individual' had been sitting there – right there, in the chair on the other side of his desk – less than a month ago. No – less than a *fortnight* ago. He'd sat there, for the best part of half an hour, throughout what he had insisted on calling the 'handover meeting.' How did he put it? Oh yes: *"Can't have the new boy being led astray can we? Got to settle you in, Smith. Hand over the baton properly. Tan tarah!"*

Smith shuddered at the memory. His predecessor at the tea estate really had been very odd. He had not, during the 'handover meeting,' handed over anything, other than the thing that Smith had handed straight back. The man had simply used the meeting as an opportunity to talk; to inform Smith of his peculiar ideas, his bizarre plans. Smith had tried to be sympathetic – but really! That unwashed shirt; that three-week beard; those stained teeth; those staring blue eyes! How had he kicked off the conversation? Oh yes:

"This isn't Bombay, you know. People do things differently around here."

"Is that so?"

"Don't worry about the tea bushes. They'll be fine. Perfect conditions. Bloody stuff grows itself."

"Most encouraging."

"It's the people you'll have to keep an eye on."

"Thefts?"

"No, no, no. They're pretty honest. I meant, you'll have to look after them. Protect them. Make up for what happened in my day. The guilt."

Smith had tried to keep the amusement out of his voice. "I think they'll find me a fair employer."

"That's not what I'm talking about." The man leant forward, hands on the edge of the desk; Smith leaned backwards: that smell. "Look. I started out in Simla. Over forty years ago. We had a saying up there. Gulab mein kaante hai. Roses have thorns. This place" – he gestured at the estates outside the office window – "it's beautiful. But underneath? Things you wouldn't imagine, chum."

"Think I'll manage. I saw a lot of things in the army."

The man had lumbered to his feet. "The army!" He marched on the spot. "Left; left; left, right, left … Squad – halt!" He saluted.

Smith waited until the man sat down again. "Is there anything else you need to tell me?"

"Ha! Oh yes!" The man bent over and dug in his canvas holdall. He pulled something out and placed it on Smith's desk. A length of black silk; a woman's stocking. "That's for you. Keep it. I won't need it anymore."

Smith had been silent. He had looked at the stocking.

"Now listen," said the man. "This is important. What do you know about the hierarchy?"

"I don't understand you."

"I mean, who runs this outfit?"

"As the estate manager, I can assure you that from now on I shall be running this – 'outfit.'"

"Ah!" The man had leaned back in his chair and nodded, as though Smith had confirmed his suspicions. "So he hasn't spoken to you. Yet."

"Who?"

"Babu."

"Who the hell is Babu?"

"He's been away for a while. During the war. But you'll know him when you meet him. One leg. His eyes … But maybe it will be different now. The war's changed everything. Bloody Germans. Destroyed more than they will ever understand."

"You appear to be suggesting that an individual named Babu will have some influence over the management of my estate. Have I understood you correctly?"

"I'm not saying it's right. It's not. You'll have to change things. God, how I wish I'd never worked for him! All those people … Poor sods."

"You worked for him? While in the employ of Bombay-Burmah?"

"We all did, you fool! We were all Babu's people. All of us. Everyone except Hampson, who ran back home when he realised, and Parry, who got called up before he was needed. Got drowned, Parry. Fell off a troop carrier in the Atlantic. Hampson didn't last long either. The usual thing. Whispers, telling him what to do."

"Who is Hampson?"

"Never mind. Before your time. Point is, it was wrong, helping Babu. But, back then, it seemed like we had no choice. Babu scared the hell out of us. The way he looks at you. We provided for him, all those years. It was either that or crossing the bridge with Babu's slit-necked slave. And I came damn close to that, every now and then. Still do. The guilt, the guilt, the guilt. It will drive me mad!"

Future tense? Smith had thought. Really? "You've lost me. What exactly do you mean?"

"Their faces, that's what I mean. Their eyes. I see them every night. In the bushes. On the walls. Even Varma – I thought he'd be too strong, with his mind, but no, even Varma got taken. Ummattaka. Babu wanted them that way. Said they were easier like that. They see the bridge more easily. Hear the Englishman's whispers more clearly. Not me, though. No fear. I look after my eyes." Tyman nodded at the stocking on Smith's desk.

"'Them', 'they' – who are you talking about?"

"Labourers, mostly. Easiest to pick on a labourer."

"Your labourers worked for Babu too?"

"Worked for him? You could say that! Yes, you could say that!" The man laughed, or tried to, before doubling up into a smoker's cough. "Varma was the worst. The one who comes back to me most, I mean. He was a good man. Didn't deserve Bedlam."

"Bedlam?"

"Too bloody nosy. That's what did for him. Hampson should never have let slip about the ummattaka puchi. So it was Hampson's fault, really. Clumsy of him. So why should I bear all the guilt? Why? I'm not going to! No more! The war changed everything – well, this is changing too!"

There was a short pause. Smith had summoned all his limited powers of diplomacy. "Look. I can see you have had a difficult patch, but well done for keeping the estate going through the bad times. Really. But now you can forget all that, eh? Put your feet up. Get the first boat back home."

"England? Ha! There's nothing for me there. The memories would do for me. Even here, they're bad. But in England, they'd be all I have. No, I've got to fix things here." He leaned forward over the desk again; Smith flinched. "Do you know how to get rid of a memory? To rub away guilt?"

"Er – no. Positive thinking?"

"There's a woman. In a blue sari."

"I see."

"Somewhere near Srirangapatnam. She has the power of redemption. The gift of forgiveness. All she does is touch you."

"Mm."

"Not like that, you fool. That's not what I mean. I mean, she touches you and – you're clean. Clean. All the things you've done – they're annulled. It's like being born again."

"Magic touch, eh?"

"Everyone knows about her. Everyone round here, anyway. Talk to your workers. Talk to the mali. Everyone knows about the woman in the blue sari. She doesn't show herself to everyone, mind you."

"I believe you."

"But who can help her? She's always looking for another, poor thing. Always searching. Always giving, always forgiving. Never receiving."

"Well. I wish you the best of luck. Listen – I am most grateful for the handover, but I really need to get on." Smith had stood up. "The tea won't pluck itself, eh? You know that better than me!"

The man had lumbered to his feet and saluted. Smith returned the motion. Humour him. Then he remembered something. "Oh – look, please take this, would you? I appreciate the gesture, but I have no need of it. Honestly." Smith gestured towards the stocking.

"As you wish, chum." The man reached over and picked it up. "None so blind as those that will not see. Unless it's those that can't help but see. But shut the windows at night, hm? And listen – " Tyman lowered his voice and pulled back his lips in a grimace that was, perhaps, intended to be a smile. " – just don't meet Babu, alright? Just refuse to see him. One-legged bastard. The way he looks at you." As if reminded of something, he wiped at his own eyes, one after the other, with the stocking.

❖

That was how the meeting had ended. And now – this letter. Smith read the cogent sentences again.

'With regard to the individual found dead in the River Kaveri, ten days ago – I assume you have read the reports – '

Yes indeed, thought Smith. The paper had been most irresponsible. Cause of death not drowning, but strangling. The silk ligature – a woman's stocking – had still been around the corpse's neck. Cue lurid Victorian tales of Thugs and so forth. Hardly what was needed in the current environment, what with Independence, and anti-British sentiments still to the fore. Yes, most irresponsible.

' – we are now informed that items found on the body, together with the identifying characteristics of the deceased, unequivocally indicate that the individual was Charles Tyman, the previous manager of your estate.'

Probably his own fault, thought Smith. Strutting around like a maniac. Ticked off the wrong people. They wouldn't have known he was doolally. Should have gone back to England. Bloody fool.

'We do not believe that this reprehensible murder was in any way related to Tyman's period of employment at the Bombay-Burmah Trading Corporation. Nevertheless, we urge all employees to be vigilant, particularly under current circumstances.'

There was a tap at the door. Smith put the letter face-down on his desk. "Come in."

It was old Somu, the estate manager. Worth his weight in gold, they said. But he looked nervous. "Yes, Somu?"

"Sir, a visitor."

Smith frowned. "I have no appointments."

"Yes sir. But he will not go."

"Well, who is it?"

Somu hesitated, turning his head slightly as if to ascertain he was not overheard. When he replied, his voice was soft.

"Sir – it is Babu."

"*Babu?*"

"Yes, sir. Babu has come."

Beyond the open window of Smith's office, the jungle's chirr ceased, revealing a profound silence; and as if to replace sound with scent, through came tones of jasmine, of liguster and lily, of musk and madder. And then, approaching the office along the corridor, scarcely discernible at first but increasingly distinct, the ryhthmic double-*clunk* and single step of one who walks with wooden crutches.

Smith frowned. "Send him in," he said. "Send him in."

☾

FIVE GARLANDS

"Relatively undisturbed patches of forest, or 'sacred groves,' have been sites of worship towards gods, deities and ancestral spirits ... for as long as 400 years [and] are especially common in the Western Ghats ... what is especially unique for the sacred groves of this region is the frequent presence of idols, shrines or temples devoted to serpent-gods ... These ... are not necessarily synonymous with actual living snakes, but are divine beings or deities which are depicted as displaying the same physical features as snakes, with a specific allusion to cobras."
- F Yuan, et al., "Sacred groves and serpent-gods moderate human-snake relations", People and Nature, 2, 111-122 (2020).

We still don't know why the Sarpal Tea Corporation sent Joki de Souza to Mansholi's dark jungles and hidden fears, half a century ago. After all, Joki was from Goa; his first language was Konkani, and he'd spent his adult life among the English-speaking professionals of Bombay, a thousand miles to the north. He could neither understand the Tamil spoken on the Mansholi estate, nor read its looping, curling script; nor, at first, find meaning in damp garlands around a black clay god, there in the cicada-humming southern hills.

Furthermore, the corporation's many employees included others who lived closer by and whose temperaments and backgrounds better suited them to a Mansholi posting. What could Joki offer that they could not? Why send this city boy to the back of the South Indian beyond? Such questions bring only polite evasions, and shrugged shoulders that speak of the passage of time. The mystery remains: and Joki de Souza does not.

But even after forty years, we can, perhaps, discern Joki's whispered story. We read it between the lines of dog-eared diaries; we trace its outline in pencilled pictures; we hear it in the faltering accounts of old men, in what they say and do not say. It tells us of a pattern drawn in soured milk and scattered marigolds. It insists that Joki's story cannot end with cold ashes taken by a cold river.

❖

On a July afternoon in 1974, Joki de Souza walked out of the Sarpal Head Office and into the cloying Bombay heat. The sun was low in the sky, so he shielded his eyes with a copy of the *Times of India*. Meandering along the stained pavement, squinting at traffic and waving at taxis, he was indistinguishable from any of the other ten thousand office-wallahs in the seething, swarming city. Just another young man with a damp shirt and a briefcase, leaving just another office block on just another road. Joki's briefcase, however, was unusually heavy: in that July, he was burdened with a decade's worth of accounts from the Mansholi estate. An exercise in 'prudence,' as he would have said. He shifted the briefcase from one hand to the other. Perhaps he muttered something as he walked; something in accountant-speak, no doubt. *It is unbalanced*, maybe; or, *inappropriate transactions*.

A thousand miles south of Bombay's fevered cliques and venal commerce, the same afternoon sun that shone on Joki also shone on the foothills of the Western Ghats. There, it found a way through the Mansholi jungle canopy, and illuminated a formless idol of black clay, making a starry constellation of its white spots. It brightened the marigolds scattered in front of the effigy, and warmed the small dish of milk set among the flowers. It accentuated the darker ground at the base of the idol, where some rich liquid had stained the earth. It roused the flies, which skipped from milk to wet soil and back again in bloated joy.

Two men stood in front of the shrine. The shorter one, his face mottled by the irregular patchwork of an old burn, peered at his companion through thick lenses; a supplicant's smile dimpled his pale scars. The other, bent to one side by a withered leg and supporting himself with a brass-ferruled stick, surveyed the tableau without expression; his dark eyes oddly intense, his face strangely ageless. He nodded towards the shrine, without looking at his fawning disciple.

The piebald man adjusted his glasses and stepped forward to pick up the dish of milk. He held it up in both hands. And the man with the bad leg and the fierce eyes drank back the fly-blown, curdling mixture as though it were ambrosia.

❖

But the narrative requires some context. Who was Joki de Souza, man and boy, and what was Mansholi to him? Unfortunately, Joki's beginnings are almost as mysterious as his ending. True, we can draw his family tree; in fact, we can follow its trunk all the way back to a Portuguese adventurer, a trader of cinnamon and cardamom, whose diary the family guarded – reverentially wrapped in paper – throughout Joki's childhood. But the tree had few branches, and fewer still in recent years. So Joki left no close relatives; certainly none that can be found today to pull out prints of Joki in bleeding colours, to recall his falls and scabs. And there are no neighbour's children to recount childhood misdemeanours, no ageing 'girl next door' to look back at lost love with misty eyes. We do, however, have Joki's sketch-books. We also have Harpreet Singh, Joki's best friend from high school and college days. Mr Singh's testimony is most relevant to Joki's final weeks, but also gives a flavour of his friend's childhood.

In brief: Joki was an only child, produced by surprised parents well after they had given up all reasonable hope of offspring. He was brought up among the elegant Portuguese villas of Goa, in a home where English was spoken as much as Konkani. The drawings in Joki's earliest sketch-book – betraying a talent still unrefined but full of promise – show a house of books and brass ornaments, typical of the sophisticated liberal elite of India.

"Always drawing," says Harpreet. "Always carrying around his damn papers and pencils." He shakes his head, but as he thumbs through Joki's artwork he produces a rare half-smile. The sketches are eloquent. Joki's father stands, ramrod straight, every inch the army man. You almost don't need Harpreet to tell you what he says: *Pictures, boy? Nobody makes a living from pictures. You'll get a proper job.* Joki's mother, on the settee, has a sad smile. "She would have known she had cancer by then," says Harpreet. "She tried so hard to get Joki married before she died, but he just wouldn't." Towards the end of the sketch-book, the drawings change perceptibly, not in style but in tone. The needle-sharp realism now is melded with a sadness of composition. Joki's mother is everywhere, because she is absent. You see her in the bowed head of her husband, in the chairs that are empty. "Joki never forgave himself. But he never married either."

There is one more picture from Joki's childhood: a full frontal of the de Souza villa, from the outside. The sky is pregnant with rain.

"He drew that when he put it up for sale," says Harpreet, "just after his father died. University isn't cheap, after all. I was watching over his shoulder when he drew. But it was sunny, you know. Poor Joki."

At the age of twenty, then, with his parents gone and no close relations on either side of the family, Joki found himself entirely alone in the world. Life was challenging, but he persevered. And eventually he found a niche in the Accounts Department of the Sarpal Tea Corporation. We can imagine Joki's relief – Sarpal was one of the world's pre-eminent tea-producing companies, winner of the Golden Leaf award eight years in succession, a giant of a company with estates all over India. A job for life surely. And he'd be based in Bombay – what better place for a refined young man with no dependents? The restaurants; the art galleries!

"I moved to Bombay a year later," says Harpreet. "We saw a lot of each other. I'd say he was happy, mostly. Life isn't always easy for gentle people, you know? I think he liked his job. It wasn't art, but it gave him a living."

Harpreet's account is supported by corporation records: in spite of his diffidence, Joki did well. Soon, his remit included monitoring and control of the budgetary performance of the Mansholi tea estates. *Idyllic*, says Harpreet; *idyllic*. Indeed: of all the domains of the mighty corporation, these plantations, nestled in the foothills of the great Western Ghats like green gems on a rumpled quilt, are the southernmost and the most serene; perhaps too, the most beautiful. But for Joki, it seems, verdant Mansholi was only a set of double entries: twin columns of tidy numerals, nothing more. So long as the numbers met his budgeted expectations, cool, beautiful Mansholi was of no further interest. And the corporation's annual reports suggest that Mansholi was dully predictable – satisfactory profits, year after year after year.

So why, one month before his death, having only been with the corporation for three years, did Joki requisition a set of archived photocopies of the Mansholi accounts – over a *decade* of records? It is as though he had heard a sibilant exhalation, a whisper in the dark: *It is unbalanced.*

◆

"Miss Raganathan?"

"Hello, Joki! What brings you to Personnel?"

"Just need a bit of help with a spot-check at one of the estates. I want an independent audit done, and I was wondering if you had any thoughts on who we should send."

"Has somebody been naughty again? It's Simla, I suppose."

"Not this time. In fact, it's about as far away from Simla as you could get. Right down the south. Mansholi."

Miss Raganathan was facing away from Joki during this conversation, her attention mostly taken up with the contents of a filing cabinet. Now she stiffened and stopped walking her fingers through the hanging files. When she turned around, she was smiling broadly.

"Mansholi? That's my part of the country."

"Aha! Then who better to advise me on how to proceed?"

"But I must say, I'm a little surprised. We've never had any concerns there before. What's wrong?"

"Well, nothing *wrong* as such, not precisely wrong, no. In fact, their results are in line with expectations. But I'd still like a closer look."

Miss Raganathan wrinkled her brow prettily, and gave Joki a quizzical half-smile. Joki squirmed.

"It's just that the variances are a little *too* invariant, you know? Being too predictable is as suspicious as being too variable. And now that it's been flagged up, I'm obliged to look into it, you see?"

Miss Raganathan didn't really see; the half-smile had gone, but the frown remained.

"It's not the *entire* set of Mansholi plantations," Joki continued. "Just one of them. Kalisholi."

"Ah, Mr Kannan's estate."

"'How do you manage to remember everybody's names? It's almost scary!"

"It's almost a requirement for being Head of Personnel."

"Of course! The youngest ever Head, I believe?"

"Mm-hm."

"Anyway, perhaps you've had problems with Mr Kannan before?"

"No. Never."

Behind the hum of the air-conditioning, the muted chaos of Bombay traffic pulsed against the closed window. For Joki, the impulse to drop the whole affair grew: *Kannan is not your problem,* something said. But he suppressed the cowardly impulse, chin raised: *It's my job.*

Miss Raganathan sighed, pushing back stray hair from her forehead with both hands, as though she were faced with a particularly onerous task. Her expression gave Joki a sudden insight into the qualities which had *really* made her the youngest ever – and only ever female – Sarpal Corporation Head of Personnel.

"Your proposal is that we incur all the expense and inconvenience of a Mansholi spot-check, because you *can't* find any discrepancies? Yes?"

"That's not quite fair. I just need to confirm things are as they seem to be, that's all. You know, for prudence."

"Look, Joki. I really think you should focus on matters closer to home. You'll have your hands full with the year-end accounts. Why make problems where there are none?"

"It shouldn't take long – surely we can spare somebody? Maybe the financial controller that we sent to Simla last year?"

"You mean Chauhan. He's done more than his fair share of off-site work recently."

"*Somebody* needs to do it."

"Is this really about a bit of – what do you call it – invariance? Or is there more to it?"

"That's what I'm going to find out." Sometimes, Joki's diffidence sloughed away to reveal a stubborn core.

Miss Raganathan turned away, and pulled open the drawer of another filing cabinet.

"Something occurs to me – one second, please." She took out a file, opened it and scanned the opening page. Joki recognised his Sarpal employment record: date of birth, date of recruitment, position. Next of kin: 'none.'

"So: all about Mr de Souza. You've been with us since 1970. You've been promoted regularly. But you've never been seconded to any part of the company outside Head Office." She looked up, smiling, and Joki's heart did a little backflip. "An ideal opportunity, wouldn't you say?"

"It's hardly the best way for me to spend my time. We usually get the FCs to follow up this kind of thing. Like Chauhan. You know."

Miss Raganathan perched herself on the edge of her desk, holding Joki's file to her chest with one hand. She adjusted the position of a brass paperweight – a goddess entwined by a cobra with five heads; dark hoods fanned out above the figure's head. *We protect,* the serpents mutely declared; and, perhaps, *we avenge.* Her lips moved briefly, as though she were silently working through a mathematical problem. Then she looked up at Joki with a winning smile.

"I know it's below your level, Joki – but actually, maybe it works for the best. I've noticed that there's a bit of an 'us-and-them' culture developing in Sarpal. You know, *us* in Head Office, and *them* out there in the estates. I've been thinking for a while that we need to get out there and see them a bit more. Encourage teamwork." She stood up and took a step towards him. "And you haven't visited any of our plantations. Not once."

"But as you just said, we've the year-end accounts coming up – "

"All the more reason to sort it out quickly. And it will tick the 'be more visible and proactive' box in your list of performance targets."

"Well, yes, but – "

"But?"

"I wouldn't know where to start with the arrangements – "

"But *I* would. And I can clear it with the boss. Leave it to me." She smiled at Joki again, and that was that.

◆

We have seen a photograph of Miss Raganathan. In 1974, the corporation produced a small, short-lived monthly magazine – called *Tea Times,* in the inevitably twee nature of these things – for circulation among employees. Back-copies of this ephemeral publication remain in the corporation archives; the December 1975 edition has a short piece outlining new pension arrangements, and next to the byline – 'J. Raganathan' – is a head-and-shoulders image of a woman in her late twenties. Even through the grainy nineteen-seventies printing, we can see that she is extraordinarily beautiful. That fact is relevant, because normally, according to Harpreet Singh, Joki was easily pushed around by pretty girls. And we can be quite sure that to become Head of Personnel – at her age, as a female, in the India of 1974 – Miss Raganathan was capable of pushing very hard. It's probable, then, that she would have significantly influenced the outcome of her meeting with Joki. But perhaps she was pushing at a half-open door. Life is not pleasant for a young man with no family and no income, so, having found a career, Joki would have been determined to keep it: once the Mansholi anomaly had been flagged, he had no choice but to address the issue. Perhaps he asked himself, why *not* go to the far tip of the great subcontinent, to this country within a country, and undertake the audit himself, in person? Perhaps it made sense, at the time.

◆

Mina Singh swirled her glass of water, making the melting ice-cubes chatter and tumble. It had been so hot under the stage lights. The tiny Chhabildas theatre was stifling at the best of times, but in July? Insupportable! She looked across the table at Joki and Harpreet.

"So, guys, what did you think?"

Harpreet raised his own glass, solemnly. "It was, my dear, a veritable – "

"A veritable *tour de force*," Mina interrupted. "You always say that. Joki, what did *you* think?"

"Well, I must say it was a really interesting take on an old story – "

"*Interesting*? That's what people say when they are trying to be polite!" Mina contrived to look disappointed. "You didn't like it, did you? You didn't like my performance?"

That wasn't what Joki meant, but Mina liked to tease him. All she had to do was bat her eyelashes and turn on the charm that had conquered the stage, and Joki became a tongue-tied wreck. It was so funny.

"No, no, Mina, your performance was fantastic. You're always, it's always beautiful, you know that."

"Yes, she does," said Harpreet, rolling his eyes.

"All I meant was, you know, I hadn't seen the serpent demon Takshaka portrayed in quite that way before, which was really *interesting* – "

"There! You said it again!" Mina extended one delicate hand towards Joki, palm up, while looking around the restaurant as though to invite other diners to share in her offended disbelief.

"Mina, please," chided Harpreet, but he was smiling.

"It's supposed to be *experimental* theatre, after all," said Mina, but she desisted from the game and leant back in her chair. She had shared a biriani with her husband, and their plates were clean. Joki's fish curry, however, remained half-eaten. Harpreet glanced at his old friend, mildly concerned.

"Not finishing your food, Joki? Was it okay?"

"It was delicious. Really. Just not that hungry today."

"Perhaps the play spoiled your appetite. No, I'm kidding! Look, we haven't heard your news, old friend. What's new in the tea business? What's the corporation brewing up these days?"

Joki considered for a while, looking into his glass of water as though it held a better answer than any he could produce.

"Nothing new, really. The tea business doesn't change much ..." He raised one shoulder slightly, in the hint of a shrug.

"But?"

"The fact is, I've got to go away for a few days. Some place in Tamil Nadu called Mansholi. It's miles away. If you went any farther south you'd fall off Kanyakumari."

"Joki, that's fantastic! It's *lovely* down there. Why are you being so negative?"

"Not so fantastic to live in some jungle cabin for a week. Imagine the sanitation. And think: no restaurants, no theatre. No libraries."

"Nonsense," said Mina, smoothing down her shalwar kameez. "There's more to life than all that."

"Mm."

"Look," said Harpreet, "it's a great opportunity to see more of the country. You haven't been out of Bombay since you moved here. And before that, where? Goa is hardly representative of the subcontinent. Anyway – a change of scene means new material for the artist, no?"

Joki brightened. "Yes, that's true. And that reminds me – I brought the drawings you asked for. From when we were kids. Mina, have you seen how fat Harpreet used to be? Keep the sketch-books for a while, if you want, but take care – the charcoal can smudge."

Childhood reminiscences, the merits of Goan cuisine, the latest Bollywood gossip – their conversation was little different, probably, from the talk at any other table. But that was the last time Mina and Harpreet Singh saw Joki de Souza.

◈

Some facts are not in dispute. We know that Joki asked Personnel to provide him with the phone number of the Kalisholi estate manager, Mr Kannan. We know that Personnel could not do this: Mr Kannan *had* no phone number. Kalisholi was isolated from the rest of the Mansholi plantations. Running a phone line along the narrow road that cut through the jungled hills had been deemed impractical. It would be necessary, therefore, to contact Mr Kannan by post. A memo outlining this logic – along with details of Joki's itinerary – is buried in the corporation's records. It is signed with scribbled initials: *JR*.

We know too that Joki, as suggested, wrote to Mr Kannan, indicating the date and nature of his visit. We know this because we have seen the letter. And we know that Mr Kannan received the letter because we have seen, on the letter itself, the black cursive of his cryptic, sinuous annotation: *For Saunders*. But the Corporation has never employed anyone called Saunders.

Other matters too are unresolved. In particular, we don't know who phoned Subayah, the manager of the plantation just down the road from the troublesome Kalisholi estate. All Subayah will say – he is an old man today – is that someone from Personnel spoke to him. Someone who had seen Subayah's application for leave to attend the birthday of his niece in Madurai. By chance, this person said, Joki de Souza would arrive at Madurai airport on the day Subayah planned to return to Mansholi. Perhaps Subayah might give de Souza a lift? Of course, Subayah agreed. It was only natural, he says.

Harpreet Singh today is also an old man. But his mind has stayed young; in any case, to support his testimony, he gestures to the bookshelves in his study. These hold volumes on South Indian folklore, in a variety of languages; indeed, his familiarity with this field is one reason for our visit. But there is another reason, and this too is manifest on the bookshelves. A row of thick exercise books: diaries, filled with the untidy handwriting of one who writes much, and writes quickly. To look at this shelf is to see the evolution of India: moving from left to right, the faded, yellowing, poor-quality notebooks of the seventies are gradually replaced by newer, hard-backed items with stronger covers. Only the handwriting remains the same: on the spine of each diary is written, in English, the years and months to which it corresponds. Mr Singh takes a 1974 diary from the shelf, where it nudges Joki's sketch-books. It falls open on the pages dated July, as though this month has been relived many times. Indeed, if required, Mr Singh can recite some passages – for example, Joki's phone call – from memory, verbatim.

Perhaps such feats of memory become possible when one is accustomed to remember for two. For today, sitting in his study, surrounded by film and theatre posters reminding him of what his wife once was, Harpreet Singh must face what she now is – an old body with a broken mind, wrapped in a wheelchair. He reminds her, again and again, of one part of Joki's story or another, but is met only by a sad echolalia.

"You remember Joki, darling, don't you?"

"Don't you?"

"You know, poor Joki?"

"Poor Joki?"

❖

Today, a single-track road still slices the jungle between the main Mansholi tea plantation – the one that Subayah managed – and the smaller Kalisholi estate. The road passes close to, but not through, a village: a little community accessed only by dusty paths that meander between boulders and lantana brakes, beneath neem trees and scarlet flame-of-the-forest blossoms. On one of these paths, close to the road, a speckled idol still mutely accepts the gifts of passersby. Even today.

Indeed, all these – the road, the paths, the village, the idol, the jungle – are largely unchanged since Joki walked to his death down the same narrow road, almost five decades ago. You can go there now, and see the marigolds and milk on the stained dust, as always. You can hold up Joki's sketch, and compare his memory, captured in black charcoal, with the hot tableau at your feet. It is as though he whispers in your ear: *Count them. Count the garlands.*

Look at his sketch, then, and count. There are four garlands around the speckled god. Four.

❖

The Monday after his dinner with the Singhs, on the 14th July, Joki set off for the remote south: reluctant, perhaps, but also determined. He was driven, in a corporation car, to Bombay airport. There he boarded an Indian Airlines flight to Madurai. The drone of the plane's engines and the drop in temperature sent him to sleep for a little while; soon, however, a stewardess – silent and unsmiling – shook him awake in order to offer him a livid-orange, cellophane-wrapped sweet. He sucked on this contemplatively, looking at the great Deccan Plateau sliding away beneath him: a flat landscape of dun browns, burnt siennas, and pale greens. Occasionally a sinuous, silver-grey ribbon stretched itself across this dry earth, side-winding its way between geological irregularities, seeking the lowest points on its serpentine course to the ocean.

Joki was in that neutral, reflective state of mind that reaches all travellers from time to time, the profound fatalism that comes from the recognition that no man is the master of his own fate. But the juddering touchdown and straining brakes of the plane jolted him out of this mood, and when the cabin crew opened the aircraft doors, the dry heat of Tamil Nadu annihilated the aircraft's carefully cooled interior climate, leaving only a regretful memory of comfort. Joki had arrived in the South, a foreigner in his own country.

❖

In the July of 1974, India was a troubled country, and its troubles dominated the newspapers of this period: their faded print complains of Indira Gandhi, of social unrest, of relations with Pakistan. But if you leaf diligently through the repositories in the grand offices of the *Times of India*, opposite the even grander Chhatrapati Shivaji railway station in Bombay, you will find a brief note buried towards the back of one of the late July editions.

Tirunelveli, Tamil Nadu: Spate of kidnappings. Residents complain that persons are taking young girls. Five have gone missing in July. Police say their fate is unknown.

Just that. It is typical of the style and depth of reporting of the time. Today, if you mention it to old Subayah he shrugs his shoulders and remains silent. When you point out that Tirunelveli is hardly thirty miles from Mansholi, and that the girls went missing just before Joki died, he only shakes his head, as though bemused by the oddities of life.

❖

Subayah had been waiting at the airport as arranged. Joki, after collecting his luggage – weighed down by accounts and artists' materials – and edging through the crowds, had seen a large, paunchy individual, with a hooked nose and a perpetual weak smile. For his part, Subayah's initial impression had been of a sensitive and perhaps ineffectual young man, but he soon realised the inaccuracy of this assessment – it rapidly became clear that Joki de Souza had come to do an audit, and it damn well would be done.

"Mr Kannan is very careful. I can't see him making any mistakes." Subayah changed gear yet again, and the Madurai traffic edged into gridlock under the furnace glare of a South Indian sun.

"Good. That's what I like to hear." Joki shifted his weight on a plastic-covered seat that had been cooked to a painful temperature in the airport car-park.

"He has his own ways of doing things, you know? But we all do in Mansholi. It's not Bombay. You need to understand that."

"Mm-hm."

"Give and take. That's how it works down here."

"Mm-hm."

"Mr Kannan runs a very tight ship. I'm sure he'll show you all that when he comes back."

"Comes *back?* What do you mean, back? Is he away?"

"Well, yes. That's why I'm standing in for him today. You didn't know?"

"No. We've had this audit booked for some time now, and it takes priority over other matters."

"Mr Kannan has particular habits."

"*My* habit is to carry out audits at the designated time. And if Mr Kannan is not there to answer my questions, so much the worse for him."

"I think he plans to return tonight. Yes, tonight, but perhaps not until late ... I'm sure he'll come to you."

"He'd better."

Subayah decided to change the subject.

"I think you'll find Kannan's house comfortable. The situation is good. It's not like the city, of course, but it's pleasant. You'll be helped by Mr Kannan's bearer, Muthu. He does all the cooking and cleaning. He'll give you no problems, but damn, he's ugly! In Tamil, Muthu means pearl, but I tell you he's more like the swine!"

And so on: and perhaps Subayah's attempts at genial conversation made the long, hot car journey less tedious than it might otherwise have been.

❖

Mr Kannan must have received Joki's letter well before Joki's arrival in Madurai. And at some point subsequent to its receipt he wrote 'For Saunders' on the letter, in his flowing, looping hand. But what then? Perhaps he got up from his desk in the Kalisholi office and looked through the window, his dark, fierce eyes taking in the serried bushes and shade trees of his emerald domain, the hunched pickers with their baskets full of green leaves. Perhaps he limped out of the office, leaning on his brass-tipped stick, and walked haltingly along the narrow jungle road. Perhaps he left the road and dragged his leg down a dusty path and past the black clay idol planted at the wayside like a sacred milestone, its dark surface speckled with white. And, finally, perhaps he returned to his house, the planter's bungalow on the hill – for that was where his stick was found, was it not? But then – where? We do not know. We only know that he had not returned by the time that Joki arrived.

❖

Joki and Subayah drove through vistas of increasing rurality: long, flat plains sporadically punctuated by acacia trees rising above scrawny cacti; level crossings at which the road jumped train tracks that stretched emptily away to opposite horizons; occasional massive, dark grey boulders sitting individually or in clusters in the flatlands, as though dropped there by a frightened god. Occasionally, they passed through crowded towns where they were forced to slow to walking pace while milling people stared unashamedly through the car windows. But as the journey progressed, towns were replaced by villages where crops were spread on the road to be dried in the sun and threshed by the infrequent traffic. Here, the noise of the car brought children out to laugh and wave at them, shouting "*Ta-ta, ta-ta, ta-ta.*" Mostly, the roads were clear; other than an occasional bullock cart blocking their way, the travellers were unimpeded.

Eventually, the monotony of the plains was broken by the far-off blue rumour of hills, and then, slowly but inexorably, the low, southernmost reaches of the great Western Ghats rose before them. The countryside too started to change, dust browns replaced by the impossible verdancy of paddy fields; acacias superseded by banyans, neems, and little orchards of banana and papaya trees. Then the first gentle slope, followed by an immediate decline, as though the ground had looked up but lost heart. But with growing courage it raised itself again, up and up, into the foothills where the Palni range merges with the Cardamom Hills. The air became cooler; the vegetation more lush, the trees taller, the shade deeper.

After a particularly steep ascent, Subayah drew up on the roadside to allow the over-heating Ambassador to recover. Once the engine had been turned off, Joki became aware of an all-encompassing, deafening, rasping trill – the only evidence of legions of cicadas hidden among the jackfruit trees and vines. They stood for a while, revelling in the cool air and listening to the grinding chirr of the invisible ones.

"How far now?" asked Joki after a little while.

"We're very close. Less than an hour. We go over the hill in front of us, and then down again."

"I'll have to do it all over again in a few days. In reverse."

"Maybe."

❖

Listening to Mr Singh expound the traditions of the South, we get the impression of a dialogue that has been repeated many times over: a script dog-eared from many rehearsals and repetitions, in which key passages are underlined by Mina's joyless echo.

"Snakes are particularly venerated, even today. Maybe it's because they shed their skin, as though they are starting afresh, so they are associated with death and rebirth."

"Death and rebirth."

"Or maybe it's because they are seen more often in the monsoon, so they are linked with fertility, with good crops. In fact, the reason they are more evident in the rainy season is because they get flooded out of the holes where they live. But it is what people believe that matters."

Mina grasps an invisible assailant, pushing at the threatening air, while her face spasms in fear and revulsion. Harpreet puts a hand to her shoulder.

"And it's interesting that snakes may become associated with a particular site, even a particular building, over many years. Did you know that, in some parts of India, they may be regarded as part of a property? Yes, the deeds of a house may actually mention a snake, if one is known to live under its walls. As if it were a creature of purpose, a guardian. Isn't that strange?"

❖

Perhaps the lowered temperatures had a rejuvenating effect, or perhaps Subayah's one-man marathon of driving made Joki feel a little guilty. In any case, Joki offered, after their rest among the cicadas, to be chauffeur for the remainder of the drive. Like many large men, Subayah had problems with his joints; it was a welcome relief, then, to rest his knees from the repeated gear changes necessary to coax the Ambassador up and down hills and around hairpin bends. In truth, for Joki too the change must have been welcome. With the car windows open and the fresh wind blowing through, with the hill road winding through cool, dark jackfruit jungle, with no traffic to speak of – how different from driving through the congestion and fumes of Bombay! One minute surrounded by untouched forest looming over the car, the next driving past a sheer descent from which they could see the diminishing ranks of the Western Ghats trooping towards the tip of India. One minute cruising down an empty road, the next slowing to let a family of langurs, dark faces framed by silver fur, cross in front of them. It is very possible that Joki was enjoying himself. And then, rounding a corner, where the hill dropped steeply away to reveal an expanse of tea bushes, he saw it: a blanket of delicate green covering soft gradients interspersed with occasional shade trees, like an emerald flock guarded by thin shepherds. For an instant, he felt as though he had been shrunk down and dropped into a carefully manicured, magical landscape.

"There you are – the jewel in our crown. Mansholi." Subayah's pride was unmistakable. "Tell them in Head Office, will you? Tell them how beautiful it is."

And it was self-evidently, utterly beautiful. Joki had seen tea plantations before, of course, in photographs and in the company literature freely distributed by the corporation. But pictures had not prepared him for the verdant reality: a commercial crop, yes, but also a great, well-tended, much-loved garden, framed by the mighty Ghats and cradled by the gentle Cardamom Hills.

No doubt Joki was tired after a long day of travel; quite possibly he was looking more at the view than at the road. Whatever the reason, his attention had wandered, and at first Subayah's shout served more to freeze him in shock than galvanise him into action.

"Watch it, watch it, *watch it!* Brake, man, brake!"

Joki stamped on the pedal and felt the soft, sluggish brakes of the old Ambassador slowly interfere with the vehicle's momentum. Then they caught, and the car went into a skid along the disintegrating tarmac. But he held the vehicle straight, and they stopped safely.

The road was empty of traffic; Joki twisted in his seat to look through the back window, but could see nothing on the asphalt's surface. Yet Subayah was already out of the car and jogging back with the awkward, lumbering run of the overweight. When Joki caught up with him, he was standing in the middle of the road, breathing heavily and looking at the ground, looking at something moving slowly in the dust, moving but going nowhere.

❖

"Anyway, as I was saying, there are many customs in the South about snakes. But most of the myths are about cobras. One of them goes like this. After many years a cobra's poison becomes thicker, becomes solid, like milk turning into cheese. Then it becomes a jewel in the head of the cobra, something that it keeps in the hood, a precious pearl."

"Precious pearl."

"And this pearl is like a lantern, it gives light, and the cobra uses this light to find its prey. Searching, in the dark."

Mr Singh holds his hand up, palm forward, fingers together and slightly cupped, in imitation of a cobra's erect hood. He turns it slowly from side to side, the very essence of a snake searching this way and that for some frightened creature.

◈

It was the first snake Joki had ever seen. It repelled him. Perhaps it was because of the unnatural way it moved, as though perpetually sliding through some dimension invisible to man, writhing around and against itself as if in transports of agony or pleasure. Perhaps it was because mortal injuries arouse as much revulsion as pity in the observer. He could see clearly where the car tyre had passed over its body, half-way along its length; dust and small stones had been crushed into its skin, and the body was flattened there, with a sharp bend where its broken innards were pushed against the inside of its skin, like a kink in a hosepipe. Blood leaked from this area, darkening the pale grey tarmac.

"My God!" Joki shuddered.

As though it had heard, the snake turned towards him, raising the front part of its body from the ground. It fascinated Joki horribly: the yellowish band-like scales on the belly, the smaller scales pushed out into little bosses as it spread its hood, the ability to turn and face him no matter where he moved. And all the time, its constant whispered warning: *they don't hiss*, thought Joki, *it's not a hiss at all, it's a shhhhh or thhhh sound*. But the most impressive features of the cobra, for Joki, were its eyes. Fierce beads of obsidian, entirely black, without discernible sclera or iris or pupil, unremitting and uncompromising;

the warrior eyes of a creature that neither sought nor gave quarter, a thing that could stare out a human even from behind the pain of a broken back.

"They won't like this," said Subayah quietly. Joki looked away from the snake with an effort; he turned to face Subayah first, before his eyes followed. He was about to ask 'Who?' when he saw them. A group of villagers, five or six, had appeared from nowhere. One of them put his hands together, *namaskar*, before softly speaking to a young boy, who ran off down a path that led away from the road, through the undergrowth, and into the jungle. The others looked mutely from the snake to the travellers with an intensity that seemed, to Joki's eyes, almost murderous.

"Why the *hell* didn't you brake?"

Joki was too taken aback by the fury in Subayah's question to feel annoyed. He started to stammer out a reply, but Subayah, beaded with sweat despite the cool evening, had begun a low-pitched exchange with the men – farm labourers, by the look of them, in dhotis and vests. The conversation, punctuated with forceful gestures directed at the snake or at Joki, was conducted in Tamil. One or two phrases kept recurring: *nulla pambu,* often uttered while pointing at the snake, and more reverently, in hushed tones – *Jakkamma*. The snake now had let its head fall and partially retracted its hood. Its movements were weaker. And all the while the light was failing.

Joki was about to insist they leave when they heard a shout from the trees. The boy had reappeared, accompanied by a man. The newcomer wore a clean dhoti and an ironed shirt with the sleeves neatly rolled up to his elbows. He looked to be in his fifties, stick-thin, with greying hair, and inflamed, watery eyes set in a lined face. But what truly distinguished him was the state of his forearms; they were scattered with light-grey scars, craters covered with thin skin that wrinkled and stretched, like the surface that forms on boiled milk. Joki tried not to stare; atavistic fears of leprosy sent shudders up his city-boy spine. The man seemed to have authority, at least among the villagers, for they fell silent while he took up the dialogue with Subayah, speaking in a quiet but firm voice. He held a bottle, an old jam jar repurposed in the Indian way, half-full of some white liquid. As they talked, he passed this container from one hand to the other, casually, almost absently, the scars on his thin arms stretching and wrinkling. Every now and then he glanced at Joki with an appraising look in his eyes.

Eventually, the conversation ran its course. Subayah inclined his head in agreement and shook hands with the man with the scarred arms. Then he turned to Joki, taking a deep breath as if to finalise – or wash his hands of – whatever arrangement he had made.

"Okay," he said. "Let me explain. For these people, the cobra is a special snake, a holy snake. They call it *nulla pambu*, good snake. In these parts, they believe it is very bad to kill this snake. It is unlucky; the cobra will return and have revenge. They say that this always happens, when the cobra is killed. And they do not want anyone in their village to die because of this."

The man with the pitted arms looked at Joki, up and down, head to toe, while gently swirling the white liquid in the jar.

"Normally, we could just give some money to smooth things over. But this particular snake, this particular cobra, is known to the villagers. It has been living in these parts for many years. It is like the guardian for the village. You see how the scales make that odd line, that scar down one side, towards the tail, where its back is slightly twisted? An old injury. That's the mark of this special snake, this holy snake. So this is very, very bad."

Subayah paused, cleared his throat, and stepped a little closer to Joki before continuing in a lower voice.

"Of course, being from Bombay, you won't believe all that. But it is not the truth that is important. It is what people *believe* is the truth – that is what matters. So we must help them. You understand?"

Joki looked across to the gaggle of villagers. They were all studying the diminishing undulations of the dying cobra, except for the man with scarred arms, who still looked at Joki with that masked, calculating gleam in his eyes.

"But what can we do? How are we supposed to help them?"

Subayah looked relieved at this, as though Joki's question was in itself an acceptance, a statement of consent.

"It is quite simple. They must give a present to the cobra, a little gift of milk. He has brought it in the jar. We must pay for the milk and then give it to the cobra. It will be ten rupees; I have agreed it with him. For the moment, that will be enough. For the moment."

Subayah and the scarred man looked at Joki, waiting for a response. So Joki pulled a wallet from his pocket, removed a ten-rupee note, and proffered it to the scarred man. The man took it with the type of smile that says not *Thank you* but *I acknowledge what you are giving me; I understand that you have accepted my demands.* He folded up the money and carefully put it inside the breast pocket of his shirt, still looking at Joki like a farmer calculating the price of a goat. Subayah turned again to Joki.

"I am sorry," he said, "but there is one other thing, a little thing. They know that you were driving the car when it hit the snake. They say it must be you that gives the milk to the snake. They say this is best."

Joki looked at Subayah, half expecting him to burst into laughter, and say *No, no, I am joking,* but he did not. He just looked embarrassed.

"It's a little thing," Subayah repeated.

So Joki took the jar of milk from the scarred man. There seemed to be nothing else to do. The jar felt warm in his hands. Feeling foolish, he unscrewed the lid, reading the manufacturer's logo on the scratched metal – *Kissan.* The opaque, white liquid was frothy at its edge. Then he looked at the snake. It was still, as though it had become part of the audience to its own final act. Joki felt awkward; this was not the kind of situation his education had prepared him for.

"What do I do?" he asked Subayah.

"Just pour the milk onto the snake, over its head. It can't move far, so you don't need to worry."

"Easy for you to say," muttered Joki, but he walked towards the crippled animal, feeling increasingly uncomfortable. As he approached, the snake lifted its head from the ground, its hood starting to spread once more. Joki stopped a good distance from the animal and stretched forward, holding the jar as far out as he could, bending awkwardly so as to avoid overbalancing onto the wretched thing. He paused, watching the snake, and the snake, with its fierce, black eyes, watched him. Then, as if affected by a spasm, Joki jerked the jar of milk forward, and the milk spilled out in a white arc, splattering onto the ground and over the snake's head. The effect was immediate; the snake reared up as if to strike and then fell back, leashed by pain and injury. It writhed around itself, the flattened wound a pivot for its sinuous, urgent dance, its partner the broken, unresponsive half of its own body. Joki leapt back. He handed the jar back to the scarred man, and flicked milk from his hand. The droplets made dark pockmarks in the dust by the edge of the road.

They were all looking at the snake now, at the decreasing pace and extent of its convulsions. Eventually, its movements ceased, but still the eyes stared, hostile jet, deep as space, dark windows onto an unfathomably savage world.

Joki felt Subayah's hand on his shoulder.

"Come, we should leave now."

"What will they do with it?"

"They will cremate it and give the ashes to the river. They believe that this will help rebirth, so it can live again."

"Just as if it was a person."

"Yes. Just as if it was a person."

They walked back to the car; Subayah took the driver's seat. He found the keys in the ignition where Joki had left them. As he started up the car, he said quietly, as though talking to himself:

"This changes things ..."

❖

The young boy who ran down the jungle path to get the man with the scarred arms is now himself middle-aged. He is brusque and non-committal in the village, but if you give him a few rupees and a lift to his work at the Mansholi tea estate, he is more forthcoming. He remembers the foreigner from Bombay, and how the foreigner ran over the "good snake" with his car and gave it milk.

The episode must have had a great effect on him – even today, forty years later, you don't need a translator to understand the intensity in his voice. When you ask him about Mr Kannan, however, he falls largely silent, only saying something to himself in a hushed voice. "We provide for Kaliya, Kaliya provides for us," offers the translator.

❖

"There is even a special festival, a snake worship festival, the Nag Panchami, held always at this time of year, July or August. Always on the fifth day of the lunar month of Shravan, the fifth day of that half of the month when the moon is waxing. Always the fifth day."

"The fifth day."

Mr Singh nods his head sadly.

"And that's all well and good. But in the village near Kannan's bungalow, they made something different of it. Something that has nothing to do with Hinduism."

He holds up one hand, the fingers and thumb spread out. "Five fires. Five girls. A devil-snake with five heads. The Nag Panchami, on the fifth day of the month. You see?"

Mina is suddenly taken by a *petit mal*; her eyelids flutter spasmodically, showing only the sclera, and a thread of saliva traces the fallen geometry of her cheek. Harpreet dabs at her face with a tissue. "Every fifth year – that's when it ends, and begins again."

❖

Nothing memorable occurred during the remaining drive to Mr Kannan's house. It was dark; the road was bumpy. Neither Subayah nor Joki spoke. When they arrived, Joki could see nothing of the house beyond the yellow electric light showing through windows covered in wire mesh. As they pulled up, a man appeared, squinting at them from beneath a hissing kerosene lamp that he held before him, first to one side, then to the other. The soft glare of the lamp's incandescent mantle threw light and shadow over his features, making an exaggerated mask of his face.

"There's Muthu," said Subayah.

Once inside, the electric light of the house revealed Muthu to be a short, middle-aged man. The skin on one side of his face was covered with flat, thin scar tissue that extended onto his forehead. He unsmilingly contemplated the world through glasses with finger-thick lenses. Behind the glasses, however, his eyes were sharp and hostile.

As Muthu took Joki's bags, Subayah subjected him to a low-pitched but intense monologue in Tamil. Joki guessed that he was talking about the incident on the road, for he picked out 'nulla pambu' again. Muthu was silent; occasionally he looked from Subayah to Joki, but his expression was unreadable – horror, perhaps? In any case, Joki was beyond caring, and had other things on his mind – in particular, the whereabouts of his host.

"Is Mr Kannan here?"

"No, saar," said Muthu. "Mr Kannan is travelling, travelling, saar. He is going and coming."

"Going and coming?"

"Muthu means he's gone away for a little while, but he'll be back soon," said Subayah. "That's how they say it around here."

Muthu nodded. "Mr Kannan coming for Nag Panchami, saar. Always coming for Nag Panchami. Even now." His lips made a smile which halted at the burn scar on his cheek. "Even now."

"The snake festival." said Subayah. "They make a big thing of it in the local village. It's happening this weekend, on Sunday. People come from miles around."

Joki noticed that Subayah looked tired. He himself was exhausted, and gripped by that soul-sickness that sometimes comes to the traveller far from home. So, after thanking Subayah for his help and making some arrangements for the next morning, and after a light meal of idlis, sambar, and the small bananas with reddish skins so popular in the South, Joki escaped to the guest room and slept the sleep of the dead.

❖

"Of course, Nag Panchami is celebrated in different ways in different parts of the subcontinent. What interested me was the particular variant that seems to be practised near Kalisholi. Perhaps variant is too kind a word; perhaps I should say *aberration*."

"Aberration."

"Normally, you see, Nag Panchami is based on the story in the *Mahabharata*, where Prince Janamejaya spares the life of the serpent king Takshaka. But in the part of the country that Joki visited, there was a group that preferred to celebrate the story of Krishna sparing the life of the serpent demon Kaliya. Or rather, their version of that story."

Mina cocks her head to one side, and pulls back her lips in a rictus of despair. She looks up at the ceiling, and pants through clenched teeth. Harpreet strokes her hair; her whimpering stops, but she continues to shudder, grasping the arms of her wheelchair.

"You know about Kaliya, don't you – the many-headed serpent demon that lived in the river Yamuna? In our version of the myth, Krishna vanquishes Kaliya, but Kaliya's wives beg him for mercy, so he spares the demon. But I've heard that some people near Kalisholi followed a different legend. In their tradition, Kaliya was killed – but then was resurrected when five of his devotees sacrificed their daughters, sending the girls to the demon's underwater home. Five girls, given to the river."

We hear the ugly complaints of crows in the neem tree outside. A small breeze, harbinger of the monsoon, riffles and flips Joki's pencil sketches. Harpreet closes the window.

"You may have seen statues of Kaliya around? The five-headed cobra, protecting the goddess Jakkamma? No, not Vishnu resting on Shesha – though they are easy to confuse. Anyway, in the hills it seems that there is a group with very unpleasant practices. Jakkamma devotees? Maybe, but I don't think so. Whatever they are, it's as though they have taken an aspect of Hinduism, and removed from it all that is good and charitable, and perverted what remains. Why, or for whom, I do not know; but I know they are not Hindus. And it is clear that even today they employ live sacrifices."

The old man is expressionless, and his voice has dropped, as though his soft exposition is for Mina's ears alone.

"Live sacrifices, as if to resurrect dead Kaliya, as if to enforce the cycle of rebirth."

He pauses, and swallows.

"One sacrifice each day, for five days. Only goats, usually."

"Usually."

❖

Joki woke just before dawn – too early for breakfast, too late to sleep on. The previous day's events still dragged at his spirit, so for distraction – or for exorcism, perhaps – he retrieved his drawing materials from his luggage. He rapidly outlined one scene after another: men in dhotis; a pair of scarred arms holding a jar of milk; a sinuous shape in the dust. In each case, no more than a few charcoal strokes – the economy of the accomplished artist. But the exercise served only to reinforce memories, not dispel them. Eventually, he threw aside his sketch-books, and went in search of his host, or Muthu.

Neither were visible. The bungalow was silent: outside, the cicadas, but inside, nothing. Joki's explorations showed that, just as Subayah had promised, the residence was pleasant: tidy and comfortably furnished. But oddly, Kannan's home seemed to contain little *more* than furniture – certainly little that could obviously be attributed to Mr Kannan. No doubt the man had various personal possessions and clothing in his bedroom, but otherwise, what was there of Joki's absent host? A few books in Tamil on a half-empty shelf; a pair of sandals by the door; next to them, a heavy walking-stick with a battered brass ferrule. Otherwise, nothing: the man was little more than a pervasive absence, a human stencil, identifiable by what was not there.

The chink and tinkle of metal and china pulled Joki from his thoughts, and he followed the noises to the back verandah.

"Good morning, Muthu."

"Saar."

Muthu was laying out breakfast on a small table: a papaya, chapatis and an egg.

"Thank you. Muthu, did Mr Kannan come back last night?"

"Mr Kannan, no saar, not coming back."

"Where has he gone?"

"Yes, saar. Going and coming, going and coming."

"But *where*? Has he gone to visit family?"

"Family, saar, yes. Family-travelling, always family-travelling."

"And where is his family?"

"Yes, saar, family, family. Coming for Nag Panchami."

Joki decided to leave it for the moment. Muthu was clearly determined to be more oyster than pearl, but no doubt someone in Kannan's office would know more.

It was a pleasant breakfast. The verandah overlooked a fruit garden, protected by walls which barely kept out the jungle. To eat there was to be surrounded by the sounds and scents and cameo interludes of the hills: hornbills flapping and barging through the trees, cocking their top-heavy heads like revenant pterodactyls; lion-tailed macaques, their grey manes and beards giving them an intimidating air, like violent old men; butterflies enrobed with iridescence, flapping their crazy, jagged paths from bush to bush. A pleasant breakfast, yes, but Joki was still annoyed when he drank the last of the tea and went to collect his paperwork. *What the hell did Kannan think he was doing? If you're being audited by Head Office, it's a good idea to participate.*

Before leaving the previous day, Subayah had offered to give Joki a lift to the office after breakfast – almost as though he had not, after all, expected Mr Kannan to return – so Joki took his briefcase to the front of the bungalow, and waited, grinding his teeth. *Every receipt, Mr Kannan. Every single scribbled chit will be found and double-checked.*

❖

"You have to understand, Kaliya is not a myth to these people. He is real. Very real. Maybe he's a local man who takes the post by hereditary succession, maybe he's some kind of godman, maybe he was picked as a child because of some sign – I don't know. These things are not made public. Anyway, the mechanism doesn't matter. It's what people believe that matters. And they believe that Kaliya's life must be made to endure, with whatever sacrifice is necessary, year after year. But by the fifth year, goats are not enough."

"Not enough."

❖

Mr Kannan's bungalow still exists. The corporation still owns it, and the current manager of the Kalisholi estate occupies it. This individual may, if approached politely and provided with sufficient reason, allow a visitor with an interest in the story of Joki de Souza to look around the house and garden.

It is a typical planter's bungalow: airy, open verandahs; floors of dark terracotta tiles; an austere, white-painted bachelor's bathroom with an enamelled clawfoot bathtub. There are brass-bound rosewood boxes and tables carved into detailed filigrees with delicately inlaid ivory. Teak planter's chairs, upholstered with rattan, extend jointed arms veneered with decades of polish. Chair-arms and tables alike are tattooed with drink rings – the stamp of cold beers left by long dead, lonely expatriates fighting off boredom and madness. Indeed, the bungalow's interior is practically identical to that sketched by Joki forty years ago, except that Mr Kannan's stick and sandals and Tamil books have been replaced by the current resident's possessions.

At the back of the house, a verandah and a short flight of steps lead down into an enclosed, rectangular garden bounded by the house on one side and by crumbling, uneven walls on the other three. The walls, pock-marked with indentations that look very much like bullet-holes, shelter papayas, bananas and mulberry bushes – a tiny orchard sequestered from monkeys and deer. Behind this enclosure is a small area of semi-cleared scrub. Just beyond that waits the chirring, hissing jungle. And through this jungle, alongside lantana bushes and gulmohar trees, runs the road to the Kalisholi plantation. Joki left us no drawings of the Kalisholi estate office, but it seems likely that it too has changed little since his time. It is a small room, tacked onto the warehouse where the freshly picked leaves are stored and partially dried before processing. One of its windows looks out over tidy tea bushes and shade trees, the other looks inward into the warehouse itself.

It is difficult to find anyone who willingly admits to entering this office at any point during Joki's visit. But corporation records identify the estate overseer from that time: the man who weighed each picker's harvest and paid the labourers accordingly. He now lives in the village near the speckled idol. There he lies all day on his bed, racked by age and tuberculosis, and attended by his daughter. He speaks only Tamil – whether through preference or need, it is hard to say – but with a translator, the following story may be extracted.

"On his first day, Joki was shown into Mr Kannan's office by Subayah, who then drove away. Joki seemed angry. He was searching in Mr Kannan's office, searching in the desk and filing cabinets. He kept asking for Mr Kannan, but Mr Kannan was not there. Mr Kannan was always going and coming. Sometimes he was going for one day, sometimes more, but always coming back. Joki shut the door of the office, but everyone could see him through the inside window. He took out all Mr Kannan's paperwork, all his files. Every day, he was making notes, reading things, counting things, checking things. When he was not in Mr Kannan's office, he was in the jungle making pictures. This is what he did every day that he came."

At first, that is all the old overseer will say. A hacking cough doubles him over, and he spits bloodily into a plastic bowl on the floor. Then he mutters to his daughter; she leaves the room. We hear each of his slow breaths.

"I saw one other thing. He did not look only in the accounts that Mr Kannan had made ready, this foreigner. He also looked through Mr Kannan's desk, through his personal letters. He found a chit, a small thing. He was looking at it and shaking his head. Then he took it."

The overseer turns to one side, and mimes putting something into a back trouser pocket. He turns back, and spits again.

"Yes, he took it. Joki de Souza was a thief. And I told Mr Kannan so, when he returned. That is all."

Certainly Joki must have worked his way through receipts and bank statements, double-checking and cross-referencing, like a terrier trying to dig out a rat. And it seems likely that he continued thus during his few days at the estate, burrowing deeper and deeper until, at last, he had something. Without Joki's personal testimony, we can't be certain of what that was, of course. But when Harpreet came to Mansholi to collect Joki's possessions, he found, in the back pocket of a pair of Joki's trousers – alongside Joki's letter to Mr Kannan, with Mr Kannan's enigmatic footnote in the margin – a chit, a "small thing." It is a delivery note, written in clumsy English: 'Sari for wedding (small size, colour red, gold). 5 item. Deliver to Kannan, Sarpal estate, Kalisholi 6201.'

Perhaps the chit Joki found is an irrelevance. Perhaps the cause of his growing concern really was some tedious accounting irregularity. A careful analysis of the Kalisholi accounts would help clarify this; but when asked, the Sarpal Corporation's archivist – a fussy babu from his balding head to the polished black shoes on his feet – shows us the shelf on which a folder marked 'Mansholi Accounts 1964' rubs shoulders with 'Mansholi Accounts 1975.' He clicks his tongue in disgust – such sloppiness! – but does not let it end there. He pulls out the Mansholi Accounts Requisition Record – for the Sarpal Corporation keeps records of record requisitions, does it not? He opens the book, determined to shame those who failed to respect the corporation's history.

The Requisition Record tells us little, but perhaps it tells us enough. In the Requisition Date column, 'June 3rd, 1974' is stamped in red ink. In the Recipient column, 'de Souza' is printed in faded blue biro; next to this is Joki's firm, neat signature. The return date is 'July 7th, 1974,' a whole five weeks on; there is no signature for this. And the next requisition date is 'July 15th, 1975,' a year later. The recipient, however, is identified only by the initials 'JR' and an illegible scrawl of a signature. There is no return date. The archivist raises one contemptuous eyebrow, his meaning clear: *This would never happen today.*

❖

Mina wanted to accompany Harpreet to Mansholi, but he dissuaded her. "It would have been upsetting," he tells us, "and there wasn't much to bring back anyway: just sketch-books and a few clothes." Destiny turns, perhaps, on such small decisions. Would Mina have been safer with Harpreet? Certainly, she would not have been left by herself, back in their Bombay apartment, while Harpreet explored Kannan's bungalow and garden. She would not have received her visitor on her own. Indeed, had she not been alone, perhaps there would have been *no* visitor.

In any case, Harpreet went to Kalisholi unaccompanied. He leafs through Joki's charcoal memories to illustrate his own.

"This is the garden behind Kannan's bungalow. You see the tops of the walls, how uneven they are? Half-fallen. They are much older than the bungalow; it is obvious. So the fruit garden once was the location of another building. And look here."

Mr Singh points to another sketch. It shows two small stone pillars, built into or against a white wall. They look old, very old; nevertheless, the undulating carvings on their surfaces are distinct: snakes entwined in a vertical design similar to that of the ancient Greek caduceus. When you tell him that the pillars are no longer there today, that the garden wall now has an iron-barred gate set into it at that point, he shrugs.

"So the stones are no longer there. Nor is Mr Kannan."

"*Kannan!*"

"And one other thing – just here, between the pillars, at the foot of the wall ... you see?"

Mr Singh points at the sketch. There is a hole in the ground, between the pillars, as if something had tunnelled into the earth beneath the wall's foundations. He holds his hands together, thumb-tip to thumb-tip, fingertips to fingertips, making a circle to show the size of the burrow.

"The hole's entrance was smooth, smooth; as if through much use." He slowly clasps his hands together, rubbing palm against palm as if to wipe away an invisible contamination.

❖

The last drawings in Joki's sketch-book are hurried and out of character; bizarre, even. One would almost say they were drawn by another, but for the characteristic style – fluid strokes that capture their subject's essence, atmospheric chiaroscuro achieved with charcoal and pencil and thumb. Nevertheless, the subject matter is disturbing. It is as though, while in Kannan's bungalow, Joki saw a succession of nightmares played out in front of him and was compelled to capture them as they occurred. A beautiful woman sits on a throne; she smiles cruelly while her feet blaze and burn. A half-formed, man-like thing with the bloat of death holds out a hand, as if begging or bestowing. Next to him, in English, Joki has written: 'Forgive me, mother.' And below that: 'I agree, I agree.' One page is given to a blind ape; its tongue lolls out between bared teeth, and its fingernails curl like claws. It holds an abacus of five rows; the first four rows have, respectively, two, three, five and thirteen beads, but the fifth row is bare. Next to this fifth row is written a number: '89.' The beads in the group of five are shaded black; the others are left without colour. On subsequent pages, abstract patterns resolve themselves into repeated snake and moon motifs. Eyes appear frequently: dark, fierce, staring from bushes and shadows, or making constellations in a dark sky; sometimes a face shapes itself around them, curiously foreshortened, as though it were peering forth from another world, another dimension.

The last image – separate from the others, and with a different mood, as though done, perhaps, the next day – is the most normal, and yet also the most disturbing. Just a face, a man's face; a curiously ageless face, with oddly intense eyes. But the remorselessness, the pitilessness, the intensity of hatred that pours from it is without parallel. It is as though the king of demons had visited Joki and tortured from him a portrait.

We know that Joki walked down to the village on the night of Sunday, 20th July. Lonely, perhaps, or scared; or tormented by the silent bungalow and the images of madness he caught on paper. Whatever the reason, it has died with Joki. But what he saw survives as the memory of a memory, in Harpreet Singh's account. The phone call: the last time Harpreet Singh heard Joki de Souza's voice. Mr Singh points to the text in the diary, but quotes Joki's words from memory. His recital still carries something of the fear and urgency that the original must have had.

❖

"I noticed them when I was going home. They'd left the festival just before me. I know I shouldn't have followed them, but I did. I saw Muthu, Mr Kannan's servant. He was with the man with the scarred arms and some others. All men, except for one girl, a young girl, maybe five years old. Muthu was walking in front with a lantern, holding a long pole.

"I followed them carefully. The moon was very bright, but I kept to the bushes, just off the path, so they didn't see me. They walked from the village down to the river, onto a stretch of sand like a little beach, and I watched them from the jungle. I couldn't see everything, but the moon was so bright, I saw enough. They lit a fire on the beach and stood facing the river. I could see the black, dead ashes from previous fires nearby. Four sets of ashes, four. And the new fire made five.

"They started chanting, but very softly. They all faced the river. The man with the scarred arms held a goat.

"The child was dressed as though for a wedding, in a red and gold sari, with lots of gold jewellery, and a garland. You know. Her eyes were heavily kohled – it had smudged onto her cheeks. And she had gold things tied to her ankles. They looked heavy, because she was walking awkwardly. She kneeled down on the sand, next to the river. The man with the scarred arms led the goat up to her and held its head in her face. Then another man hung on to the goat while the one with scarred arms took out a knife, cut its throat, and pulled its head right back so that the blood went into the girl's face. And I know it's horrible, but I saw it – she was drinking it.

"She was drenched in blood, and everybody was very quiet. I could hear the water lapping at the banks and the fire crackling. Muthu fixed his lantern to the end of the pole and held it out over the river, as far as he could reach. The water was silver where it reflected the light, but otherwise it was black, black. The girl got up and started walking into the river. Nobody was forcing her, she just did it. I don't think she knew where she was. I thought she was just going to wash the blood off, but she kept walking slowly out into the dark water, staring at the opposite bank. I followed her gaze; there was someone there, standing in the water, his arms held out. It was hard to tell in that light, but I think he was an old man, a European. And I think he was crying. I looked back at the girl; she kept walking, walking until her head went below the surface. Only the garland was left, floating on the water. I suppose that's what the weights round her ankles were for. It was horrible. I looked to the opposite bank again, but Muthu was holding the lantern over the floating garland, and I couldn't see beyond its glare.

"Then – and I tell you, it happened, I saw it – up from the river came a man. I don't mean he came up like a swimmer surfacing. There was no splashing, no big intake of breath. He just came up as though it was a natural thing to walk up from the bottom of the river. First his head broke the surface, and then his shoulders and chest as he got closer to the bank. He came up from under the garland, so that it hung around his neck as he rose up. And as he came farther out of the water, I could see that he had something wrong with one of his legs, he was limping. He walked up to the fire. He was naked, and painted black, black as tar, but with lots of little white dots all over him."

Joki paused, his breath coming in shudders. Harpreet, appalled, took the opportunity to try to calm his friend down.

"Look, this is not something for you to deal with. You need to tell the estate manager, this chap you're auditing, Kannan. He'll know who to contact in the local police."

But there was something else troubling Joki. Over the crackling phone line, Harpreet Singh heard his friend's voice raise and break with emotion.

"Don't you understand? Kannan didn't take his stick! I found it in the house – don't you see? He left his stick behind – when he goes, wherever he goes, *he doesn't take his stick ...*"

❖

Subayah admits that Joki made a phone call from the office in Mansholi on the day that he died. At least, Subayah remembers that when he went to pick up Joki on Monday morning, the day after the festival, Joki insisted that he be driven not to Kalisholi – where there was no phone – but to the main Mansholi office, to use Subayah's phone immediately. Subayah did not listen to Joki's phone call, he says; of course not. When Joki had finished, Subayah simply drove him to the Kalisholi office, as Joki requested. And then Subayah left Joki to his business. He did not come to pick up Joki at the end of the day, because he understood that Mr Kannan had returned that morning, and would be taking over as host.

Today, sitting in his living room, Subayah's recollections of the events of forty years ago seem fragile. He is often silent, and often shrugs. As we leave, he stubs out a Charminar cigarette in the ashtray on the table by his chair. Next to the ashtray is a small brass figurine – a standing figure entwined by a cobra, a five-headed cobra. Subayah touches it briefly.

❖

Harpreet looks down at his hands. Outside, the wind has died. The monsoon has changed its mind. Even Mina is silent.

"There is one more thing. On the last day, when Subayah came to pick him up – you know, when Joki demanded to be driven to Mansholi, not Kalisholi, so that he could use the phone there – on the way, he made Subayah stop by the jungle path. He went to look at the shrine, the speckled idol. I think he already knew what he'd find, but he went anyway. Before he phoned me."

Mina holds her breath. The ceiling fan blades chase each other in slow circles. Harpreet looks down at his hands, which tremble in his lap.

"There were five garlands around the speckled god, he said. He counted them."

For once, Mina remains still, as though listening, or remembering.

"I would have pursued it," says Harpreet Singh. "I would have pursued it to the end, with the police, and through the newspapers, if necessary. Mina could have made a big stink about it, with all her Bollywood connections, and she would have. But when I got back from Mansholi, she was ill. She was like this."

"Like this."

Mr Singh weeps silently into his balled fists. "What could I do? I had my own problems. What could I do?"

❖

Oddly enough, the final part of Joki's story is both the most documented and the least clear. In an entity as large as the corporation, the death of an employee on corporation business cannot go unnoticed, even where the employee has no family to fight his corner. Thus, we have a circular from Miss Raganathan:

'Further to the announcement this morning, I am very sorry to confirm that Joki has indeed passed away. We understand that the cause of death was snake-bite and that he has been cremated locally. In memory of Joki, who was so popular with us all, the Corporation will be donating five hundred anti-venom sets to local hospitals.'

And a written memo from her to the then Managing Director:

'Regarding Harpreet Singh's insistence on personally collecting Joki de Souza's effects from Mansholi: given that Joki has no family, I suggest we just go with it – would be bad publicity to make a fuss. In any case, I understand from Kannan that Singh is already at Mansholi. In Singh's absence, I will pay a personal visit to his wife to thank her for her husband's efforts.'

A letter from Mr Kannan also exists, written in response to questions from the Managing Director:

'Mr de Souza was found in my garden, early in the evening of the 22nd July. The discovery was made by my employee Muthu. He recognised the signs of snake-bite, as such events are common in this region. The funeral was held the next day. Please accept my condolences.'

Given the tropical heat and Hindu custom, perhaps it is not surprising that the decision was made to cremate Joki quickly; but as to whose decision it actually was, that is unclear. What is abundantly clear is that neither the police nor a doctor saw poor Joki's body before the flames took it. Perhaps Miss Raganathan could tell us more, but the Sarpal archives indicate that a year after Joki's death, on 16th July 1976, she left the company and moved back south to her Tamil homeland. Unfortunately, the records are silent on her new address and occupation. Miss Jakkamma Raganathan remains an enigma.

And the Kalisholi estate? Why, it was soon back under the control of Mr Kannan, who apparently returned the day they cremated Joki de Souza. Certainly, he was there when Mr Singh came to collect poor Joki's possessions.

"I got to the house before he had arrived back from the estate. His servants were there. A man with scarred arms opened the car door for me. Muthu was inside and offered me tea. While he was preparing it, I looked around. I checked the house first, and then I went into the garden. When I looked back towards the house, I saw him. He was sitting on the verandah, watching me. As I walked up the steps from the garden to the verandah, Muthu came and gave him a glass of milk. He picked it up and drank it slowly. Black, black eyes above white froth. His walking-stick was by his chair. Flowers were scattered at his feet – marigolds."

"Marigolds."

"He didn't get up – said that he'd been unwell, unable to move for five days, and was still weak. I asked him where he'd been, which hospital, but he only smiled and shook his head. *'What about Joki,'* I said, *'how did it happen?' 'Only Joki knows,'* he said. I suggested it was an unlikely accident. He laughed: *'Accident?'* he said, *'Joki de Souza invited it.'* And then he told me where Muthu had found Joki. *'In the walled garden,'* he said, *'at the far end; by the burrow between the pillars, at the wall's base; with one arm as far down the hole as it would reach, and his head pillowed against the stone. You see? Joki de Souza wished for death; he offered himself to it.'* He added that he regretted not being here for Joki, not being there when he arrived, to warn him of the dangers of the jungle. But, from his sick-bed, he had prayed that the gods would make a bridge for Joki, a bridge to span all troubles, and lead him across it. I suggested that his prayers had been ineffective. *'Maybe,'* he said. *'Maybe.'*"

❖

In Mansholi today, you can walk down the jungle road to Kalisholi and then take the path that leads from the road. You will pass the dark, white-speckled idol. You will see milk and flowers before it, as always. In some years, you will see garlands around its black body, trailing their wet flowers in the dust. Sometimes one garland. Sometimes more.

SEEING JOHN

*"The [Indian] Government's residential schools ... have reportedly witnessed
49 suicides in just five years ... all except seven were suicides by hanging ..."*
- Suicides in Novodaya schools: 49 in 5 years
Indian Express, Dec 24th, 2018

The red-haired boy took the small metal cylinder from beneath
his bed and sat on the dorm floor, his back against the cold wall.
He turned the steel shell over and around, passing it from one hand
to another, marvelling at the smooth weight of it. At one end, two
wires, terminating in frayed copper strands; at the other, a small,
three-bladed plastic propellor. The boy flicked one of the blades,
delighting in its easy spin. He raised the cylinder to his face and
inhaled, catching a hint of oil and, more distinctly, the unmistakable
odour of newness. The motor even *smelt* foreign, here in the Salvation
Army International School of South India: the fragrance of possibility.
A battery-powered boat; maybe even a plane!

"Andrew!"

The red-haired boy looked up. Over the rough blankets of his bed,
beyond the row of identical beds, he could see Vijay standing in the
dorm's entrance. Untidy hair; plastic-framed glasses permanently
askew; skinny, scabbed knees poking out beneath khaki shorts.

"We're going now! To see John. You'd better come quick – it's Nikesh on duty."

Nikesh was the bumfluffed prefect who'd once made John drink from the toilet. At night, Nikesh walked the dorm pulling blankets from sleeping boys. During the day, he administered Chinese burns and nipple-pinches, dead legs and kicks. *If you cry, I'll give you another one. Until you stop being a little girl.* But John always cried, and Nikesh always rose to the challenge. *You'll get thirsty, crying like that. Come and have a drink. Here.* Everybody had watched.

"Coming." Andrew pushed the motor back into the toe of a football boot, and covered it with a still-damp sock. There shouldn't be thefts in a school for missionaries' children; but there were.

The two boys left the dorm, and hurried to the front of the school. A fine, hot day; not a fierce sun, here in the high mountains, but a tropical sun nevertheless. The sky was a delicate blue, shorn of the usual hill-station mists and clouds, and the low Victorian buildings of the school, once the summer residence of the governor of Madras, threw precise shadows on the ground. In front of the veranda – milling in the shade cast by its white pillars and yellow walls, pulling leaves from its borders of clipped box and low privet – two hundred boys were assembling into little squads. They had the half-triumphant, half-disbelieving air common to all children let off lessons.

"Standard Six over here!" Nikesh was scowling at them. Andrew and Vijay joined the other ten-year-olds. Seven rows of two; and as John wasn't there, one boy would have to march on his own, at the end of the squad. To be this pariah seemed unlucky, somehow, so the duty went to the weakest: a Canadian child with a lazy eye. He blinked at the others through spectacles in which one lens had been replaced by a piece of white card.

"I don't care," he said.

"Three-Eyes," said Andrew. "Three-Eyes, all by yourself."

"I don't care."

"Come *on*," said Nikesh. The boys shuffled into more exact lines, each boy on the left extending his right arm to his neighbour's shoulder so as to correct their placing.

"Now," said Nikesh. "By the left ... quick – march! Left; left; left, right, left! Left; left; left, right, left!"

Keeping a steady formation down the steep, winding drive that led to the school gates wasn't easy, but the boys were used to it – they'd been doing it twice weekly all term. As always, the driveway was sunless; the towering eucalyptus trees to each side cast a cool gloom over the old tarmac. But today, when Andrew looked up, he could see blue sky between the branches.

"Do you remember John's first day?" said Vijay.

"Yeah. Eating sick."

It should have gone so well for John. His parents were majors in the Salvation Army – *both* of them. That should have counted for something in a missionary school. And he'd come to India straight from England, with new English possessions entirely foreign to the other boys. That could have triggered popularity as easily as envy, perhaps; certainly, John's first evening at school was full of attention. But his first breakfast, the following morning, saw his stomach reject the tepid grey *ragi* – millet boiled in water, known to the boys as 'sand-porridge' – back into its bowl. The duty teacher, short-sighted and bitter, knew only that each bowl had to be emptied. That was the rule.

"Can't believe Miss Rawlins made him eat it again."

"Only dogs eat their own sick," Nikesh had said. *"Shall we give you a collar, little puppy?"*

"Left; left; left, right, left!"

Standard Six marched through the school gates, where a blue and white banner asserted 'I am the Resurrection and the Life.' They went past the entrance to the town's Botanic Gardens, where green slopes and towering cedars suggested some new Eden; they turned away and trooped down Garden Road. A street-food cart selling sweets and hot peanuts mocked them with heavy scents; tourists in bright saris and carefully ironed shirts stared and giggled.

"I reckon it was Matthew's idea." Vijay frowned; his mouth pulled to one side with the effort of theorisation. "I'm sure of it."

"What?"

"You know. The teddy bear."

John's bed had been directly beneath one of the horizontal steel rods that supported the dorm's corrugated iron roof. This transverse pole was ideally placed; when they hanged his teddy bear with a coarse, plastic rope that crushed the soft toy's pampered throat, the bear was left suspended above John's pillow. But the muddy footprints on John's pillow weren't Matthew's; Andrew was certain of that.

"Probably," said Andrew. "Probably *was* Matthew."

It was certainly easy to believe; Matthew had always had 'difficulties'. He'd once caught a slow-worm and pulled the reptile in half in front of the other children. Andrew had seen it all: the pink stumps, one in each of Matthew's hands, and the wriggling that gradually ceased while Matthew's grin slowly broadened. And Matthew pushing one bloody end into John's face. *"Look – the little girl's got a bindi."*

"Left, right, left!"

They'd turned off Garden Road now; this was a quieter part of town. No tourists, no street vendors. At the top of a small hill, the Union Church raised to the cloudless sky its crosses and pointed arches. Like the Salvation Army School itself, the church had been painted in white and yellow. On a day like this, with the way its walls threw back the sun, it almost hurt to look at it.

"We should have told a teacher."

"Suppose so," said Andrew. Vijay just didn't get it. You don't tell teachers anything. You just don't.

John had taken down his hanged teddy bear himself. By standing on the headboard of his bed, he could just reach the rope where it met the steel rafter. When he untied the knot, the bear fell onto the dirtied pillow. He carefully removed the rope from the bear's throat, and fluffed up its neck where the cord had separated the toy's stuffing and scarred the fur. He brushed it down and put it back under his pillow, very gently. Then he coiled up the rope, and walked out of the dorm. His head was high, and he held the rope close, as though it were a gift. He didn't say anything, he didn't look at anybody, and he didn't bother cleaning the mud from his pillow.

"Left, right, left! Squad ... *halt!*"

Andrew looked up. The younger children were already climbing the stone steps that led from the street to the church. Mr Thomas, with his pointy beard and his eyes that never met anyone's, was at the top of the steps, beside the reverend, discussing whatever it is that the headmaster of a Salvation Army School would discuss with a reverend. From behind, Andrew could hear Standard Seven approaching: *left, right, left.*

"Do you think John's parents are here yet?" he asked. "I can't see them."

It had taken John's parents two weeks to get back from the Salvation Army conference in America. First, they had been difficult to contact; then, the storms had grounded all flights; then the backlog of stranded passengers had made it almost impossible to get an internal connection; then they were put on a waiting list for flights to Bombay; then they had to stay in Bombay overnight before getting another plane to Bangalore; and finally they had to hire a car to drive to Ooty. So Nikesh had said, relaying half-heard teachers' talk through his boy's moustache.

"Maybe they're inside," said Vijay. "Come on."

Andrew and Vijay went up the steps together, unconsciously co-ordinated. *Left, right, left.* Small plants poked out from between the stones; the sun-warmed metal hand-rail was rough with blistered paint. Three-Eyes, wheezing with asthma, tried to overtake them; Andrew pushed at him, but stopped when he saw that the reverend was watching. He was a big Irishman, the reverend, a kind man, and normally full of smiles. Today the kindness was masked by something else, and his eyes were deep and full.

"Line up, boys," said Mr Thomas, his eyes fixed on a point just above Andrew's left shoulder.

Standard Six joined the queue of children at the entrance to the church. Three-Eyes ended up at the back again, next to the bigger children of Standard Seven. Andrew picked at the wart on his palm; somewhere, crows squabbled. Then, as though in response to a signal from within the pale stones of Union Church, the line began to shuffle forward.

"Some of the teachers have seen him already," whispered Vijay. "He looks great, they said. Nikesh told us."

Andrew didn't answer. He didn't believe anything Nikesh said. Anyway, to talk now – *here* and now – surely would be sacrilege. The church was so bright and peaceful: the walls washed with fine sunlight fresh-filtered by stained glass; the soaring arches supporting the remote, white ceiling; the bouquets of fresh flowers; the clear silences; the small, sweet fragrances. In such a place, at such a time, it was easy to believe in Heaven.

To his left, in the shadowed corner stacked with hymn books and piles of cheap, curling paper – Scripture quotations and illustrated Bible stories – Andrew heard soft movements. A man; a European, head bowed, one hand to his face. The hand slipped down to finger the old-fashioned silk scarf around the man's neck: Andrew saw an old face, a mouth that made soundless prayers. He'd never seen a grown-up cry before, and behind his embarrassment, the boy felt a twinge of fear. *If adults too are weak, then who is strong?* The man turned to him: his lips shaped words. *Come to me, all ye who are weary and heavy laden.* Andrew shuddered, and turned away.

Ahead of Andrew, the queue of boys hesitated at the transept, before filing around to the right and then back down the other aisle, where teachers were ushering the boys into seats. Andrew could see that some of the little ones were upset. But Standard Six had reached the front now. Andrew stepped forward, suddenly weak, his heart hammering.

Seeing John, there, cocooned in white cushions and pale wood, was like seeing a pretty memory of him made flesh. His hair had been carefully combed to one side; it glistened, as if fresh-washed. A garland had been placed around his neck: pushed up to his chin, it made a dog-collar of marigolds that covered his throat. His hands were arranged on his chest as though he were praying, or making a final *namaste* to his classmates, but Andrew could see that his thumbs were tied together with fine thread. And now that Andrew looked more closely, not at the embalmer's work but at what lay beneath, he saw that John's lips made a secret smile, as though he knew who'd taken his toy motor and hanged his teddy bear, but it really didn't matter anymore.

THE MIRROR

"Pune's historic Yerawada Central Prison has a ... retail shop, where you can buy products made in-house by the inmates. Biscuits, furniture, bed linen, carpets, bags, lamps, clothing, shoes – are just some of the things you can buy off the rack here ... Ladies' clothing like blouses, Paithani sarees (INR 2000 onwards) and jewellery are widely available during festival season."
- *https://lbb.in/pune/yerwada-jail-shop/ Accessed 24th Nov 2020.*

In Yerawada, Maharashtra, there is a wall. Stone on dark-grey stone is set in paler mortar, to a height of forty feet. Barred windows accentuate the wall's clear purpose; a set of massive ledge-and-brace doors reiterate it. As if by afterthought, the corner-stones and crenellations of the portico are painted bright yellow and blue. This colour scheme extends to the high double-doors, which are yellow with a broad, central blue band. Yet the wall's stone-grey dominates; the eye leaves thirsting for colour.

This dull rampart, a legacy of the British, is the external face of Yerawada Karagruha, Maharashtra's state jail. Since 1871, Yerawada has held inmates of every hue – con-men, rapists, politicans, film stars; Gandhi and Nehru, Sanjay Dutt and Ajmal Kasab – and their ectypes are found there still among its four thousand *qaidis*. Most of the incarcerated can take heart from the prospect of release, but not all: in 2004, twenty-five of the four thousand are on death row. And one of the twenty-five is a man in his sixties with a tired face. Cross-legged, surrounded by all the woven colours of the rainbow, he listens to the machines' clangour and finds bright memories there.

Who is he, you ask? And why has he been waiting for death for twenty years? Ah – you want the *beginning*. As if it were possible to unpick time and find an origin! As if we are not bound to follow the thread; to trace the warp and suffer the weft; to weave that pattern to which we are forever blind ...

Very well: *beginnings*. Perhaps we should start in Bangalore, where two men, Hemal and Sunil, work for the All-India Textile Company. ATC is owned and run by members of Hemal's extended family; Sunil is a comparative outsider. Perhaps this asymmetry, which contaminates an otherwise genuine friendship, is our origin: after all, a mis-set loom must make the pattern go awry.

But perhaps the first stitch is more significant than the start of the thread. Consider: soon after the two friends joined ATC, Hemal's uncle persuaded Hemal's other relatives, during an ATC board meeting, that ATC should invest in two adjacent holiday homes, in Ooty. For the use of employees above a certain level: which, in practice, meant management's family and friends – and which is how Hemal and Sunil's families began spending their summer holidays together in the high Nilgiris. Yes, that's a kind of beginning; but still it seems far removed from the end.

Suppose then we start with Hemal's other half Pushpa and Sunil's better half Padma, and the women's shared love of needlework? Look: in the summer of 1964, they sit together in the living room of the larger of the two holiday homes, sewing. They are happy; but somewhere, Pushpa has a pack of cards which fate has seen fit to order *just so*. And somewhere else – oh, it's just a game! – Hemal and Sunil hack their way around steep fairways while the nearby Hunt scents prey.

Look more closely. While their mothers talk, the children fret and sigh. Pushpa's twelve-year-old sons, Nilesh and Darpan – as unlike as twins ever could be – squabble over a chessboard. Nilesh, who is as aware of his good looks as Darpan is unconscious of his ugliness, shows off to Padma's daughter, Yogita. She is only eleven, but already has a power over the boys that they will never understand. Parvati or Kali? You decide. Listen: in the hills, the jackal wakes.

Yes, perhaps that's where it all started: up among the grey mists of the Nilgiri Hills, seven thousand feet above sea level, in the town known to Tamils as Udhagamandalam, anglicised by the British to Ootacamund, and abbreviated by all to Ooty. And if you wish to pin down inception in time as well as place, then surely it started in 1964, the year that Bollywood released *Sangam*. Remember, in one of the scenes from *Sangam*, Sundar, whose destiny is to lose both love and friendship, pursues the lovely Radha across Ooty Lake. *Oh, Mehbooba*, he calls, as the rowboat glides on. In Yerawada, forty years later, the *qaidi* with the tired face replays each scene, each song, in his mind. *Oh, beloved!* He runs colour through his fingers, and cocks an ear to it, and shudders at the echoes. Warp and weft, o ye little people.

So: let's say it started in the Ooty of 1964, if it started anywhere. There. There's a beginning for you.

Part I: The pack

"Good *shot*, man!"

Sunil's admiration was sincere; from an unpromising position by a eucalyptus stand, Hemal had wielded a nine-iron to perfection. His stroke had scattered mud and fragments of grass over the rough, but the little white ball followed its pre-ordained flight, bounced, and rolled onto the green, close to the pin. Hemal was laughing. "I thought it was going to be unlucky thirteen – but it's turned out okay."

"There is still time for bad luck, *yaar*."

"After that rain, I think we've had our share, don't you? My feet are soaking."

"We'll warm ourselves up at the nineteenth hole."

"Imported whisky! Always planning ahead, Sunil. Talking of which…" Hemal's pause was full of words.

Sunil gritted his teeth, and avoided Hemal's eye. *This again.* He peered at his bag of clubs as if he had mislaid something essential.

"You can't plan everything." Sunil made his tone jocular. "Sometimes you just have to let things happen."

"But not always. Not where the kids are concerned. Their future is our obligation."

Sunil thought about Hemal's children. He'd always liked Nilesh. Difficult not to: good-looking and gregarious, the boy's charm was evident. His path in life, surely, would be smooth. *Darpan*, however ... Sunil took the putter his caddie had found for him, and lined up his shot.

"Family is everything," continued Hemal. "Don't you agree?"

Sunil avoided the question, as though to concentrate on the game. He swung the putter; the ball scuttered past the hole, nearly to the other side of the green. Behind him, his caddie let out an exasperated sigh and a muttered "*Aiyaw* ..." Sunil frowned.

"We've organised things for Nilesh already," said Hemal. "A good match; a second cousin twice removed." He took his own putter, and walked across the green with Sunil. "Just looking for Darpan, now."

"A nice boy," said Sunil. He pictured Nilesh's twin: his bony face, his bulbous nose, his squat body; the way he sulked in corners, never saying much, never joining in, but never going away either. As though his dharma was to just *be* there, a mute witness to other people's lives, darkly reflecting their faults and foibles, like a sullen reminder that all is vanity. So different from Nilesh. Sunil kneeled, head close to the ground, to assess the contours of the green.

"But we need to firm things up. Can't wait forever."

"Of course not," said Sunil. A small hope ignited in him. He stood up. The wind whipped at his face, threatening more rain. "You must have loads of options."

Hemal shrugged: *Modesty forbids, etc.* "And you? Surely it's time to make plans for the beautiful Yogita?"

Somewhere behind the thirteenth green, well beyond the rough that surrounded it, a distant cacophony arose: high-pitched barks and yips. The sound of dogs that scent blood.

◈

In the living room of the larger of the two guest-houses, Pushpa and Padma sat with their backs to the main window. Behind them were the white mists and trees, the high peaks and valleys of the Western Ghats; before them, lying in folds and falls of saffron and indigo, their shared passion of needlework. Cascades of glowing silk, shot through with filigrees of colour and light, lay across their knees. Padma was creating a fine, subtle harmony of soft green and warm gold, but Pushpa's cloth glittered and winked and returned a thousand sharp fragments of image – for she was embroidering a sari in the Shisha style, in which countless small, reflective discs are sewn into the fabric in intricate patterns. It is delicate and immensely time-consuming work. But she enjoyed it, and both women chattered endlessly as the exquisite needlework progressed – on one side, the pale, elegant beauty of Padma, and on the other, as if through a glass darkly, the angular features and prominent nose of little Pushpa.

The children, by contrast, were quiet, subdued perhaps by the damp Ooty weather. Yogita, Padma's daughter, just eleven, was curled up in an armchair, lost in a book. She was reading, yet again, the story of Parvati – Parvati who won the heart of Shiva by shedding her unwanted aspects in the form of black Mother Kali, whose consort is the jackal. Having retained only her virtuous qualities, the story goes, Parvati presented herself to Shiva in the form of a golden beauty fit to be the consort of a god, indeed of a god who is the epitome of masculinity. Yogita peeped over the top of her book. Nilesh and Darpan were playing chess in front of a gently hissing fire of eucalyptus wood: Nilesh tall and fair like their father Hemal, Darpan short and dark like their mother Pushpa. Darpan looked up, and caught her eye, and held it for a second with that odd stare he had; but then his brother moved a knight – *check* – and he looked down again.

"Losing again, little brother!" Nilesh spoke to Darpan, but looked at Yogita. Darpan said nothing, and Yogita went back to her book, musing. In the fireplace, resin popped; outside, a thin mist collected on the hill opposite, as if searching for warmth among the eucalyptus trees. It had stopped raining, but still everything dripped.

In fact, the weather had provided a bone of contention for Pushpa and Padma. Should they risk a walk around Ooty Lake? Or should they take the safer option of the cinema, beyond any reach of rain and its distressing effects on hair and clothing? The merits and demerits of each option were complex and manifold. Padma put aside her embroidery in favour of a small packet of snuff tobacco. She took a pinch between finger and thumb and inhaled sharply – *one, two* – while Pushpa emphasised her arguments with a threaded needle. The fire spat; the women debated. Eventually, Pushpa put aside her needlework, delved in her bag and brought out a small, slim box. There was nothing for it, she said, but to seek the wisdom of the pack. She shuffled carefully: eyes closed, chin up, frowning with concentration. *A black suit means the cinema; a red one, the lake.* Padma rolled her eyes, but smiled and drew the five of spades. And so, the bone was discarded.

"Nilesh! Darpan! Come now. You can finish the game later."

"It's finished," said Nilesh. "I've won, again." He glanced at Yogita; Yogita smiled.

"No, Nilesh! My king can still move! It's not checkmate!"

"It'll be checkmate in two moves. Look."

"Don't fight, children. Finished or not finished, we're going to the cinema. Now. Yogita! Stop reading *now*."

So Pushpa put a guard in front of the fire, Padma took another surreptitious pinch of snuff, the children pulled on jumpers ('It's *still* too big for you, little brother!') and all five piled into a creaking white Ambassador. And after ten minutes of driving down the winding, broken tarmac leading from the guest-houses to Ooty town, and after parking on a street, and walking a little further, they found themselves outside the Assembly Halls Cinema. Giant posters in tones of sepia and red showed Raj Kapoor looking troubled, Rajendra Kumar looking desolate, and Vyjayanthimala looking tragic. At the bottom of the posters, in red letters, the word *Sangam;* and beneath that, for the benefit of non-Hindi speakers, its English translation: *Confluence.*

◈

Sunil looked down at the golf ball. Moisture held in its dimples caught the light and winked at him. *That barking; what the hell is going on?*

Sounds like a hundred dogs have gone mad. And what are those other noises?

"So?"

"What? Oh – Yogita?" said Sunil, as though none had been further from his mind. "Well, you know, Padma has the final say in all that." It sounded feeble even as he was speaking; both knew that Padma would accede to whatever Sunil proposed. But Hemal inclined his head as though in sympathy.

"And Padma, I am sure, will understand. You know what she said the other day, when the kids were playing together? *The three of them are like cousins.* That's what she said. Pushpa told me."

Sunil didn't reply. Hunched over his club, he gave the impression of absolute concentration. This time, the ball ended up close to the pin. "That's better."

"Just like cousins," Hemal repeated, as he lined up his own putt.

"If you sink this, the game's beyond hope. Again. Don't know how you do it."

"I know the course pretty well. I've been playing here since I was a kid, remember? My uncle used to bring me here. You know, our very own Director of Manufacturing." Hemal straightened up without playing his stroke. "Yes, he's helped me in many ways. I know he'll help the kids too. Like I said – family is everything."

Especially when your family pretty much owns ATC, thought Sunil. But it was true; Hemal's sons would always have a place at ATC. There would always be a good job for each boy; always a good home for each boy's wife.

Hemal was no longer interested in his ball; he held Sunil's eye. "So what do you think?"

"Well." Sunil wiped grass from the head of his putter. Then he looked towards the pin; and beyond it to the edge of the green; and beyond that to the rough, where sparse trees appeared from the mist. *Surely that's where the noise is coming from?* "I'm very pleased that you should think of us. Really." *Darpan? And Yogita? No!* He shuddered.

But the sounds had drawn closer – very close. A confusion of shouts and barking, as though men were trying to break up a dogfight. And beneath all that, a thudding, felt as much as heard, as if of some great weight pounding the earth.

❖

In 1964, the legacy of the British is still evident in Ooty; it lives on in the place names, the buildings, the very traditions of the town. Consider: just as Hemal and Sunil approach the thirteenth green, damp but undaunted in their pursuit of a very British sport, another very British pursuit is approaching them at pace through the bushes and woods. Yes, it is the Ooty Hunt – horses, dogs, scarlet-clad riders and all. Indeed, the Hunt is the spitting image of its English namesake in all respects save one: there are no foxes in South India, so they hunt jackals.

And at the same time as these streams of Britishness approach their confluence, where quiet fairway and fleeing quarry will surely meet, Pushpa and Padma and the children are exiting the Assembly Halls Cinema, built in 1901, just after the death of Queen Victoria. They find themselves on Garden Road, the boulevard that leads from the town's central intersection, Charing Cross, to Ooty's Botanical Gardens. Here is Higginbotham's Bookshop, with its shelves of P.G. Wodehouse and Nevil Shute, and there, Spencer's Department Store, with its shelves of everything. It is as though interwar England once held up a mirror to itself, and the reflection remains in Ooty. The image is dimmer today, more blurred and distorted; but in the sixties it is sharp indeed.

In any case, then, as now, any holiday-maker who visits Ooty will, like the crowds leaving the cinema, find themselves on Garden Road: tourists follow their destined trail, just as the oil-man's blinded buffalo circles the pestle and mortar to which it is yoked. And just as inevitably, just as crows fly to a carcass, Garden Road draws the scavengers: the beggars, the voyeurs, the purveyors of hot peanuts wrapped in cones of newspaper, the owners of stalls selling street-food "made with real ghee." But among these motley hopefuls, there is today one with a little more colour than the others, and, perhaps, a little more dignity. He comes from a tradition far older than the Anglo-Indian mores of Ooty. He is an intercessor between the mortal and the astral; the nexus between earth and eternity. He sells destinies.

❖

"Boys! Stop fighting!"

"The film made Darpan cry, Mam! He's like a *girl* – "

"Shut *up*, Nilesh, I never–"

"Boys! That's enough. Nilesh, be *quiet* – here they come."

Yogita and Padma had gone to buy sweets: now they returned with cellophane-wrapped, orange-tinted balls of stickiness. And as Yogita offered them around, Darpan became, all at once, aware of a subtle change, a change that operated on a level where words are too small for meanings. A new thread had been set in the loom; a new colour had entered; the pattern now grew differently, in fractals of new joys and new pains. *Warp and weft, oh you little people!* Before the film, Yogita had been only Auntie Padma's feisty daughter, the girl who would sometimes play cricket with the boys, and sometimes slyly watch them from behind a book. But now, she was possessed of that delicious secret, that infuriating feminine power – Parvita *and* Kali – that both emasculates and inflames. How so? No doubt the tragic romance of *Sangam* had played its part; doubtless the subdued half-light inside the Assembly Halls Cinema, delicately illuminating the slimness of Yogita's wrists and the dark cascade of her hair, had also contributed; but there was more to Darpan's sudden, overwhelming love than these happy chances. As if inscribed in the constellations, it was simply right; that he should love Yogita was, quite simply, *right*. Indeed, surely there was something of the tragic Bollywood hero about him: could anyone see him, walking thus in front of Yogita and Nilesh, and not also see the role to which he was born? Darpan puffed out his chest and lifted his chin. He would be *Sangam's* Sundar; Yogita would be Sundar's Radha. He wouldn't actually have to *shoot* himself like Sundar, of course, but Yogita would have to love him. Of that, he had no doubt.

Behind him, Nilesh said something in a low voice, and was answered by a suppressed giggle. Darpan turned, and saw Yogita, with her hand to her mouth, gazing at him, her eyes shining, while Nilesh looked away, expressionless. Darpan's heart swelled; *she understood!* Yes, Yogita understood; he could tell by the way she was looking at him. She too must have felt the *rightness* of it, the intertwining of destinies.

Darpan would be kind to her, and she in turn would be grateful and devoted; Nilesh would visit them, sometimes, and look on their blissful marriage with wonder and, yes, just a little jealousy ... poor Nilesh. Darpan's swagger became more deliberate and pronounced.

❖

Over his legs he wears only a pristine dhoti, the pedlar of destinies, and only chapped sandals on his feet, but otherwise he has acknowledged the Ooty chill – so far removed from the savage heat of his native Madurai – with a thick jumper, and a scarf that is wrapped around his neck and over the top of his head. He sits on a small, fold-up chair, before a small fold-up table, on the pavement of Garden Road. Here he waits, just in front of a patch of waste ground, where weeds wrestle with the debris scattered by a busy town. A thin plastic sheet, printed with a geometric pattern in faded red, covers the table.

On this plastic sheet are a number of objects. One is a framed picture of a seated Shiva, with Vasuki the snake coiled around his neck. The reds and bright yellows of Shiva's jewellery are gaudy against his pale blue skin; Vasuki has a black back and a turmeric-yellow belly. Next to Shiva is a portrait of the goddess Jakkamma; she is entwined by a five-headed cobra. The snake's hoods are spread protectively above her head, like a dangerous parasol. A fresh-cut marigold lies at Jakkamma's feet.

Also on the table is a pack of small envelopes, made of thin cardboard: each a little wider than a playing card, a little longer, a little thicker. The envelopes have wide borders of scarlet along their longer sides. Between these borders is a pale area on which numbers and letters are handwritten, in Tamil. The envelopes are neatly stacked one on top of the other.

But the most prominent item on the table is a delicate structure of polished rosewood, strengthened with brackets and bosses of brass. It is perhaps a foot wide and sixteen inches high, and maybe five inches deep. Its upper part consists of a box-like compartment, the lid of which is now open to its fullest extent, restrained from falling backwards by cords. Opened in this way, the lid is held just beyond the vertical, so that the paintings on its inner surface are proudly displayed: garish representations of Buddha, Jesus and again Shiva. The compartment revealed by this open lid is empty, but its dimensions would perfectly accommodate the scarlet-edged cardboard rectangles.

The lower part of this structure, beneath the open compartment, comprises a pair of cages, side by side. Each cage is fronted by a door of delicate vertical bars. One is empty, except for a grey dust of dried guano on its floor; the other holds a rose-ringed parakeet: a green-feathered jewel with a red collar and a knowing eye. It seems too colourful for the cold, dim clouds of Ooty – indeed, the parakeet is a bird of the hot scrub and intense light of the plains – but nevertheless, it is here, barred and boxed, set between some wet waste ground and a busy road in a cold town high in the Nilgiri Hills.

Tourists who are going to and from the Gardens will have to pass him, this man with his gods and goddesses and his caged parakeet; and those who have gone to the cinema can't help but see him as they emerge into the real world, their heads full of what-might-be. So the astrologer waits, and his bird looks out from its cage; first with one eye, and then with the other.

❖

Hemal and Sunil, their children's destinies briefly forgotten, turned towards the unseen commotion. And then, from the bushes behind the rough, a dark shape erupted and raced across the fairway; a creature with a grey coat and a thin, vicious face; a dog-like thing that ran like a thief chased from his village, bitter and unrepentant. The cunning trickster, the snarling coward, the companion of gods: the jackal. Straight after him came the bullying pack, mad with the hope of death and blood, pink-tongued and rolling-eyed, and behind them, the thumping, frothing horses, and the ramrod-straight riders in knee-length scarlet coats and green collars: turbaned Sikhs and bare-headed Rajputs. The fairway shuddered under the impact of hooves;

saucer-sized divots were kicked up.

"Wow!" said Hemal. "So that's the Hunt! Look at those guys!"

"Look at the mess they're making of the fairway."

"You can reposition your ball if it ends up in a hoof-print. It's in the club rules – Uncle told me. As I said, he often plays here."

They watched the riders disappear into the mists and bushes, chasing a pack that chased a shadow in the Ooty mists. Hemal took a step closer, and lowered his voice.

"And, while I'd like to think that I've kept my ATC job all these years due to ability alone, maybe Uncle also helped. This is the real world, right? And, no offence, but I think my relationships have also done you no harm. Guilt by association, perhaps?"

"Ha ha," said Sunil.

Hemal didn't smile. "Like everyone says, it's not what you know, but who you know. And if you don't know the right people, the pack turns on you. Ask the jackal." He looked down to take his shot. His putter found the ball at the central, lowest point of its pendular arc; the ball rolled smoothly across the green and disappeared into the hole. The caddies grinned at each other.

"Yes, they'll turn on you," said Hemal. "No question."

Sunil walked over to his own ball. Something heavy dragged at his insides; odd how he could be in fresh air, at the top of the Nilgiris, and yet feel caged. Like a butterfly pinned to a board, like a snake caught in a cleft stick, all notion of choice was, surely, illusory. *A wealthy husband for your daughter, and the assurance of your own continued employment – you know what you must say.* But Yogita; poor Yogita! He looked towards the eucalyptus woods; even the trees seemed to be listening. *If only they'd find another girl ...* Sunil took a deep breath. Poor Yogita!

"Perhaps you are right, Hemal. Darpan and Yogita have so much in common. Just like cousins."

Hemal smiled; a slow movement of his lips that had something in it of triumph, but little of joy. "You agree?" he said. "You agree to the marriage?"

Sunil picked up his ball. It was so close to the hole, there was no point in playing it. "I agree."

In the distance, the barking reached a crescendo; but whether of joy or disappointment, Sunil could not tell.

❖

"Twenty-seven cards, *behen*. This is the number of Nakshatra, of holy stars. Ashvini, Bharani, all holy stars. Each card has picture of god or goddess. Mary and Jesus also. You see, I make Pambu-babu pick a card for you, then I say fortune for you. You see."

"Pambu-babu is the name of the bird?" Pushpa contrived a sceptical expression, but her eyes gleamed.

"Yes, yes, Pambu-babu. I bring him from Meenakshi temple. Very holy bird. Ten rupees for your fortune, *behen*."

The children examined the parakeet in silence; and the parakeet examined the children, first from one side of its head, and then from the other: *That was your past; and this will be your future.* It worked its pink beak as though chewing on a morsel of wisdom, and scratched its neck with one scaly grey claw. Yogita put her finger to the bars, and clucked gently at it. Darpan remembered how *Sangam's* Gopal had placed his hand on Radha's, and how she had let it stay there, eyes downcast. He remembered the tragedy of lost love and the sweet joy of reconciliation. He reached out.

"Careful, Yogita. It may bite."

Yogita jerked her hand away as though a scorpion had crawled onto it. "Don't tell *me* what to do!"

Darpan blinked: his smile faded, but was too nervous to fully die. On the other side of him, Nilesh snorted.

"Darpan wants to hold your hand, Yogita. He'll be singing *Oh, Mehbooba* in a minute."

"I'd rather hold hands with a camel!"

"At least a camel would be *tall*, cousin ..."

Nilesh knew just what to say to raise a black rage in his brother. But Darpan had no response; the usual infuriation triggered by his sibling had been replaced – so suddenly! – by an unprecedented pain. This was worse than the normal taunts from his bigger, stronger, cleverer, better-looking twin; this carried the humiliation of secret love played out on a public stage. How could they know of this new, private thing, this sudden new colour in the cloth?

"*Haan!*" Yogita was laughing now, but without humour. "*Haan!* But maybe Darpan can sing better than a camel ... show us, Darpan!"

"Sing for us, Darpan!" Nilesh grabbed his brother's face with one hand, thumb on the left cheek and fingers on the right, so that Darpan's mouth was forced into a pout. "Sing! Like Sundar sings for Radha!"

Lacking the tools for formulating a subtle riposte, and – the shame of it! – with tears coming to his eyes, Darpan tried to push his brother away. But, as always, Nilesh was stronger, and Darpan himself was shoved backwards: another humiliation in front of the divine, hateful Yogita. And, as always, once started, Nilesh would not stop – he struck a pose in front of Yogita, and started to sing in a Bollywood parody:

"*Oh, Mehbooba, tere dil ke paas hi hai meri manzil-e-maqsood, Oh, Mehbooba*" (*Oh, Beloved, my destiny is to be next to your heart ...*)

And Yogita just giggled helplessly.

❖

What of the *qaidi*? In 2004, he has been imprisoned for nearly twenty years, while the Indian legal system grinds through appeals, one after the other. But this has not stopped him contributing to the jail's cottage industry, namely the manufacture of clothing. For Yerawada has its own textile mill, of which the primary product is prison garb, made not only for Yerawada's inmates but also (at profit) for those of other jails around the country. It is not a sophisticated operation; it relies on devices from the last century, antediluvian behemoths of iron and wood constructed in Dudley or Manchester or Birmingham. But they function still. In fact, there is something intimidating in the scale and power of the machines, their rhythmic cadences and metallic screams. They seem alive but insentient; automata that know nothing of the human scale, giant iron spiders spinning webs of cotton. But their names are incongruously zoological: Small Porcupine, Hopper Feeder, Mule.

❖

"Listen, dear, shall we get the children's fortunes told, with the bird? Just for fun."

"Let's just get back before it rains again."

"But my dear, you just don't see parrot astrologers in Bangalore! And it's only ten rupees."

"Pushpa, we've already spent money on cinema tickets, *and* we've said that the children can buy something from the shops."

"Only ten rupees!"

"Let's just go. The children aren't even interested."

"We'll ask them." Pushpa nodded at the children, bringing them into her circle of *what-might-be*. "Children, you'd like to have your fortunes told with the parrot, wouldn't you?"

Yogita declined; however, the boys, under Pushpa's pointed regard, were more acquiescent. And why not? Truth is a shattered mirror strewn; why shouldn't a bird's eye resolve part of that broken image?

Pushpa bent down, close to the parakeet's cage, and squinted through the bars. As she did so, a sudden gust of wind blew up, raising dust and making the parakeet flap its wings in displeasure. Something caught in the back of her throat, and she had a small, lady-like coughing fit.

"My dear, if you're going to do this, hurry up, before anybody pushes in." Padma nodded towards a gaggle of tourists who had paused nearby. Darpan turned; among the onlookers was a lone European. He was large, middle-aged, perhaps older; his neck was muffled with a silk cravat, and his bald head glistened as though oiled. He looked at Darpan with the unashamed stare more typical of the very young or the very old, while Pushpa bargained.

"*Arré, bhai,* half-price for the children, okay? Five rupees for him, five rupees for him, *haan?*" Pushpa's voice broke up as she coughed again.

"*Aiyaw ... illay ...*"

And so the negotiations proceeded, mainly in English, with an occasional admixture of Tamil and Hindi, until they had agreed, inevitably, on fifteen rupees for the two. All the time, the old European watched them, as though a connoisseur of transactions, occasionally raising one hand to adjust the thin scarf around his neck.

❖

The *qaidi* with the tired face walks past the Small Porcupine, pausing only to kick aside some cotton waste on the floor. He passes the Mule, once the apotheosis of the mechanised cotton mill; this too holds no interest for him. He no longer notices the odour of raw cotton or the clatter of machinery, but fibres catch in his throat, and he coughs drily as he walks. Now he finds himself in the weaving section, with its hand-operated looms and finished fabrics. Here, the *qaidi* with the tired face stops; here, where the longitudinal threads of the warp are set and the weft is gently pulled between the warp's delicate struts – this is his demesne.

He sits cross-legged on the floor. On one side a box of tiny mirrors, winking with memories; on the other a basket of coloured threads containing all the hues of creation. He cocks his head, as though to discern a divine tone, a golden bell, behind the cacophony of industry and incarceration.

❖

"Okay, children, who's first?"

"Me, Mam!"

"Mam, Nilesh is always first, it's not fair –"

"Darpan, it really doesn't matter ... Nilesh, come here ..."

Nilesh stood in front of the caged parakeet and sneaked a triumphant glance back at Darpan and Yogita. Then he turned to the astrologer with one of his winning, Nilesh-smiles: *am I not the most fortunate of all?* The old man looked from Nilesh to Darpan and back again, and pushed up his glasses with one finger. He took his pack of cardboard envelopes, shuffled them, and placed them in front of the cage. The wind picked up again, and Pushpa coughed. Darpan glanced behind him; the old European, now much closer, moved one shoulder in what might have been the smallest of shrugs.

The astrologer raised the sliding door in front of Pambu-babu's cage. The parakeet looked out at him, bright-eyed. The old man made a gesture in front of the cage, a rapid chopping motion with his open palm. Pambu-babu waddled out to the stack of envelopes. He quickly removed the top three with his beak, flinging them to one side as if to hurry fate. He paused, head cocked, then threw aside another. Then he took the topmost envelope, dropped it in front of the astrologer, turned and weaved his way back to the cage. His long green tail dragged across the plastic mat with a dry rustle.

The astrologer closed the cage door and picked up the envelope chosen by the parakeet. He opened it and took out a card. It had Tamil writing on one face, and a colourful image on the other.

"Tsk! We can't read this." Pushpa was annoyed. "Can you say it in Hindi, or English?"

"I tell in English, madam. It is no problem." The old man put the paper on the table, and showed them the side with the picture. A four-armed goddess on an ornate throne, covered in jewels and garlands, with a leafy branch in one hand. "Pambu-babu gives you Goddess Shakthi. This is your fortune." The astrologer hesitated, looking at the Tamil and searching for the English words. Nilesh craned forward, as if to hear better.

"You are lucky, clever. You are getting rich. You have child. But there is problems." The astrologer frowned. He squinted over Nilesh's shoulder, as if the onlookers could help with the translation. Darpan turned; the old European was still there, motionless, yet closer still, and now to one side. It was though he obeyed a different geometry; or as though his co-ordinates remained invariant while this reality flowed and changed around him.

"You must remember," said the astrologer. "Forgiveness changes fate." The astrologer nodded, happy with the words. "You can forgive, or not forgive. You must choose. This is your fortune."

Nilesh sauntered back to Yogita. "Hear that? Lucky, clever, and rich."

Now Darpan came forward. He felt somehow burdened, as if beneath a weight of attention, of observation – the European? Pambu-babu ruffled his feathers. From somewhere behind Garden Road, a church bell rang, slow and clear. The astrologer re-shuffled the pack of envelopes, and the process was repeated. They looked at the picture chosen by Pambu-babu: a blue-skinned god carrying a trident. The god whose name means *jackal*.

"Pambu-babu gives you Lord Shiva," said the fortune-teller. He turned the paper over to show the scribbled Tamil script, and looked from Darpan to Pushpa and back again. "Now I say fortune."

Behind Darpan, Nilesh nudged Yogita and said something in a low voice.

"You are skilful. You have success, money. You will marry. But you have much pain. Here." The old man patted his chest. "But less pain if you forgive. Forgiveness makes different life. Remember." He paused, wrestling again with language. From behind Darpan, close as skin, distant as starlight, came a whisper: *But some sins are unforgiveable ... do you agree?*

"Pah!" said Padma. Reverting to Hindi, she said "What kind of horoscopes are these? We've wasted enough time and money – let's just go!"

Pushpa nodded vigorously. "Yes." She turned on her heel, chin up. "Children – come now."

Unwilling to walk with the others, Darpan loitered, staring at the parakeet; what was in its mind, this little thing? And as he looked and wondered, the dull Ooty clouds broke apart, pushed away by the same wind that had blown dust into Pushpa's throat and lungs, and a ray of sun caught the parakeet, making of it a thing of green and rose flames. They burnt with the sound of sitar chords, like strings of celadon and cinnabar, branding Darpan's senses and hillocking his skin in the way that great music can. Then the clouds returned, and all was quiet again. The bird cocked its head and settled down on its feet. It fixed one grey eye on Darpan; its pupil contracted as though to focus on a fault in the fabric of destiny, a loose end that needed tying.

"Darpan! Come *now!*"

❖

In the Yerawada textile mill, the *qaidis* have traditionally used the basic, over-and-under weave that you would expect for fabric destined for prisoners' clothing. In 2004, however, the management has become more ambitious: if simple cloth makes small returns, surely better material will make bigger returns? It is obvious. And so the mill is experimenting with the manufacture of Paithani fabrics, fine silken weaves inculcated with intricate patterns. Paithani work is labour-intensive – it takes a day just to set the silk threads on the loom – but time is abundant in Yerawada. And the resulting saris and shalwar kameez, fit for weddings and gifts, will command a high price. The initiative should be profitable; the Yerawada management is pleased.

Perhaps this is why the *qaidi* with the tired face, alone among the death row residents, is allowed to participate in the textile operations. He knows how to grade and choose the silk yarn, and how to set the Paithani looms. Only he can advise on the motifs and patterns to employ: peacocks or parrots, Muthada or Panja geometrical designs. Without him, the Paithani product line would have been stillborn.

❖

"He will marry, yes; but he will marry a camel."

"Poor little Darpan. Look how his jumper sleeves come over his hands."

"You know, Yogita, once I saw him looking at himself in the mirror, with *one of Mam's saris wrapped round him!*"

"No!"

"So when he gets married, maybe *he* will have the nose-ring. Not the camel."

"And he will have a camel-baby!"

"Don't be angry, Darpan. You must forgive us, remember? The parakeet said so."

And so on, and on, until, on the way back from the parrot astrologer, they stopped at Spencer's Department Store. Nilesh and Yogita paused at the section of books and jigsaw puzzles, but Darpan, carrying something bruised and aching in his chest, walked on: blindly, without direction, anywhere just to be away from the others. And then, as though it had always been there, always waiting, just for him, just for this moment which always was and always would be, he saw the penknife. It was on a tray, one of several identical items, but slightly separate from its brethren. And somewhere inside him, a small voice said *"Take."*

So Darpan put it in his pocket – and it was part of the *rightness* of things that when he did so, there was no one looking at him, that he was invisible, hidden in a bubble of collective inattention. He re-joined the others; his new treasure, heavy as destiny, pressed knowingly against his thigh. And from this point, it was as though Darpan had grown another layer to his shell – as though the mirror had been re-silvered. The jibes and giggles of Nilesh and Yogita had lost none of their pain, but their power was lessened, *reflected*, for he now possessed something that was his alone, something hidden from the other children; and this very fact warmed his soul.

❖

"It's all arranged, Pushpa. Sunil has agreed to match Yogita with Darpan. At last!"

"How wonderful! But Sunil should be approaching Darpan to make a proposal, surely?"

"Everything will be done correctly, dear. He'll come and offer Yogita when the children are eighteen.. We agreed. Until then, don't tell the children, okay? It'll only cause embarrassment."

"It's funny, but Nilesh was teasing Darpan only today. About Yogita. Almost as though he knew ... Oh, Hemal, this is *so* exciting..."

Certainly, Pushpa was overjoyed by the prospect of making complicated wedding arrangements; perhaps she was also happier to discuss these arrangements than admit to money spent on cinema tickets, shops and parrot astrology ... In any case, she and Hemal were happily asleep before the rain returned, and long before the jackal wailed from the hillside above them. Indeed, throughout the night, they were disturbed by nothing more than Pushpa's small, dry cough, which had persisted since that sudden wind blew dust into her face while she was glaring at the fortune-teller's parakeet.

❖

It is night; the rain has stopped pounding the corrugated iron of the guest-house roof. In the dripping silence, a jackal howls from the hill: the sound of the eternal outcast. The dog of sorrows, despised by men, Kipling's Tabaqui, two-faced and lying, a fox in a wolf's coat, the trickster of the Mahabharata and the consort of Black Mother Kali the destroyer. It is the same jackal that ran from the Ooty Hunt that morning, the hunt that interrupted two golfers at the Gymkhana Club's thirteenth hole. *If you don't know the right people, the pack turns on you.* Perhaps the confounding of the Hunt explains why there is something of mockery in the jackal's call, something of the pariah who yet survives, against all odds; but mixed with that defiance is the sorrow of the exile.

In the bedroom shared by the boys, Darpan hears its ululation, and finds there some inexpressible meaning. He gets up and walks across to the other bed, the coir matting rough on his bare feet. The fire has subsided to a collection of glowing embers, but still gives light enough for him to see Nilesh's face. The shadows make something strange of it; it is as though the soft red light has captured an echo of the future – here is Nilesh the *man,* tall and strong, with his fine brow, his aquiline nose, his thick, wavy hair. So different from Darpan, who, the mirror tells him, womb-mate or not, is cast from some other mould – squatter, with a broader nose, and features that even now, softened by youth, cannot be pleasing. Their mother's son, just as Nilesh is their father's.

Darpan bends forward slightly, so that his face is directly above Nilesh's, and – slowly, quietly – collects a tongueful of saliva in his mouth, and then pushes it forward, through pursed lips, so that it falls on Nilesh's face. Nilesh twitches in his sleep, and his breath catches, but he does not wake. The jackal calls again; Darpan returns to his bed. He feels that something meaningful has happened, but cannot formulate the words to interrogate his experience, not even to frame its description. It is as though circumstances arrange themselves in such a way that things *must happen as they do*; as if Darpan himself were only a medium that reflected events occurring in some plane of existence more real than his own. That the jackal cried when it did; that Darpan was awake to hear it; that Nilesh was deeply asleep; that Darpan decided – no, was *compelled* – to get up from his bed and look at his sleeping brother – events so shaped themselves that, somehow, it was right, indeed unavoidable, to spit on Nilesh's face while he slept. It was part of the *rightness* of existence, an unbreakable thread forming a great pattern that spread out in all directions, forward and back, this way and that, somehow encompassing the gleaming penknife and the parakeet and Yogita with her eyes shining and the dying light of the eucalyptus fire. Darpan falls asleep marvelling at the infinite, destiny-rich mystery that he has discovered.

Part II: The sari

In June 1967, the monsoon was slow to arrive, and Bangalore was caught in a sultry pocket of humidity. By day, the inhabitants stamped fractiously about their business, cursing the thousand small discomforts, while verges and walls pushed out a sudden green bloom – Bombay creeper and Indian mallow. At night, humidity made sleep rare and precious; frequent power cuts forced even those with air-conditioning to sleep with windows thrown open, gasping for a fresh breeze. It often seemed that half the city lay awake, listening to the predatory whine of mosquitoes within, and the furtive scrabble of the bandicoot rat without. But for Hemal and Sunil, the summer brought welcome news – thanks to ATC connections, they had finally become members of that snobbiest institution, the Bangalore Club. They celebrated, one Saturday, with the club's own-brew lager, served up at an outside bar on the club's perfect lawn.

"Pulled a few strings," said Hemal. "One of them was attached to a cousin. He's a permanent member. He shouldn't really propose anyone unless they're personally known to him, but, well, you'll be a relative by marriage soon, won't you? Can't get more personal than that."

"Thanks," said Sunil. "Appreciate it." He looked over the grass, neatly trimmed for the last one hundred years, and absorbed the elegance and haughtiness of the club buildings. "Fantastic. Let's have dinner here with the girls. My treat." He nodded, and smiled. *It's not what you know, it's who you know.* But Hemal, for once, had no answering smile.

"I'm sorry, Hemal – I should have asked. How's Pushpa? Have you had the latest results through yet?"

"Yes. Looks like she's stuck with it. Nothing we can do, the doctor says."

"I'm sorry."

"It's okay. There are worse things than arthritis."

"I don't understand how it came on so quickly. Three years ago, she was fine – I remember her sewing away when we were in Ooty."

"Exactly. That was the origin of the trouble, apparently. When she got ill, that holiday, remember?"

"Eh? I thought the hospital said that was bird fever, or something?"

"Parrot fever. Psittacosis, they call it. Usually it's mild, apparently, but if you're unlucky it can trigger serious issues, like joint problems. Pushpa was unlucky, I suppose. Got dealt a bad hand, so to speak."

"How on earth did she get parrot fever, anyway?"

"God knows."

"Can't the doctor do anything to make her more comfortable?"

"Oh, he gave her some tablets, but they do nothing. Pushpa threw them away. She's taking those Ayurvedic powders of Padma's instead. They seem to help her sleep, but she still can't do her needlework, and it's driving her crazy."

"Ah – the famous Shisha sari. Don't worry, Hemal – she'll get back to it one day, you wait. Medicine advances all the time."

But Pushpa never sewed another thread, nor a single additional mirror, into her half-made masterpiece. Her disease progressed inexorably, twisting fingers and wrists into knotted bone; needlework was impossible. Sometimes she would rub and stroke her clubbed knuckles on the fine silk, as if cold mirrors could soothe away swelling, as if smooth threads would lubricate her corroded joints. But they did not.

❖

The *qaidi* with the tired face has produced works of rare beauty during his time in Yerawada; but this sari, his latest creation, is exceptional. He holds the delicate cloth, and examines its pattern of silvered discs; they wink brightly at him, like so many single eyes, catching the light when he moves the fabric. Each glint a glimmer of something lost, something that can only be found through the refractions of memory; each glint a wink that speaks of the complicity of sorrows. Wink – the teardrop in the air; wink – the blood catching the light; wink – *Oh, Mehbooba*, as the sunlight catches the ripples on Ooty Lake, where Radha flees unwanted love; wink, wink, wink.

It takes months to weave and embroider a Paithani-Shisha sari; but the *qaidi* with the tired face is grateful for an occupation, for being outside his stinking cell for a few hours a day. He sits, cross-legged, on a mat on the floor; to one side of him, his silk threads – spun from a rainbow surely, in Kusumbi red, Pophali yellow, Neeligunj blue, and Brinjal indigo – and to the other, the tray of little glass discs with silvered backs. Sometimes a guard approaches him, all swagger and *lathi,* to remind him of his position.

"Why you here, *qaidi*? Murder, *haan*?"

The *qaidi* pulls a golden thread through this finest of fabrics – *under, back up, over and through* – and listens to the delicate play of tone on tone.

"That is why you hang, *qaidi*. But first you make women's clothes. *Accha,* sari-babu."

❖

In that year of the late monsoon, the boys turned fifteen, and Yogita fourteen. But girls are faster to become women than boys are to become men, and while Darpan and Nilesh showed some promise of broadness of shoulder – Nilesh more so than Darpan – Yogita's graceful curves were now unmistakable. It was a magical time; she had not yet grown so apart from the boys that she would not be seen with them, not so self-aware that she would no longer spend time with them. And one day, she went with them to the maidan to play *gilli-danda*. The simplest of games: the cricket of two sticks. One bigger, one smaller.

As always, Nilesh went first. He placed the smaller stick on the ground, resting it against a pebble, so that it sat with one end down and the other in the air, like an unbalanced see-saw. He hit the raised end of the see-saw with the bigger stick, so that the shorter stick jumped vertically into the air to shoulder height, spinning rapidly, end-over-end. At its zenith, he hit it again, very hard, and ran between the batting position and the mark while Darpan chased after it.

"Eight runs, little brother! Your legs are too short. But you can have a turn, now. See if you can actually hit it, okay?"

Darpan walked slowly back, examining the smaller stick. It wasn't the best; too thick at one end, splintered at the other. Difficult to make jump vertically into the air; and that would make it more difficult than normal to beat Nilesh. Darpan brought out his penknife, the knife that he had carried with him almost continually – and, until now, continually kept hidden – since he stole it in Ooty three years previously. He whittled away at each end, rotating the stick in his left hand while his right hand applied the knife to peel off thin shavings. Like sharpening a double-ended pencil. Nilesh and Yogita came closer.

"What are you doing, little brother?"

"What does it look like?"

"Where'd you get the knife?"

"None of your business." Darpan had now trimmed the stick to a needle-sharp terminus, a wicked singularity, at each end. He held it up to the cloudless South Indian sky and squinted at each pointed tip.

"Pfff! So Darpan has secrets!" Yogita's contempt filled the maidan. "How *exciting*! How *important* he must be!"

Darpan just looked at her, rolling the sharpened stick between his fingers. He still loved her, achingly; and also he hated her, passionately. Nilesh turned away, and as Yogita followed him, he inclined his head towards her, and said, in a voice that Darpan was intended to hear – but also, insultingly, intended to believe to be part of a conversation from which he was excluded:

"Ah, Yogita, you know little Darpan's biggest secret,? It's the Shisha sari he is making to wear for his *hijra* parties."

"What!"

"Yes, really! Can't *wait* for Father to find out – "

What happened next was always going to happen. It was part of the pattern of existence. Darpan knew it – even before he placed the sharpened stick on the ground and gave a short downward blow to its upward pointing end, he knew it. Not at an analytical level; not at a level that can be articulated; no, he knew at some deeper, visceral level that the future trajectory of the stick was fixed, that it was inevitable that – once he had hit it a second time, in mid-air, with perfect timing and infinite venom, with all his strength – Nilesh would turn to look back at him, lips bared wolfishly over his white, regular teeth, turning just as the stick went whipping towards his face, end over sharpened end, the fresh points – pale where the bark and sapwood had been trimmed away – winking as they flipped through the air, through the preordained, exactly *right* trajectory until the stick embedded itself deep in Nilesh's eye. Now Darpan knew why he had sharpened the stick so; it was part of the inevitable, unavoidable *rightness* of destiny. If he had intended to bring about that result at any other time, even if some demon had offered him the riches of the world and Yogita at his feet to send the wooden needle through the air just so, with just such an effect, he could not have done so; but at that particular moment in time, no other result was possible.

Darpan would always remember the shocked silence, followed by Yogita's cry of alarm and then the rising scream as Nilesh raised his hands to his face, palms upward, as though seeking blessings from heaven. Others on the maidan paused, and turned to stare at the good-looking boy with the stick in his eye. There was not much blood, at first; the missile itself plugged the wound it had made. But there were tears, and as Nilesh, receiving no comfort from above, bent down in pain, a drop of crystal ran down his nose – so finely shaped – and fell through the air. As it fell, it caught the sun and winked at Darpan, a little glint of joy; and deep inside Darpan, a small voice sung in pleasure.

❖

While Nilesh bled on the maidan, Pushpa and Padma chatted in Padma's sitting room. The ceiling fan thrummed; its breeze teased at a strand of Pushpa's hair, pulling it across her face. She pushed it back with one twisted, swollen hand, and waved the other at Padma.

"Listen, my dear. Darpan is fifteen now. We really must start planning the wedding."

"But Pushpa, it's *years* away." Padma unlidded a tiny brass snuff-box.

"I know, I know. We don't actually have to *do* anything. I'm talking about *planning*."

"I really don't think it would be a good idea to let the children know about this just yet." Padma quailed at the thought of Yogita's likely reaction; the girl had become so wilful recently.

Pushpa sighed. "If you insist. Though I really can't see the problem, my dear. But we can *discuss* things, at least. Like, where should the wedding be. Things like that."

"Where? I don't know. Somewhere in Bangalore, of course." Padma arranged a pinch of sniffing tobacco on the back of her hand, and bent over it.

"But you see, my dear, I was thinking of something else." Pushpa's eyes gleamed; she stretched out a leg to ease one aching knee. "I was thinking of Ooty."

"Ooty! We're not Bollywood moguls, Pushpa!" Padma wiped at her nose.

"Come on. It would be so picturesque. And it was in Ooty that we first talked about the marriage, wasn't it? It just seems right to celebrate it there." Pushpa nodded. "It just seems *right*."

"The cost! Sunil would have a heart attack."

"Look, Hemal is very keen on the idea. His family, you know. There are expectations. So there will be ways of offsetting costs. I know it."

Padma absorbed the vague offer. "It would certainly be romantic. The lake, the hills. It's all very *Sangam*." She closed the snuff-box, and put it away in her bag; she'd kept her tobacco and brown powders with her at all times since she'd found that Yogita had been surreptitiously trying them.

"Exactly. But talking of romantic matters, you must promise me one thing – *don't buy a sari for Yogita*."

Padma looked at Pushpa, but said nothing.

"Yogita must have the one I've been making. You know." Pushpa knuckled away the strand of hair again.

"But Pushpa – you can't work on it anymore, with your poor hands."

"No. But Darpan can. I am teaching the boys needlework, you see."

Padma raised an eyebrow.

"Their father doesn't need to know, of course."

Padma raised the other eyebrow.

"Don't look at me like that, Padma. Darpan is actually very good. Nilesh *could* be, I'm sure, if he only tried." Pushpa rubbed her hands together, as if searching for movements her fingers could no longer make.

Padma's eyes widened still further, but Pushpa was lost in the world of *what-might-be.* "How *romantic!*" she repeated, clasping her twisted, crippled hands to her chest.

❖

Darpan held the needle up to the window, so that the sky made its eye blue. He threaded it, squinting against the brightness, his mind travelling where it would. There was little about last year's *gilli-danda* accident, he reflected, that he regretted. He had hurt Nilesh in a way that had never before been possible; a hurt which had gone some way to balancing the account of their shared childhood. That was good. At the same time, he had actually had some effect on Yogita; he knew, as surely as if he had pressed his ear to her soft breast, that he'd made her heart jump and race. Yes: for the first time, he'd had power over beauty; and that was very good. And finally, since losing his eye, Nilesh had become more distant, and spent more time out of the house; and that was also good, because the sarcastic barbs and put-downs came less frequently. That said, Darpan still shared a house with Nilesh, and the subtle insults still came. To escape his twin, however, was increasingly easy: his mother's obsession with finishing the Shisha sari became more urgent each day. Nilesh would make increasingly ridiculous excuses – *"I've got earache, Mam, it gets worse if I sew,"* – and that suited Darpan very well, for he was drawn to the work as if each stitch led to the resolution of his life's pattern.

Indeed, for Darpan the sari's sum was more than its silk and mirror parts; its hues and tones made a number that was incalculable. For it was woven, surely, from yarn spun in some dimension where colours were tangible, where the eye can hear and skin can see. It was as if the cloth had fallen from a sphere in which a saffron silence were shot through with deepest violet, where its small discs chimed as cold as trembling stars, their yellow radiance imbued with the texture of thread; where gravity fell in silky waves and folds, warping the cloth without changing it. Whenever it lay across Darpan's lap – nine yards of silk and cotton that contained the best of creation – he was undone. The colours and pattern held his eyes and drugged his mind; they triggered a visceral pleasure that also had something of the spiritual. It was as though his soul were soaked in hues that resonated with those at his knee, and the harmonies echoed through all time. As though to look at the sari were to ring a great bell, to feel it chime in Bhagwa gold and yellow, and then to hear its echoes return in indigo and porphyry ...

"Darpan! Stop dreaming! And *listen* to me– you won't learn anything if you don't listen. You're not a little boy."

"Yes, Mam."

"You see the pattern – the little mirrors are sewn in here, here and here. With the yellow thread. You try one while I watch."

"Yes, Mam."

"That's it – under, back up, over and through ... then repeat. Good. You have a talent for this, you know? I wish Nilesh would make more of an effort, because he *can* do it when he wants, I've seen him – and where is that boy, anyway?"

"He's gone to play tennis with Yogita."

"Tchah! He *knew* I wanted him to help with the needlework today!" Pushpa glared into the distance before turning back to Darpan. "But I particularly want you to do this, and you have some ability, so maybe it's all to the good."

Indeed, it came easily to Darpan, cross-legged on the verandah and surrounded by that cloth of Paradise. Here, with the sari's folds caressing his skin, he explored a universe of tangible colour unknown to Nilesh and Yogita, a secret far greater than the stolen penknife, greater even than the secret understanding that things *must happen as they do*. No longer was he little, ugly Darpan; he was a traveller through dimensions measured in the hues of eternity, a pilgrim on a silken road of sound and light. He pushed the needle slowly through the delicate silk, revelling in the soft friction of saffron on indigo, the fricatives of tint and tone. And as the yellow thread tautened again under his downward pressure, he thought he heard the remote chime of a golden bell.

❖

The sounds of the jail mill are omnipresent: the eldritch complaints of metal and the groaning of wood; the oppressive, repetitive hammering that rises up through the floor; and the shouted obscenities of guards and *qaidis*, in Hindi and Marathi: *Sali kuta! Kutte ki jat! Randi ka baccha! ... Randichya! Gandchodya!* The stained concrete, the smell of sweat and cotton, the infernal noise, the infinite small cruelties of man – this is your life, *qaidi*. Until tomorrow.

But if the *qaidi* is conscious of this deadline, he does not show it. Cross-legged on his mat, he sews with the same slow, focussed deliberation that he has always shown. He has put away his box of little mirrors; that work is done. Today he is finishing an impossibly delicate operation, a viridian tracery, a collection of living shapes in green gossamer. All around the margin of the sari, he is embroidering groups of tiny birds, three in each group, beak to tail, in a circular arrangement. Each has a slender, rose-pink collar around its green throat; each looks out to the unknown future with one eye, while the other is held eternally to the unchanging past. Rose-ringed parakeets, of course.

He heaves a sigh as he finishes the last bird, and with that, the sari. All that remains now is to sew the YK label – Yerawada Karagruha, the brand – into the hem. But someone else will do that.

❖

Returning from ATC one afternoon in 1969, Hemal enjoyed the curious lightness, the weightlessness, of the man who has no particular worries. Within three years, both Nilesh and Darpan would be married to carefully matched girls; thereafter, both would have guaranteed careers in ATC; and at present, Pushpa's arthritis, although not improving, had stabilised under her regime of Ayurvedic creams and powders. *If you don't push fate, fate will push you,* he thought. *And I prefer to do the pushing.* He smiled; perhaps he smirked.

But as he got out of the car, Pushpa's maid scuttled out of the house, fists to her mouth, leaving the door open. From inside, Hemal could hear Pushpa's voice, wailing and shouting. *Now what?* He followed the sounds through the hallway to the sitting room. The tableau was almost absurd: Pushpa shrieking, waving her knobbled little fists in the air; Darpan, sitting on the sofa, his face bruised, rubbing at his neck; the curtain half-ripped from its rod, spilling its blue on the floor. And everywhere, everywhere, the loud silence, the solid absence, of Nilesh.

"What – ?"

"Nilesh! He just went mad, Hemal! Look at Darpan! I thought he was going to kill him! Look!" Pushpa placed a clubbed finger under Darpan's chin and tilted it back so that Hemal could see the marks left by Nilesh's hands.

"But why? What happened?"

"I don't know! I don't know!"

"Darpan?"

Darpan shrugged. "All I did was congratulate him on his bride. Our lovely second cousin twice removed. I said I was sure they would be very happy." He moved his hand from his neck to his bruised eye. One corner of his mouth twitched.

"Pushpa!"

"Why *shouldn't* I tell them about their wedding arrangements? It's time for them to know! They're seventeen!"

"There's a time and a place for such discussions. Where's Nilesh?"

"Gone! Gone!" Pushpa waved at the window, and then sat next to Darpan, pressing his bruised face to her shoulder and reaching an imploring hand to Hemal, as if asking him to rewrite the past.

"Mm. He'll come back when he's hungry. *Then* we'll talk."

Nilesh did indeed come back, though he showed no signs of hunger; and he did indeed have a talk with his father, during which his one good eye remained as dark and expressionless as the black eye-patch over its dead twin. But he was carefully polite to everyone. He expressed appropriate contrition for the damaged curtain, and accepted an appropriate penance. He even apologised to Darpan, with an easy grin: "I just misunderstood, little brother – I thought you were saying my future wife was *ugly*, you know?" But the charm was eggshell-brittle; all could see what seethed beneath it.

"The problem is, he's always had whatever he needed," said Pushpa, later. "Now, he goes mad if doesn't get whatever he wants. It's *horrible* when he's like that. He looks at you as though he doesn't know who you are – or who he is."

"He's just got a temper. That's all."

"You didn't see him, Hemal." Pushpa rubbed cream into her hands. "He scared me. Really, he did."

❖

The *qaidi* with the tired face sits with his back against a cold wall. In the half-light of the Yerawada night, he sees through his barred door other barred doors. He wonders briefly about those who are behind those other bars; what must those other lives be like? And why can't this life be exchanged for another, more satisfactory reality? The cages are interchangeable; why not the contents?

He puts his hand to one side of his face, and squints through the cage door. Outside, a wind blows clouds from the moon, and an old light silvers the floor of his cell. Somewhere, twenty-seven holy stars shine on all the manifold destinies of this earth. He shivers, and puts a hand over the other eye. Now he can see nothing; but wasn't it always so?

❖

"How is she?" Padma spoke without turning as Sunil entered the room.

"The same. She'll come to terms with it. Even if I have to keep her locked in her room until she does."

"School will be starting again soon."

"So? If she wants to see her friends, she'd better behave. How did she even find out about it?"

"Pushpa told her kids, and Nilesh told her."

"Pushpa – the silly bitch! I thought you'd told her to wait until we managed the news in our own way?"

"I did, Sunil. And she said she wouldn't say anything until we were ready. But you know what she's like."

"Silly bitch!"

From Yogita's room, they heard the sound of something breaking. A mirror? Padma sighed. *What is it about children today? They seem to think real life should be like it is in films.* "Look. She's not calming down, so let's give her a little help." She opened her handbag, pulled at the zip of an inside pocket, and extracted a small sachet of brown powder.

Sunil frowned. "Snuff? How will that help?"

Padma didn't look at him. "It's not tobacco. I use it sometimes, to help me sleep."

"Is it safe? From the doctor?"

"It's Ayurvedic."

"From that place behind Commercial Street?"

Padma hesitated. "Yes."

"I didn't know you were having trouble sleeping. Anyway, if it works, it works. I'm going to the office now. Tell her I expect to hear some sense from her when I get back."

After Padma had delivered a cup of heavily sweetened tea to Yogita, she returned to her own bedroom. She licked the end of one finger and dipped it into the sachet of brown powder. Then she put her finger back into her mouth, and rubbed the powder all around her gums and the roof of her mouth.

She sighed deeply, walked to the bed and lay down on her back. As she stared at the ceiling fan – *round* and *round* and *round* – her pupils expanded and her breathing slowed. *She just needs to learn that marriage isn't like in stories. You don't always get who you want.* She wiped at a sudden wetness on each cheek, turned on her side, and let her eyelids slowly close.

❖

In 1972, the Indian Wildlife Protection Act was passed; five years later, the Ooty Hunt would bow to pressure and accept that it could no longer pursue jackals, or any other animals, with dog and horse. But in 1974, the jackal still ran from the Hunt, and still survived to cry at the black night. The twins, still as unlike as ever twins were, were twenty-two years old, and Yogita twenty-one. The marriage of Darpan and Yogita loomed perilously close; prompted by Hemal, and encouraged by talk of a discount negotiable by ATC (*"Contacts, my friend. It's all about who you know"*), Sunil had booked a venue near Ooty. Hemal had told him about it. *"Remember those tall iron gates by the side of the road, just as you're coming into Ooty, from the Ghats? No? Well, anyway, it's behind those gates, about a mile. The Big House, everyone calls it."* It was indeed 'big': a sprawling arrangement of pillars, archways, domed roofs and small towers that was more like a small palace. The kind of place where film stars or politicians would marry; surely this would be acceptable to Hemal's family? Hemal certainly seemed to think so; and certainly Hemal's various relatives nodded kindly at Sunil if they passed him in the ATC corridors.

And, as if to confirm Yogita's future security, these same corridors welcomed Darpan and Nilesh before the year was out. Any water-cooler grumbling regarding the recruitment process was stilled by the twins' obvious abilities; they worked hard and learned fast. Sometimes, in fact, it seemed that they were competing, and competing more intensely as the wedding preparations crawled on. Like identical magnetic poles that resist more the more closely they are apposed, the demands of family and work that brought them unwillingly together also increased their mutual repulsion. Sharing the same birth, living in the same house, working in the same part of the same company; it was as if two incompressible lives were being forced into an existence designed to accommodate only one – an existence whose possibilities shrank by the day. All felt the rising pressure; even Pushpa was relieved, when, less than a month before the wedding, the brothers' schedules at last diverged. Darpan was required to attend a one-week training course at ATC's Hyderabad facility, where he would wrestle with cotton's bestiary – the Porcupine and other monsters – and learn the operation of different looms. Nilesh, however, would not be required in Hyderabad until after the wedding. And so, when the car came to take Darpan to the airport, Nilesh watched silently, arms folded, his one eye glinting.

"I wish you and Darpan would behave as if you were family!" snapped Pushpa, waving at the taxi.

"But we do," said Nilesh.

"Three weeks until his wedding, and you cannot even smile at each other. And speaking of weddings – "

"Mam, please. There's nothing more to say."

Nilesh, as usual, was unmoved by Pushpa's glare. Having declined to marry the second cousin twice removed so carefully chosen, and having refused all other attempts to nudge him toward marital stability, he was a source of embarrassment and anger to his parents; a thorn in their traditional flesh. But he'd made it clear he would go his own way, and that was that. And although nobody was aware of any girlfriends that had lasted any length of time, it was hard to believe that he'd lacked opportunity: the eye-patch that punctuated his film-star good looks had somehow given him an aura of danger, a piratical, swaggering menace that, when combined with his charm, sent girls weak at the knees ... *Why* won't he marry, Pushpa would wail; but nobody could answer.

"Nilesh! Don't walk away when I am talking to you."

"Sorry, Mam." He grinned, and Pushpa wilted. *Such a beautiful young man.*

"Remember, on Saturday I am going shopping with Padma. Your father will drop me off on Commercial Street, on his way to the club."

"Playing snooker with Uncle Sunil?"

"Of course. But what I am saying is – "

"No, Mam, I'm not coming shopping, thank you. We've already got everything I need for the wedding. Anyway, I've got plans for Saturday."

"What plans?"

"Why, getting ready for dear Darpan's homecoming on Sunday, of course."

Saturday was a fine day. Perhaps it was chance that Yogita told the maid to take a day off when Padma and Pushpa were trawling the sari shops on Commercial Street and her father was playing snooker with Hemal at the Bangalore Club. Or perhaps she just wanted some time alone to prepare herself for the wedding. But in any case, Yogita was as clean and pretty as a new-bloomed lotus when Nilesh dropped by; and Nilesh was freshly showered and shaven, with a wolfish grin.

❖

Two weeks later, just before the wedding, the families found themselves, once again, in Ooty.

"Your big day tomorrow, little brother. Feeling nervous?"

"Nilesh, stop teasing him and get ready."

"Ready for what, Mam?"

"You *know* what! We're going to the Big House, to make sure everything is ready."

"I thought Yogita's parents had already done that?"

"Well, yes, but we're just going to have a look anyway."

"*You* are. I'm going to have a round of golf."

"Nilesh!"

"What? I'll see it all tomorrow, and if it's not ready by now, there's nothing I can do about it."

And so only Pushpa, Darpan and Hemal drove to the Big House that day. The iron gates were pushed back, and the drive newly gravelled, the beds of marigolds and chrysanthemums freshly weeded, the lawns neatly cut. The stands of eucalyptus formed a dark counterpoint for the bright gardens, and washed the air with that pervasive, unmistakable fragrance. The house itself was festooned with strings of coloured light bulbs: "Just *imagine* how it will look in the dark!" breathed Pushpa, as Darpan helped her out of the car.

After the obligatory tour, Darpan left his parents rehearsing dull details with the event manager. He walked through the gardens in search of the promised cliff-top view to the plains, but the mists had rolled in, and he saw only endless grey: a featureless panorama that invited introspection. *What is this that I am? What does it feel? And why are things like this, and not some other way? I am to marry Yogita, so why this sickness within?*

He paced on, watching his feet on the wet grass: left, left, left-right-left ... Someone else walked too, close enough to notice, far enough away to be made only a half-formed shape in the mist, a shadow of a body's shadow. And then, the echo of a whisper: *Some sins are unforgiveable ... do you agree?*

Darpan stopped. The shape that walked with him paused too; as Darpan looked at it, it half-resolved, as if drawing substance from the damp air. A large figure, pale as rice, oddly familiar – but then back to a dream of a memory. *"He will marry, yes – but he will marry a camel. Poor little Darpan."*

Humiliation after insult, year upon year.

Unforgiveable. You deserve a better life. Do you agree?

The uncountable injustices.

A better life. Do you agree?

"Yes," said Darpan. "But first I will take what I am owed in this life. No matter what the consequence, I will collect the debt."

There must be balance.

"I agree."

❖

In Yogita's bedroom, the night before the wedding proper, silence grows. With hennaed hands, she opens a compact mirror, and places it on her dressing table. From her bag, she takes a small plastic sachet. She opens it, holds it at an angle and taps at it until a scattering of dark dust is deposited on the mirror's surface. Then she turns her attention to a paper packet with an orange label: Dholakia Snuff. She adds a pinch of this to the mirror's surface. Finally she takes a nail file and, with small chopping and pushing motions, mixes the brown tobacco with the darker powder. The tool makes a cold *chink-chink* sound on the glass, and the aromatic tobacco releases its scent; but beneath it there is another odour, bitter and sad. She brushes the last brown granules from the nail file, and puts it away. Then she applies a cut-down drinking straw to the powder, presses her nostril to one end, and inhales sharply: *one, two*. Her eyes half-close, and she smiles, absorbed in the sudden clarity of sound. The drip of rain; a distant bell; a jackal; and somewhere, surely, the grinding of huge cogs, as if a great machine were drawing slowly closer.

❖

Dawn approaches; the *qaidi* with the tired face has stayed awake the whole night through. And why not? Who could sleep before such a day? He runs his hands around his throat – *under* his chin, *back* up each side of his neck, *over* his nape and *through* his hair: *good.* In the silence, he hears sounds beyond Yerawada's walls. A bell. Parakeets. The jackal's cry. Rain on a tin roof. *Oh, Mehbooba.* Memories more concrete than the bricks he leans against. *Oh, beloved.*

He waits, and wonders, and wonders: what is this little thing inside him that wonders what it is? And what transformation awaits it? Does the thread break here? Or does it join another pattern? He listens to the footsteps in the corridor. He hears them stop outside his cell. Realities elide.

❖

The backdrop to a wedding is always the muttering of relatives. Its continuity habituates the ear; one ceases to notice it. But it persists: *"Why is the sari not red? Most unusual! Most inauspicious! And why do they look so glum, the bride and groom? Such a strange wedding ..."*

Darpan exchanges garlands with Yogita; a susurration of marigolds and jasmine. Together, they intone the normal affirmation: "Let those gathered here witness, we accept each other willingly and amiably. Our hearts run together like a confluence of waters."

The families trade gifts; Yogita accepts the *mangala sutra* necklace – black beads on a turmeric-yellow thread – signifying her married status. *"Look how her shoulders droop – you'd think she'd put on a buffalo's yoke!"*

Hemal, slightly drunk, declares that Yogita has accepted Darpan, and begs Darpan's family to accept Yogita in turn. Agni, the sacred fire, is lit; a shaven-headed priest intones Sanskrit mantras; bride and groom pace around the flames. Yogita leads for the first three circuits, and Darpan, smiling weakly, leads for the final one. *"He looks terrified – a boy, not a man!"*

Darpan dips his finger into kum-kum powder (oh, the clash of a scarlet cymbal!) and marks the parting in Yogita's hair. His hand trembles. *"Look at that! He's taken too much powder. It's gone into her face."*

Yogita blinks and tries to knuckle away the irritant; her eye runs red. But nothing will stop this ceremony; this marriage made, surely, in some reality's heaven; this union dictated by twenty-seven holy stars and the colour of gold. Now, indeed, bride and groom are tied together with a knotted cord. *"He'll need more than a little string to keep that one – you wait."*

Finally, the blessings of the priest. There. It is done.

A wheel moves; another cog clicks forward in our great machine. Outside, the mist curls and threads its way through the dripping eucalyptus.

❖

Who'd have thought a wedding night could be so cold? Anger, clumsiness and shame, disgust and humiliation: this is the palette from which the marriage bed is painted. *"Look at him – poor Darpan."* But it ends, soon enough.

When Yogita comes back from the bathroom, she finds Darpan holding the Shisha sari she had worn for the wedding; the sari into which – over so many years! – he had sewn his sorrows and his soul. He is holding it to his face, half-deafened by its ochreous tones and porphyrian harmonies; he is silently weeping. And Yogita knows that her contempt for him can never be measured.

Somewhere, a jackal calls. Odd; you don't usually hear them so close.

Eight months and one week later, in December of 1974, Yogita delivers a baby. It is a fine, healthy boy, and they name him Daman.

Part III: The rope

Rope for the purpose of hanging a man by the neck until he is dead is not easily acquired. It is not sold in hardware shops or market stalls. It is made expressly for the purpose; it is different from other ropes.

In India today, there is only one source of hangman's rope – Buxar Central Jail, near Patna in Bihar. Just as Yerawada produces clothes for the country's *qaidis*, so Buxar produces the rope to hang them, if required. This rope, this special rope, is made from Manila hemp, which in fact is not hemp, but a type of banana grown in the Philippines. Manila hemp is imported by manufacturers in the Punjab, who process it into yarn, and sell the yarn to customers – including the rope-makers of Buxar jail. And the Buxar rope-makers, if asked, will use this yarn to produce hangman's rope – but only, they insist, according to unusually specific criteria.

Firstly, with regard to length, the rope must accommodate a fall that is a precise multiple of the height of the convict. Too little, and instead of having his neck broken, the *qaidi* will die painfully by slow strangulation; too much, and the *qaidi* will fall too far, and be decapitated by his own momentum. This is not a theoretical risk: the American state of Arizona adopted the gas chamber in place of hanging after Eva Dugan had her head torn from her shoulders during her 1930 execution. Other examples have occurred before and since. But rending of flesh and cartilage has never happened with Buxar ropes, for Buxar's experts know the golden ratio: between drop and arrest, the rope must allow a fall that is precisely 1.6 times the height of the condemned man. A number that itself hides among Fibonacci numbers, and which is therefore evident throughout Nature ...

Secondly, the rope must be made to a thickness sufficient to bear the convict's weight without breaking. Normally, three-quarters of an inch is sufficient, but this assumes an appropriate number of twists per inch, the standard number being three. Thus, the Buxar experts must adjust both thickness and twist according to the weight of the prisoner.

Thirdly, elasticity. The rope must have sufficient give to ensure it does not break or unnecessarily cut into flesh, but not so much that it fails to transmit the necessary force required to separate the vertebrae of the *qaidi's* neck. The key factor is hydration – a bone-dry rope is more likely to snap during the fall. The experts at Buxar claim that sixty-seven percent relative humidity during manufacture is ideal, and smugly note that Buxar's proximity to the Ganges provides them with these perfect conditions. Does the *jallad* have any complaints, they ask; is he happy with our products, the prison hangman? To which the answers are no and yes, respectively.

But finally, and most importantly, once the rope has been manufactured with due regard to length, strength, and flex, it must be treated to ensure that these carefully designed properties are preserved: to prevent the rope stretching or shrinking, to avoid it becoming brittle or dry during storage. To this end, the team at Buxar applies – each day for three days – ripe banana, butter and wax. The Manila hemp soaks up these unguents, and changes colour in the process, turning from a uniform straw colour to a deep turmeric-yellow, darkly flecked where the banana flesh has turned black. The end result is a flexible, smoothly running creation, which can be coiled and knotted without kinking or tangling, yet is not so greasy as to be unmanageable. If you pick it up, it slips easily through the hands as though eager to fulfil its destiny; and it has an odd smell, strong but not unpleasant, somewhere between a clean farm animal and a tub of ghee.

Perhaps each hanged man dies wondering, from beneath his woven black hood: "What *is* that smell?"

❖

It is 1979. Nilesh sits in his car. He is parked close to Tannery Road, that part of Bangalore the police know well but rarely visit. Here are bootleggers and gangs; hooch-drinkers and heroin addicts. And here is where Nilesh buys little sachets of powder from one he knows. But they are not for him.

The transaction complete, Nilesh resumes his journey home. The stop-start traffic, the roadworks, the mopeds and auto-rickshaws: he sees none of these. They are too familiar to note. He sees only his brother's face; and Yogita's; and understands that, somehow, realities have melded. Threads have gone awry, and become tangled, and made a bizarre, ugly pattern. He is living another's life, while another usurps his own.

At home, he goes to his bedroom. He sits on the bed, his one eye focused on nothingness. Absently, as though without volition, he picks up a pillow. Without looking at it, he presses it between his hands until his thumbs and fingers meet; and then he strangles the soft, beautiful neck he has found, crushing until his arms shudder with the effort.

❖

Padma sat on the edge of the sofa. What *was* it about Yogita and Darpan's house? Everything was comfortable, everything in perfect taste: the books and antiques, the brass and the rosewood. And yet, it never felt like a home. More like a stage, set and waiting for something to happen. She looked at Yogita, sat opposite to her, and made a smile.

"Daman has turned into such a fine-looking boy!"

"Mm-hm."

"His father must be very proud, *haan*?"

Yogita looked at her fingers; one side of her mouth pulled down. "Yes. He is."

"He will be ten soon. What shall we give him?"

Yogita shrugged. "Anything. You decide."

Padma clasped her hands together. She interlaced her fingers, released them, looked at her palms, and then put them together, fingertips upward.

"Yogita, my dear..."

Yogita raised an eyebrow.

"I did not sleep well last night, my dear. Not well at all. Your father snores so, and I had a headache."

"Mam..."

"Don't look at me that way, my dear. You know your father won't let me buy my medicine anymore. And I don't know how *you* manage, by the way."

Yogita sighed, opened her handbag, and retrieved a large leather purse. "'How' doesn't matter." She snapped open the purse catch. Without taking her eyes from Padma, she took out a number of items and placed them on the side table. Then she hunched over the table; Padma went to sit beside her.

"What a funny little penknife."

"It's Darpan's. He's going crazy looking for it. Like a child." Yogita pressed the blade into the mixture of powders, pushing the granules this way and that. The knife's edge winked in the light, and the mirror winked back.

"Well, *give* it to him."

"Of course. One day." Yogita closed the penknife, and put it back in her handbag.

"He's your husband, my dear! You should remember that."

"Husband? For the moment."

"What *do* you mean?"

Yogita raised one shoulder slightly, as if to shrug off the question. But then she said, in a lower voice: "I've had enough, Mam." She raised a hand to her throat.

"Yogita – is Darpan hurting you?"

"That weakling? What could *he* do!"

"But then what is the matter?"

Yogita hesitated. "More and more, I understand my role, Mam. And I don't like it. Because you know what it is? It's just to give myself – or rather, to be given. To accede to demands and requests. Darpan, Auntie Pushpa – others. It's like I'm currency. A greasy old rupee note, fingered by everybody."

"Yogita!"

"My life must change, Mam. Because if it doesn't, something will happen. I don't know what it will be, but I know it will be terrible."

"Yogita, listen to me. You have a good husband and a beautiful child – and family obligations. Remember that, mm? And stop this talk. Please."

Yogita sighed. "As you wish, Mam. Here." She picked up the compact mirror; two little piles of powder waited neatly on its smooth surface.

She held the mirror out to Padma in one hand, and offered her a cut-down paper drinking-straw with the other.

"Of course, my dear, if there is anything wrong between you and Darpan, you must tell me." Padma bent over the mirror, straw to nose, inhaling sharply.

"How could there be anything wrong, Mam?" Yogita's voice was dully monotone; like a young child reading a script. She took back the mirror. "As you always say, I have the perfect marriage." She took another straw from her bag.

"Just like your father and I."

For several minutes, neither spoke; Yogita at one end of the sofa and Padma at the other, both with their legs crossed – Yogita left-over-right and Padma right-over-left – both with their hair tied back, both in red and black shalwar kameez. Then – as if it were rehearsed – each turned to look at the other, as though mother and daughter were seeing each other for the first time.

❖

The *jallad* is happy to talk about his work. He has hanged more than twenty men over the last forty years. His routine is precise, his preparations exact. Once the date of the execution is fixed, he inspects the gallows. He pulls the iron lever, and perhaps he oils the lever's joint. He checks the working of the trap. He tests the strength of the scaffold, using sandbags in lieu of a man. He ensures, once again, that the drop accommodates the golden ratio of 1.6.

The day before the execution, he checks the rope – that smell! – and if he has any concerns, he will rub in more ripe banana. When he is happy with the hemp's quality, he will tie the noose. Then he coils the noosed rope neatly, and leaves it on the gallows stage.

One more thing: the hood. He folds it in four, and places it next to the rope. For some reason, he ensures that its edges align with those of the wooden platform. He does not know why he seeks such parallels; out of respect, perhaps. *We are all brothers, all slaves of fate.*

The next morning, before anyone else arrives, the *jallad* goes to the execution cell. He fixes the rope to the gallows. Then he waits.

❖

As Yogita spoke, she twisted the phone's sprung cord around her fingers. Round and round; release; and round again. Sometimes her hand left the cord to emphasise a key point, to cut at the air; but her interlocutor was blind to these elegant signals.

"It is as it is. We have to stop."

...

"Because I want to. I want to change my life."

...

"Then you should be happy for me."

...

"Yes, I know that's not what you meant. Now try to understand what I mean. I am changing *everything*. Everything."

...

"You have no idea, do you? I feel dirty, contaminated – every inch of me, inside and out. I could stand in the Ganga for a year, and I would still be unclean. You know what I did last year, when Mam and I went to Kovalam for a weekend? I went to a godman. Yes, a godman. I asked him for guidance. How can I peel off this skin, I said, this filthy skin, and start again? How can I burn the dirt from my innermost soul? What must I do? He had no real answers, or so I thought. *Sister, bathe in the river, and forgive others. Forgive everyone.* That's all he said. Forgive! How can I forgive, when my life has been stolen? And whom should I forgive? The gods? The universe? But then I thought – I, Yogita, I too am not blameless. Oh, in so many ways, I am not blameless! From my childhood to today – so many wrongs. Had I just said *No:* to my parents, to him, to you – all would be different. For all of us."

...

"What I mean is, I have to move on from my own culpability, somehow. It's weighing me down as much as any injustice. Maybe that's what the godman meant – forgive *everyone*, including oneself."

...

"Don't you understand? It's not that easy. You can't just say 'I forgive me,' and that's it, everything fixed. Forgiveness has a cost. It's a transaction. I guess the cost is different for everyone, and everyone has to set the price for themselves, and deep inside they know whether the price is fair or whether they cheat themselves. And this is the price I must pay, okay? To move on, I must change everything. I will do it as kindly and gently as I can, but *this* – you and I – this stops now."

...

"No. You have no rights over Daman. I have cared for him; you did nothing."

...

"Don't speak to me like that! You want me to tell your family? You know I would – "

...

"No! Enough, now!"

Yogita replaced the phone. One hand went to her throat, and found there her *mangala sutra*. She looked around the living room – the tasteful, co-ordinated, expensive, soulless furnishings – and then turned her face to the window; to the blue and infinite sky.

❖

Sunil paced the room. "That girl needs to be careful. She'll go too far."

"She's unhappy, Sunil. Why don't you speak to Hemal, and he can speak to Darpan?"

"Don't be ridiculous! You know what that family are like. If there is even a *suggestion* that she's thinking of leaving Darpan – " He shook his head, and threw his hands in the air. "I don't know what they'd do, but it wouldn't go well. Do you think they'd keep me on? There are at least two of Hemal's cousins who want my job."

"There are other jobs, my dear – "

"Other jobs? With Hemal's family blackening my name? You *stupid* woman! There'd be nothing for me in Bangalore. We'd have to leave. But where to? These jobs don't grow on trees! Stupid!"

"My dear – "

"Here's what we'll do. They just need some cooling off time, Darpan and Yogita, yes? Or Yogita, anyway. So we'll pay for them to have a holiday. In Ooty. I'll book that guest-house we used to stay in, when the children were young." *When everything was simple, and all were friends.*

Padma wiped at her forehead. The ceiling fan was on full, but still she was sweating. And that headache – she could hardly think. *I need some medicine. Oh, Yogita, why are you so difficult?* "It's a good idea, Sunil, but I wonder if they are quite ready for that."

"They can damn well make themselves ready. We'll look after Daman while they're gone, so no excuses."

"And how will you get the holiday home at such short notice?"

"At this time of year? Nobody is on holiday now. I'll check at work tomorrow, but I'm certain it will be free."

And indeed, both holiday homes were available, and – with Hemal's support – booking one on Darpan and Yogita's behalf was easily done, holiday consent being quickly obtained on 'health grounds.' There was some grumbling among other employees, but as always, the family did as it wished, and so the grumbling was muted.

❖

"You *will* take the sari with you, won't you, dear, and have some photos taken? Just to keep Pushpa happy?"

"I'll do it if she wants. But I don't think the photos will keep her happy for very long."

"It's a lovely idea. So romantic."

"Mm."

"Are you all right, Yogita? You seem preoccupied."

"I'm better than I have been for years, Mam."

"You don't seem very happy. We thought the idea of Ooty would cheer you up."

"Sorry, Mam. And thank you for organising a holiday for Darpan and I. It's actually very timely, because there are things he and I need to discuss. Or rather, things I need to tell him. It will be easier if we are on our own."

"It worries me when you talk like that, dear. The holiday is supposed to bring you together, remember?"

"This is my life, Mam, and from now on I shall do what I think is right, not just what keeps everyone else happy. And I know that will affect you too, Mam, and I'm sorry, but it's all for the good."

"Yogita – *please*. Remember your father's position."

"How many lives is that position worth, Mam? How many years of unhappiness?"

"But you're causing the unhappiness, Yogita!"

"If so, better I were gone. But before I go, I want to help you too,"

"What do you mean?"

"You know what I mean, Mam. The 'medicine.' It will kill us both. I have decided – after this Ooty holiday, I will have no more of it. No more sachets and straws, no more lost hours. But we can't stop on our own. So I have booked us both in to see the doctor. The day after I get back from Ooty. Okay?"

"Yogita!"

"It's happening, Mam. Change is coming. It will hurt us all, but it means new life. We don't have to just exist in others' realities; we can make our own."

❖

The *qaidi* looks at his little audience: the doctor, the magistrate, the prison superintendent, the *jallad*. Their faces make barriers: on this side life, on that side death. Only the *jallad's* eye has any warmth.

High in the wall, a small window frames the young day's sky. The dawn is hardly half an hour old: but its canvas already hints of the blue of utmost heaven. As if azure and caerulean had come together to make a colour without a name. The *qaidi* shudders with delight; and as he does so, something green flashes across the window. It is there and gone in an instant; only the *qaidi* sees it, but all hear the parakeet's diminishing call.

The *jallad* gently guides the *qaidi's* hands behind his back. As he ties them with cord, he whispers something: *"Forgive me, brother; we are all slaves of fate. Oh brother, forgive me."* And the *qaidi* starts to laugh. He laughs while the *jallad* ties together his ankles; and he laughs still while the *jallad* pulls the black hood over his head.

❖

Nilesh adjusted his eye-patch and looked around the table. All the food was gone. Beyond the empty plates, his mother and father were talking; they had forgotten he was there. Pushpa's eyes gleamed, and she waved her twisted, bony hands to emphasise one word or another.

"So I said to her, 'Darling Yogita, you *must* do this for me, you simply must.' Because it is true that she will not always be young and beautiful. And when will they be back in Ooty again? Who knows? Maybe not for years."

"Pushpa, this is supposed to be a holiday for *them*. They don't want to spend it doing things to keep *you* happy."

"Oh Hemal, they don't mind! How could they? Anyway, it *is* for them, as much as for me. Imagine what a beautiful memory it will make ..."

"What's going on? Darpan and Yogita are going to Ooty?"

Pushpa rolled her eyes. "Nilesh, do you never listen? We've been discussing this for the last thirty minutes."

"Sorry, Mam. I was concentrating on the lunch. Anyway, I thought you were talking about a sari."

"I *was*, Nilesh. That's the point."

Nilesh looked at Hemal; Hemal grinned. "Your mother has insisted that Yogita takes her wedding sari – you know the one that she started and Darpan finished – "

"Even *you* did a little of it, Nilesh, remember?"

" – takes it to Ooty, when they go there on holiday next week. Why, you may ask – "

"Why?"

"Oh Nilesh, it will be lovely!"

" – and the answer is that your mother insists that Yogita wears it out on the lake, on one of those rowboats, and has a picture taken of her doing so."

"Just like Radha, Nilesh! In *Sangam*!"

"So when are they going?"

"On Friday, dear. The day after Daman's birthday. For a whole week. Isn't that nice?"

Nilesh pushed his plate away. His usual grin had disappeared. "Bit of a funny time to have a holiday."

"I think your brother needs a little rest. He hasn't been himself recently. Not at all." Pushpa nodded firmly. "I've been quite worried."

"We think he and Yogita are having some troubles," said Hemal.

"Ah."

"Don't suppose you know anything about it?"

"Nope."

"How *could* he know anything about it, dear? You know he and Darpan never talk to each other!"

"Apparently," said Hemal, "and we don't know the details, but apparently she is being pestered by some man. He won't leave her alone."

Nilesh was very still. "Who?"

"She won't say," said Pushpa. "She won't even tell her parents. Or Darpan, I understand."

"Do we have a name?"

"She just calls him the infatuated fool. So Padma says."

"Infatuated fool," repeated Nilesh. He looked down, and was silent briefly; then raised his head again, with his normal grin. "Are you sure she's not talking about Darpan?"

Pushpa glared at her son. "Why can't you just be *nice* to each other?"

Nilesh stretched, lazily, like a cat that thinks it might be hungry. He placed his hands on the table, and looked up and to one side, as though thinking hard. "Well, Mam, since you insist, maybe I'll pop up to Ooty this weekend myself. Spend a bit of time with my brother and his lovely wife."

Pushpa and Hemal looked at each other.

"This is supposed to be for them to have some time to themselves, Nilesh," said Hemal. "That's why they're leaving Daman with us."

"I know. Don't worry, I'm actually going to stay on the golf course all day. Don't expect I'll see Darpan at all."

They stared at each other, father and son; Hemal said nothing, but Nilesh smiled. "I'll see if I can get a birdie," he said.

❖

The pedlar of destinies waits on Garden Road. The parakeet nibbles at the cage bars. Mists fall; the astrologer shivers, and pulls his coat around him. He is too old to sit outside like this, waiting for tourists. But that is his lot in life.

He shuffles the pack, mixing fates and fortunes, re-ordering joys and sorrows. Why should this person receive this card, and that one another? Why not?

❖

It is the day before Darpan and Yogita leave for their impromptu holiday in Ooty. The family gathers for Daman's tenth birthday. Uncle Nilesh, a great favourite with the boy, bends over the child to give him a present. The child accepts it with a smile, turning towards Yogita in his pleasure, and at the same time Nilesh too looks at Yogita with his one eye.

And there and then, as they both look to Yogita, man and boy – each with the same pale skin, and aquiline nose, and wolfish smile, and perfect teeth, and strong jaw – it is as though there is some kind of mirror between Nilesh and Daman: a mirror which sees Nilesh the man, eye-patch and all, but reflects Nilesh the boy, as he was on the night when Darpan was summoned by the jackal to spit on his sleeping brother's face. An instant which poisons eternity; an image which contaminates all possible futures, and which Darpan sees with agonising clarity. But Nilesh misses the revelation so apparent on Darpan's face, for he is talking to Daman again, and his eye-patch is turned towards his brother. Yogita too is intent on the boy. And so they gaze at the child, their son, adoringly, unaware that Darpan now possesses this momentous, dangerous truth.

Reflect, Darpan, reflect: are some sins unforgiveable? Do you still agree?

He knows the answer; he has always known it.

❖

Nilesh took the Friday off work to drive up to Ooty. He opted for the route through the Bandipur-Mudumalai wildlife parks, driving too fast, as though he had urgent business to complete. He only stopped once, in the foothills, just before the road contorts itself into the famous series of hairpin bends that lead to the Nilgiri peaks. Even so, it took him seven hours to reach the odd little guest-house between Ooty and Coonoor.

Once in the guest-house – while Yogita and Darpan sat silently in front of a fire in ATC's Ooty holiday home – he paced the room, his flesh rising under the cold air's touch. He pulled aside the curtains; their blue shrieked at him. One of the curtain's fastenings was awry; the hook hung untidily. Nilesh looped it into its eye, without thinking, his mind in some other reality.

Infatuated fool. Some words are unforgivable, are they not? He wiped at the skin on his cheek, and adjusted his eye-patch. Unlike modern eye-patches, which have foam padding and rounded edges designed to fit snugly to flesh, it was just a square of thick, black cloth, made from a doubled sheet of fabric, in which the warp is as black as the weft, woven in the standard over-and-under manner. It was held in place with an elasticated cord which passed around Nilesh's head, over one ear and under the other. Oddly enough, the eye-patch was made from the same cloth as the hoods for men who are to be hanged.

❖

In the holiday home, Yogita gazed into the fire. The discussion had been honest; the air was heavy with it; truth hung there like a cloying mist. Darpan had walked out afterwards; he was still gone. She opened her handbag, and took out her compact mirror and the little penknife. She would give it to Darpan when he returned, for it was time to right wrongs. And this medicine, this would be the last of it, never again; but oh, how she needed it now!

❖

It is night. The jackal wails. The mists curl. In the bathroom, he stares at the mirror. Who is this thing that stares back? He looks down at the sink. On its edge, there is a crushed paper drinking straw, stained brown at one end.

He opens the bathroom door, and goes to the sitting room. On the sofa, in front of the fire, Yogita sits, leaning to one side, as though the sofa arm had caught her slow collapse. Her bag is beside her; its contents spill over the cushions. Money; straws; a packet of snuff; a sachet of brown powder; and a little silver penknife. She sees him; she tries to sit up, but the drug is too heavy, and she falls back. Her lips move: A smile or a sneer? No matter. He grasps her neck with both hands, and pulls her from the sofa to the floor, where he sits astride her, looks into her dilated eyes and crushes her throat, forcing the black beads and turmeric-yellow cord of her *mangala sutra* necklace into her flesh.

He remains sitting on her body for a little while. Then he reaches for the little silver penknife – stolen in Ooty, eighteen years ago. *Take.* It is *right* that it is here, and right that he opens it now and uses it to saw off dead Yogita's nose and slice off her ears.

The blood slowly pools; it catches the electric light of the wall lamps, making a high scarlet harmony. He dips one finger into the singing incarnadine, and marks the parting in Yogita's hair with her own blood, red as kum-kum powder. *Oh, Mehbooba.* Finally, he goes to the bedroom and searches through Yogita's things until he finds the Shisha-embroidered sari, the glorious orchestration that Yogita had worn for the wedding. He puts it on the floor and starts cutting it into tiny, tiny pieces.

When his brother finds him, he is sitting on the floor by Yogita's body, surrounded by downy fragments of silk and innumerable little round mirrors, which he is pushing back and forth on the floor, making abstract patterns into which he gazes intently, as if seeking some deep truth in the scattered reflections.

❖

In the writhing mists, something moans. It speaks in English: *No, no: I wanted none of this.* But there are none to hear. It beats on the window with soundless fists; it weeps tears of no substance. Eventually, it moves on, head down, if head it has; a shadow of no consequence, a wish without agency.

◈

It is so good to be friends. In 1964, Yogita is eleven, and the boys are twelve. The children are being looked after by Pushpa, for Padma has gone to hunt for bargains among the fabric shops of Bangalore's Commercial Street. Pushpa is teaching the children about inauspicious and propitious times.

"Now, listen children, say after me: Mother Saw Father Wearing The Turban on Sunday. You see? Mother Saw Father Wearing The Turban on Sunday, for Monday, Saturday, Friday, Wednesday, Thursday, Tuesday, Sunday. It's easy, isn't it?"

The children repeat the mnemonic dutifully, but are somewhat bemused. The only thing that holds their attention is the delight in Pushpa's dark, bony face as she explains how to remember the inauspicious periods for the days of the week.

"So you see, children, the Rahukalam times go in that order, starting from seven-thirty in the morning, yes? And how long is each Rahukalam period?"

"Ninety minutes!" chorus the children.

"Yes! So Rahukalam is from seven thirty to nine on Monday, and from nine to ten thirty on Saturday, and so on ... Mother Saw Father Wearing The Turban on Sunday."

Nilesh makes himself an impromptu turban from the end of Pushpa's sari, before being pushed away, and Darpan and Yogita laugh to each other. Yes, it is so good to be friends.

"But listen children, there are not just the Rahukalam times to avoid, there are also the Yamagandam times. These are *very* inauspicious. I will tell you how to remember these times another day."

"What time are we leaving for Ooty, Auntie Pushpa?"

"Good question, Yogita. We are leaving at seven thirty a.m., which is auspicious for Saturday."

"If we are coming back on a Wednesday, what then?"

"For starting a journey on a Wednesday, Nilesh, the propitious time will be between ten thirty and twelve."

"And if we leave at seven thirty a.m. on Wednesday?"

Pushpa's dark face grows serious, and she clucks with her tongue like a worried hen.

"Tsk, tsk, no Darpan, that is very bad. Seven thirty on Wednesday morning, this is Yamagandam. This would be very bad, very unlucky."

And she shivers with distaste, and goes back to her silks and Shisha mirrors.

❖

In 2004, *Veer-Zaara* is released. Like *Sangam*, this film deals with the eternal triangle; like *Sangam*, it has a strong vein of tragedy; and, like *Sangam*, one of the main characters is in the Indian Air Force. This character is incarcerated in a prison cell, and much of the film comprises flashbacks from his cell, where he languishes, a *qaidi* with a tired face.

In Bangalore, there is a late-night showing of *Veer-Zaara* at one of the cinemas close to Commercial Street. It is barely a hundred yards away from the place where in 1974 Padma was shopping for saris when Nilesh was impregnating Yogita; when Hemal and Sunil were enjoying a long lunch at the Bangalore Club; and when Darpan was diligently learning about Small Porcupines and Mules. Tonight, a tired man is in the cinema audience, for to stay at home this night, the night before the hanging, is unbearable. As the on-screen story unfolds, he follows it with an eye which glistens a little more than is explicable by the make-believe sorrows of cinema. Indeed, a stray tear rolls down his face, catching the light reflected from the screen, and winking at whoever should see. But nobody sees.

❖

The *qaidi*'s hanging is scheduled for seven thirty a.m. on a Wednesday morning, in June of 2004. They make him take his shoes off outside the execution cell: he had been weighed without shoes when they took the measurements demanded by the Buxar rope manufacturers, therefore he must hang without shoes. Such are the regulations. His bare feet recognise the rough coir matting, and he pushes a tongueful of saliva forward to moisten his dry lips. He feels the black cloth of the hood, with its over-and-under weave, as they put it over his head. He hears the *jallad*'s well-meant prayer, and laughs at fate's mocking smile. *Oh brother, forgive me!* And as a black-flecked length of turmeric-yellow rope is slipped around his neck, his very own *mangala sutra*, his Vasuki the snake, he cannot but wonder: *What is that smell?*

❖

The *qaidi*'s brother is at the family home, sitting with an old, old woman. She is dark and tiny, and her hands are crippled by arthritis. Her son holds them, and tries to warm them, but it is like trying to animate the knuckled wood of a pair of dead sapling stumps. Her eyes are dark and empty, as black as the patch that bisects Nilesh's face with its dark diagonal.

"*Yamagandam ...*" she whispers, as the clock on the wall moves to seven thirty. And at that precise moment the *jallad* pulls a lever to send Darpan on his last journey, and the silk-smooth, odd-smelling rope snaps his jaw back after a drop of exactly 1.6 times his height. His bare feet twitch, toes wriggling as though in delicate ecstasy, as though he had just heard a remote, golden bell.

In the tamarind trees outside Yerawada's grey walls, the rose-ringed parakeets squabble and laugh over the dropping fruit. And in the house, Nilesh weeps, for without Darpan, how can he tell who and what he is?

❖

In 2005, one year after Darpan is hanged, a famous Bollywood actress is in Ooty. She has come to participate in the making of a film, and is now walking down Garden Road with the slow, self-conscious tread of those who wish to be watched. To ensure that she *is* watched, she is wearing a splendid Shisha sari, recently purchased at enormous cost from a very fashionable Mumbai boutique. The sari's margin is embroidered with groups of little green birds, bill to tail, three in each group; and in the hem of the sari is a little label bearing the letters YK.

She stops in front of an old man sitting at a fold-up table. A man who shuffles and flips dog-eared destinies in his clumsy old hands; a man who sees the future and the past through thumb-thick, plastic-framed lenses. A parrot astrologer – how quaint! You hardly ever see them anymore.

"Twenty rupees for your fortune, *behen* ..."

The opportunity is too good to miss; the photos taken by adoring fans and paparazzi can only be good publicity. The fortune-teller clears his throat, and squints at her through the thick glasses that he never liked. Mist curls.

"Your fortune, *behen* ..."

Warp and weft, o ye little people. Warp and weft.

THE EXCHANGE

"An original seed source in Nandi resulted in the Mysore Hybrid, the most widely planted eucalypt in India (about 500,000 ha., or 1.2 million acres)."
- The Eucalyptus: A Natural and Commercial History of the Gum Tree, Robin Doughty, 2000

There's no such thing as cold flesh on the seared plains of South India; there, even the dead are warm. But you still need fire, and fire needs fuel; and as Mother had used up all our fuel the previous day, naturally I had to go and get some more.

"I'm hungry," I'd said as Mother shooed me out the door that morning.

"You'll eat tonight. Hurry now, before the fire goes out."

Eat tonight? Only if there were still food left after Krishnamurthy's visit. Handful after handful of rice had disappeared into his mouth, last night; and as though to make room, out came words and more words, as he talked through the evening. Outside, his new motorbike had gleamed in the dark, like an armoured messenger from a future world.

"How can he eat so much?" I'd whispered to my mother.

"Ooty is miles away. He's been travelling all day. So he's hungry."

My father always said that Krishnamurthy's family was cursed, but I never could see why. Cursed, to live in Ooty, up among the peaks and clouds, where money falls from the sky? True, six of Krish's seven older siblings were girls, which was bad luck, but they're all married off now. His younger brother, who would have been my age, died four years ago, and that's bad too, but it happens. But his older brother Venkataraman made eucalyptus oil at his own distillery; a real businessman! And Krishnamurthy himself was luckier still, sitting in his shop, protected from sun and rain, selling pretty things to tourists. *Call me Krish, like the tourists do.* They had money, that family; they ate well; and, above all, Venky was married, and Cousin Krish surely would be soon.

"If only *we* were cursed."

"Don't say such things! Go now!"

So off I went to collect the cowdung that we'd patted into little cakes and left to dry on the sun-scorched rocks overlooking our village. Village, I say; but it's no more than a collection of huts jumbled together at the foot of a stony hill. Hill, I say! It's no more than a mound of rock and cactus. When I was younger, my mother told me that this stony lump, this province of scorpions, was the start of the Nilgiris, those great mountains which marched perpetually on my childhood's horizon, blue and remote. But now I'm older, I know that's nonsense.

I peeled off yesterday's crop of dung-cakes – now crisp and light – and piled them onto the square of grubby cotton that I'd brought with me; I twisted the cloth corners together and slung the sack over my back, while my stomach gnawed at itself. Whenever Cousin Krish visits, we go hungry the next day.

When I got back to the hut, Krishnamurthy and my father were squatting outside, drinking tea, their shadows lengthened and deformed by the rising sun. They watched me as I went inside.

"He's sixteen now," I heard my father say. "He'll do. And he'll work hard."

I put the cowdung fuel-cakes on the ground next to the chulha stove, narrowing my eyes against the stinging smoke. As usual, Mother knew what I was going to ask before I did.

"It's agreed," she said. "It's an exchange. It's business." She wrapped the end of her sari around her mouth and nose, poked cloying smoke from the fire, and wiped at her eyes. But she wouldn't look at me.

And that's how I found out I was leaving home to work for Cousin Krish.

❖

I knew what was going on. Part of it was Krish getting help, but only part. Part of it was economics; if I was in Ooty, there'd be one less to feed at home. And Krish would send my wages to Father, of course. But there were deeper currents still; I had felt them pulling at me for at least a year. There, always unspoken, but weighing heavier each passing month: the question of *marriage*.

There are no girls in our hamlet, none; we can't afford such walking, eating, dowry-debts. But those who can afford them – in the other villages where the ground is less dry and stony, where the soil can bear paddy fields and papaya trees and groves of toddy palms – they can keep their baby girls. And later they can marry the girls to whoever they please, for there are so few of them. But none would give their daughter to the son of a subsistence farmer; that was clear. Nobody wants to see a dowry handed to one who has no money of his own. We never spoke of this directly; it was always spoken *around*, as though a solution could arise from the silence between words. Unusual, then, that the issue had raised its head the previous evening, when Cousin Krish had moved the conversation from how well Krish was doing to how well his brother Venky was doing.

"But Venkataraman has two daughters to marry off," said my father. He flicked his fingers at the air, as though to dismiss the fiction that Cousin Venky was fortunate; as though to remind us all of the curse.

"All in good time," said Krish, smirking. "Arrangements will be made. But speaking of arrangements, maybe now is a good time to talk ..." He glanced towards me.

"You, Yajan," said Father, nodding in my direction. "The motorbike will be cool enough to clean, now." It was too dark to do anything outside, but nobody argues with Father, so I went around the back, to where Krish had parked his machine under the thatched lean-to. The bright chrome; the black rubber! Such an other-wordly mount: it was as if the *hamsa*, that magical bird ridden by Brahma, had alighted by our little hut. I stroked its smooth contours, and gripped its handlebars. I sat astride it, and looked to the horizon; above the Nilgiris a blue star gleamed, and I felt the pull of destiny. *One day, I will be happy.*

When I came back, the house was heavy with silence. Krish smiled at me; the fire billowed smoke; my father wafted his hand at a mosquito.

Yes, I'd wondered at the time what was going on. And now I knew.

❖

It only took me a night to come to terms with the arrangement. After all, it answered so many questions; with a job in Krish's shop, I would no longer be just a farmer's son – I would be *eligible*. It could solve both my problem and Cousin Venky's problems; or one of his two problems, at least. That had to be why I was being sent up there; it had to be. So I welcomed the idea of leaving home for cold Ooty, high up in the Nilgiris. Anyway, who wouldn't want to visit the most famous of all hill stations, atop the greatest of our southern mountains?

"Full of tourists," said Mother, squatting by the chulha, making a little dung-cake pyramid. Through the window, I could see Krish and my father tying Krish's bag to the back of his shiny motorbike. The machine winked at me in the morning sun. "And film stars. They throw money away. All you need to do is pick it up."

"What are their names again?"

"Who?"

"Venkataraman's daughters."

Mother hesitated; I couldn't see her face.

"Lakshmi and Nalini. But listen ..."

"Mm?"

She hesitated again, looking back to the open doorway. The men's shadows stretched across the pale dust outside, grotesquely mimicking their lazy gestures as they talked. She looked back down to the stove, and lowered her voice.

"Just keep yourself to yourself. That family – they're ..."

"Cursed?"

"They deserve it! They're remorseless – remorseless! Their younger brother – "

Her fists were clenched; she knuckled at an eye, and then took a step towards me and gave me a hug. She hardly ever does that. "Don't do anything foolish, Yajan. Alright?"

"Alright."

Half an hour later, we squeezed onto the back of Krishnamurthy's motorbike, Krishnamurthy and I and Krishnamurthy's bag; my father was at the front. I'd never seen him drive a motorbike before.

"Why are you driving, *Appa*?"

"Mind your own business."

"Are you driving us all the way to Ooty?"

"Just to Mettupalayam."

Well, that was far enough; Mettupalayam is in the lower reaches of the Nilgiris. So I had to jam myself against my bony cousin all the way from our village to this town in the foothills. But with each brief stop, the Nilgiris were bluer and bigger and more full of promise. *I will get married up there,* I told myself, looking at eight thousand feet of azure; *I will get married to a beautiful girl, and we will live in the mountains, next to the clouds, where tourists throw money in the air, catch it who can.*

I will be happy.

At Mettupalayam, my father dropped us at the bus terminus. He didn't even stop the engine. As soon as Krish had got his bag, my father just turned the motorbike around, crossed to the other side of the road and set off back, swallowed up instantly by gaudy lorries and dusty cars. I couldn't believe my eyes.

"He's keeping the motorbike?"

"It's a gift. Come," said Krishnamurthy, walking off without looking at me. I scampered after him, clutching my own tiny bag of possessions, and before long we'd squeezed our way onto the Ooty bus.

Krishnamurthy found a seat near the front; I stood while the bus wound its way through the foothills and then up the mountains, hairpin bend after hairpin bend. The continuous, swaying turns of the bus, and the all-pervasive diesel exhaust, sickened me, but I held back the nausea. And after a while, as we climbed higher and higher, behind the stink of straining engines and men's sweat I detected something purer and sweeter. Not just the cooler air of Coonoor and Ketti, but something else, something cleansing and invigorating.

That was the first time I smelt eucalyptus; and nothing now can remove the magic of that first scent, not even the knowledge of what stenches it may cover.

❖

When we finally arrived in Ooty, my legs trembled from the effort of keeping balance for hours. But I was so excited, I hardly noticed that; it was all so foreign. The bus stand was just by Ooty Lake; I'd never seen so much water; never. And I'd never felt so cold; intermittent mists slid damply over Ooty's puddled streets and chilled my core.

"Walk faster," said Krishnamurthy, who'd put on a jumper. "Exercise will warm you."

But I couldn't walk faster than him, as I didn't know where I was going. He strolled casually along, pointing out the main features of the town as though he owned them or were somehow responsible for their construction.

"The racecourse. The bazaar. Garden Road."

So many shops! And just as everyone had always told me, there were tourists everywhere: Westerners; Chinese; Bombayites looking like film stars. Maybe they *were* from Bollywood. I swear, I could almost smell the money.

"The cinema; many good films. Paramasivan, the fortune-teller." Cousin Krish nodded to an old man with thick glasses, sitting at a fold-up table set back from the pavement. On the table, a caged parakeet fluffed up its feathers against the cold. Paramasivan nodded back at us, squinting at me curiously.

"The exchange?" he asked.

"My cousin," said Krishnamurthy. We walked on, while Paramasivan shuffled and flipped his cards, waiting for customers. When we crossed the road several yards later, I glanced back; the old man was still looking at me.

"Government Gardens," said Krish, nodding towards glimpses of neat lawns and bright flower-beds. "Up there, the international school. Here, Commercial Road."

I wondered which of the enormous shops that lined Commercial Road was Krishnamurthy's. I wondered how long it would be before I became his trusted lieutenant, running the business in his absence, an indispensable creator of profit; how long before Venky *begged* me to marry one of his daughters.

But we turned off Commercial Road, and followed little side streets; the roads became narrower and more pot-holed, the buildings smaller and dirtier; well-fed tourists were replaced by stray dogs and men with lined faces.

"Mukurti Street."

That was the first time I saw the Englishman. He was sitting on a plastic chair outside Mopuvan's Cafe, on the opposite side of the street. Mopuvan had to put his two chairs on the pavement, because there wasn't room inside for anything more than the wooden counter piled with idlis and sambar and sweets and hot peanuts. At the Englishman's elbow, a metal cup steamed gently on the table between the two chairs; in his fleshy hand, he gripped a small cone of newspaper, from which he took peanuts, one by one. He was breaking up the nuts between finger and thumb, and carefully flicking the fragments to a gaggle of sparrows at his feet. Shockingly wasteful! My stomach briefly turned on itself again. But I forgot my hunger for a second, he looked so odd: a huge, bloated creature, all white and sagging; a man of fallen flesh from which the blood had been washed by age. As he sat there, neck muffled against the cold with a white scarf, he turned his bald head from side to side, surveying Mukurti Street. Like a giant maggot in old meat. He saw me looking at him, and held out one great hand, palm upward; whether to offer something or ask for it, I could not tell. I shivered.

"Come," said Krishnamurthy. I followed him a little way down the street. "Here."

He'd stopped before a one storey building. It had once been painted bright yellow; now, like the other buildings on the street, its paint was faded and stained, and the lower surfaces of its walls were stippled with the black dirt thrown up by heavy Ooty rains. The right-hand side of the building was a closed shop-front, with a sign above: 'Krishnamurthy Trading,' in red Tamil script on a white background. To the left, a door; left of that, a high, small window. Krish unlocked the door, and we entered.

We were in a concrete-floored room lit by a single bulb. In the corner, a charpoy with disarrayed blankets; next to that, a small stove and a pile of wood and kindling, among which I could see the elegant points of eucalyptus leaves. On the other side of the room were cardboard boxes filled with oddments and oddities: pieces of worked wood and raw timber, knobs and bosses of brass, small mirrors, tins of polish, jars of screws and nails, pieces of broken furniture.

"You sleep there," Krishnamurthy said, pointing to the heaped collection of junk.

I looked again. What I'd taken to be a group of planks leaning against the wall was a door held awry by a single hinge. I pushed it open, making it scrape and judder over the floor, and looked inside. A high window, too small for even a child to squeeze through. Dark walls, stained floor. A charpoy. No blankets. No stove.

"It will be cold, Cousin." I was shivering uncontrollably now. He looked at me, eyebrows raised, as though I was some kind of idiot.

"What, you've brought no blankets? No warm clothes?"

As if we needed any of that on the searing plains. As if my tiny bag, which he'd seen me carrying all the way from home to here, could have contained any of that. He pulled a plastic suitcase from under his charpoy, and took out an old blanket and a scarf.

"Here. But this will come out of the money that I am sending your father."

Later, wrapped in the old wool, and filled with the dahl that Cousin Krish had heated on the stove, I was warm enough – just – to fall asleep. Not warm enough, however, to sleep beyond the very early hours. But it wasn't so bad: my hope blanketed me that first morning, and fired me with optimism. I revelled in the strangeness of my new situation – the cold air, the far-off, lonely note of a jackal, the sound of Krish snoring in the next room. I thought of Lakshmi and Nalini, and wondered if they were pretty, while a grey dawn grew in the window. Odd thing: as I lay there, I heard the sound of shuffling steps in the street, and of murmuring voices. A man's voice; gently, softly pitched, as though comforting a child or a lover, passing my window. *He's here,* it said. *He's here.* It was too cold to get out of bed, but I got no more sleep.

❖

Mukurti Street was a world away from the upmarket shops and cafés of tourist Ooty; it was a world to itself, with its own characters and community. I saw the same clutch of people every day, and within a fortnight I knew several by name: Paramasivan the parrot astrologer, stumping along with his caged bird and his little fold-up table and chair, on his way to tell the future for the tourists of Garden Road; Cheliyan, the one-eyed goldsmith, squatting on the ground, his mouth applied to a thin pipe through which he blew into a tiny clay smithy until the embers glowed white; gloomy Yalamudhan, the embalmer, with his bistouries and brass pumps, his clamps and cottons and trocars and oils, making his living from dying; Mopuvan, the street-food chef, grinning at his trays of syrupy sweets and spicy pakoras. And every day, pretty much, the same noises: first, outside my window in the early morning, the soft murmuring and the shuffling footsteps; later, Cheliyan's son Harikumar chivvying along his idiot brother on their way to school; the rasping of crows, the squabbles of pi-dogs; sometimes, distant bells from a church, sounding out the Christians' version of death and rebirth; and occasionally, Mopuvan's wife shouting that he'll go the same way as Venkataraman, if he's not careful, look at poor Venky's mother, one son gone and who's next, and if nothing changes she'll douse herself in kerosene and burn in front of him, you wait and see! I soon learnt that she often made such threats; but Mopuvan just smiles and waggles his head and leaves another cone of peanuts on the table next to the Englishman. He does this without looking at his client, as though the peanuts were placed there by way of decoration only, and if someone picks them up and eats them, why, what business is that of Mopuvan's?

Yes, Mukurti Street: litter and puddles and dogs; one giant step from Commercial Road, and one small step from a slum. Not the kind of place where you'd expect the rich to come and throw their money around. But somehow Krishnamurthy made it work to his advantage.

"Think about it," he said. "All the antique stores on Commercial Road – the ones selling *real* antiques – they're doing their best to look like Western shops, Bombay shops. But why do you think tourists come to Ooty? To see the same shops as they see at home?"

"No?"

"No. Bombayites maybe, but foreigners want the 'real India.' So they make an effort, they walk around a bit, they go down little old Mukurti Street, and there they find Krishnamurthy Trading – no glitz, no hullabaloo, a picture of Ganesh on the wall – so then they think they've found the real India, don't they? So we keep the prices lower than Commercial Road, and they believe they've got a bargain, don't they? Everybody's happy. Shut up now."

A clutch of tourists had come into the shop, and Krish scented profit. He went through his usual act: ignore them until they actually say something; act all surprised to find such a thing as a customer in a shop, of all places; feign reluctance to sell anything. I didn't understand the words Krish used – he spoke in English – but I knew what he was saying. *Very old pieces. Very fine. Maybe two hundred years. See, ivory inlay. But I am only selling to shops in Bombay. Business to business only.* This never failed to make them desperate to buy. Soon he'd sold two jewellery boxes to a European woman with tattoos and a ring through her septum.

"Do you think she knows what she looks like?" I asked, as she counted out money with red-freckled fingers.

"Shut up, Yajan."

"Why? She doesn't understand Tamil. None of them do."

"All customers are beautiful, no matter how ugly. Remember that."

We went to the door of the shop to watch the tourists meander away down Mukurti Street.

"And anyway, some of them *do* speak Tamil. The older ones. Like him." Krish nodded at the great, bloodless creature across the street, with his peanuts and his sparrows.

"Who *is* he?"

"The Englishman. Damn him!"

The anger in Krish's voice surprised me. "Why? What's he done?"

Krish picked up a piece of wood and started sanding it. "Done? He hasn't done anything. It's what he makes others do." He blew dust from the wood, and wiped it with his palm. "Once he latches on to you, he just won't let go. Drives people crazy."

"What do you mean?"

"Never mind. Forget it. Give this a polish, will you?"

That night, or soon after, the dream first came. I thought I'd woken, and saw the door to my room ajar. I got up to close it; I couldn't bear to sleep next to that black opening. But as I pushed it shut, something resisted. Something was on the other side, pushing back. I braced my legs, I set my shoulder to the planks, I strained every muscle; but I was forced back, back, by an unimaginable momentum. And then the darkness came in.

That woke me up, of course. I huddled the blanket to me, guarding the little warmth I had, and – inevitably – listened to the shuffling and murmuring outside. *He's here.*

❖

I soon understood Cousin Krish's business. He made antiques. Sure, sometimes he traded real antiques – old brass pots, perhaps, swindled from the plains villagers on one of his parasitic visits – but mostly he made his own. He was skilful. He'd get off-cuts of eucalyptus wood from the sawmill; he'd sand them down and stain them up like rosewood, these scraps of planking; then he'd nail them together and put brass or copper bands on the corners, or iron bosses on the panels; and suddenly there was an antique box worth eight hundred rupees. For a cut of the sale price, one-eyed Cheliyan sometimes helped Krish with the metalwork, melting down copper wiring from stolen electrical cables and hammering it into decorative lock-plates or delicate filigrees. The amount of care that went into those pieces – they were worth as much as any antique, and that's the truth.

But after working for Cousin Krish a whole month, I still hadn't met Cousin Venky, or his daughters. Two girls, not yet married; I couldn't help being curious. Especially now that I was working in a *shop*, not a paddy field, as eligible as a god. Anyway, wasn't I here to find a wife? Wasn't that part of the point?

"Why aren't you married, Krish?"

"Not the right time. Too busy."

"Are Cousin Venky's girls pretty?"

"What's it to you?"

"Well …"

"The real question is, will Venkataraman and I get ugly if you go Eve-teasing his daughters. Behave."

A little later, I tried again. "Krish, I haven't seen Cousin Venky since I was very young. Shouldn't I go and meet him?"

He gave me a sharp look, before returning to dig at a resinous knot in a thin panel of wood.

"Yes. At the right time."

"When *is* the right time to visit Venkataraman?"

But before Krish could answer, we were interrupted.

"Venkataraman?" enquired a hoarse voice from the shop door. It was Yalamudhan, the embalmer. He swallowed, painfully, his face contorted into a rictus of greeting. People said that the corpse-chaser's throat had been eroded by the astringent chemicals he inhaled while hunched over his lifeless clients, as he hollowed them out and drained them for their loving families. But I couldn't imagine him sounding any other way; that voice was made for that fallen, pitted face.

"You are visiting Venkataraman? I've just come from him."

Something must have shown in my face; Krish glanced at me, and then laughed.

"Don't worry, Yajan – Venky is still with us! Yalamudhan is *his* client. Not the other way around. Right, Yalamudhan?"

"For the moment," said Yalamudhan.

"The only people who profit from death," said Krish. "Yalamudhan and my brother Venky."

"No," said Yalamudhan, seriously. "Not the *only* people, Krishnamurthy. As you know." He looked at me closely, up and down, as though wondering how I'd brush up once dead. Then he turned to Krish. He cleared his throat, grimacing with discomfort. "In fact, Venkataraman has a message," he announced. "The exchange is overdue, he says, and -"

But Krish leapt up from the mat where we were polishing brasses and shooed Yalamudhan out of the shop, talking in a low, urgent voice. He came back after a couple of minutes; but something about the glint in his eye and the set of his jaw made me reluctant to ask what Yalamudhan had meant. I continued polishing old brass in silence for a while.

"I don't understand," I said, after I guessed it safe to speak. "I can see how deaths are good for an embalmer's business. But what's in it for Venky?"

Krish snorted. "Are you kidding? Have you any idea how much eucalyptus oil it takes to stop a corpse from smelling? To keep the dead skin looking soft and plump?" He gathered together the gleaming brass bosses and plaques and dropped them into their box. "A lot. Trust me. An awful lot. Yalamudhan doesn't need oil very often, but when he does need it, he makes a big order. And that makes Venky happy." He got up; the metals clinked in their box. "And *that*, believe me, you don't see very often."

"So, Krish?"

"What?"

"When *is* the right time to visit Venkataraman?"

But Krish wouldn't commit himself.

The next Saturday, however, I saw them. Venky's daughters had come to the bazaar to buy vegetables, and stopped off at the shop to give Krish a message. Nalini was about twelve, and Lakshmi the same age as me. Nalini was pretty, but Lakshmi was utterly beautiful. The face of a goddess, gifted with skin from heaven. If she noticed me, she didn't show it. Her younger sister goggled at me as though I were a talking monkey, but Lakshmi saved all her words for Krish.

"Uncle Krish, Father asked us to tell you that he is wondering how things are going."

"It's all under control."

"Father is getting angry. He is shouting a lot. He says you don't tell him anything."

"He knows where I am."

"Father is very busy with the distillery."

"I am very busy with my shop."

She caught me staring – I just couldn't help it – and looked away, clasping her bag of shopping in front of her like a shield.

"Uncle Krish ... Mother is angry too." She sounded like she was about to cry; and it was all I could do not to jump up and hug her and tell her I'd protect her from anything, anything.

"Okay! Okay!" Krish took a deep breath. He put down the brass pot he was polishing, and briefly closed his eyes. "Okay," he said again. "Tell him that I've done my part. It's cost me a lot. Don't I walk everywhere now? From now on it's up to him to move things along. Okay?" He turned to me; his face closed, angry. "Actually, Yajan, *you* tell him. The girls will take you to meet your Cousin Venky. It's the right time. Go now, and tell him I say he has to arrange the business himself. Okay?"

The girls looked at me; Nalini all big-eyed, Lakshmi expressionless. Or almost expressionless; I swear I saw a smile, suppressed as soon as it appeared. My heart jumped.

"Now!" snapped Krish. I wondered why he was annoyed.

We walked off down Mukurti Street, the girls walking a few paces behind me and whispering to each other. We passed Mopuvan's, and the Englishman held out his hand to me, while the sparrows squabbled at his feet. I cringed with embarrassment; I thought I heard Lakshmi giggle, but couldn't be sure. I glanced back towards the cafe, and caught a glimpse of Mopuvan inside. He grinned and nodded his head, and mouthed something at me.

The girls called out directions as we climbed out of Ooty, going up the dirt tracks that led off into the mountains. Left, they would shout; right! No, that way! And then they'd whisper to each other. They wouldn't talk to me or answer my questions, but I didn't mind. I was in love.

The track climbed steeply; and after half an hour, we'd left Ooty far below. I could see the lake spread out, and tourist pedal-boats going in little circles; there the botanical gardens, and there the bus station. It was quiet up here, and peaceful; a breeze took the scent from the eucalyptus leaves and spread it around me and over me and, surely, over the two girls walking behind.

Yes, the smell of eucalyptus is forever associated with love, for me.

"There," said Lakshmi. I thought I heard a smile in her voice; and when I turned, she was pointing across a small stream to a clearing; to a house-sized mound of dead eucalyptus leaves and branches, in which I saw a doorway-sized opening. Steam, or smoke, was percolating through the top of this mound. A eucalyptus oil distillery.

"Father's inside," she said. "Father! It's the one that Uncle Krish brought from the plains!"

A man appeared at the distillery doorway. He was wearing a pale long-sleeved shirt and a dhoti; on his head, a length of grey cloth wrapped into a simple turban. I could see some resemblance between him and Krish; but he looked bigger and stronger; also older, more tired and care-worn. A man who didn't sleep much. He looked me up and down as we approached.

"Come," he said. My smile went unanswered. "Come inside."

The girls continued up the path, giggling, and I followed Venky through the smoky entrance. It was gloomy within; what light there was came from the two open entrances, one at each end of the distillery, and from the flames and glowing embers beneath a large aluminium drum. This drum, large enough to accommodate four grown men squatting down, was the still. From its conical lid, a pipe rose vertically and then kinked downwards, leading into a smaller drum, full of water, set in a pit.

Venky disconnected the pipe and took the lid off the still, raising clouds of steam which caught in my throat. He poked a stick into the drum, tamping down a mass of leaves darkened by heat and gleaming with moisture, before adding armfuls of fresh green eucalyptus fronds from a pile on the floor. Then he secured the drum lid and reconnected the pipe at its apex. At no point did his eyes leave me; cold, black embers, they locked on to me while the steam rose and swirled around him, rising from his clothes and head as though he himself were being subsumed into the distillation, as though his own essential oils were being released by a hidden furnace.

"Seen this before?"

"No."

"You heat up the eucalyptus leaves in the drum. Steam them. There's water in the bottom. The steam evaporates the oil and takes it out through the pipe at the top. The oil turns back into liquid as it cools, where the pipe is submerged in water. Here."

He jumped down into the pit, took a battered jug, and carefully drew off the top layer of liquid from the smaller drum.

"The oil rises to the top. You draw it off – so. And then you bottle it."

He reached behind him, and took a small, clean bottle from a box. He carefully decanted oil from the jug into the bottle. Then he replaced the jug, picked up a metal screw-top, and climbed out of the pit to stand next to me. I noticed how strong he looked: middle-aged, but unbreakable. He closed the bottle tight, and handed it to me.

"Eucalyptus oil. The finest. Cures all kinds of problems. Problems you might never imagine. It preserves you."

A little oil had dripped down the side of the bottle; it soaked into my fingers, feeling cool and clean. I raised it to my face. That scent!

"It preserves you," repeated Venkataraman.

"Very good." I said. I wasn't sure what else to say. I held the bottle up, so that it was framed against the light of the doorway. The liquid was pale yellow; a thin, light oil, not the viscous kind that flows slowly. It looked like straw-coloured water. "Very good." I tried to hand it back, but Venky shook his head emphatically.

"No. Keep it. You'll need it, one day. And there's plenty of it." He gestured vaguely at the still, at the wooden struts of the walls holding back years of spent eucalyptus leaves. "Plenty."

I passed the bottle from hand to hand, awkwardly; it might stain if I put it in my pocket. But I was grateful for it; and even Venky seemed to soften as he saw me smiling.

"So how are things with my lazy brother?"

"Oh – I almost forgot. He says it's up to you to move things along. He asks that you arrange the business yourself." I said this casually, as though I knew what was going on. Venky's eyes hardened again; the still's fire spat and hissed, but the temperature had dropped.

"*Did* he?" His voice was soft, menacing. "Well then. How should I do that?" I didn't know what to say; I just stood there while he stared me down. I found myself thinking: *He's seen some things, this man; and I hope I never see them too.* The silence grew while Venky's hard eyes burned into me like black ice; I looked around the distillery, hoping to find something to comment on, to break a growing tension that I just did not understand. Jugs and old rags hung from the unmade struts that held back the dead leaves; and the dead leaves, each covered with a soft, years-old layer of fine white ash from the distillery fire, poked their points between the struts. Like the talons of a devil, straining to catch lost souls. A floor of beaten earth; an empty newspaper cone, trodden flat. And in one corner, two charpoys, side by side, with neatly folded blankets. Someone sleeps *here?* I thought; but I said nothing.

"Why have you come here?" asked Venky, making me jump.

"I wanted to greet you ... my father sends his regards ..."

"No. I mean, why have you come to Ooty at all?"

"To work for Cousin Krish. There is an agreement."

"The exchange?"

"I suppose so."

"You know about this?"

"Yes. I work for Krish, Krish feeds me and gives me a bed. And sends money to my father."

"Ah! And what's in it for you? Apart from eating and sleeping?"

"Well ..." I squirmed a little. "I'm learning the business. I'm learning how to make money. From tourists."

Venky said nothing. He was very close.

"And there's nothing at home ... it's hard."

Those hard, cold eyes. What could they have seen, to be so dark?

"Our neighbour's son, at home – he's ten years older than me – and he's never married! Never!"

I could no longer look at Venky. I focused on his feet in their battered black sandals; on his toes dusted with grey cinders. But when he spoke, his voice was soft; something about the tone seemed familiar.

"Listen. To get married, you'll need money. And to make real money in Ooty, you need a bit of English. To feed off the tourists. With English, you can work anywhere in the town: the shops, the cafes, the hotels, anywhere. Understand?"

I nodded.

"There's an old man, an Englishman," Venky continued. "In Mopuvan's shop. You've seen him?"

"Yes."

"Ask him to teach you. Make an agreement with him. You help him, he'll help you. Understand?"

"An exchange?"

"Exactly."

I could look at Venky now; he had a small, grim smile. But his eyes were black stones.

❖

That night, the dream came again; only, something had changed. The door was ajar, as before, and when I tried to push it shut, I was pushed back, as before, and as before, the darkness came in, blacker than the night; but now something stirred behind the darkness, something as pale as a snake's belly. It came forward slowly; like a dead fish rising to a river's surface, buoyed by its own gases. And as it came, it murmured to me.

I woke to hear low voices outside my window again. This time, curiosity got the better of my cold flesh, and I slid off the charpoy, still wrapped in my blanket, and walked over to the wall. I stood on tiptoes and peered over the sill of the window.

It was just getting light; across the road, I could just make out the sign that said '*Mopuvan's Cafe. Chai. All sweets made with real ghee.*' Two figures, their backs to me, were walking across the road. One turned back briefly, as though he felt my gaze; it was Cousin Venky. He was walking with the Englishman; he had one arm around the Englishman's waist, and the other under one of the Englishman's arms, supporting the old man as he waddled and heaved up the steps to Mopuvan's. Venky held the chair while the old man squeezed himself into it, and then bent low and said something into the pale thing's ear. The Englishman nodded; up and down went his big old head, up and down, but slowly, majestically, as though he had just understood an eternal truth. Venky turned and left at a brisk walk.

The Englishman couldn't see me, in my dark room, peering out over the sill; I was sure of that. But he stared in my direction, motionless. It was unnerving; as though I were the focus of some strange attention, for some incomprehensible reason. I went back to the charpoy, and huddled myself down, knees to my chest. Later, when I got up and looked out of the window again, Mopuvan had opened up his cafe, and the Englishman was cradling a tea and a paper cone of hot peanuts.

❖

"Krish?"

"What? Look, if you put this kind of handle on, you need this kind of lock. You see? Otherwise they don't match."

"Yes, okay. But Krish?"

"What?"

"What is it between Venky and the Englishman?"

"What do you mean?"

"I saw them together. In the early morning. Venkataraman helped him into his chair outside Mopuvan's."

Krish's head was bent low over the newest antique, adding a lock to its lid. He adjusted the position of the decorative lock-plate – another small masterpiece from Cheliyan – moving it by minute fractions of a degree, and then started carefully twisting down the screws to hold it in place.

"Well?"

"Look. It's difficult to say no to the old man. He's got a way of asking." Krish held the box at arm's length, and examined his handiwork; the polished wood glowed deeply, the brass shone brightly. When he spoke again, it was more to himself than me.

"It's like trying to push away mist. But each one diminishes him. And after *this* one – "

"Venky said I should ask him to teach me English. He said I could get any job I wanted if I knew some English. He said I should make a deal with the Englishman."

Krish was silent for a second. He looked out of the shop-front, across the street, to where the Englishman sat with his untouched tea. Then he looked back down at his jewellery box, and blew a tiny speck of dust from its gleaming surface.

"Yes," he said, turning the box around, looking at all its angles. "Yes. That's a good idea. You should do that. Make a deal."

To be honest, I didn't like that answer. Partly because I was reluctant to speak to the Englishman; something about that pale mass of flesh repulsed me. But I confess, it was also because Krish's response was almost insulting; it was as though Krish didn't value me at all, as though he'd be happy to see me leave and work in a hotel or something. As though all my polishing and cleaning and running around had been for nothing! The more I thought about it, the angrier I got, and the more I decided it was about time I started keeping the money I earnt. Yes: the only way to get married and start a family was to keep my money; and the only way to do that was to find another job; and the best way of doing that, in Ooty, was to learn some English.

I'd decided. I would go and talk to the Englishman. I'd wait for the right time, that's all.

◈

Paramasivan peered at me through his thick lenses. He narrowed his eyes to better focus; the effort pulled his lips back from his gapped teeth, and made his grey stubble stick out.

"Are you sure you know what you're doing?" He squinted at me again, and Pambu-babu, sitting on Paramasivan's hand, flapped his clipped wings.

"Yes. It has taken me much careful effort to acquire this skill." *You cut a piece of wood to size; you nail it on.*

"I appreciate this. No need to tell Krishnamurthy."

"Mm-hm." Cousin Krish was away, that Saturday morning, but in fact he wouldn't have minded us giving away this particular bit of wood to repair Pambu-babu's cage; it was too knotty to make into a Mughal-era jewellery box or a hundred-and-fifty-year-old table. And I wanted to look busy in case Lakshmi walked by; she needed to know I was a good worker. That couldn't do me any harm.

Paramasivan leaned back, chin raised, looking at me. He held the bird loosely in two hands now; it spread one wing in protest, the feathers rustling like paper on the old man's skin.

"Listen – let me tell you your fortune."

"No need. I know where I'm going in life."

"No, you don't. You really don't. Look, it's free. No charge. Okay?"

I knew what he was doing. I fix Pambu-babu's cage, he tells me my fortune. Debt cancelled. An exchange.

"Okay," I said. "Very kind of you." I tapped the last tiny nail in, and showed him Pambu-babu's cage, with its new back panel.

"Good." Paramasivan slid up the cage door with one hand; Pambu-babu jumped off his other hand, and once inside did a quick about-turn, sticking its head back out to better see us. The old man didn't shut the cage door, but placed his fortune cards in a little pile in front of the cage. He looked at me, expressionless; a man who reads the stars.

"Your fortune, then," he said. He made a rapid, chopping motion with his hand: the signal for Pambu-babu to perform.

I never tire of watching parakeets pick out fortune cards. The way they sidle up to the pile of rectangular, scarlet-trimmed little envelopes; the way they pick up and discard one after the other until they have the very one, the only one, that hides your future; the way they drop this gilded rectangle in front of the astrologer; the way that this one old man now holds your destiny in the cracked skin of his swell-knuckled old hand! I don't believe any of it; but I love to watch it.

Paramasivan picked up the envelope that Pambu-babu had selected for him, and took out the slip of paper it contained. He showed me the picture on the front: a much-garlanded god, carrying a spear, with a peacock at his feet.

"Pambu-babu gives you Lord Murugan." I looked at Pambu-babu; he'd scuttled back into his cage, and turned one grey eye on me.

Paramasivan turned the card over, and read from the handwritten scrawl on the back.

"You work hard. You are a kind person. But you do not value yourself enough. You must make your life in *this* world. Do not walk into other's dreams. Do not agree to everything. You must only consent with the greatest of care."

Paramasivan put the slip of paper down on the work bench, picture-side up, so that the god observed me with his eternal smile.

"This is your fortune," he said. "You understand? Consent *only* with the greatest of care." He nodded vigorously, blinking rapidly, and pushed his glasses back up his nose with one finger. "The greatest of care. Will you remember that?"

"Well," I said. "I don't know if I should consent to remember that. One has to be careful."

I felt sorry about making a joke out of it; Paramasivan took offence, and stamped off, clutching his parakeet cage and muttering to himself. After he'd gone, I noticed that he'd left Lord Murugan behind. I picked up the card, and read the handwritten Tamil on the back. It only had the first part of the fortune. Nothing about *this world* or *others' dreams*. Odd.

I stood in Krishnamurthy's shop-front, and casually looked up and down Mukurti Street. The usual sights; white smoke rising from Cheliyan's portable smithy; Mopuvan's wife walking past his cafe, looking as black-tempered as burnt demoness Holika, and just as likely to emit poison from her breasts. "Nine years his mother's had to put up with it! Nine years, and four of those grieving!" she screeched. Mopuvan rearranging his trays of food; he grinned to himself as if at some secret joke. The Englishman throwing nuts for sparrows; he held out his fat hand to me, yet again. No tourists; that is, no customers. No Krishnamurthy to badger me into sanding or polishing or sweeping.

Good. I drew a deep breath and set off across the street.

There it was; that feeling again. As though I were being examined, as though I were the focus of some incomprehensible attention. I looked up and down the street; to the left, Cheliyan, squatting on the pavement, had stopped blowing through his pipe; his one eye was fixed on me. To the right, Mopuvan's wife had stopped her angry march and half-turned to look at me over her shoulder. In the cafe, Mopuvan's head was down, as if he were closely examining his snacks; but his eyes were up, watching me. It was as though in that instant, life stopped and held its breath. But then a dog started barking; and up the street, I thought I heard the grating shriek of Pambu-babu.

I could have stopped right then; I could have turned round, gone back to the shop, and polished a few boxes. And I almost did; something felt wrong. *Everything* felt wrong. But as I looked down Mukurti Street again, I saw Lakshmi walking towards me, carrying the groceries. She looked so slim and beautiful! I remembered why I was doing all this; and I swear, she gave me a secret half-smile and inclined her head, just slightly. *Go on,* she was saying; *go on.* And I went.

The Englishman watched me as I approached. He stopped crumbling peanuts, and put the half-empty paper cone on the table. For some reason, my heart started thumping. Why? He was just an old man.

I stood in front of him, closer to his bulk than I'd ever been. Now I could see exactly what kind of thing he was. Not just bald, but entirely hairless; no eyebrows, nothing. Just old, pale flesh, white as animal fat, smooth as candle wax; a man of adipocere. There was something odd about his skin; it glistened, as though secreting some oily liquid. His eyes were almost as colourless as the rest of him: the irises a pale, washed-out tint that might once have been blue or brown, the sclera a pale, delicate straw-yellow. Around his neck a white silk scarf, wrapped tight, like a bandage; its edges were brown with dirt.

Now I was here, I didn't know what to say. But he saved me the trouble.

"You here to talk? Yes?" His Tamil was odd, but understandable.

"Venkataraman told you?"

"Venkataraman tell me, yes, yes." Something pulled up his mouth at each corner; I understood that he was smiling. But he had no teeth; none at all. Just straw-coloured gums lined with wet craters.

"How long have you lived here? In India, I mean." I couldn't help myself asking. There was something timeless about him.

"Long time. Long, long, long time." He waved up, towards the eucalyptus-covered slopes that looked down on Ooty. "Longer than the trees." He bent forward in his chair, as though to examine me better; something frothed at the corner of his mouth. I fought the impulse to run.

"Venky said you might teach me English."

"Yes. Oh, yes." His manner was off-hand; as though it really didn't matter. He showed me his yellow gums again. "But first we talk?" He was holding his hand out. "Yes?"

Talk about what? I thought. Stupid old man. I caught a divine, fleeting scent: eucalyptus oil. But beneath that joyous fragrance, something foul and old and rotten. I looked at his extended hand again; a flabby, naked offering.

"We talk." He was insistent, the old man. "I must tell you things. Many things." He nodded his head emphatically; he smiled again. A false smile; but not for deceit, so much as to veil something: unimaginable sorrow, perhaps, or unforgivable guilt. *What had he done, this man?*

"I will tell you." His hand was still there. "I *must* tell you. You agree?" I reached my hand to his – slowly, slowly.

"Agree, and I tell you – " he said, as I grasped his hand " – *everything!*"

His grip was inexorable; I could no more pull my hand away than pick up a water-buffalo. It wasn't power that he brought to bear so much as irresistibility. There was a dead weight behind his hand, a mass that had built and built over countless years and now would not, could not, be repudiated. I felt the unimaginable momentum of it; I sensed it, pale as a snake's belly, foul as rotting fish. The accumulation of guilt upon sin upon guilty sin, forever.

"You understand!" His pale old eyes locked onto mine; they gleamed with something – tears? "You understand!"

And do you know, at that instant, yes, I understood. I understood what Venkataraman's hard eyes had seen, but refused to examine. I understood why Mopuvan would not look at the Englishman, and why Mopuvan's wife was so scared. I understood where Venky and Krish's younger brother had gone, and why. I understood the immense burden of existence.

And with that understanding, something subtly shifted on Mukurti Street. It's hard to explain; it was as though I were seeing everything from a slightly different angle. The same people, the same geography; but dimensionally shifted in some inexpressible way. Cheliyan blew more vigorously through his pipe, and the white smoke rose higher; the church bells tolled more quickly, maybe, and at a subtly different pitch; the dogs barked different barks. Behind the Englishman, Mopuvan arranged a tray of sweets, head down; his grin had gone. I looked behind me, towards Lakshmi; her dark eyes never left mine as she passed me, and she smiled, but her smile was cold, cold. At the end of the street, Paramasivan stood, shaking his head. He raised Pambu-babu's cage and held it to him, with the greatest of care.

❖

I don't know how long I listened to the Englishman. Long enough for Lakshmi to marry Krish, maybe, and for her belly to swell. Long enough for Venky to move out of the distillery and back to his wife. Or maybe those were just images of how things are in some other world, or how they are in every world, and how they will be in this one. I don't know; often, when he talks, I cannot tell where his world begins and my mine ends. *The woman in the blue sari; her child lost; her feet swinging in the air.* Madness and despair; death after death after innocent death! Such inconsolable grief; such unforgiveable guilt; such pointless existence!

The Englishman nods; but I see tears on his cheeks. Yes, I know. I know now. The one irreducible sound of this universe, the one that arises behind each great silence: the sound of weeping. We are the unwantable, the unforgivable; I agree. Let me seek a happier existence, then, a new reality, across the bridge. You will become mist, and I, smoke.

I pour the eucalyptus oil over my head. I rub it into my hair, and then work it into my face and shoulders, my chest, belly and legs. I feel it cool my flesh in the mountain air. I look down at my feet; the ground is dark where the oil has run off my skin. I pick up the box of matches.

€

THE TOURIST'S STORY

"Sentiment, legend and an oft-quoted poem have combined to invest this spot with glamour; a glamour intensified by its romantic situation and the potent charm of dusk and moonlight on the stretch of river which in a lovely curve slips silently along, or when in flood, foams madly past ... For many years, the house and furniture did remain as he left them."
-'Scott's Bungalow', in 'Seringapatam', by Constance Parsons, Oxford University Press, 1931

There is a place, near Mysore, where the Kaveri feeds the impossible green of paddies; where the imported car has yet to compete with the bullock cart and the bare foot. To find this blessed region, go by train to a certain rural station; once there, choose a gharry-driver with an honest smile. Ask for the old bungalow, from the Raj. Everyone knows it.

Go inside. The building is drenched in expatriate melancholy; its tiled floors mourn the warmth of young feet, its high ceilings whisper of old losses. The foreigner's children died, and he left. Perhaps bereavements are more bitter when they are borne in a foreign land. Certainly, the house has a story to tell. But I have another. There is no beginning or end to it; it's not that kind of story. It is an echo of an echo of something missed.

This day, the day I remember, I walk from the house, for a little way, and some more, to the river. I go to that place where the banyans half-hide a clutch of abandoned temples: their walls washed by time's monsoons, their floors swept by dead leaves. Like broken shells in an old nest, the buildings gape at the breeze. I look through their doorways, but do not enter.

I walk on. At the sand-silted shore, where the river slows, one of the temple buildings stands alone. From its walls, steps lead to the bank's edge, and down into the water. I peer at them; pale stones descending to unseen depths. I take pictures, as tourists do.

I still have them; I still look at them; I still think of her.

I put my camera on the ground, and shade my eyes against the sun with my hands. The steps draw the eye down, down. Where white treads fade into a green world, I see occasional movements. Sometimes quick glimmers, as of a fish's belly. Sometimes a slow, dark shadow, moving closer, as though curious but cautious; always on the edge of sight.

Then I feel it: eyes on my skin. I look across the river, to the opposite bank: nobody. But, next to me, on the ground, from the corner of my eye: a small, silent movement. A trickle of water, the tiniest of rivulets. It follows the dry slope downwards, past my sandal, pushing aside the dust. It pools on the topmost step.

I turn around, and see her. Water runs from her as if she has just stepped from a bath; her sari clings to her in folds of gold and red. She looks at me, and I swear she recognises me, this woman I have never seen before. I see it in her eyes, and it disturbs me in a way I cannot express.

In the banyan's branches, the shriek of a parakeet; feathers brush rich dark leaves with the dry rustle of a silk fan unfolding.

My smile goes unanswered. With a muttered apology, I start to retrace my steps, back to the old bungalow. I walk for only a few minutes before realising that my camera case is too light. Cursing, I turn again. I make my passage noisy, so as not to alarm her with a sudden return; I whistle, I beat aside moonflower with a stick, I kick at stones.

My camera is on the ground, where I had left it. Like a gift. The steps are as pale and pristine as before, except for one thing. Wet footprints; leading down, down into the water. Yes, leading into, but not out of, the unpeopled river; disappearing, evaporating before my eyes, in the heat of the Mysore sun.

One day I will return to that place of bullock carts and bare feet. I will take a gharry to the old bungalow, and walk from there to the banyans, and from there to the river's bank. I will go down those pale steps and into the water.

I will go to that place where there is movement at the edge of sight.

TWILIGHT OF THE GODMAN

"Sabbe satta ummattaka" [All worldlings are unbalanced]
- Attributed to Buddha ~500 BC

"Are you a devout man, Yalamudhan?"

The question was posed by old Paramasivan. He asked as though half-joking; but that meant he was also half-serious.

"After all, you see so many dead – do they persuade you that the soul survives the body? Or do their bodies convince you that life begins and ends with flesh?"

Yalamudhan sat on an old box and cradled a mug of *kallu* – his third from a potent batch brewed behind Mopuvan's Cafe on Mukurti Street. The palm wine had softened this odd man's edges, and that in turn had encouraged questions from his guests. He took another long sip before answering.

"Do I believe in God, you mean? That's what you're asking."

The bare bulb that hung from the ceiling bathed us all in a yellowish light; it tinted Yalamudhan's sclera with jaundice and found deep shadows in the pits and wrinkles of his face.

"Do I believe in God? Let me tell you this – I have *seen* God!" He leant back, chin up and mouth set, daring us to laugh; but we did not.

When he saw that we listened still, he continued, more softly. "Yes, I have seen God, with my own eyes."

Paramasivan, who feels the cold more than the rest of us, poked short-sightedly at the fire, and revived a small flame. Some of the others shifted position, trying to find comfort on Yalamudhan's thin mats. Nalini, full of her first child, stood by the doorway: too shy to sit, too curious to leave. Nobody spoke.

"You know me as Yalamudhan the embalmer, who lives alone in this poor house on Mukurti Street." He waved his arm at the room; a gesture which took in the cracked plaster of the ceiling, the blackened fireplace, the bare walls. "But I have not always tended corpses, and I have not always lived here in Ooty, in these chill mountains. Once I was married. I lived with my wife on the warm lowlands, in a village set on the banks of the Kaveri, near Srirangapatnam."

In the fireplace, the dance of a small flame, and the hiss of hot gases. In the air, the tang of eucalyptus wood.

"My wife died giving birth to our first child. No, save your sympathy – life is as life will be. My father helped me with the baby – my mother too had passed away – and it grew into a wonderful little boy. My brother assisted too, as far as he was able."

Yalamudhan cleared his throat: wet gravel on leather.

"As the child grew older, my employment increasingly took me away from home. But I had no concerns for the boy. After all, my father was there: wise as ever, fat with good health, and eternally fortunate. So I thought. And my brother – as strong as a water-buffalo, albeit with the mind of a child – was both staunch protector and eager playmate for my son."

He took another sip of *kallu*; but it could not soften a voice so hoarse that listeners swallowed in sympathy.

"What employment, you say? At that time, I was assistant to a veterinary physician – one who specialised not in farm animals or domestic pets, but in wildlife. In those days, India had few such people. Consequently, we travelled widely: from the Palni Hills in the south up to Mudumalai and Bandipur; to Kanha in Madhya Pradesh; and even as far north as the lion-parks of Gir and the Corbett National Park by the Himalaya. Such places I knew! Such creatures!"

Behind Yalamudhan's ravaged face, we saw jungles aglow with golden orioles and flame-tree blossom; in his cracked speech, we heard the cicada's hum and the soft pad of the tiger.

"I would help my employer wherever he needed help – catching animals, feeding them, caring for them, curing them. And, yes, opening up those that had died, to understand why death had come. Poachers or disease? And if a disease, what form?"

One of the younger listeners – probably Harikumar, who finds it difficult to be silent – asked if that was how he had learnt to embalm.

"Yes! Sometimes we needed to take dead animals, or parts of them, back to my employer's offices. For tests." The embalmer straightened his back and raised his head; for a moment, we glimpsed a younger, stronger Yalamudhan. "So yes, I learnt how to keep the putrefaction from dead things; how to stop them stinking in the summer's heat, how to stay their mouldering in the monsoon. And I became very good at it."

He looked around at us; we made small noises of assent.

"So that was my life. Now, one day, my employer told me that we had been called to the Theppakadu elephant sanctuary." Yalamudhan pointed at the wall with his chin; a gesture which spoke of the two-hour drive north from Ooty to the jungles of Mudumalai. "Someone had found an injured elephant in the hills nearby – could we help? Naturally, we left immediately – but by the time we'd driven to Theppakadu and then trekked through the jungle by foot, it was too late. The crows had already started, and the jackals would soon come. 'Poachers,' I said, for it was clear that the animal had been shot. Even so, my employer insisted on doing a post-mortem, then and there. And when we opened up the carcase, we found a baby elephant, all snuggled in the womb."

"Still *alive?*" blurted Harikumar. Nalini shuddered, her hand over her rounded belly.

"Of course not, fool! No, the baby was as dead as its mother. My employer looked at me, and said, *'Here is a test for your embalming skills, Yalamudhan.'* Naturally, I protested; a baby elephant is too heavy by far for a pair of men to carry through the jungle. And even if we got it back to the jeep, we had not brought sufficient embalming chemicals for something so large. But he smiled, and said: *Just the head, Yalamudhan. Just the head."*

Mopuvan muttered, "What has this to do with God?" But we all ignored him, and Yalamudhan gave no sign that he had heard.

"So we cut off the head, put it in a sack and half-dragged, half-carried it back to the dirt track where we'd left our jeep. There, I flushed out its blood vessels with preservative, and cleaned and oiled its skin. I placed it in the plastic barrel we used for transporting organs, and added what embalming fluid we had. Not a full procedure, but enough to halt the decay until we got back to Mysore. That was the day's work done, I thought, and I turned my mind homeward: to my father, my brother, my young son.

"But as I was tightening the barrel's lid, my employer wrote something on a piece of paper. When he gave it to me, I saw that he had scribbled down an address. An address here in Ooty. *'Listen, Yalamudhan,'* he said. *'I have a task for you. Take the baby elephant's head to the man who lives here, at the big house, and do what he asks. Three days' work, perhaps four. He will pay you well."*

"What big house?" asked Harikumar; but Yalamudhan waved his question away.

"I raised various objections of a practical nature. How to get there? What about my son, at home? But my employer had all the answers. I was to remain in Mudumalai for the rest of that day and overnight, sleeping in the jeep; the next day, I would drive to Ooty with the head, and commence work for the gentleman at the big house. My employer would make his own way back to Mysore immediately. There he would see that my family were informed of the situation. *'Why can't I go to Ooty today?'* I asked. *'They are not ready,'* he said. *'And anyway, there is work for you here. Do a survey. See how many lion-tailed macaques you can find. A detailed survey – from now until mid-day tomorrow. Only then take the head to the big house. You understand? Only then."*

Yalamudhan frowned at the memory, and shook his head.

"There are no such macaques in that part of Mudumalai. But I acquiesced, of course; he was my employer, and if he wished me to look for animals that were not there, what else could I do? Harikumar – where's that jug of *kallu?"*

Harikumar stood to replenish Yalamudhan's cup; shadows flickered and spasmed on the stained wall.

"So for the rest of that day, and half the next, I paced the jungle, notebook and pencil in hand. I saw muntjac and Malabar squirrels; chital and langur; butterflies as big as my hand whose iridescent wings glowed blue as gods. But I saw no lion-tailed macaques. In the late afternoon, as instructed, I took the jeep and drove to the address I had been given. To the big house. You'll know where I mean, although you won't have seen the house itself."

The fire spat while Yalamudhan described the place: a track, barred by tall iron gates and white pillars, leading off the road between Ooty and Coonoor. We nodded; we'd all seen the black metal bars a thousand times.

"The gates are always shut," someone said. "Always."

"Yes. Nevertheless, on that day, they were open. So I drove in, and up the track. The unmade road twists and winds between great old eucalyptus trees; they are tall, and their branches overhang the road. Even on a bright day, that domain is sunk in endless twilight. But when the mists come ..."

Yalamudhan was silent for a moment; his eyes were closed, as though to shut out the darkness.

"Anyway, the road takes you higher and higher; you'd think you were going up Dodabetta. But soon you emerge from the trees, and there's the big house. Covered verandahs, white pillars, balconies and towers. The summer residence of a maharajah, I'd have said – perhaps one of the Wodeyars of Mysore. Or maybe it's older still – the zenana of a wealthy nabob? One of Tipu's cruel follies? I don't know. It was beautiful, but in a joyless way. Like a dried bloom. I felt it would crumble into dust at the sound of laughter. Behind it, I saw high slopes where eucalyptus clutched at grey clouds; in front, the Ghats fell to the sunlit plains."

We were still, all of us, our small discomforts forgotten. Nobody would have guessed Yalamudhan had such words in him. It was as though the story were telling itself, in Yalamudhan's hoarse voice, and the man himself were only a mouthpiece.

"I parked the jeep in front of the great house. Clipped bushes. Marigolds glowing in weedless beds. The dying sun; the long shadows. And, most noticeable of all, the deepest, deepest silence. I heard nothing but a far echo of someone shouting in the valley below. And that made the place feel lonelier still, somehow."

A shy, shuffling sound betrayed Nalini, whose feet were weary of her six months of pregnancy, finally slipping into the room and squatting down on her heels, behind us.

"I thought I saw movement from the house: something blue that waved from a first-floor window before being snatched away. But then my attention was drawn to the ground floor. A man was watching me from the verandah. He was beardless and shaven-headed. As he approached me, I saw that he limped as if one leg was shorter than the other. And he was dressed like a priest – white dhoti and shawl, *tilaka* marks on his forehead. I didn't recognise the marks: two white bands, curving upward at each end like a smile; superimposed on those, five red dots."

"That's a Shaivite *tilaka*," said Mopuvan. This led to a short argument, which ended with general agreement that Mopuvan, being a Toda, was not well-placed to know about these things. This Mopuvan good-naturedly accepted with his usual grin. But nobody could say for sure what that *tilaka* signified, if it was not Shaivite. Yalamudhan, gazing into his mug of *kallu*, made no comment during the discussion; finally, however, he shook his head and said, very quietly, as if to himself: "Not only was it not a Shaivite mark – it was not even Hindu." But few heard him.

"So, the man?" said Mopuvan, by way of apology for his interruption.

"He was expecting me; that was clear. *'Bring it inside,'* he said. He spoke like one accustomed to command; but nevertheless – and despite his bad leg – he helped me get the barrel up the steps onto the verandah. Then he opened wide the windowed double-doors, and we walked the barrel across the threshold. Inside the barrel, the head lurched from one side to another, and the embalming fluid slopped and splashed."

Paramasivan took one of Yalamudhan's last logs and placed it on the half-dead fire, with a sidelong glance at our host. But the storyteller gave no sign that he had noticed.

"Indoors, the silence was more oppressive still. The big house held its breath; its very walls watched me. So I felt. But I had work to do. *'Put it on this,'* said the priest, if that is what he was, pointing to a trolley. A long, metal table on wheels, like the ones they use in mortuaries. We heaved the barrel up and over the edge of the trolley, making the steel bed clang and the wheels groan. *'Now follow me,'* he said.

"I pushed the trolley after him as he limped through room after great room. All empty. All silent except for the trolley's wheels and my footsteps. It felt like a place awaiting resurrection. Some of the walls had murals – scenes of myths that I did not recognise, portraits of monsters for which I had no names. These pictures looked fresh and new; the gaudiness of their painted demons was at odds with the gloom in this house of endless twilight. At last we came to a room brighter but less grand than the others. Here, apparently, we were to stop."

Yalamudhan cleared his throat again, grimacing with discomfort. In the hearth, the new log hissed and popped as resin boiled from its knots.

"I looked around the room. It was both crowded and empty – like a half-filled store-room. I saw first an antique box, set on a little table by itself, just inside the doorway; near that, on one wall, I saw a painting of a Mysore tiger mauling a British soldier; and then I saw pipes and taps, benches and ceramic sinks, jugs of various sizes, and an aluminium tub big enough to bath in. And then I noticed more surprising items, arranged on shelves and benches – things I immediately recognised. Carboys of formaldehyde and glutaraldehyde; bottles of methanol; tubs of humectants; threads and glues that can hold fast wayward flesh; oils that scent dead skin and preserve its suppleness. And the instruments! Steel trocars from Switzerland, Swann Morton scalpels from England, syringes and hoses and gooseneck adaptors from Germany! I tell you, they had bought the best. *'Is this sufficient?'* the priest asked me. *'For the work that you do, is this sufficient?'* His words fell into a dusty silence. *'This suffices,'* I said, *'but the other arrangements?'*

He shook his head, as though such matters were of no consequence. *'Your expenses will be met,'* he said, and gave me directions to a guest-house on the way to Coonoor. *'As for payment, I think you will be satisfied.'* And he fixed me with his eyes and mentioned a sum for three days' work, to start the next morning, that was more than I normally earned in three months."

Yalamudhan was silent, briefly; and Nalini heaved a little sigh.

"That surprised me, but now I understood why the veterinary physician was willing to lose my services for a little while. If the man from the big house was paying me so much, how much more would he have given my employer in compensation, not to mention in consideration for the elephant's head itself? I felt the draw of money too, of course; but above all, I was scared. What influence must he have, this man who dressed as a priest, to live in such a place, to pay so highly? And what else might he do – for example, if one displeased him? I tell you, power flowed from him like cold air from a mountain's peak; to meet his eyes was to accede to his demands. So I agreed to the offer made by the man from the big house; but also I resolved to work quickly, to the best of my ability, and leave as soon as possible. Besides, I missed my home, my son."

Paramasivan poked again at the fire; the new log had failed to properly catch, and now smoked blackly, refusing to share its warmth. Yalamudhan got up from the antique box he sat upon, opened it, and took a fistful of crumpled paper from inside. This he threw on the fire; the papers blazed up, making Paramasivan, huddled close to the hearth, start in surprise. The old man moved forward as though to grab the flames, before checking himself and leaning back. He shook his head and pushed up his glasses with one finger, while Yalamudhan continued.

"I took my leave of the so-called priest and drove to the guest-house. Within an hour, I was congratulating myself on the small fortune that awaited me, and by the morning it was as though I had already spent what I had yet to earn. A cricket bat and ball for my son, a moped for my brother, a radio for my father, new clothes for all. Such were my thoughts as I drove to the big house the next day.

"Again, the gates were open, the driveway gloomy, the priest waiting, the house silent, clean, empty. Again, we walked through the house to the embalming room. The elephant's head had been removed from the barrel, and placed in the aluminium tub. On the benchtop next to the tub were a number of gaudy, shiny things: a garland of plastic flowers; a bowl of imitation sweets, again of plastic; a gold-coloured crown, made of cheap tin sheet and clumsily painted; a tin axe, poorly made and brightly painted. Like children's toys, all of them. But more than this – there, on the trolley, obscenely naked, an insult to the vision, was a *headless human corpse!*"

Our mugs of *kallu* were forgotten; our gasps and exclamations stopped our host's harsh voice. Someone said "Yalamudhan – this is too much, now. Nobody can believe this." But once quiet had returned, the embalmer continued, impervious; it was as though the story had opened up a well of memories, and he was compelled to draw from it until dry; to drench us with the recollections in which, perhaps, he drowned himself each dark night.

"The priest pointed at the head, at the gewgaws of plastic and tin, at what lay on the trolley. *'We have an agreement, you and I,'* he said. *'I think you know what you must do.'* I feigned ignorance; I begged, I wept, I made other offers – I tell you, I offered everything! – but that demon in a priest's guise was implacable. *'You will do this,'* he said. *'You will make Ganesh.'"*

"Don't judge me; you can't understand unless you were there, unless you had looked into that madman's eyes and seen what waited there, what lies beyond darkness, beneath evil. I feared for my life in that silent house of twilight. So I proceeded. I started by completing the embalming process begun in the jungle: careful cleaning, and fresh fluids and oils. Then I repaired the damage that the baby elephant's head had suffered during its travels. I did my best, but still it looked nothing like Ganesh, nothing at all. And then – with bile burning my throat – I started on the human corpse.

"The body was that of an overweight old man, dead for perhaps two days and starting to stiffen. I washed out its cavities. I massaged and flexed its unresponsive limbs. And when the embalming was done, I arranged the body: I bent the fingers of the right hand around the cheap tin axe, and tied them in place with thread; I glued the bowl of plastic sweets into the left hand. Finally, I stitched the baby elephant's head onto the corpse's shoulders. I pinned the tin crown in place and tied the plastic garland around the neck. And when I looked on the abomination I had made, I tell you, I wanted to die.

"Nobody had disturbed me while I worked; I saw no one, and heard nothing except, perhaps, a child crying in the distance. Now, silence fell like dust – but in that great silence, I heard someone draw breath. I looked up from my creation and found the priest-man observing me with an expression that I could not read, but which was close to joy. Exultant, yes; and, somehow, hungry. *Now, follow me,* he said. *Bring my servant Ganesh.*

"We went to a different part of the big house, to a wing that stretched away from the main part of the building. My breath came in sobbing gasps as I pushed the trolley; Ganesh is heavy, but guilt and fear are heavier still. Soon we entered a long, narrow room, like a great corridor. The only windows were small and set high in the wall, and the only light in the room came from these small openings. Along the walls were ranged mechanical items and machinery that I did not recognise: structures of dusty cogs and ratchets, networks of fine filaments bound in cobwebs. At the far end of the room were three empty chairs. Big, strong, high-backed chairs, almost like thrones. *There,* said the priest, pointing to the left-most chair.

"Getting that dead weight from the trolley to the chair – truly, it was like a nightmare. We lay the chair on its back beside the trolley; we slid the corpse off the trolley and into the chair, he supporting the head and I the body. Then we dragged the seated god to his position by the other two chairs, and tipped him upright. This almost led to calamity – Ganesh's head tipped forward and would have torn itself from his body, had I not caught it. Even so, some of the stitches came loose around the neck, and the tin axe bent.

"It took me another hour to set Ganesh correctly on his throne – fixing the head upright, wiring the axe-wielding hand into position, tying down the hand that held the plastic sweets, bending one stiff leg so that its foot rested on the opposite knee. None of this was easy. But in the end, it was done. *There,* I said, *it is finished.* The devil-priest turned to me. *'No,'* he said, *'no, it is not. This is but the first day of the three days that we agreed.'*

"I objected, naturally. *'My son,'* I said, *'my family.'* He laughed. *'Do not concern yourself about them.'* And before this monster, my arguments dissolved like salt in water. Nevertheless, in my head, I thought to flee as soon as I'd left that half-lit domain of madness; I would get in the jeep, I told myself, and drive, drive back to my family. But the priest had anticipated this, for when we took the trolley back to the embalming room, he pointed to the old box I had previously noticed, on a table just inside the doorway. An antique box, with brass-bound corners, decorated with copper filigrees and iron bosses. *'Open it,'* he said. I did so: it was full of rupees; full, I tell you! *'Touch them,'* said the priest, *'feel them.'* I ran my hands through those dry-greased notes; I picked them up and let them fall back, light as feathers, heavy as fate. *'They are yours,'* said the priest, *'on the third day.'* I turned to him, intending to bargain, to negotiate; to say, *Pay me for what I have done, and let me go.* But he looked at me with his black, black eyes, and I saw again what lives in the infinite night, and what it might do to men such as I, and I could not speak. I could not speak.

"In my bed that night, in the guest-house, I justified what I was doing in all the ways you might expect. There was no logical difference between embalming humans and embalming animals, I told myself; with life gone, they are both but matter. Doubtless the man's demise had been natural, I avowed; doubtless the head had been removed after death, perhaps for medical science; doubtless the hideous procedure had some purpose beyond my understanding; and so on. But you all know it was money that shut my mind to the obvious concerns, and fear that made me return the next day.

"Again, the gates were open, the driveway gloomy, the devil-priest waiting, the house silent, clean, empty. Again, we walked through the house to the embalming room. On the trolley, as I had dreaded, another headless corpse; but this time the body was of a young man, with a strong physique – a bull-buffalo of a man. And on his chest, another head, but this time of a monkey. Nearby, the accoutrements of the new god: a gaudily painted mace, a cheap tin crown, a plastic garland. *'Today,'* said the man, *'my servant Hanuman comes.'*

"Everything went as before, but more smoothly, more quickly. You see, one can become familiar even with such work as that. Towards the end of the day, we took Hanuman to the throne room – where Ganesh waited as we had left him – and tied the new god to the chair on the right. I remember that his body leaked scented oils and acrid formaldehyde. And just as our Ganesh looked ridiculous, with his over-sized, misshapen, lop-sided elephant head, so our Hanuman looked bizarre, with a too-small monkey head on a sturdy physique. Each god an absurdity, yes, but somehow not laughable – only sad. Also distasteful, blasphemous; it was as though one had spat on the sacred. I looked at the gods I had made, at my handiwork, and hated what I had done. The shame has never left me. And as I left the embalming room, I saw the money box, and thought of what was owed to me for my efforts to date, and knew, *knew,* that no payment would adequately balance my weight of guilt. I turned back, intending to say, *Enough!* But I only met the devil-priest's eyes, and he looked into me, deep and cold, and he saw the ugly thing I call my soul, and laughed. *'We have an agreement,'* he said."

Yalamudhan paused; somewhere, a jackal called. "And then I realised I *had* to return the next day. It was no longer a question of *should* or *shouldn't*; some contracts cannot be broken."

Outside, the dark evening had turned into black night; the Ooty chill crept under ill-fitting doors and raised tiny bumps on our flesh. Paramasivan shifted closer still to the fire, and Nalini drew the end of her sari around her head.

"The third day, then. The mists that morning were thick and heavy; they condensed on the jeep's windscreen like gossamer rain. They made black shadows of the eucalypts that lined the driveway. The devil-priest, wrapped in a woollen shawl, shivered as he waited for me – but his eyes burned. *'My last day,'* I said. *'Yes,'* he said.

"The body that lay on the trolley this day was that of a young child, a boy. And he was blue; I mean his skin had been painted blue, every inch. The paint had been applied thickly; in some places it had cracked into a mosaic, like a dry river bed. This body was not headless, however; rather, it was wearing a cardboard mask in the likeness of Shiva – you know, a third eye on the forehead, and a crescent moon on the brow. Imitation adornments of Lord Shiva lay waiting: a plastic *trishul* trident and plastic snake. *'Go to it,'* said the priest, *'but see that you do not remove the mask, for this is a holy thing.'*

"So I proceeded. On this occasion, for no reason that I could see, the devil-priest did not leave. He stood close behind me, breathing quickly, almost as though he had been running. All my first fears of this dark house and this incomprehensible man returned, and my hand trembled as I took up the trocar. I know you won't believe me, but I swear to you, I had no choice; I began the procedure; I inserted the trocar head just below the boy's navel. And I swear, the body shuddered then – as though it were asleep and attempting to break through a nightmare's paralysis. I looked at the priest, who stood behind me still. His fists were clenched, his eyes wide and staring. *'Continue!'* he shouted. *'Continue!'* So I resumed; after all, dead bodies do sometimes move as muscles relax and joints accept gravity.

"First, I flooded the body cavity with embalming fluid and closed the abdominal incision with a suture. Then I turned my attention to the circulatory system. I scraped blue paint away from the relevant areas of the throat, over carotid artery and jugular vein respectively. Then I made an incision in the jugular, ready for placement of the drainage tube; but – horror of horrors! – the blood pulsed and flowed from the cut in spasms – it left the boy's vein with the skip and stumble of a dying heart – slowed – and ceased! I stepped back, aghast, and then turned to that monstrous devil-priest, as mad as he was evil. *'What have you done?'* I said. *'What have you made me do?'* But he became enraged. *'Fool!'* he roared. *"Would you question this god, or his dreams? Continue!'*

"I did not continue. Something broke in my mind; I became a creature only of action and reaction, heedless of contracts or consequences. I picked up a carboy of formaldehyde, raised it high, and threw it at the priest, as hard as I was able. It caught him across the groin, and he fell to the ground. The carboy shattered, spraying glass shards and toxic chemical across the floor. As I ran from the room, I took the money box, without thinking, as if by reflex; behind me, I heard the devil-priest, choking on the vapours, but shouting still: *'The agreement, fool! It remains; it remains!'*

"I ran, ran through rooms of endless twilight. The house began to wake now, as though in response to the priest's shouts – I heard answering calls, rapid steps, and echoes of other sounds, scrapings and mechanical groans, sounds whose meaning I could not guess. It was as though a great machine were coming to life – or dying.

"I have no recollection of getting into the jeep and driving down through the heavy mists and black trees. But I do remember finding the iron gates shut, at the bottom of the driveway; I remember pulling at them with all my might; I remember the rust cutting into my hands, and the silent, dripping trees around me.

"When I had opened the gates enough to get the jeep through, I drove out and away, as fast as the winding road would allow. I headed down past Coonoor, making for the plains, away from that domain of madness. I wanted nothing more than to be home again, with my father, my brother, and my dear son."

Nalini's knuckles were pressed to her face. Harikumar's mouth hung open, as if he had forgotten his jaw were there. Old Paramasivan, impassive, stared myopically into the glowing hearth.

"The road was poor in those days, and had been made poorer still by that year's monsoon. I could travel at only half the speed we would go today. Nevertheless, I drove until sleep could no longer be denied. Then I left the main road, headed into the country, and parked up on a dusty road, far enough from the closest village for me not to provoke the curiosity of its inhabitants. I lay on the back seat, with one hand on the money box. I slept, after a fashion; but whenever I shut my eyes, I saw only a blue-painted boy, in a mask, shuddering as the trocar entered his belly. He has never left my dreams, this boy; he has never left.

"I woke often, that night, tortured by some variant of what I had seen in the big house; but each time I woke, I found comfort in the hard angles of the old box. I imagined my homecoming. I thought of how I would walk through the door and empty the box's contents on the ground, so that my son could walk on a carpet of wealth. I dreamt that we would be as rich as Mughals, as Sultans."

Outside, there was a change in the wind; the hearth belched a little smoke past Paramasivan, and Harikumar coughed.

"Probably none of you have lost a child," Yalamudhan said, looking around the room. "Most of you are too young. Ah – Paramasivan?" The old fortune-teller nodded slowly, and pushed up his glasses.

"Yes – my daughter. She was five. The river took her, they said." Paramasivan's face showed no emotion; *These things,* it seemed to say, *are written in the stars.*

"Then only Paramasivan can understand, truly understand, my feelings when I finally reached my home the next morning. To find your house empty; to comfort yourself with one foolish possibility after another, each less likely than the last – *they have gone to the market, they are hiding to play a joke* – to suppress, time and again, your worst, nagging fears until they burst forth and take you by the throat and push your face into that which should have been obvious from the outset!

"But still I called out for them, even after I knew; and eventually our half-deaf neighbour appeared. *'Why are you shouting so, Yalamudhan?'* he asked. *'My family,'* I groaned, *'my family. My father, my brother, my son. Gone, gone.'* He was puzzled. *'But they went to join you,'* he said, *'a man came and gave them money, and an address, and said that you waited for them in Ooty. So they went. Maybe five days ago.'*

"I remember little of the next months. It's clear that I went mad, but I recall only unconnected scenes from this mental descent: iron gates that were always shut; dark mists and darker trees; police who paid me no attention, unless to beat me; my employer's offices, at first empty, and then rented out to a textile merchant. I do not know in what order to place these images. But I do know that I became a creature first of ridicule, and then of fear, wandering the countryside near Srirangapatnam, sleeping on dirt and eating thorns, screaming in temples until my throat's lining tore . Some began to call me the godman; but I would laugh and gibber at this, and attack them when they came to offer me food and drink. *'Give me not sweets or milk,'* I would rail, through my swollen tongue. *'Give me your children, that I may make of them things wondrous and immortal! Let me adorn them with tin crowns, let me give their flesh the hue of azure!'*

"Eventually, I understood that I was close to death – and I wished for it with all my heart. So, one day, I scored my flesh with sharp rocks to hasten the departure of life; I lay in the sun and asked it to burn me to nothingness. The sky was so bright and clear that day; the blue so profound that it weighed on me. As though *blue* were a thing of infinite substance. I closed my eyes, with the intent of opening them never.

"I travelled inward, to the depths of myself, to annulment; it was so close, that joyous oblivion. So close. But hands pulled me back. Soft, strong hands; they brought me to my feet, and a voice said, *'Come.'* My eyelids were stuck together as if by glue, so I could see nothing, but the hands guided me and sat me down against a tree trunk. I felt dirt being washed from me with a damp cloth, and my eyelids bathed; my mouth was opened, and thorns pulled from my tongue. Now that I could see, I found my helper was a woman, a young woman in a blue sari, hardly more than a girl. She made me drink a little, and then said, *'Walk now; you must go home.'* I said, *'Sister, I don't know where that is.'* She answered, *'I will show you.'*

"So we walked through the hot afternoon, and into the evening. In fact, I do not know how long we walked. Perhaps it was days. I could hardly move, and mostly it felt like she was carrying me; I could not see how she could be so strong. We reached my home, my family home, as it was getting dark. There I fell into a sleep that was – for the first time since my flight from the big house – untroubled by dreams of the blue boy.

"She nursed me for days, that young woman; she would leave me in a dreamless sleep every night, and reappear just after I woke. She gave me simple food, and water, and she helped me wash. One day, as I rested, she cleaned my house. It had been untouched since my madness descended and I went wandering, but all our possessions were there still. Even the antique money box from the big house; that too. *'Nobody will enter your house,'* said the girl. *'They fear the godman.'*

"I asked her not to call me that; and then I asked who she was. But she didn't answer. I noticed that she was gathering certain things together into three bags. One had a few belongings of my father's; another some things of my brother's; and a third a few items that belonged to my son. Nothing of any great value, you understand –

just old clothing and so forth. *'What are you doing?'* I asked. *'Come,'* she said, *'bring these things, and the money box, and matches, and see.'*

"We went outside. People stared; not at her, but at me. We walked to the bank of the Kaveri. *'End what has gone,'* she said. So I took the three bags and emptied them out onto the clean sand. More people had gathered now, but I ignored them. I looked only to the girl in the blue sari, while the people looked only at me. *'How will you light these pyres, Yalamudhan?'* she asked. The onlookers gasped when I opened the box and took from it great handfuls of rupees. *'Madman!'* they shouted, as I pushed the vile paper into the piles of clothes. But I continued until the box was nearly empty of its paper sacrilege. *'Now, Yalamudhan,'* she said. *'Here is forgiveness, here absolution. And here, release. Now.'*

"Some of those watching made as if to rush forward and take the money, but I had only to grimace to make them retreat. Truly, they feared the godman. But before proceeding, I asked the girl: *'Should there not be a priest, a ritual?'* Some in the growing crowd shouted vulgarities at me, but she in the blue sari only laughed. *'God needs neither,'* she said. *'Only kindness.'* So I lit the fires and watched the blue smoke rise into the bluer sky, until all the embers were dead and all the cruel crowd dispersed; until I was alone before three heaps of white ash."

We were silent, all of us; even Harikumar. In the fireplace, the log had burnt down to pale cinders. Paramasivan took off his glasses, and wiped them on his scarf; Nalini bit at her fingernails; the others were still.

"So, you ask me, do I believe in God? The answer is *Yes* – for, as I said, I have seen God." Yalamudhan nodded in slow emphasis; his cheeks were wet, and his hands followed the angles and iron bosses of the old box he sat on. "Yes, I have seen Her, seen Her with my own eyes, and she was dressed all in blue."

☾

THE DAIRYMEN

"Our first experience with ultraviolet light as a field tool occurred about 1945. As an aftermath of a lecture on desert survival to a local association of 'Rock Hounds,' one of the members related the following incident: 'While searching for fluorescent rocks at night, I observed a highly fluorescent "rock" at a distance of about thirty feet. When I got close to it, the "rock" started to move away ... '"
- H Stahnke, "UV light, a useful field tool"
Bioscience, 22, 604-607 (1972)

Thirukumar sits on one side of the table, and I on the other; between us waits the old wooden chessboard. This Thiru adjusts and re-adjusts, fraction by tiny fraction, until its planes mirror those of the table. Nailed to the board is a metal tea-strainer; its wire-mesh dome is fixed above the board's very centre, as if to cage geometry. To my right, a twelve-volt powerpack enjoys similar precision, centred between board's edge and table's edge. Here, however, Thiru's careful symmetry is desecrated: two tangle-prone wires, each ending in a crocodile clip, uncoil from the power unit in disordered spirals. Thiru paws at them, frowning, but their helices defeat his linear needs. He tuts, and positions them in the usual way: one crocodile clip grasping the mesh of the tea-strainer, and the other gripping a pair of metal forceps. Then he sighs, my brother, and runs his hands through hair uncut since we started the Dairy.

"Harikumar? Ready?" he asks.

"Sure am, dude." With my gloved left hand, I pat the Thermos of dry ice; with my right, I wave a glass capillary tube. The tube has a rubber bulb at one end, which I squeeze between finger and thumb. "All systems go."

Behind Thiru, a small shadow moves inside one of the translucent plastic boxes stacked against the mud wall; through the window comes the moaning and keening of Krishnamurthy's aunt. *Oh, my son.* It is early, but the heat of the day threatens.

"Okay," says Thiru.

For once, my brother meets my eyes with a level stare; I nod, to acknowledge the implied significance of this, our final session. But truthfully, this last milking means less to me than it does to Thiru. If it doesn't work out, I'll find another way. I always do. But Thiru – well. Black or white; all or nothing; perfection or rejection; that's Thiru.

He turns and reaches to the stacked boxes. Two hundred of them, their surfaces dated and numbered in blue marker-pen; each carton a cube of side similar to that of a CD case. He pauses jerkily, as if pulled by strings, and adjusts one of the stacks. Poor Thiru! The higgledy-piggledy columns drive him mad, but Krish's aunt has no straight lines in her hand-built, mud-walled hut; no right angles against which to set the square-sided containers, no level floor to support the concept of perpendicularity. And so, the untidy piles of boxes lean this way and that, teasing my brother's sensibilities. I smile at his futile efforts: poor Thiru!

I've had that smile since the day I realised my brother was different. He was ten years old, and I eleven, and Mukurti Street was all agog with the imminent wedding of Venkataraman's daughter Lakshmi. Mopuvan, the cafe owner, was doing the catering, and Thiru and I had gone to watch him slaughter a chicken. This was an intimate affair: rubbing shoulders in the tiny yard behind the cafe, we smelt the ebb of the bird's warmth; we heard feathers leave flesh with the sound of slowly ripped cloth; we saw pinpoints of blood stipple the hillocked skin. The slap and stink of the gutting; the joyous flies all a-buzz! I was nauseated; it was though some small thing inside me also had had its throat cut, and also struggled and kicked its life away. I never ate meat again, no matter how our father glared at me from his one eye. But Thiru just watched the passing of life as though it were a flow of data; an equation to solve.

Yes: poor Thiru.

My brother picks up the first of the translucent boxes. He checks its number against the handwritten log hanging on the mud wall.

"Last milked: three weeks ago. Number of feeds since last milking: two."

He knows that already, as do I; the routine is unbroken since we started, ten months before. But checking the log is part of the process, and Thiru needs process. Take the tracks away, and the train grinds to a halt.

He makes as if to return to the table, but pauses, attempting once again to straighten the ramshackle towers. As he turns away in defeat, we hear the old woman outside: "Oh my son," she wails, "oh my son!"

Most people would ask questions if their tiny two-room dwelling were, without warning, invaded by two young men and two hundred empty boxes. But Krishnamurthy's aunt barely noticed. *"She's mad,"* Krish had said, and it was true. When we first parked our rented jeep in the hamlet, we were met only by dust and dogs, and, somewhere, a distant, hopeless wailing. Most of the villagers were at work – hunched over their paddies, we guessed, or herding skinny goats through the thorns. But one at least remained: an impossibly wrinkled old man, squatting under a neem tree. Pushing wet betel around his rotten teeth, he pointed out a hut set apart from the main cluster of baked mud walls and sun-bleached thatch. *"The old woman? Follow the sounds; find the weeping."* And indeed, as we approached the hut, the wailing grew louder.

We clapped and shouted outside the door, but nobody came, so we walked around the back. And there, beneath a leaf-roofed lean-to, was Krish's aunt, a sheen of sweat on her bald head, her white sari yellowed with the years. She was on her knees in the dust. Her arms, free of any kind of jewellery, were raised, as though in supplication or retribution, and she was crooning a funeral lament, sometimes softer, sometimes louder. Before her was a black-burnt carcase of twisted metal. Hung with soft white filaments tugged by the breeze, it looked like a tangle of dark driftwood that had caught thin seaweed and hung it out to dry: a harvest of many tides. In fact, it was the wreck of a motorbike, burnt down to its metal skeleton, and now shrouded and hung with long, grey, human hair. Beneath it, the ground was black with old fires.

Unconscious of our arrival, the old woman continued without pause: a Tamil lament for a lost child. *"You always helped me, you gave light to my life and joy to my days of pain and toil. You were the father of my unborn grandchildren. Where are you now, o my son?"* Her earlobes, stretched and pendulous with the weight of long-gone jewellery, trembled at her words. Yep, Krish was right; you can't get madder than his aunt.

Thirukumar brings the box back to the table. He holds it up to the light, checking that the shadow inside is on the floor of the box, not somehow clutching the underside of the lid. That hasn't happened yet, but you don't take chances in the Dairy. He places the box on the table, and slowly peels back the lid, holding the box very still. He puts the lid next to the box and adjusts it minutely, always questing the parallel. Then he picks up the forceps, trailing crocodile-clip and power-pack lead, and carefully reaches down into the plastic container. A quick dart of the hand, and the forceps emerge, holding a wriggling, twisting *Buthus tamulus* by the tail. I make myself ready; capillary tube in my right hand, my gloved left hand steadying my right forearm, both elbows resting on the table.

"Go for it, bro."

Thiru brings the scorpion close to the tea-strainer; its legs scrabble and grip on the mesh dome, and the electrical circuit is completed. Its tail starts to pulsate and jerk between the forcep arms; the last two segments shudder in spastic delight, and the hooked sting's tip grows a tiny drop of cloudy liquid. I advance the mouth of my glass capillary to the milky venom, and capture the precious harvest in the tube.

One done, one hundred and ninety-nine to go. We continue our unchanging routine: Thirukumar puts the scorpion back in its box, lids it, and records the date of milking in the log-book, while I, with my hand gloved against cold-burn, take the sample bottle from its dry ice nest in the Thermos and unscrew its lid, one-handed. I insert the end of the capillary into the bottle, and press the rubber bulb to eject the venom cargo. I work quickly, imagining the venom freezing inside the capillary and shattering the tube. Thiru says that wouldn't happen, but I don't want to risk spraying the room – or my eyes – with tiny glass shards dripping with *B. tamulus* toxins. I think of Krish's aunt, shuffling around in bare feet, and shudder.

When Krish's aunt finally turned her back on the hair-hung motorbike carcase, that day we first arrived, she made to walk past us as though we were geckos on the wall. No surprise, no greeting, no response to my greeting. Thiru, typically, went straight to the point.

"Why were you doing that?" he asked.

"My son."

"It's a motorbike."

"It's all that's left."

"Is he dead? A motorbike accident?" (Sheesh, Thiru! Subtle as a Jagannath cart!)

"Who knows?"

"When did it happen?"

"When did what happen?"

I decided I'd better intervene.

"Amma, we are friends of Krishnamurthy. Your nephew. From Ooty."

This time, she looked at me, and raised her hands to her bald head. One of them found a long grey hair, a lonely survivor, and she pulled it out, blinking at me through watery eyes.

"Krishnamurthy?" she said, winding the hair around her finger.

"Your nephew. He asks if you might let us stay in your lovely house, while we set up our business. We'll be no trouble. We'll bring food, and cook. You can eat with us; we'd be honoured. Here – please take this."

I presented her with a box of sweets – burfi and gulab jamun from Mopuvan's Cafe, back home in Ooty. She took the box absently.

"Krishnamurthy? He eats too much." She shuffled through the back door and into the house. We followed her. "Krishnamurthy. Curse him."

She seemed to accept our presence without question, and we helped her out as much as we could. Sometimes she ate with us, and sometimes she just watched us eating, as though puzzled by the activity. She never asked why we were there or what we were doing.

Thiru places another scorpion on the electrified mesh. This one is reluctant to release its precious bounty, so I stroke its abdomen with the capillary tube; the extra irritation is sufficient to entice the fluid from its sac.

Perhaps no scorpion is beautiful; but *B. tamulus* seems especially ugly. Its common English name is the red scorpion, but it's predominantly yellow. Not the bright yellow of fruits or flowers, but the yellow of pus, of putrefaction. On the six segments of its fat, strong tail, the colour becomes progressively darker, reaching a dull orange at the hooked sting; the plates on its back are dirty grey. Its dust-pale pincers are thin and delicate, as pathetic as a gharial's snout, but cocked pugilistically, perpetually at the ready; the tiny black eyes on top of its head are robotically hostile. What kind of awareness can such a thing have, as it waits under rocks for beetles and baby lizards? Dust and death and the joy of the glut; that is the sum of its existence.

"So why are we doing this, bro?" I don't need to ask, of course; I just want to hear him tell me, that's all. The repetition comforts me. Also, I love it when he loses himself in numbers. It's like putting a gasping fish back into water, and watching it swim. "How is this going to make us rich?"

"The market value of one litre of *Buthus tamulus* venom is eight and a half million US dollars, which is sixty-five million rupees."

Yep, scorpion venom is the most expensive fluid in the world, according to Google. We confirmed it by phoning up Anant Biosolutions, in Coimbatore. *"Yes,"* said the lady scientist we spoke to, *"yes we need* B. tamulus *venom for our research, and yes we pay the market price for it. About five hundred rupees per microlitre."* We couldn't believe our ears.

"Each scorpion produces approximately twenty-five microlitres of venom per milking, which is twenty-five millionths of a litre. This represents twelve thousand, five hundred rupees per scorpion, per milking."

"Twelve thousand, five hundred per scorpion? *Hazaar!*"

"Thus, to milk two hundred scorpions is to generate stock worth two and a half million rupees."

It had only taken us a few days to collect two hundred scorpions; they're dirt-common around the hamlet where Krish's aunt lives. During the day, we'd walk around the stony little hill behind her house, turning over rocks to reveal one *Buthus* after another, snugly folded in their little scraped-out homes. More productive still was to search by night with the old mercury vapour UV lamp that Thiru had found in Ooty market. The label on it indicated it had come from the Cosmic Ray Research station just outside Ooty – they'd obviously chucked it out when it stopped working. But Thiru had fixed it somehow. So at night, we would drive out into the countryside, leave the jeep idling and connect the UV lamp and convertor to the engine battery; then we'd walk to the limit of the extension cable, in a big circle around the car. And invariably, in each location, the ultraviolet would show up a few *B. tamulus*, fluorescing cold blue in the hot night. Once we found a pair dancing claw-in-claw, in some kind of freaky courtship. Another time we found a giant black scorpion, big as my hand, tearing a lizard to pieces; but we had no use for that.

"Therefore, ten milkings of our herd provides an asset worth twenty-five million rupees. Two and a half crores." Thiru looks me straight in the eye again. "This is our tenth session."

We'd built in a contingency, of course, to allow for market fluctuations. One crore each; that is, ten million rupees apiece – that was the real target. For me, to buy a small guest-house back in Ooty, so I can sit in its garden making money from tourists until I die. For Thiru, to fund a PhD in Cambridge.

"Tell me again, bro – why Cambridge? Why not Heidelberg or Harvard?"

Thiru puts the lid back on the box of Number 127 before answering. This topic is too important for him to discuss and at the same time do.

"Cambridge gave birth to physics! First came Isaac Newton's *Principia*, the revolutionary treatise on classical mechanics; his seminal work on optics, his invention of calculus. Then Young's wave theory of light, Stokes' development of vector calculus, and the establishment of the Cavendish Laboratory under Maxwell, whose theories of electricity and magnetism were vindicated after his death. Afterwards, the atom's dissection by Thomson and later Chadwick; then Wilson's cloud chambers, Rutherford's nuclear fission, and the first controlled nuclear disintegration by Cockroft and Walton."

Thiru is gazing into the middle distance, where subatomic particles follow their seductive trajectories. The cloudy whirl of the electron, the squat momentum of the neutron; for him, these are manifestations of something like the divine.

"And from India, Cambridge embraced Ramanujan the mathematical prodigy, and Subrahmanyan Chandrasekhar, who showed that the mass of a white dwarf could not exceed 1.44 times that of the sun. In Cambridge, Jayant Narlikar and Fred Hoyle developed the Hoyle-Narlikar theory of conformal gravity. And above all" – Thiru looks me in the eye again – "above all, Cambridge welcomed Homi Jehangir Bhabha, father of the Indian nuclear programme and founder of the Tata Institute of Fundamental Research, whose work on the absorption of cosmic radiation led to the establishment of the Cosmic Ray Research Centre in Ooty!" He drew a breath. "Knowledge old and new is in the very stones of Cambridge, and I *will not study anywhere else.*"

"You'll fit right in, bro!" I hold the capillary tube as if it were a gun, and pretend to shoot him. Unsmilingly, he gets up to retrieve the next *Buthus.*

The annoying thing is, Thiru would have aced the entrance tests for any university in the world. But during the first of his final school year exams, doubtless on his way to his usual hundred percent, he'd noticed the normal Higher Secondary activity – students' friends and relatives clustered outside the windows of the examination hall, handing in answers and cheat sheets. It was no more blatant than any other pre-university exam session, in any other year; but this year, Thiru was there. He asked the invigilator to do something; and when she wouldn't, he got up, ripped his paper in half, and stormed out. *"Since the exams are meaningless, I will not take them,"* he said. *"From now on, I will teach myself."* And teach himself he did; but there's a limit to the amount of particle physics research you can do from a tiny house on Ooty's Mukurti Street.

I look into the Thermos flask. "The dry ice is getting a bit low," I say. "And we've only got enough in the box for a couple more refills."

Dry ice is critical to our whole operation; we have to keep the venom deep-frozen, or it will degrade. Something to do with the nature of the toxins; some of them are enzymes, and if they don't get flesh to eat, they eat each other, I guess. This cold storage requirement almost stopped the whole project; how do you keep something at minus twenty Celsius in an off-grid hamlet on the baking plains of South India? We looked at solar-powered freezers, but Thiru muttered about watt-hours and battery capacity, and rejected the concept. In fact, the answer was just a few doors down from us on Mukurti Street: Mopuvan, the cafe owner. He operated an ice-cream franchise in Ooty, renting out little carts to local kids who'd push them along Garden Road selling cones to tourists. So how was the ice-cream kept frozen, without electricity, in a cart? *"Dry ice,"* said Mopuvan. *"There's a distribution centre in Mettupalayam. Use my account number, you can get it cheap."* So, once a week, Thiru and I drive from Krish's aunt's house to Mettupalayam, buy six bags of dry ice pellets, and bring them back in a thick polystyrene trunk.

Thiru makes a small, precise tick in the log-book hanging from the wall. Number 173: milked. I continue talking to his back.

"The point is, if we drive to Mettupalayam for more dry ice, we'll have to delay the meeting with Anant Biosolutions."

"No. We've arranged the meeting. The last milking will be done by midday. We'll eat, and then drive to Coimbatore. The dry ice *will last.* And once they buy it from us, the storage *will be* their problem. Plenty of time."

Thiru was right, logically, but I couldn't help being nervous about it. It just didn't feel right. You milk the last scorpion, you drive off to a biotech company with a small bottle of frozen liquid, and you come back with twenty-five million rupees. There just didn't seem to be enough *process*. Something was missing. But Thiru was implacable.

"Are you sure the meeting's set up?" I ask.

"I spoke to Dr P. Patel. By telephone. She agreed to a meeting."

"But we never got anything in writing."

"She has a PhD from Cambridge. I checked her CV. On the internet."

"So?"

"So she *will be* reliable. She will understand the importance of truth, of consistency. She is a Cambridge-educated scientist."

I suppose Thirukumar and I got our interest in science from our father. Not that he was a scientist, as such; he had no education. But we'd watch him at his cunning alchemy, and when you analysed his occupation, it was all physics and chemistry. On fine days, he'd sit down on a mat outside our house on Mukurti Street, and put his portable smithy on the pavement in front of him. He'd fire up this thick clay vessel, and hoarsely blow into it through a long tube, blow until its coals glowed white. In a crucible, he'd soften a small nugget of gold, then place it on an iron ingot and tease and hammer it until it took on its final form – the decorative pendant of an earring, perhaps, or a bead for a bride's *mangala sutra* necklace. Other times he'd take a spiral of stolen copper wire and melt it into a glowing bleb; we'd look on, entranced, as he made this formless thing into a delicate filigree, a decoration perhaps for the antique boxes that Krishnamurthy manufactured, just down the road. But the real base of his trade – performed in clandestine operations in the yard behind our house – was not gold, but lead. This he would melt into a silver-grey puddle and pour into moulds shaped like rings or pendants. When cool, the leaden simulacra were hung on a hook-shaped negative electrode which itself was suspended, a few inches from its positive counterpart, in an empty glass tub. Then Father would take that secret, oh-so-preciously guarded jar of fluid from its hiding place and carefully pour its contents into the tub, until both electrodes were immersed. We'd often seen him make up fresh stock of this magical liquid by dissolving a carefully measured grain of gold in cyanide-based solvent. To watch solid wealth disappear into shapeless poison was a fearful thing, and my brother and I would gnaw our own lips with the tension. But the gold was still there, in solution; its retrieval required only the application of electricity. So, Father would turn on the power supply, sending a precisely controlled current through the submersed leaden jewels and their liquid bath; and we would watch, Thiru and I, as the voltage slowly drove dissolved gold to the negative electrode and deposited it, atom by atom, on the leaden jewel templates. When I was a kid, I thought the lead was actually being transmuted, but Thiru seemed to instinctively know the real chemistry of electroplating.

Thiru replaces the last scorpion in its box, and makes the last entry in our paper log. I eject the last droplet of precious venom into the sample bottle, screw on its lid and push it down into the dregs of dry ice. Then I close the Thermos.

It's done. It's done.

I smile at Krish; his expression doesn't change. Inside the hut, all is quiet. Outside, Krish's aunt increases the volume.

"*O my son, my son; why did you leave your good home for the cold mists of death? You will never have children. You will never bring joy to me now, o my son.*"

"Amma?" I call. "We are going to eat now. Please come and join us." She stops moaning, and I hear the soft slap of palms on bald pate; but she stays outside.

After lunch, we top up the Thermos with the last of the dry ice from our store and put our precious cargo in the rented jeep. Driving to Coimbatore in the heat of the day will require every last frozen pellet; but Thiru is confident. "It *will* last," he says. However, we are both silent throughout the journey, and whenever I look at Thiru, he is either running his hands through his hair or is hunched forward clutching his knees. I put a CD on, some heavy metal to psych us up. Rock is the only kind of music he likes; anything else just goes over his head. And after a while, even Thiru relaxes somewhat.

Getting into Anant Biosolutions is a bit of a palaver; security isn't expecting us, for some reason, and won't let us in without ticking the appropriate box. But there are only two boxes: *University* and *Company*, and we are neither. Thiru embarks on a long and detailed explanation, but I cut him short.

"We are representatives of Buthus Tamulus Extractions Limited," I say. Thiru starts to object, but I silence him. Sometimes it's easier just to give people what they expect.

But 'Buthus Tamulus Extractions Limited' kind of backfires, because when Security phones through to Dr Patel's secretary, she says she's never heard of the company. Security looks at us with suspicion.

"Tell her we have scorpion venom for Dr Patel," I say. "A lot of it. As agreed."

The guard is unconvinced. He blows through his moustache, and scrutinises our dusty jeep and our dusty sandals; then he glances down at his own carefully ironed khaki trousers, his polished boots.

"Why would she want scorpion venom?"

"It is very valuable. It is for research, for making new medicines."

"But it is a poison, not a medicine."

I grind my teeth, and once more stop Thiru from starting an aggressively intellectual monologue.

"Please – trust me, it is very important, and she asked us to bring it. Just say to her, we have scorpion venom. Please?"

Eventually, he consents to phone her again, and eventually we are let through. But all the while, the dry ice sublimes.

Dr Patel keeps us waiting in the hot foyer. When she finally appears, pushing through the security turnstile, I recognise her from the mugshots on the Anant Biosolutions website. *Dr Preeti Patel: Head of Drug Discovery.* But in the mugshot she is smiling, whereas now she is wearing a 'what's-all-this-about' frown, which deepens when she sees us sitting on the edge of our seats – me clutching a cheap Thermos flask, Thiru tugging at his unkempt hair. I bounce up enthusiastically, nudging Thiru.

"Dr Patel? Very pleased to meet you." I make the usual introductions; I guess she won't speak Tamil, so I use English. She nods at us vacantly.

"Just remind me, please – you are here for ... ?"

Something clutches at my insides; fury or fear? *Thiru – you said you'd spoken to her! You said you'd arranged the meeting!* But Thiru is talking; I've bottled him up too long, and this is one step too far. He takes his hands from his hair and talks rapidly, addressing her ankles.

"We spoke by telephone, twice. The first time was on the 18th May, at eleven fifty-five a.m. You said that Anant Biosolutions wanted *Buthus tamulus* venom. You said you'd buy as much as we could get. At the market price. The second time we spoke was on the 28th November. That's when you agreed to this meeting."

"Ah. I do remember that call. It was – um, yes. Anyway, I expected some kind of diary meeting request or email confirmation, which I never got. So I guess the meeting never got into the system."

"You have a PhD from Cambridge." Thiru says this as though it explains all that has passed and guarantees all that will come. He is still looking at her feet.

"Look," I say. I take the lid off the Thermos, and offer the open mouth to her so that she can see the sample bottle. "That is pure *Buthus tamulus* venom. It's been kept in dry ice since harvesting. It's taken us nearly a year to collect."

In her face, something hidden comes to the surface and is quickly suppressed.

"Are you sure? I mean, you know how to distinguish *Buthus tamulus* from other species?"

Thiru snorts. "Obviously!" he snaps. I cringe.

"Venom collection is not simple, you know," says Dr Patel. "If you don't milk them carefully, they get stressed. And then you get not just venom, but other secretions too. The contamination makes the venom unusable."

Thiru snorts again. "We used the latest electrostimulation method, published last year. Fouad and Halmet, 2008. The product *will be* perfect."

She is interested; I can tell by the way the shutters have come down, the way she keeps her voice neutral and her face expressionless.

"How much is here?"

"Fifty millilitres. The product of twenty-five microlitres per milking, from two hundred scorpions, milked ten times each. At the current market price – "

"Thiru! Let Dr Patel see for herself."

She takes the Thermos, and angles it so that she can look inside to where the sample bottle rattles around with the last few dry ice pellets.

"We'd have to check the purity. A quick run through the mass spec. Are you okay with that?"

"Sure," I say. But Thiru raises his head. For the first time, he looks at her directly.

"What size sample will you use? For the mass spectrometer." *Good point, bro!*

She smiles at him, suddenly laying on the charm. "Maybe a microlitre. The machine's very sensitive, so we don't need much. Don't worry."

"One microlitre is worth five hundred rupees."

Her smile remains fixed. "But we have to check it. You understand that?"

Thiru slowly nods. His gaze doesn't leave her eyes.

❖

Thiru has different kinds of silences: an angry silence, a frightened silence, a sad silence. The one that he inflicts on me as we drive back to Krish's aunt's hut is different; it's an end-of-everything silence. I haven't heard it before, not even after that time he'd walked out of the Higher Secondary exams. I'd like to cheer him up, but I don't know what to say, and anyway when he's in non-speaking mode there's just no point.

I am driving too fast, but everyone deals with things in their own way. When a cyclist weaves in front of me, I brake hard, and the Thermos shoots off the back seat and rattles around on the jeep's floor. But we arrive safely, and in record time.

I get out of the jeep and look up at the sky. There's no light pollution where Krish's aunt lives; the constellations are stunning. As I walk around the car, I pick out Nakshatra stars glowing in the night: there Vishakha; there Swati; and there bright Chitra, so white it is almost blue. Thiru is still sitting in the passenger seat, his fists clenched in his hair. It looks painful. I retrieve the Thermos from the back, and open Thiru's door.

"Come on."

Under the light of a wind-up lantern, we go into the house. Krish's aunt is still moaning around the back. We take our plastic boxes, our Dairy, outside and stack them next to the jeep. I start up the engine again, and open the bonnet so that I can hook up the UV lamp to the car battery. I hold the lamp aloft while Thiru carefully releases the scorpions. In the jasmine-rich night, they glow as blue as Lord

Shiva's skin; we watch their cold fluorescence slowly fade as they leave our circle of imperceptible light, as though each were a bright dream leaving a black-lit stage.

When Dr Patel returned, after an hour, I knew what she was going to say. I could see it in her brusque tread, in the belligerent set of her shoulders. Get rid of them, said her body, in every language in the world. I looked at her while she gave us the briefest of brief, unapologetic explanations, but I wasn't listening. I was just looking, and thinking that she had never had to confront a single real challenge in her life. You can always tell; such people have a bloom on their skin that real hunger has never brushed away, a confidence that real hardship has never dented. She's seen injustice her whole life, I thought, but never experienced it. Rich parents, the right university, a PhD in America or Europe, and back to India to lord it over the rest of us. I envied her so much; for a minute I hated her.

It's okay; I'll win out somehow, I know I will. It's Thiru I'm worried about. We walk back to the hut, listening to Krish's aunt.

"*O my son. You will never know what wonders the world held for you, what riches and joy. O my son, you will never share such joys with me.*"

"Thiru? You okay?"

He is silent.

"*O my son.*"

"Thiru, listen. You'll still get to Cambridge, okay? We'll make it happen."

"No. I *will never* study again."

"Dude! Don't go all-or-nothing like this. There are grants, government schemes. Someone with your brain – "

"No."

"*O my son – you will never see your mother grow old.*"

"But *Cambridge*, bro!"

For no good reason, we walk around the back of the hut, to where Krish's aunt crouches before her altar of hair and black steel. An oil-lamp has turned her face into a skull of shadows and light.

"*My son, my son. Never, never.*"

"Cambridge?" says Thiru. "You want to know about Cambridge?" He spits to one side. "Go and look in the Thermos. That's Cambridge."

"*O my son. You will never know the dreams I had for you.*"

"Just go and look."

I'm a bit puzzled, but okay. I take the wind-up lamp and go into the hut. I pick up the Thermos and shake it. Something skitters and rolls inside. I open the flask, and out falls the sample bottle. It's warm now, but as Dr Patel said, the contamination had rendered it valueless anyway, so who cares? I pick up the bottle, and look at the clear liquid; so much effort, so much investment, for this mouthful of worthless fluid.

Odd that it's gone clear; the poison was cloudy-white when secreted. Like milk, in fact. I look at the little container again; a standard laboratory sample bottle: transparent, cylindrical, flat-bottomed, with a plastic screw-on lid. On its side, I see some faint writing – marker-pen that has been carelessly rubbed away.

"*Never, my son, never.*"

We'd never written on the sample bottle. There was no need.

I don't know how long I sit there, digesting this, running through the possibilities in my mind, and wondering how to manage Thiru. I have to wind up the lamp several times.

"*O my son, my son.*"

When I go outside again, Thiru is on his knees in the dust, beside Krish's aunt. The motorbike carcase has a fresh harvest of hair, rich and black against its older, greyer blanket, and Thiru's scalp is hillocked with dark points that gleam in the lamplight.

"*O my son, where are you now? You will never return to me.*"

Thiru reaches to the oil-lamp, and holds something over its flame. A clump of hair – it catches and flares up. He throws it to the ground beneath the motorbike wreck, and the dressings of the dead steel briefly blaze and stink in the warm, South Indian night.

☾

BALANCE

"Who will search the wide infinities of space to count the universes side by side, each containing its Brahma, its Vishnu, its Shiva? Who can count the Indras in them all – those Indras side by side, who reign at once in all the innumerable worlds?"
- Brahma Vaivarta Purana, ~AD 1500

"That linker particles have not been observed since 2059 only adds to their mystery. In retrospect, their sudden disappearance, together with the dramatic loss of key Bhabha-Yamada personnel in the same year, signalled the end of a remarkable period in the annals of the Institute."
- The Bhabha-Yamada Institute: A History, Aiko Tanaka.
Chandra Corporation Scientific Press, Bengaluru, May 2064

FLOWPOINTS: INCALCULABLE-514229

I thought it was a monkey at first, because of the noises. And then I thought, monkeys do not come here: these high peaks are too cold for them. So I walked from my shed up to the eucalyptus grove, from where the sounds came: there, where the mist makes its own shadow.

Professor S. Tharakan was naked. His mouth was black, from soil that he had pushed into it. Not to eat, I believe, but to stop breath. He had not succeeded; biology strives always to exist, despite everything, despite anything.

Blood ran down his cheeks and into the soil around his mouth. He was on his knees, one hand against the trunk of a eucalypt: as though to say, We are brothers, the tree and I. But the trunk's bark was scratched and bloodied.

He took his hand from the tree, and pawed again at where his eyes had once been, as if to assure himself that they had indeed been put out.

Such noises he made.

I did not find his eyes.

❖

"What next? Will *you* start believing in ghosts, too? This is 2059, not 1759! We're *scientists,* remember! And I expect everyone at the Bhabha-Yamada Institute – including whoever replaces Suresh – to *behave* like scientists!"

Chandy ignored the slur. If Vinayak would rather lambast Suresh Tharakan's character than discuss the post Suresh had so tragically vacated, then so be it; but Chandy John would rise above it. No job was worth bad-mouthing a colleague – particularly one in poor Suresh's position.

"From what I saw, Suresh was very diligent."

"He almost broke the Cage! That is *not* my idea of diligence!" Vinayak Mulgund chopped at the air with his hand; behind him, hill-station mists writhed against the office window. And behind *them,* knew Chandy, the Ghats fell away to the warm South Indian plains, two thousand metres below. *Where home once was.*

"But even when the Cage returns to full operation – when it simulates the full range of alternative realities – there's no guarantee it will reveal another source of linker particles. It's possible that the particle flux, and the energy flow it mediates, is a one-off; once it reaches zero, that's it."

"No!" Outside, the mist thinned. Something on Vinayak's desk caught the sun and winked at Chandy John: Tipu Sultan's famous mechanical toy, scaled down to paper-weight size. A metal Mysore tiger mauling a metal British soldier. "Listen, Chandy. The particles have been reaching us, ergo there is a channel, a bridge, by which they arrive. If one bridge fails, another can be built. If one channel is blocked, we use the Cage to find another. I know it to be possible. I *know* it!"

Chandy hesitated. Vinayak had thrown too much Bhabha-Yamada research money at the linker particle project to back down; he'd have to be gently guided towards more productive avenues. Not that the linkers weren't worthy of study – they were, quite possibly, the most disruptive discovery in physics for a century or more. How else to describe the advent of a new sub-atomic particle that – by one interpretation of the data – seemed to flow from an *alternative reality*? Especially one that, by *any* interpretation of the data, was orders of magnitude more energetic than OMG – Oh-My-God – particles, themselves previously thought to be the most kinetically extreme of the cosmic ray family. Chandy's colleague Wehmeier, with clumsy imagination, had wanted to call these extraordinary objects OMGG particles – Oh-My-*Great*-God – but Vinayak had vetoed Wehmeier's proposal. No; the particles would be called OMVs – Oh-My-*Vishnu*. A new physics for a new age – the *Indian* Age! Vinayak's influence, however, had its limits: Institute comics soon asserted that OMV stood for Oh My Vinayak, and the acronym never replaced 'linker particle' in the Bhabha-Yamada physics lexicon.

But even the most sceptical conceded that Vinayak was right about one thing – this new particle, which made an OMG look as impressive as a dropped ping-pong ball, did indeed promise a new physics. Experimentation at the Planck scale beckoned; *"India shall blow bubbles in quantum foam,"* Vinayak had proclaimed; social media had frothed. But now the linker particle flow, its origin still obscure, was in decline, and Vinayak seemed to think the world was ending. If Chandy wanted Suresh's job, he'd have to treat the Bhabha-Yamada director with kid gloves.

"If we focused more on identifying the linkers' exact origin – "

"The point is not where the OMVs come from – though, if it makes any difference to you, I am happy with your reading of Deutsch's many-worlds thesis – but how they get here. The route of transfer. And that is where Suresh failed me. Catastrophically."

Vinayak picked up the metal desk toy. By turning a small wheel between finger and thumb, he could make the tiger's head move up and down, up and down, as though it were tearing out the throat of the soldier.

"Let me be clear. I reward results. And the rewards will be great, *very* great, if – "

Chandy John waited. A familiar electronic whine dopplered past the window: an auto-hamsa, taking its cargo of scientists from one part of the Institute to another.

" – and *when* the OMV decline is reversed."

When an auto-hamsa is crushed by a juggernaut full of moon-ore, its metal shell ribbons across tarmac like yellow apple-peel. Chandy John pushed the image away. *Stop.*

"You understand." Up and down. Up and down.

"The Cage hypersim does what it does. We can't dictate the results. We can only sit in the Cage, observe the simulated realities that the Cage reveals, and react." Chandy John smiled, trying to take the accusation out of his response.

"But Suresh's reaction was unsatisfactory. Obviously. Or we'd have another OMV bridge." Up and down. *How long does it take one soldier to die?*

"I don't know what he saw. But if you think I'm the right person for the job, one of my first tasks – after verifying the Cage sub-systems – would be to examine his methodology and repeat his last simulation run."

"The methodology is perfect. I designed it myself. The fault was in the observer."

Chandy John smiled again, this time to hide disbelief: *Vinayak* designing a state-of-the-art hypersimulation protocol? But Vinayak was no fool, and his black stare increased in hostility.

"Remind me – why *do* you wish to join Bhabha-Yamada?"

And there was a question more difficult than any posed by sub-atomic physics. Vinayak's point – for his queries often were disguised statements – was that Chandy John's options were limited. With

Europe in ruins, America turning on itself, and China accelerating its eastward metastasis into Australasia, Indian particle physicists largely had to choose between, on the one hand, the Bhabha-Yamada Institute, and on the other, the Chandra Corporation – in Bengaluru's techno-hub – where Chandy currently worked. Chandy John's job search, however, was prompted not by ambition but by personal factors: not least the noiseless scream of bereavement that filled his empty house each night. *Dawn, my loveliest. Abhishek, my dearest. How can anyone live with such loss?* To stay in Bengaluru was impossible; to return to the palmyras of his native Kerala, impractical. Also, Bhabha-Yamada offered the teasing hope of resolution; maybe even the guilty hope of companionship.

The silence became uncomfortable. "I feel like I need a change," Chandy John said, finally.

Vinayak's ageless face showed no expression. "We are of course aware of the sad loss of your wife and son. We commiserate. But – forgive me – are you certain you are ready for a position of this nature?"

"Life goes on."

"Sometimes."

Without dropping his gaze, Vinayak began collecting up the documents on his desk. Chandy John's CV, his letters of recommendation, copies of his last three publications: all were collected into a small pile of wasted carbon and ink. The desk's tableland – bare except for a glass of water, a clutch of Ayurvedic powders and the tin soldier's infinitely protracted death – spoke teak words to Chandy John: *There is nothing for you here.*

"Time for my presentation," Vinayak said, at last.

Chandy John followed Vinayak's bobbing Gandhi cap and matching grey kurta to the Institute's main lecture theatre. *Blown it,* he thought, and shrugged at Aiko and poor sad Wehmeier as he took the seat they'd saved for him in the front row.

"Not good," he murmured, in response to Aiko's mouthed question. "Looks like I'm staying in Bengaluru."

Aiko squeezed his shoulder, making an *'oh no'* face. Wehmeier waggled his hand in a gesture that could have meant anything. On the stage, Vinayak fussed over the audiovisual set-up while the audience murmured and shuffled. Chandy John looked around: the familiar Bhabha-Yamada melting-pot. Mostly Indians and Japanese, reflecting the Institute's history. A knot of Chinese defectors, huddled together for mutual support. And, of course, the usual scatter of Europeans. Chandy knew their stories without asking: refugees, washed up on Indian shores like so much flotsam. These, however, had been saved from begging in the street by their recondite expertise: dark matter, black holes, big data, hypersimulation programming. The West's pain, Vinayak often said, is India's gain. So he willingly provided temporary contracts to these desperate people; nevertheless, the foreigners would never progress beyond Senior Scientist level – Vinayak Mulgund would see to that. Europe burns: Jai Hind!

"Ladies, gentlemen." Vinayak's voice, amplified by the pitch-perfect sound system, hushed the fidgeting audience. "You know I place great value on my time; I value yours equally, and therefore will be brief."

As Vinayak went through the usual protocols, Chandy John's mind wandered to the usual places. *Dawn. Abhishek. The pyre's blue-grey column. You sent them into the juggernaut's path.* But then, triggered by that curious instinct of *being watched,* he turned and met the expressionless gaze of an old man. The curve of the front-row seating gave them a mutually uninterrupted line of sight. Odd: someone that age surely should be Lab Head or higher; but Chandy John knew all the Bhabha-Yamada nobility and didn't recognise the man now staring at him. Poorly dressed, even by a scientist's standards; more like a labourer than a lecturer. He did not smile, but neither did he look away; as though in seeing Chandy John, he had identified an aberration worthy of study. For a moment, Chandy John was troubled by a vague sensation of being out of place – an impostor in a foreign reality.

Vinayak's voice changed in tone, and pulled Chandy John's attention back to the stage. "Finally, an announcement. You are all aware of Suresh Tharakan's situation. Most of you will also know, by name at least, Chandy John, from the Chandra Corporation Institute of Technology, who was Suresh's key collaborator in the discovery of OMV particles."

Chandy nodded and gave a half-wave as faces turned towards him.

"As you know, Suresh is unlikely ever to return to the lab. But his senior scientists, Aiko Tanaka and Jurgen Wehmeier, have ensured that our cosmic ray work has continued seamlessly." Vinayak nodded towards the front row. "To lead our effort in this new field, however, we need someone capable of filling the gap left by Suresh. I am very pleased to state that we have offered the position to Chandy John, from CCIT. His involvement with the OMV discovery made him an obvious choice."

And that was how Chandy John heard of the offer he couldn't refuse. Beside him, Aiko punched the air, and leaned towards him. Her hair stroked his cheek as they hugged. Jasmine; musk; the sweet warmth of friendship. Odd thing: as the applause grew and spread, he thought he heard a man's whisper: *This changes nothing – do you agree?* He pulled his lips into a smile, and nodded at his new colleagues, and tried not to think of yellow ribbons on grey tarmac.

❖

I perceive him more often, now, but less clearly. A dark shape, a pale shadow, a whisper in the mist. Why are they so scared? Begging hurts none. One might as well run from an empty bowl. Yet Professor S. Tharakan could not bear to contemplate that beggar's offering; he sought to annul what his own eyes saw. And now the hospital orderlies watch him through each live-long day and each eternal night.

Later, I will go to the detector fields. To keep them proper, yes, all free of weedy growths; but also to partake of their symmetry. To stand in the centre of an array is to be a node in two nets: that described by the detectors and that described by the spaces between them. There, my position is quantum-like, in that to locate it is to change it. Like an electron in a cloud.

We have that much in common, he tells me.

❖

After Vinayak's presentation, Chandy John escaped to the OMV laboratory. This squat accretion of concrete – all sharp angles except for the circular, domed add-on that housed the Cage – was the ugliest part of the Institute, but enjoyed the best location. From the lab's perch above the rest of Bhabha-Yamada, Chandy could look down on the steep arrays of cosmic ray detectors, set in the grassy slopes like waist-high pagodas of grey plastic. Below them was the campus – the apartment block, the cafeteria, the library and lecture rooms. And behind that, he knew, lay Udhagamandalam – the hill station once known as Ooty, and so favoured by the British that they tried to turn it into Surrey – while all around, the Nilgiri peaks marched on, cascading down to the plains in one direction and to the coast in the other. Today, however, the mists had swallowed all but the nearest of the serried detectors, and the surrounding mountains were no more than a suspicion of unseen mass.

"Your new empire," said Wehmeier, from his desk. He already had half an eye on his simulation program, and fidgeted at the keyboard. "We should have a catch-up, *ja*? Show you the latest numbers."

"Let's save that for when I start, Jurgen. Anyway, first I'd like to go through Suresh's files. Everyone okay with that?"

A brief silence roared of unspoken things; nobody looked at the one desk that was clear of physicist's clutter.

"Of course," said Aiko. "I'm sure they'll give you immediate access to his data, under the circumstances. I'll ask. But Chandy – "

"Yes?"

"Suresh wasn't himself in the last few weeks."

"I understand. Vinayak told me." *"Suresh began seeing things,"* Vinayak had said. *"Patterns in numbers. Shapes in mist. Ghosts."*

That silence again: Aiko glanced at Jurgen, and Jurgen's thousand-yard stare drilled through his screen and into a universe of universes. Beyond Jurgen, Chandy John could see the closed and locked titanium door, set into a titanium frame that was, he knew, contiguous with the hidden framework of the Cage's domed housing. Above the door, a light was set into the wall, alongside a warning in red capitals: FLASHING LIGHT MEANS EXPOSURE BREACH: CUT HYPERSIM IMMEDIATELY.

"Anyway." Chandy John stood and hooked backpack straps over his shoulder. "It's been a long day."

"Of course. You must be tired. You're staying in the old guest-house, the one on the way to Coonoor?"

"Yes. Back home tomorrow morning."

"You know that they've moved Suresh to NIMHANS now? You could visit him, if they'll let you."

"NIMHANS?"

"National Institute for Medical Health and Neurosciences. On the Hosur road, pretty much next door to you in Bengaluru. He's in one of the special wards – suicide watch, with a room to himself."

"I'll definitely drop by. Thanks, Aiko."

They stood in the doorway of the OMV lab, and shook hands. As Chandy John turned to the grassy slopes and detector arrays, he saw a hunched, drab figure shuffling up the path towards them: the old man from the lecture theatre, who had stared at Chandy so oddly.

"Who *is* that?"

Aiko followed his gesture with her eyes, and then dimpled. Her smile seemed to follow a flawless geometry; its arc an expression of the formula for perfect joy. Dawn's had been the same.

"Thirukumar," she said. "Old Thiru, the Institute legend. He's been the handyman at Bhabha-Yamada since it was the Ooty Cosmic Ray Laboratory. Sixty years, maybe more, Suresh told me. He should have retired a decade ago."

Wehmeier nodded, and gnawed at a fingernail. "In a way, he *is* retired. He spends half his time in lectures, and the other half in front of his store." He pointed at a small shed, with a corrugated iron roof, set between the topmost detector array and the eucalyptus woods. A fold-up chair propped the shed's door open.

"True. He'll sit there for hours. Just staring into the mist, or reading physics papers." Aiko shook her head. "Let's hope Vinayak never realises."

Wehmeier turned back to Chandy John. "Something you should know – Thiru was the one who found Suresh, at the top there." Wehmeier nodded towards the eucalyptus trees on the hill behind the OMV laboratory. "He was opening up his shed in the morning, and heard sounds coming from the trees."

"I thought Suresh was found in the Cage."

"No. He ran the program late that night, it's true. He left the hypersim on; it took me a month to repair. But the autolog shows that he left the Cage in the early hours. And then, as far as we can tell, instead of going back down to his apartment, he went up to the top, where he – did what he did. Thiru found him in the morning. Naked, bleeding, clawing at the trees."

"That must have been so difficult for the old man – seeing something like that."

Wehmeier shook his head. "Thiru has not the personality that is affected by externalities, I think. He understands neither grief nor joy. In my opinion."

As they watched, the old man stepped between two of the solar diode posts that lined the path, left the stamped gravel and walked to the array's centre. He bent painfully over one of the cosmic ray detectors, brushing at its pyramidic housing as if to remove debris left by the mountain winds: like a crippled old Daitya come down from heaven to tend the puny dwellings of men.

❖

In the guest-house that evening, Chandy John found himself listening to the silence that dogs the solitary traveller. Silence that is not silence: inaudible echoes, unheard whispers.

Guilt follows you; this night and each dark night, forever.

He stood, shaking his head as though to see off a fly, and walked around his room, studying the famously odd decor of the old guest-house. On one wall, a glass case containing five butterflies pinned to a white cork base: each butterfly entirely black, black as sin, wings and body and all. On the wall opposite, a framed batik print: the spread hoods of cobras protecting a stern goddess from a marigold sun. On a third wall, blue curtains which hid the room's single window with their old, damp cloth.

And each night declares your life's sum unabsolvable, your soul as irredeemable as rotten fruit. Don't you agree?

"Shut up," said Chandy John, into the empty room. He turned to his device and clicked on the newsfeed: *China declares absorption of*

Papua New Guinea into its 'Eastern Protectorate', ignores Australian protests; Fall-out from European disaster has made North Sea a dead zone, say scientists; California militias routed by Mexican Army. His mind overflowed with evidence of human folly; nevertheless, he could not escape the persistent feeling of some task unfinished, some question unanswered. Had Vinayak raised something for him to action? Something about the Deutsch hypothesis perhaps? He went over the interview dialogue; at the point the many-worlds theory came up, he'd been speaking to Vinayak's back while Vinayak stared through the window.

"Deutsch's idea was that alternative realities can interact with each other, because some of their aspects are fungible. So other realities can – maybe, I grant you, at a level largely invisible to us – influence us in some way. And I think that the energy imbalance represented by the linker particle – sorry, OMV – flow could be a manifestation of that. They show where one reality leaks into another."

Vinayak had remained silent for a long while. Finally he had nodded and turned to face Chandy John.

"Fungibility? A preposterous word for a small component of an ancient concept. Had the Europeans been more broadly educated, they would have recognised their little theory as being encompassed by Yoga."

He had paused to drink from his ever-present glass of water.

"Yoga, of which the literal meaning is yoke, and the metaphorical meaning is Union; Union as in the conjunctions of the Nakshatra, the holy planets; Union as in the mating of souls; Union as in the absorption of spirit into the cosmos."

Metaphysical claptrap, Chandy John had thought at the time. But now he wondered if Vinayak had half a point. Indeed, if we accept Deutsch's thesis of different, quantum-entangled realities ... what is *fungibility* other than a manifestation of *union*?

Vinayak's words kept returning, like a brainworm: *"Union, which annuls all the worlds' pains. Don't you agree?"*

His device bleeped, and he pounced on it with relief.

"Aiko?"

"Chandy – sorry to bother you, but I thought I'd let you know I spoke to IT. They've emailed you a read-only access code for Suresh's data files."

"Fast work! Thanks, Aiko. I'll have a look later."

"No problem. By the way, something struck me: how are you getting back to Bengaluru tomorrow?"

"The nine thirty bus from Coonoor."

Chandy John could almost hear the frown behind the sigh. "Listen, Chandy, you *must* start using hamsas again – you know that, don't you? Buses aren't practical – or safe."

"I like buses." The reality, of course, was that Chandy John preferred to risk dacoity rather than face the accusation of two empty seats in an auto-hamsa; and would far rather listen to the chatter of the poor than to the ceaseless whispers that a hamsa would only amplify. *You put your own ambitions first. Again. Didn't you?*

"If you want me to come to Bengaluru and help you pack, I'd be happy to."

Chandy John knew what she was saying: *If you can't be in a hamsa by yourself, I will sit with you.*

"That's really kind, Aiko. But it's fine. I'll manage." Some ghosts must be faced on your own.

"I'm glad you're joining us, Chandy."

"Thanks. Thanks, Aiko." Something warm ignited, deep inside Chandy John; but he stamped it out.

"Chandy – can I mention just one other thing?" Aiko's voice had developed an anxious edge.

"Of course. Go for it."

"Jurgen is angry. Really angry. With Vinayak."

"Who isn't?"

"This is different. Vinayak's been altering the hypersim program. Without discussing it with Jurgen. It makes things very difficult."

"Ah. That explains something he said; something about designing the methodology himself."

"I just thought I'd raise it. You might find a record of the changes in Suresh's Cage files. It would really help Jurgen if you did. Vinayak just ignores him. You know."

"You did right to tell me. Thanks again, Aiko."

After Aiko's warm voice, the cold air felt yet more old and dead. Almost involuntarily, Chandy John hurried to the window and yanked aside the curtains, as though they sought to suffocate him. Something gave: a fastening dangled, hanged, as it were, on a blue thread. Outside, the moon-silvered grass of the guest-house lawn darkened. Mist rose up from the ground and hunched against the pane; on the glass, condensation coalesced into droplets and trickled downwards. Chandy shuddered, closed the curtains again, grabbed his mobile and retreated to the bed.

While running through the day's harvest of e-comms – *delete, delete, delete* – Chandy John found the email that Aiko had mentioned. He retrieved the access code, and logged into the Bhabha-Yamada system: 'Welcome, Visitor. You have no new emails.' Suresh Tharakan's data files and notes were, as expected, orderly and logical. 'Linker particle mass/energy predictions' ...'Lack of concordance with Cygnus X-3 source' ... 'Energy imbalance' ... 'Reverse extrapolation: Linker meta-peak every 65 years' ... That said, there were some unusual observations, as Vinayak had intimated; some, in fact, were downright crazy. In one file, Suresh had displayed linker particle frequencies using a helicopter plot. The extrapolation showed a mad spiral towards a central zero, like water down a plug-hole. If that were true, the flow would disappear with unprecedented speed – indeed, in a matter of weeks. Ridiculous! The scientist in Chandy John smirked; but some ancestral part of him felt its hackles raise. As for the alterations to the hypersim program that Aiko had mentioned – there were no Cage files in Suresh's data files at all. Not one. *Something to speak to Vinayak about.* In fact, Chandy could find only one coding file, on its own at the bottom of Suresh's column of folder icons. The filename looked like a default: '17022059.' The date it was created, presumably: four months ago. Not like tidy, fussy Suresh to leave a file outside a folder, still less to leave one without a meaningful title.

Almost accidentally, Chandy John double-clicked. And as he scanned the one thousand, five hundred and ninety-seven lines of code that was not code, each line comprising the same two words, he shook his head in pity. At the window, the curtain hook swayed on its blue thread: a pendulum that measured invisible currents.

Fatigue won; he closed the file, shut down his device and nuzzled under rough blankets. *Poor, poor Suresh. Just like Aiko said – he was losing it towards the end.* Something dragged his eyelids shut; thoughts welled.

Oh My Vishnu; Vishnu the Blue, Vishnu the Preserver, Supreme Being of the Hindu trinity, greatest of the great five. Vishnu, who dreams the universe into reality while pillowed on the coils of the serpent Shesha. How many dreams might one god have?

Why not exchange this dream for another?

Do you agree?

Outside his window, the mists hung still and dark, as though listening.

FLOWPOINTS: 514229-28657

"It is to stop him hurting himself." The orderly, a buffalo-shouldered Sikh, nodded at the broad canvas belt around Suresh's waist; canvas straps affixed to wrist cuffs prevented the patient from reaching above his midriff. Suresh raised his hands slightly, as though to affirm the arrangement. "He's no danger to anyone else, so I'll leave you alone. But you'll get little sense from our Professor-ji." The orderly turned, his blue tunic straining to accommodate its outsized owner; the NIMHANS logo on his back – a swan on a pond – stretched out of shape as he opened the visiting room door and ducked through it, moving crabwise. From the corridor, a faint smell of faeces and the thin wail of another inmate; the latter, at least, was abruptly cut off by the click-clack of the latch.

"Suresh," said Chandy John. "Suresh, this is Chandy. Remember?"

Suresh, perched on the edge of his bed, remained motionless. The pair of circular gauze pads on his face, held in place by a transverse bandage, made a chimaera of him: a man with the compound eyes of an insect. Beneath the bandage, his face was set into an unmoving mask: drawn cheeks and down-turned mouth, lips pulled back over eroded gums and uneven teeth.

"I've come to see how you are. Can you hear me? Suresh?"

Suresh closed his mouth briefly and swallowed; he made as if to reach to his face, but dropped his hands back to his knees when they were halted by the belt cuffs.

"I'm going to join Bhabha-Yamada, Suresh. To continue our – your – work on linker particles and fungible realities. Can we discuss new data from time to time? I'd really appreciate your insights."

Suresh stiffened, opening his mouth as though in sudden pain. Then he shuddered, and nodded to himself.

"Fungible!" He said the word as though it tasted rotten; as though it contaminated his mouth.

"That's right, Suresh – Deutsch's theory."

"To lose such love, so cheaply."

"Suresh?"

"A wife. A child. Their fragile, priceless affection. These things are not *fungible*."

Something twisted deep inside Chandy, as if to wound his soul. "Suresh – please."

"How many years? And how much pain? Urgh!" He shuddered, and his face spasmed as though he were about to vomit.

"Do you need more analgesia? I can call someone ..."

"I called out. In the Cage. But only the mists came, and what the mists hold. He showed me what was, and is, and what might be. Ah! I could not bear it!"

"Please – you're upsetting yourself. You are safe here in hospital. You are being cared for."

Suresh shook his head. "I could not bear it. I shut my eyes to it. I held fast to the tree – but his story grows in each tree's heartwood. I heard it in the peeling bark."

"That's over now, my friend. Forget it. We're going to make you better."

"He comes, and his echoes come, and echoes of his echoes, this night and each dark night. Such grief, he brings! Such guilt!" Suresh balled his hands into old man's fists: papery skin over humped knuckles.

"Suresh. This is Chandy. Remember? I am real – your nightmares are not."

"Your wife: she wore a blue sari."

"Dawn was English, Suresh. She never got used to saris."

"I saw her. In the woods. But even she cannot redeem such as I."

"Okay. Suresh, I don't think I'm quite connecting with you today. But I just wanted you to know that we're all thinking of you. All of us at the particle lab, all of us at the Institute. I'll come back and see you soon, hopefully with Aiko and Jurgen. Okay?"

"Without eyes, one cannot weep."

As Chandy got up, Suresh shifted in his seat, and swallowed again; a white froth had appeared at each corner of his mouth.

"Suresh – are you trying to say something?"

But it was not until Chandy opened the door that Suresh spoke.

"The cycle has turned now for three hundred years. Why should it not turn and turn again?"

❖

There will be balance, one day.

There are so many equations. Some are beautiful. Some ugly. But all must balance; one side against the other.

Last night, I was woken by the tap-tap of a goldsmith's hammer. Yet there have been no goldsmiths on Mukurti Street for sixty years or more.

Perhaps this is what it means to be old: the past echoes into the present. Angle of incidence equals angle of reflection. But what is it that reflects those dead sounds?

He was weeping again, today, in the mist.

One day, there will be balance.

❖

Three months passed, during which Chandy could neither dispel the nagging sensation of questions left unanswered in high Udhagamandalam, nor completely define their import. Such whispers had been, to some extent, drowned out by the noise of moving from Chandra Corporation to Bhabha-Yamada; but on his first day back in the mountains, surrounded by stacked packing cases, they were exposed, naked and insistent, by the cool silence of his apartment. Aiko's texted invitation to meet in the Bhabha-Yamada cafeteria therefore offered a welcome escape route, and Chandy fled his new residence for a meal that his stomach didn't really need.

"Was it okay? The hamsa ride from Bengaluru?" As she spoke, both hands holding a tray, Aiko nodded towards the far end of the cafeteria. The place was busier than usual; the latest intake of recent graduates milled around like puppies in a new home. Chandy John followed Aiko past the crowded refectory tables in the centre to the small four-seaters by the cafeteria windows. Outside, the clouds were lit orange by a Nilgiri sunset.

"Oh sure, sure, no problem."

In fact, when the hamsa's lemon-yellow fuselage rolled up to his house in Bengaluru, Chandy John had briefly struggled with an elision of realities: not just a wistful dream but the certain knowledge that, when he tapped in his PIN and the hamsa doors opened, he would see Dawn and Abhishek smiling out at him. Of course, there'd been nothing within but the familiar electronic murmur: *You are travelling in a Hamsa Corporation autonomous vehicle. Please confirm that your transport is satisfactory.* He'd set his hamsa account preferences to English, two years ago, because Dawn found it easier; now, changing the preference to Malayalam would seem like a kind of betrayal.

To live on, when those you loved most have crossed the bridge ahead of you – that is betrayal.

"Did you get any sleep on the way? Or are you one of these people who can work in a hamsa?"

"Neither sleep nor work, on this occasion. I couldn't mute the damn thing. Had to endure '*You are travelling with Hamsa Corporation, the world's pre-eminent provider of autonomous vehicles, we thank you for your custom*,' every fifteen minutes, for six hours."

Aiko dimpled, hand to mouth, and Chandy John wondered why beauty existed and what it meant and how it had such power. And then guilt rose and bobbed like a corpse on a pond. *Is Dawn over, then? The pyre's blue smoke dissipated? Well?* Yellow ribbons. *You sent them away. What price ambition, Chandy John?*

"And your new apartment? Everything okay for you?"

"Fine thanks, Aiko."

"You're on the same side of the apartment block as me, right? With a view up the slope to the particle lab?"

"That's right. I can keep an eye on you all from my sofa."

"In the evenings, I often just sit and watch the light fade and the moon rise. It's beautiful, when the skies are clear."

"I can believe it. Got to be better than a view of Bengaluru concrete." Chandy John peered at his salad: a 'Toda Special', claimed the cafeteria, hinting at cheese made from fresh buffalo-milk, but the white slab on Chandy's plate looked as processed as a slab of plastic.

"I hope you won't miss CCIT too much? Everyone says it's a good place to work, and Vinayak is, well, Vinayak."

Chandy John rolled his eyes. "I know. Fifty years ago, he'd have been going on Hindutva marches and lynching foreigners. Like some BJP throw-back."

"You think? Suresh always said Vinayak wasn't any kind of Hindu, not even an extremist."

"Maybe. But it doesn't matter; whatever he is, we have to work with him. The politics of science. Anyway, to answer your question, I couldn't stay in Bengaluru. Partly because of the memories, but also – "

"Yes?"

"Well. Bhabha-Yamada is on top of the world, and Bengaluru is down on the Deccan. Upwards just seems like a natural direction of travel, you know?" Now that he expressed it, it sounded feeble. "Everything goes up, if it can. Growth is upward motion."

This is what I meant to say. To leave Bengaluru's techno-hub for high Udhagamandalam, atop the blue Nilgiri mountains, is simply to follow an ineluctable flow. All things strain to escape earth's dull pull: plants, hope, smoke, souls. All seek some kind of confluence among the peaks, or beyond; some kind of absorption; smoke into sky. Some kind of union.

"Lots of things move in the other direction, Chandy. Water. Cosmic rays."

"Yes, Aiko. You're right." *Yes, but: steam, mist, clouds. Sublimations and evaporations. We all fall; but still we strive. That's the point. And cosmic rays simply pass through us on their own journey towards their own summit. Their alignments are not ours.*

"Something I need to ask you, Aiko. At some point, I'll need to re-run Suresh's last hypersim. Obviously, the lab-books and autologs have all the key information – the program version, the main settings, significance limits, all that. But I need to know about the things that don't get recorded. Can you help?"

"Things that don't get recorded?"

"You know. Everybody has their own way of doing things, conscious or unconscious. And it's hardly ever written down. Maybe you saw Suresh do something different?"

"Once you're in the Cage, nobody can see you. You're on your own. At least – " Aiko hesitated, and looked towards the window. The sun had gone. "Look. The only thing he did differently, as far as I know, was that he took something in with him. Something that Vinayak gave him. And I only know that because Vinayak went half-mad looking for it, afterwards. He was more concerned about this whatever-it-was than about poor Suresh."

"Strange. Some sort of data-sink? I'll ask Vinayak."

"Good luck. Have you managed to get any idea of what he did to the program yet, by the way?"

"Not yet. I've got a meeting scheduled with him at the end of the week. I'll raise it then."

"Thanks. Okay – I've got to go. I'm expecting a call from my parents." Aiko stood, forehead marred by a tiny frown. "Are you not eating your sandwich?"

"Just not hungry. Travelling doesn't agree with me, I suppose."

"I understand. But do take it back to your apartment – you'll be hungry later."

"In fact, I thought I'd pop up to the lab and look over the Cage, so I'll eat it up there. Walking up that hill has got to give me an appetite."

"Too true! See you tomorrow, Chandy."

"Good night, Aiko."

❖

He does not speak to the others as he speaks to me. He asks only to set his grief against theirs, and to agree on the differential. Indeed, I do not understand why they always seek to die. It is only an equation, and equations must balance. Numbers have no bias.

If he were a number, what would he be? A variable in which the numerator is constant and the denominator grows continually? But he cannot be a number, for he is not infinitely divisible. His sum is not in this world, nor counted in any numbers I can figure.

Unless it is zero.

◈

To walk into the Cage was, at first, claustrophobic. The domed ceiling and circular chamber of its windowless housing were lined with wires and circuitry, giving visitors the impression that they had been shrunk and trapped within a hard drive. The feeling of *capture* was exacerbated by the mesh which had given the Cage its name: a filigree lacework of fine wires, making a dome within a dome. This fine metal network, connected to the circuitry on ceiling and walls at multiple points above and around, did indeed resemble nothing more than a very large birdcage; a prison for those who wish to fly.

Centrally positioned on the floor within the Cage, incongruous and battered, was an old office chair of the type that sits on a wheeled tripod and swivels according to the sitter's whim. And gaffer-taped to one of the arms of the chair, its spiralled wires leading to a ground level connector, was a large on-off switch. Nothing more; for nothing more was needed. The simulation program was made ready in the particle lab proper, adjacent to the Cage. The observer would enter the Cage – closing the mesh door behind them with the greatest of care – and sit; and then, when ready, would push the switch, and expose themselves to all the infinities of every eternity.

Chandy sat in the chair, sandwich packet on his lap, immersed in the Cage's dead air and brutal silence. Grief, he reflected, is like a drug; when you've lost everything you love, it's all that's left to you of those you lost, so how can you give it up? But then a stronger part of him rebelled: stop this self-indulgence! Look at Jurgen: not just his family, but his country – indeed most of the entire *continent* he called home – are smoke and ashes. Yet he continues. Look at Aiko: those parts of Japan that escaped the rising sea are now under Chinese control; PRC soldiers trample cherry blossom each day, and each week she hears more horrors from the country of her birth. Yet she too, she continues. What makes *your* grief so special, Chandy John? Is it not – *fungible?*

No – Jurgen and Aiko can blame externalities, but I – I cannot. Had I not chosen ambition over family, we would still be together, somewhere, Dawn and Abhishek and I. Chandy swivelled on the chair, so that it faced towards the Cage exit. *There is no pain like mine.*

He got up, catching the sandwich as it slid off his knees; the packet was smudged black. His hands too. A finger, run along the chair arm, collected a berm of fine black dust. *Electrostatic precipitation? Something to talk to the team about.* He binned the food on his way out of the lab; the door lock clicked into place behind him, and he hunched under his coat. *Oh, for the warmth of Kerala!* And then, that under-the-microscope sensation again; involuntarily, he turned to his right and looked towards the trees. There was a figure among the detectors: Thiru, snail-pacing from his shed to the path. He had a blue plastic sack in one hand, and an electric torch in the other. Chandy couldn't tell whether the old man was looking at him or not, but waved, just in case. Thiru made no answering gesture.

As Chandy walked past the sensor at the top of the path, the solar-powered diode posts that lined the walkway flickered into life, delineating the track's gentle, descending curve. Gravel chinked beneath his shoes; cool air washed him with the clean tang of eucalyptus. Towards the bottom of the path, the apartment block raised its black angles, a dark mass against a star-speckled sky, and he tried to identify his living room among the ranks and rows of windows. Counting up and along gave him a candidate, but he must, he thought, be in error, as it was clearly occupied. Someone, a man, stood pressed to the window, his face palely illuminated by one of the external downlights of the building. Had the apartment light been on, he'd have been visible only in silhouette, but the window was unlit; he stood there in darkness, watching Chandy John.

❖

Dr C. John walks as one who is weary and heavy-laden. Perhaps it is because he has no family now. Dr A. Tanaka, who is beautiful and sad, told me. The Bangalore flyover collapse, eighteen months ago. The concrete contained iron pyrites; in the presence of water there was a transfer of electrons from iron atoms to oxygen atoms. The key equation is $4\,Fe^{2+} + 4\,H^+ + O_2 \rightarrow 4\,Fe^{3+} + 2\,H_2O$. Rust splits concrete into sandy rubble. The differential was such that they died beneath the juggernaut.

When a man is hanged, his feet balance the exact centre of the Earth against the infinite void. Period is independent of amplitude in a simple pendulum.

If there were love within me, and I were young, I would love Dr A. Tanaka; but she loves Dr C. John.

If there were balance, the net of grief would be a centreless circle, and all pain null.

❖

Chandy John's apartment was on the second floor; hardly worth taking the lift. He climbed the stairs slowly, as if burdened, counting each tread silently: a rosary of steps. The fire door creaked as he pushed it open; he turned to the right and walked past a series of doors, all identical except for the number affixed to each. At Apartment 89, he stopped, tapped his PIN into the lockpanel, and pushed open the door – but immediately paused, hand on the hallway light switch. An odd effect: it was as though an echo from inside the apartment died as he entered. A child's laughter; someone singing an English nursery rhyme. *Little boy blue.* Neighbours, perhaps. Chandy listened, head cocked: but heard only a familiar silence. He closed the apartment door and continued through the hall; thin tracks in the carpet led to the HumVac autocleaner, parked in its charger by the front door. Its standby diode winked at Chandy John, as if to say that life were no more than an electronic jest.

In the living room, he leant against the windowsill, face against the glazing. As Aiko had said, the aspect from this side of the apartment block was pleasant. On a clear day, he would look up to the green slopes and precise arrays of cosmic ray detectors above Bhabha-Yamada, all framed by the surrounding stands of eucalyptus. Better still – thanks to the minimal levels of light pollution here in the mountains – on a clear night he would see his boyhood obsessions and lifelong companions: the stars, the stars, the stars. Like tonight, indeed. Beyond the black silhouettes of eucalyptus and up, up, in the unimaginably populated sky: such distant, complex beauty! There Chitra, the bluest of all stars; there Krittika, or the Pleiades; and there, the giant, eternal moon. In Chandy John's childhood, its cold face had been unsullied silver; now it displayed the slurry of Chandra Corporation's mines – visible even from Earth – like a black *tilaka*. But even as he delighted in this cosmic tapestry, mist gathered behind the moon-milky OMV laboratory at the top of the hill, smothered the Cage's domed housing and then rolled down the slope and over the serried detectors towards his apartment. Soon it reached his window and pressed against the glass, like a forgotten guest seeking admittance. His flesh rose in tiny bumps.

Listen.

He stepped back. The apartment was so cold.

Listen.

Chandy shook his head. Time to unpack his bedding; it had been a long day.

Listen. This silence is insupportable. It whispers to you of those who are no longer here: a roar of nothingness that deafens you. Exchange it!

"It's time to move on," said Chandy John. He had the feeling that he, or someone very like him, had said this before: today, or many years ago and many times since. As he turned and walked away from the window, he felt his stomach clutch emptily: the tiresome demands of flesh that existed without purpose.

Do you agree?

Chandy turned, first one way, and then another, as though the bare surfaces of the apartment might furnish an answer. The silence built a wall, higher and higher. He shuddered, overcome by an immediate, pressing sensation of utter solitude.

You are alone, because you sent them away, and they died.

According to the Hamsa Corporation database, someone, it must have been Dawn, had said *'Hamsa, stop'*; maybe Abhishek was carsick. Their vehicle had turned into a lay-by on the great Bengaluru flyover, built in the 2030s to take congestion out of the city. That the giant pillar supporting that particular section of the flyover chose that particular moment to announce its decades-old illness was a coincidence of fate, a cosmic joke, that Chandy John still could not fathom. *Poor-grade material,* they said, *riddled with iron. Should never have been used. But standards were different in those days. And pre-climate change, there was less rain.* But there it was: years of monsoons had reacted with the iron and turned the pillars to columns of talc. Sick concrete syndrome. The fall would almost certainly have killed them; but, as though fate wanted to be absolutely sure, their hamsa fell into the path of several hundred tons of semi-processed moon-ore travelling at eighty miles an hour.

Chandy had avoided hamsas ever since – even their colour triggered a kind of heartsick nausea – until today's final journey to Bhabha-Yamada. To enter that (different, but fungible) vehicle, this morning, was to feel the old, vibrant reality – the reality before the flyover collapse made realities bifurcate, and left him in the wrong one – nudging this new, dead one. The older one had felt so much more authentic. How could such vivid lives, such joy and energy, simply cease? It made no sense. During the journey, to avoid looking at the emptiness in the opposite seats, he'd twisted to one side, his face to the shatterproof glass. The hamsa followed the road beneath the flyover, weaving between Chandra Corporation moon-ore juggernauts, and Chandy John saw swarms of construction bots ratcheting and juddering up and down guide cables, their metal jackets glinting. Still reinforcing or replacing each of the hundreds of flyover pillars, nearly two years later.

"You are travelling with Hamsa Corporation, the world's pre-eminent provider of autonomous vehicles. We thank you for your custom."

Somewhere, Dawn and Abhishek had stopped in a different lay-by, or had travelled to Abhishek's grandparents in Mattoor on a different day, or had not travelled at all, or had travelled with Chandy John. Somewhere, they lived still; somewhere else, Chandy John had died with them.

"You are travelling with Hamsa Corporation ..."

Somewhere, spending time with his family had been more important than another weekend in the lab, more valuable than another swathe of numbers.

"You are travelling ..."

"It's time to move on!" Chandy identified the packing box that contained his bedclothes, and upended it on the sofa. Enough for one day, he thought.

Enough for two lives? Or three?

Enough.

FLOWPOINTS: 28657-1597

"So," said Vinayak. This was his 'method': an introductory comment of no meaning followed by a hostile stare. Chandy John had developed a counter-gambit within a week of joining Bhabha-Yamada: he simply met Vinayak's gaze and remained silent until Vinayak deigned to share his thoughts. Other staff, he knew, were intimidated into babbling nervously; he suspected Vinayak enjoyed this.

"Suresh's final simulation run."

"Yes," said Chandy John, and let silence take its course again. Vinayak refilled his glass of water from a small jug. Chandy John noticed a lump under the skin of Vinayak's throat, like a goitre, that moved each time he swallowed.

"It is time to replicate it."

"Not quite."

Outside, the sun cut neat shadows from a crepe-paper lawn. Through the open window, Chandy John heard a far-off bell: the Union Church, perhaps, down in the old part of Udhagamandalam. Vinayak reached for his glass, and took a small packet from the sachets ranked next to the Mysore tiger desk toy. He shook some powder into his water, very slowly, with both hands; like an alcoholic trying to conceal a tremor. Green dust fell outside the glass and made a Holi splatter pattern on the teak.

"I was making a statement; not asking a question." Vinayak articulated each word discretely; precise nails tapped into a polished sentence.

Chandy John took a deep breath. "Vinayak, you're asking us to run the hypersim based on a program altered in ways you're not sharing with us. If you've made improvements to it, that's wonderful, but we need to know what they are. What have you pointed it at? What exactly are we looking for when we sit in the Cage? You can't expect us to go in there half-blind. It's unreasonable."

Very gently, Vinayak placed the empty sachet against the mechanical Mysore tiger. The death of the tin Englishman filled the room with silent echoes. *He's been screaming for three centuries,* thought Chandy John. *Slowly dying, ever since Tipu Sultan fought the British for the right to rule the South.* When Vinayak spoke, Chandy had to strain to hear.

"It seems that you wish to tell me what I cannot expect. I will let that pass, for the moment. But let me tell *you* ..." Vinayak paused; something had caught in his throat, and he coughed spasmodically, as though the office air choked him. When he continued, his voice was eggshell-brittle. "Let me tell you what I *can* and *do* expect. You saw the pattern, did you not? In Suresh's data?"

"The precipitous decline in linker particle – sorry, OMV – flow? And the prime number relationship?"

"Yes. The transfer bridge is failing." Vinayak shuddered. "And the rate of failure follows a Fibonacci prime number relationship. Each successive flowpoint quantum – a lower Fibonacci prime. The energy decrease is catastrophic – catastrophic!"

"On that point, I do wonder if we are seeing an artefact. I can think of no reason for the OMV flow reducing in a manner corresponding to Fibonacci primes."

"Artefact? Look! Look at the last measurement!" Vinayak angled a monitor screen towards Chandy. "Multiple repetitions. Different instruments, different methodologies. All give the same measurement: an OMV quantum of 28,657."

"But if the artefact is at the OMV side, not our side – "

"Enough speculation! The point is that the flow is declining far more quickly than I could have expected. At a level of 28,657, we can expect only seven more transfer events – and the last of those will be negligible ..." Vinayak's breathing was deep and laboured; his chest shuddered with each intake, as if it were pulling precious air through wet cloth. "Naturally, therefore, I have re-engineered the hypersim program to increase the probability of another bridge being formed. You don't need to know the details of the changes. You only need to run the hypersim from the Cage, in the normal way, and when you see an OMV source, you need to grasp it. With both hyper-simulated hands, as it were. That is what I *expect*."

Chandy John chose his words carefully. "It's fantastic that you have that kind of expertise. But the hypersim program – it's Jurgen's baby. And he's very good at what he does. How about bringing him up to speed with – "

"Listen. The foreigner has a job. If it fatigues him, I can arrange that it is no longer a problem for him. Understand?"

And if poor sad Wehmeier is out on the street, why, so are the three other Euro-refugees he supports. "Yes. I understand."

"Good. Now, when do you intend to run the program? Tonight would be highly convenient, by the way." Vinayak had pulled open a desk drawer and taken some small object from it. He held it between his two hands, moving palm against palm in gentle, circular motions, as though warming – or being warmed by – whatever he held.

"First of all, Aiko and Jurgen need to set up the hypersim for me. They will replicate the conditions of Suresh's run from autolog data, of course. But without further information regarding the programming changes, they'll have to do a dummy run, without a human observer. For safety purposes, as well as for scientific rigour."

"Then do the dummy run tonight. And the real replication tomorrow."

"I can't do a run tomorrow; probably not for days. I've been testing the Cage background circuits and sub-systems all week. My exposure is at the limit." Chandy John patted the clip-on badge at this chest; it fluoresced a dull amber. They both knew that Jurgen's, as always, would be glowing red.

Vinayak leaned back in his chair and exhaled through gritted teeth. That cold, dark stare again. Chandy John waited. Eventually, Vinayak nodded to himself, looked down, opened his drawer and replaced whatever it was he had removed. Chandy John caught a flash of yellow.

"Very well. You have one week for exposure recovery. This day next week, we will have another meeting. That *will* be immediately prior to the replication run. Understand?"

"Yes," said Chandy John.

As Chandy left the office, he glanced behind him. Vinayak was staring out of the office window into the mist. He was holding the desk toy again; *up and down, up and down.* The angle was such that the British soldier seemed to look at Chandy in supplication.

Help me. You can help me. Do you agree?

❖

The next exchange approaches. He has told me. With each one, he becomes less; yet each such diminishment compounds his pain.

I would release him if I could. Indeed, I tried; before Professor S. Tharakan found such numbers as do not balance, and the pattern they hold, I took the rope from my shed and held it to my neck. I imagined my own kicking end. Annulment.

And then I refused that path. "I do not agree," I said. But it meant nothing to me, and so nothing came of it.

And then, when the dying day made a jewelled necklace on each dripping leaf, Professor S. Tharakan went to the Cage; and later he went to the trees, and removed his clothes, and dug out his own eyes while the jackal called of nothingness to the empty night.

Should we grieve – or should we rejoice? After all, the Professor has escaped the push and pull of all worldlings' cares. His mind wanders a place, between realities, that is not a place.

But it was an inadequate balancing. The equation is an ugly one, and unresolved.

He will come from the mist, the Englishman, and pose another.

❖

"It is like feeling in the dark," grumbled Wehmeier. "A foolish way to do science." He hammered at his keyboard, then swiped at a screen, highlighting a block of code in livid red. They had been setting up the Cage and tweaking the hypersim program all day; Wehmeier had chewed the white off his nails, and now had resorted to pulling at his thinning hair.

"Sorry, Jurgen. In the end, our jobs depend on keeping Vinayak happy." Chandy John turned to Aiko's desk for support, but her chair was empty. At the end of the lab, through the open Cage door, he saw her neat profile bent over the Cage's internal filaments. "That's life, I'm afraid."

"Mm. For some of us."

"That's not fair, Jurgen. I know what you're saying, and I know Vinayak's attitude to foreigners stinks, but I'm beginning to think we – all of us – have bigger problems than that on our hands. I'm really not convinced Vinayak is completely stable and rational any more."

"For example?"

"For example, to get the okay for our next publication, I've had to agree to his unique spin on the linker particle story."

"Ah! The paper referencing Deutsch's theory." Aiko had returned; she peeled off disposable latex gloves, streaked with black powder, balled them together and dropped them into a bin.

"Deutsch? Fungible realities? Fairy stories!" Jurgen's contempt was palpable, and had been since Chandy John first advanced Deutsch as, not quite an explanation, but another piece of the linker particle puzzle. Aiko, always the quiet force behind any lab meeting, had put forward a thread and loom analogy, and Chandy John had taken it up:

"We're part of this tapestry, this universe, each of us contributing a unique thread to this closely woven reality. But all the time, the threads are splitting, each of them, to make other tapestries with different patterns, above and below and next to ours. Some threads end in one tapestry, but continue in another. Multiple tapestries, layer upon layer and rank upon rank of them, forever and ever, amen. And we're never aware of any of them other than our own. But suppose that, in some dimension, different realities become closely apposed? You could push a thread from one tapestry into another, maybe retwine it with its counterpart."

Jurgen had snorted: "In that case, Chandy, you'd see the extra thread. You can't destroy energy; it has to balance."

"Yes," Chandy had said, "but in this case maybe it's a bit like an accountant's balance sheet. Debits equal credits. If you push a negative into the other reality, it will spit out a balancing positive."

Jurgen had frowned: "Then what is it that our reality loses to balance the inward flow of linker particles?"

"I don't know Jurgen; I just don't know."

"So what does Vinayak now tell us, in his great wisdom?" Wehmeier drew down one side of his mouth; the effect was one of infinite cynicism.

"Well, he's okay with the concept that the linkers are streaming from another reality into this one. He also accepts that the linker decline could reflect the alternative realities drifting apart, such that the particle bridge – whatever it is – no longer spans the alternative universes effectively. Together with the numbers we generated, he agrees there's enough there for a paper."

Wehmeier sighed deeply, as though struggling with a disappointment that was the only real thing in every possible universe. His upside-down smile spread to both sides of his mouth. "But? There is a *but*, is there not?"

"*But* he doesn't want us to mention Deutsch. He wants us to write the paper with reference to Jyotisha."

"Jyotisha?" Aiko's smile had fled. "Hindu astrology? *Astrology?*"

"I know. I know."

"Explain, please." Wehmeier's smile – now the right way up – seemed to say: *You see where Deutsch's foolishness leads?*

"In particular, he wants us to call it the *bandhu* theory, *bandhu* being the astrological connection between the inner and outer worlds. Which he sees as a metaphor for the linker bridge. And under the circumstances – employment-wise – I am afraid we have to live with that."

In fact, Chandy John had put up more resistance than that.

"Failing to cite prior work is hardly congruent with the culture of scientific research," he had said, while the tin tiger mauled the British soldier.

"You should embrace your true culture. Not the half-formed day-dreams of a dead foreigner." Vinayak's cold anger had been palpable.

"I am happy to embrace culture and truth wherever I find them."

"And while you are employed at Bhabha-Yamada, you will find, and espouse, truth where I tell you it is found. In whatever so-called reality I choose. Clear?"

But Wehmeier knew nothing of Chandy John's efforts, and his disgust was palpable. "So. That is your problem, I think. Mine is to set up the dummy run, without knowing what Vinayak has done to my program. If you will excuse me." He turned back to his monitor, raising steepled fingers, all gnawed cuticles and angry hangnails, to his mouth.

Chandy John sighed; Aiko smiled. "It's late," she said. "You might as well leave us to it. The tests could go on half the night."

"Are you sure?"

"Of course. There's nothing else you can do at the moment."

"Okay. Thanks. Good night all. See you tomorrow."

"Night, Chandy." Aiko took another pair of gloves from the box, and looked over her shoulder towards the Cage. Wehmeier waved one hand in the air without turning around; in front of him, lines of code had been replaced by a black screen on which pale points briefly glimmered, and then spiralled inwards and disappeared, as if drawn into a central well of darkness.

As Chandy John walked back down towards the campus proper, with the dying day's sun to one side of him, the mists descended again. Briefly, he thought he saw someone – Thiru? – keeping pace with him, but realised it was his own shadow projected onto the mists to his right, among the black silhouettes of eucalyptus trees twenty to thirty metres away. As the grey cloud thinned or thickened, so the shadow appeared further away or closer; sometimes it seemed to move of its own accord, according – Chandy John guessed – to currents of air dispersing or concentrating the mist, giving the impression of, say, an arm being held back when Chandy John's own arm swung forward, or of a head dipped in contemplation when Chandy John looked up. *Wehmeier is right,* he thought. *This is how the stories of the Bhabha-Yamada ghost got started. The 'Brocken spectre' optical illusion.*

Life is illusion, came the whispered answer. *You too are a shadow in the mist.*

Chandy turned from the ever-closer, ever-darker mists, towards the sunset. The evening light had turned each droplet of moisture, on each blade of grass and leaf, into bright silver; as though the ground had grown a billion tiny mirrors that glinted and winked in delight. The little lights flicked off, and then back on again, as another cloud rolled in and past, and the cool wind made Chandy shiver; so different from his childhood home. *Right now,* he thought, *in Kerala, the sun is shining on the old churches, and fish jump in the Periyar. In Bengaluru, in the reality that was real two years and two lifetimes ago, Dawn is bathing the child, and singing some English nursery rhyme from her childhood, and I am watching and wondering how I could be so lucky.* The mists lowered, stencilling the eucalyptus trees into black skeletons, and crept down the slopes.

Some mistakes are beyond forgiveness. Don't you agree?

Driven by some vague wish, Chandy John left the path for the detector array. The damp grass darkened his shoes with moisture; the low sun made long, parallel bars of each detector's shadow. *Like threads on a loom.* He imagined the barrage of linker particles, the indescribable momentum of their journey from the depths of some reality, the numerical improbability of their capture in this one. He looked up, half-expecting to see evidence of their passage, as if the air should refract and shudder beneath this invisible bombardment; but he saw only the dark trees made into darker shadows by the mist.

FLOWPOINTS: 1597-233

"Is Aiko not here today?"

"Well ..." Wehmeier nodded towards her empty chair and shrugged. *Yes, I know she is not physically sitting in front of her console,* thought Chandy John. *That's not what I'm asking.*

"So she hasn't been in at all?"

"No."

"Is she alright?"

Wehmeier only shrugged again; he was lost in big data. Numbers go on forever. Chandy John put on headphones and spoke to his device: "Call Aiko Tanaka."

"Hello Chandy." She sounded subdued.

"Aiko – is anything wrong?"

As he listened, Chandy John looked at the sheet of A5 that had appeared overnight, stuck to the wall above Aiko's desk; an enlarged print-out of Suresh's mad extrapolation. From its vantage point it seemed to observe them all, like a unitary, hypnotic eye. The graph's spiralling pattern raced jaggedly to the centre, where zero sat like an oculus capturing invisible light from an infinite void.

"Well?" asked Wehmeier, when Chandy John ended the call.

"She's off today."

"Sick?"

"Not exactly."

"Either you are sick or you are not, I think, *ja*?"

"She's upset. She saw something, she says. Last night, after she left the Cage executing its dummy run. Something outside, in the mist."

"Pah! She saw *mist* in the mist! Everyone knows the wind makes it into shapes. Even *I* ..." Wehmeier paused, his large hands suddenly balled into fists. "She is being foolish."

"Jurgen – she says it spoke to her. In English."

But Wehmeier had put on his headphones and was muttering coding instructions to the simulation program. On his console screen, stars were born, lived their fiery lives, and died in blossoming supernovae; new constellations made divine conjunctions and divorced again; black holes opened like the maws of hell and collapsed into dark singularities.

Chandy John got up and put on his coat.

"By the way." Jurgen called over his shoulder as Chandy John reached the door. "Vinayak's looking for you. He wants to see you. Immediately."

"Wonderful."

❖

"It haunts me. I can't escape it." Aiko's voice flatlined, as though something dead were speaking. Chandy John fought the impulse to hug her. *She's not smiling,* he thought; *I've known her all this time, and I've only just realised she smiles all the time. Usually.*

"Escape what, Aiko? What do you mean?" Chandy John had persuaded her to leave the safety of her flat, and they were walking from the apartment block towards the stamped path that led up the hill to the OMV laboratory. *"And then, if you want to go back, I'll walk back with you; and if you want to stay in the lab, we'll be there with you until you want to leave, and then we'll leave too. Or I will, at least."*

"This terrible thing that I've done. The way I've failed those who needed me. Worse."

"Aiko – this is silly. Stop, now."

"But the shame doesn't stop, and why should it? It follows me, and just builds and builds and builds. And, I know this sounds mad, but it's like it's been personified. As though it's so big, so unforgivable, that it's taken on a shape, and found a voice." Aiko paused, and knuckled at her eyes. "And now, now, it's as though there's somebody else there, telling me about their own crimes, and that doesn't make it better, it just makes me realise that there is nothing good or just in this whole shitty, *cruel* world. Kind people always get crushed, selfishness always wins, and I – I am part of that."

"Now I *know* you're talking nonsense, Aiko. What terrible thing do you think you've done? Have you teased Jurgen and made him blush? Oh, I know – you booked a Bhabha-Yamada hamsa for personal use, didn't you? I shall tell Vinayak."

"It's a bit worse than that. You see, I killed my parents."

"What! Don't be ridiculous – you were on the phone to them the other day!"

"Yes. But they're dead now, and I've known for months how it would end if I did nothing, and I did nothing. When I left them, with PRC troop carriers anchored off the coast, I just knew Japan was finished. I *knew* it. But I still went – because I could, and I wanted to. And then, when it became clear that the occupation was going to be even worse than anyone had thought, I could have gone back, to look after them. But I didn't. I stayed here, Chandy."

"Aiko – it would have been madness to return. What could you have done? You'd have just been soldier fodder. Imagine what *that* would have done to your parents."

"Oh, I can construct all kinds of justifications. But in the end, they all fall down before the one fact: I failed them when they needed me, and it was the death of them."

"I'm very sorry about your parents – you should have said something – but it was *not your fault.*"

"He speaks to me, Chandy. In the mist. In my room at night. In the Cage. He shows me such – such *horror.* The things that have happened; that people do to each other. Even children. Why continue, he says; why wallow in this filth? There are better worlds, just a short step away."

"Please, Aiko – stop this."

"And then he shows me how life could be – how it *is,* somewhere else. The climate hasn't got angry, the seas haven't spilled over, my childhood home hasn't been commandeered by some pig-ignorant Communist Party of China apparatchik, and my parents haven't died on the pavement outside their own door. And you – you and I – "

Something clutched at Chandy's heart and pulled it askew. *Say something.* But Aiko had moved on.

"Exchange it, he says. This life, for a better. Do you agree? And Chandy – it's so, so difficult not to."

"There's nobody there, Aiko! You must stop giving weight to these illusions."

"This is how it started with Suresh, isn't it? Seeing things. Hearing things. And look at him now."

"No! Everybody sees shapes in the mist. All that means is that we all have the same retinal physiology. It's like Jurgen always says: Brocken spectres. Your own shadow is cast on the mist. *An optical effect known for centuries,* ja?" Chandy John's effort to mimic Wehmeier's accent was clumsy.

"Sometimes the sun is behind the shape. Not behind the person seeing it. And shadows don't speak."

"Listen. The mist and the mountains – of course we'll get odd sound effects. Echoes. Sometimes you hear a dog barking in the valley, and you'd think it was right next to you. Two minutes later, and the sound barely reaches. Combine that with lack of sleep, and the grief of bereavement, and the stress you've been under, and the propensity for the human mind to think in words – well. Really, Aiko – it's not just you." *Trust me on that one.*

Under their feet, gravel rubbed shoulders with gravel: scrape and chink. On the slopes above them, the detectors sat squatly in the grass; close to them, at the bottom of the hill, Chandy John saw a figure hunched over the ground.

"Let's go and talk to Thirukumar," he said.

The old man had been pulling up some weeds that grew around a telecomms booster unit: they lay on the grass tidily, stems aligned so as to be parallel, roots pointing one way, tips the other. He rose slowly as they approached him, with the stepwise unfolding of the elderly: knees, hips and neck in turn. He nodded unsmilingly at Chandy John's greeting before unconsciously adding to his own taciturn legend – the odd old man who respects no person.

"What do you want? I'm busy."

"We want you to tell us stories about Bhabha-Yamada. We're here for myths and legends." Chandy John tried to be jocular, but failed; Thiru just looked at the ground and remained silent.

"Stories about things in the mist. People seeing things. And hearing things. It happens to everybody, right? And it means nothing. Just tricks of the eyes and the ears. Right?"

"How can I know what others see?"

"I mean, these kinds of stories have been around for ages. It's normal. People have been seeing odd things around here for years and years, haven't they?"

"Three hundred years. He told me."

"I'm sorry?"

"We cannot blame him for wanting what he wants."

"Eh? Who?" Chandy John felt the conversation slipping away from him.

Thiru looked up briefly, and then turned his eyes to his feet again. "Begging hurts nobody, whether in good English or bad Tamil. And he is much weakened now. Less mass than mist. All momentum spent. He cannot hold you. His only purchase is what you offer him."

"Thiru – what do you mean?"

"The Cauchy momentum equation is illustrative. Where sigma is the stress tensor, and the flow velocity vector field depends on time and space. He seeks only another continuum."

And as elliptical answers go, thought Chandy, *that has an eccentricity of at least 0.9.* "Thiru – "

"Suresh accepted his offer, but reneged. His equation is unsolved. It is ugly."

Chandy turned to Aiko, but she was looking at Thiru, and through him at something else.

"I repeat: balanced transactions hurt none. And he seeks only balance. Let him go."

"*Who?*"

"I am busy." Thiru slowly squatted again; there was finality in his hunched back, in the rip of plants from damp soil.

As they left the old man and walked up the path, Chandy John tried to think of a cheerful way of brushing aside Thiru's comments without at the same time seeming patronising; but he could not, and Aiko was silent. Eventually, however, she spoke, almost to herself.

"Poor Suresh."

Chandy John welcomed an end to the break in conversation, despite the subject. "Yes. He clearly hadn't been right for a while, you know. Did you see the final entry in his personal log? The 'coding' file?" Chandy made finger-quotes.

Aiko shook her head. "No. No access."

"It was strange. Just two words, on every single line."

"Really?" She was walking more quickly now, and Chandy John adjusted his stride to keep up.

"Yes. The same two words: *I agree.* Over and over again. *I agree, I agree, I agree.* One thousand, five hundred and ninety-seven times."

Aiko stopped abruptly; Chandy John had gone forward a couple of paces before he realized. They were just over half-way up the path; below them, the mist pearled and smoked over the campus. She was looking up to the OMV laboratory, her face set in the oddest expression: mouth pulled to one side and slightly open, chin up, eyes focused on something – but what? Chandy John turned to look up the path, but saw only an endless, interchangeable grey.

"Aiko?"

She hesitated, her face still raised towards the OMV lab's angles and rondure. Then she turned towards the topmost detector array.

"Look – Thiru's left his shed open, and his chair outside – and it's starting to rain."

"I'll call him."

"It's okay, Chandy – I'll walk across and close up for him. Maybe you could tell him that on the way down?"

"On the way down? I was coming up with you."

"Thanks Chandy, but I'll be fine. I know what I need to do, now. And I know you are supposed to be meeting Vinayak."

"Seems like he's managed to tell everybody except me."

"Maybe you should turn your phone on sometimes. Really, you'd better go."

"If you're sure. But promise me one thing – that you'll take a couple of days off work and rest up. Okay?"

Aiko made no response; Chandy John searched her face, but could not read its messages; her eyes welled with an unidentifiable emotion. He tried again. "Two days off work. Agreed?"

Aiko didn't seem to hear him; but she answered. "I agree."

"Good night, Aiko."

At the bottom of the slope, something made him turn and look back. Aiko was standing in the same place, her back to him, looking upwards through the arms of shifting, curling mist. As he watched, she dropped her head and set off across the detector field towards Thiru's open shed. She walked with quick, rapid steps, as though something in the thin rain harried her.

FLOWPOINTS: 233-89

"So."

Vinayak pawed at the mechanical desk toy; Chandy John waited. The clear plastic sachets of Ayurvedic medicines had proliferated.

One of them, half open, contained a black powder; so black, it seemed to suck light in and swallow it.

Watching Vinayak fumble with the tin tiger and its tin prey, Chandy John realised, with the shock of revelation, that the Bhabha-Yamada director could no longer operate it. *Neuropathy? Stroke?* But Vinayak's gaze was as intimidating as ever.

"You have executed the dummy run."

"Yes."

"And now you will repeat the hypersim event that Suresh last created."

"Yes. Soon." Chandy John patted at his exposure badge: amber fading to blue.

"Tomorrow. But there is one other thing." Vinayak pulled open a drawer and took something out; he held it in front of him, cupped in one pale hand, so that it was hidden from Chandy John. "I wish you to take this into the Cage. You must keep it during the hypersim, and when you see a new OMV source, you must hold this up to it. So that there is an interaction. Do you understand?" Vinayak placed his hand, palm down, on the desk, and opened his fingers. The thing that he held made contact with the teak surface – *toc*.

Chandy John reached for it. Some sort of stone, perhaps, or cured resin, about the size and shape of a small egg; semi-transparent, yellow as marigold, but shot through with dull orange; unusually heavy, oddly warm. "What is it?"

"Let's say that, just as yellow filters absorb blue light, this too is a kind of medium that absorbs a kind of wavelength. The OMV wavelength, perhaps."

Perhaps something showed on Chandy John's face; perhaps it was disbelief, perhaps it was dismay. In any case, Vinayak saw it. "If you do not do this, Chandy, I will know. Trust me, I will know."

"Where is this from?"

Vinayak gave a half-shrug. "Collaborators. It's not a Bhabha-Yamada development. So keep this confidential. Yes?"

"I don't understand. Is this part of an experiment? If so, where is the protocol? What's the control? How – "

"Listen!" Vinayak's hands flattened on the desk, one on each side of the metal Mysore tiger, as though he were about to leap up and tear out Chandy John's throat. "Listen carefully. I have measured all parameters. This is an essential step. You must do this. Do you understand? You must."

"Vinayak – "

"You must do this!" He bent over to cough. The smooth mass in his throat moved beneath his thin skin as, using two hands, he picked up his ever-present glass of water and sipped.

"As I have said to you already – your job is simply a matter of competently executing a simulation, of opening up another OMV channel, a new bridge. It should have been done already. This item will help. I am sure of it."

Chandy John waited. *Let him get it off his chest.*

"So much incompetence. Suresh. The others."

"Others?"

Vinayak's eyes flicked down to the badge on Chandy John's chest. "You're turning blue, Chandy. Tomorrow, then. Don't let me down."

"It would help me immensely if I had access to the simulation parameters."

"We have been through this. All you need to do is enter the Cage and run the program. Observe the net of realities. Look for Fibonacci prime intersects: five, thirteen, eighty-nine, and so on. Find a source of OMVs. You will know it when you see it. You will recognise – certain aspects. And when you know it, reach out, holding what I have given you – in both hands, mark you – and appose it to the source. Then, everything is good. Understand?"

"I understand what you want me to do. But not why."

"That's sufficient. But remember, Chandy John – hold it tight. Use both hands. If you lose this in the Cage – my displeasure will be extreme."

As if anything could be 'lost' in the Cage! But Chandy John made no comment; he was tired of the conversation, and tired of Vinayak. Looking at his face, Chandy John had the impression of paper skin glued onto dead bone; of flesh dried down to scraps and strings; of old needs that burnt in an empty body; of utter self-absorption. What had Aiko said? *Kind people always get crushed, selfishness always wins.*

He stood, and left Vinayak's office.

❖

"Of course I can make the Cage ready for you. We've done most of the set-up already. But the finalisation step is Aiko's responsibility, I think, yes?" Wehmeier folded his arms stubbornly.

"Yes, but she's still off work. You know her situation, now."

Jurgen said nothing, but his level stare had a message: *And what about my situation?*

"I know you've had – have – a painful history too, Jurgen. But, as I said, Aiko has a particularly acute need at the moment. We have to help her. And if I don't repeat Suresh's hypersim tonight, which means starting in the next hour or so, I'll be in a very difficult position. With Vinayak. You know how it is."

Wehmeier exhaled through his teeth and dropped his head. In front of him, his screen flickered soundlessly, the visual equivalent of white noise. "Okay. Okay. I will do it."

"Thank you. Exactly as for Suresh, please. Really. The smallest details – "

"I know this!" Wehmeier stood, reaching for a pile of books and documents. "First I take the hypersim manual. Here. And a universal calibrator – here. And now I go to make the Cage good. So." He stamped past Aiko's empty desk to the end of the lab, and opened the titanium door. From Chandy John's position, he could see the operator chair within; it had swivelled around to face the Cage entrance, as though someone unseen was sat there, waiting for the door to be unlocked.

"*Scheisse!*"

"Jurgen? Anything wrong?"

"I need another calibrator. This one is faulty."

"Hang on. I'll get Aiko's."

Aiko's desk was tidy, but impressively occupied: stacks of papers and books, boxes of circuitry modules, packets of energy probes and sensor spares. After a minute of futile searching on the desk's top, Chandy sat in her chair and started pulling open the drawers. As he did so, his foot nudged something on the floor; something soft that rustled as it was dislodged from its hiding place; something that slid over itself to rest against his foot. Curious, he leant back and down to see what it was; a blue plastic bag, of the sort that old Thiru used to collect debris for disposal. Its handles, loosely knotted, made a pair of bunny ears. He reached down and pulled the soft weight towards him: the bag's neck gaped.

"Oh no. Oh, Aiko."

"Have you found it?" Coming from the Cage, Jurgen's voice had a curious dead echo.

"What? Oh, the calibrator? Sorry, not yet. Hang on." Chandy pulled open a drawer. "Ah – here it is." He took Aiko's calibrator in one hand, and the blue bag in the other. On the way to the Cage, he put the bag on his own chair and covered it with his coat. "Is this what you want, Jurgen?"

"Perfect. I will tell you when it is ready. Maybe forty minutes."

"Thanks. I'll wait." Chandy John returned to his desk. As he sat, he looked again in the blue plastic bag; he reached inside and, overwhelmed by an infinite sadness, touched what it held, feeling the purpose woven into its coils.

❖

Perhaps I left the store unlocked last night. But if so, it was locked again this morning. What thief is so considerate? And who would steal the thing of least value, and leave the rest?

That weeping shade, that mist's eidolon – he can no longer open locks or doors. He is not close enough to this reality.

Perhaps I left it somewhere yesterday, and my old memory fails me. But I do not think so. No, I do not think so.

So: who then took my rope?

❖

Chandy John had only flown in the Cage twice. The first time was soon after it had been built, in the initial phase of the collaboration between Chandra Corporation and Bhabha-Yamada. Then it had been a wonderful, secret novelty – a trap to catch the elusive linker particles in the pincers of the human mind. The second time had been to witness, to corroborate, the flow of linkers as seen by Suresh. The difference between the two Cage flights, six months apart, had been marked: Jurgen's amplification of the Cage's power – by his cunning tweaks to the underpinning simulation program – had proceeded logarithmically, and the breadth and resolution of observations, the glory of the Cage's vision, had increased pari passu. But now, a year later still, with his left hand on the faux leather arm of the chair, and his right on the hypersim switch, Chandy John felt as if he stood, blinded by mist, on the edge of a great cliff. To fly in the Cage had always been to make one's mind naked, to strip it bare before the eternal, boundless possibilities of Being that stretched before and behind, and all around, forever. But the attendant emotions had always been controlled, like the fear that accompanies white-water rafting or rock climbing. Now – who knew what might happen?

"For God's sake! It's only a hypersim!" Chandy's voice was captured by the domed circuitry around him, the echoes killed at birth. With Vinayak's yellow stone in his left hand, warm and heavy, he reached for the hypersim control with the right. He pressed his thumb down, and heard the click of the switch.

❖

The hum of the cage, the exquisite trembling of its delicate bars; the blur of the *here*, the elision of the *now!* To think one's life is but one life: the absurdity of it!

See: the world of worlds in the unutterable night. Listen: their colours sing; darkness roars.

See differently: you are but one echo in a chain of echoes, and each of those the first in another chain, forever. Death is only a pause.

Dawn. Abhishek. They echo on. Their images shudder.

To change the cosmos: flick your finger against a glass of water, and watch its troubled surface. The ripples reach, and reach, and reach again.

There, Chandy John: stretch out your hand; flick this glass or that; change this or that reality, forever.

Once, you never sent them away. Once, you went with them. Once, the bridge held firm. Once, once, once; and again, once.

Who is that? A man: a thing of shadows and dark mists. A distillation of grief. But what does he say? Look, he says. Look: Dawn is singing with Abhishek. *Little boy blue.* They miss you so much.

Only reach. That's all. Reach from this failed existence to that sweet promise.

Only stretch out a hand, and take back your stolen joy, the happiness that hurts so much to see.

That's all. Just look, hold out your hand and reach.

Just look, hold it out, and reach –

FLOWPOINTS: 89-13

"What the *hell* was that!" Not a question, but an accusation. Chandy John, fists clenched, didn't recognise his own voice.

"The exposure warning was going off. I saw the flashing through the lab window. Didn't you hear the alarm?" Aiko folded her arms; her coat was damp with rain.

"I almost had them! I almost touched them!"

"Look at your badge, Chandy."

"*Screw* the badge!" He ripped the clip-on plastic from his shirt and threw it against one of the lab windows. It fell to the sill; its red glow echoed in panes made mirrors by the black night. "What are you even *doing* here? You're still off work, remember?"

Aiko looked around the OMV lab. The empty chairs stayed mute; the only movement came from Wehmeier's desk, where a monitor winked to signal the death of another cosmos.

"I just came to pick something up." Her glance flicked to the foot of her desk. "Why are you so angry, Chandy?"

Chandy John looked back at the Cage, and knuckled his eyes. His hand came away streaked with black. "Because now – " He pulled out a tissue, and wiped at his hands. "Because now I have to do the whole damn thing over again. Thanks to you."

"Sorry. And so *sorry* for following safety regulations and cutting the hypersim. Like it says on the wall, in big capitals."

"I knew what I was doing. You didn't."

"All hail the great Doctor Chandy John, who knows all."

"Don't be pathetic."

Aiko's level stare made something wither deep inside Chandy John. She looked away, with a small smile that had something in it of despair, and walked to her desk. "Forgive my inadequacies, please. I will just take what I came for, and not trouble you again."

She bent down to reach under her desk; her hand came back empty. She looked under the desk, and then on top, and then, more quickly, in her drawers; then she glanced around the lab, and, finally, looked towards Chandy John.

"Aiko."

"*What?*"

"It was me. I found it. In the bag. I took it."

Behind him, the rising hum of the Cage spoke of the need to execute the hypersim shutdown.

"I know what you wanted it for, Aiko. I just know. And I won't let you. Do you understand?"

But she was gone, walking quickly, with one hand to her face, her high ponytail waving from side to side as if in mockery: *Goodbye, Chandy John.* He would have followed her, but the *beep-beep* of a system overload warning tied him to the lab. Another Cage breakdown was unthinkable – Vinayak would fire just about everybody.

Later, once the Cage had returned to a background exposure level, Chandy John remembered Vinayak's odd demand. He patted his pockets, looked around the Cage, and then searched the lab. Nothing other than his red-fluorescing badge. Not a hint of yellow, anywhere.

❖

In the Cage, they think to capture all possible realities. But it is they that are held, pinned by the current's flow. What kind of energy is this? No soul's spasm can escape such forceps. Their grip is adamantine; their force eternal.

Yes, he is right. It comes, again. I feel it. A balancing.

Perhaps this is the one that will break him – or replace him. And then what?

Somewhere, the wheel turns on.

❖

Chandy John found himself in his flat, with no memory of returning to it.

You are alone.

The second-person soundtrack of his thoughts had been joined by a second-person perspective. Thus, he watched a fungible Chandy John move its limbs, use the toilet, walk to the bedroom: for all the world as though it were truly alive.

You sit on the single bed, staring through the window.

Outside, the moon shone briefly through the mists, glancing palely off the gravel path that led up past the OMV lab to the old eucalyptus woods.

None of this exists. This empty apartment, the concrete walls of your laboratory, the delicate, indestructible Cage – these are mere phantasms, eigenstates dependent on observation for existence. When you do not see them, they will not be; therefore, look to another reality.

"Aiko was right." Chandy John spoke at the same time as the Chandy John he watched. "You know that. Nothing but cruelty and injustice in this shitty, shitty world. Forever."

Life is illusion. Death is illusion.

Exchange them.

Do you agree?

Chandy shook his head and went to the kitchen, driven by a mechanical instinct to escape. And there, on the centre of the table, as if deliberately placed – as if it were the nexus of all worlds and the navel of every cosmos – was the blue plastic bag he had taken from beneath Aiko's desk.

Do you agree?

He weighed the bag in his hands, as if intrigued by some purpose inherent in its shifting mass. He held it by its end and pulled the blue plastic away from that which it covered. And out slid the contents, smooth as oiled hair, coil upon coil of it, thin and strong, expertly noosed: a hemp snake that pillowed infinite dreams.

FLOWPOINTS: 13-5

Look: Chandy John walks to the steep path leading from the Bhabha-Yamada apartment block to the detector array. Mists hide the moon's scars; mountain air chills his skin. He stands for a moment, and wonders if darkness really is just the absence of light. The thing that stands with him whispers: *Do you agree?*

He flaps his hand at the first of the posts that line the path – the sensor is famously erratic – until the diodes atop each knee-high pole flicker on, discharging their solar harvest over gravel trodden flat by decades of physicists' feet. The lights make a glowing chain in the mist; each link less discrete than its predecessor, all leading up, up into dissolution.

He climbs the path, touching each post as he passes it, always watching the furthest mist-fuzzed beacon. As he ascends, he imagines that he is pulling a long, loose thread from a worn tapestry. It drags behind him over the damp gravel, like a thin tail; it echoes the noosed cord he carries.

It comes easily, this stray thread; it is not part of the pattern. Nothing holds it but the pull of accidental contiguity.

❖

The tap of a goldsmith's hammer. The clutch of a scorpion; the arc of its telson. A woman in a blue sari. Ashes by the river; the boy so alone. The clamour of the machines. The ulcer of love rejected, the agony of loves lost.

Dreams, or memories; what is the difference? All are dead.

Grief's cycle turns. Again, always, forever.

❖

Look again: at the top of the path, the breeze strengthens, and Chandy John hunches inside his coat, pushing his hands deep into his pockets. The wind rolls the mists away: darkness is speckled with light. He looks up, and the constellations wink at him as though he is part of the conspiracy of spheres.

What planets are warmed by these cold points? What unguessed beings might people the infinite variety of their landscapes? Blue gods, perhaps, reigning over sidereal kingdoms where justice is sacrosanct and colours are inhaled like heady air. Indeed, Chandy has found a new god, or discovered an old one as young as a child, and its blue head nods at him. *Come,* it says. *Come, Chandy John.* And now Chandy sees that it has many heads, in continually changing superpositions and superimpositions. *One of us, at least, will look upon you kindly, in one of our infinite dreams. Only come.*

"I come," says Chandy John.

FLOWPOINTS: 5-3

Yes: here comes Chandy John, a hollow man on a cold hill. He passes the little pagodas, collecting their nightly harvest of cosmic rays and condensation. He walks past the ugly concrete that houses his laboratory. He passes the domed shell of the Cage; the weight of silence that flows from it pushes aside the mist. He climbs the last slopes, and enters the stands of black eucalypts that wait among blacker shadows.

The trees' seed pods roll beneath his feet. Roots corrugate the ground; fallen leaves hide hollows and rocks; and the returning mists cloak the spoilt moon's light. But Chandy John doesn't stumble; something guides him. It is as though he has found some kind companionship in the dark glades; a shadow to walk him safely through the wild, resin-scented woods.

From the valley, a jackal calls: *I am alone,* it wails, *this dark night and each dark night, forever.* Chandy John throws his head back and shouts: "*I know! I know!*" And then, quietly, to himself: *No longer.* The rope's soft weight bumps against his leg.

Dawn. Abhishek. Somewhere, the pattern continues. But not here. *Do you agree?*

❖

Keep looking, Chandy John. See? You clutch the bag against your chest; through its thin plastic you feel the cord, snugly coiled. Its corrugations nudge your hand: a companionable friction. The eucalyptus trees reach up to the stars; in some reality, you stand here, not by yourself, but with your wife and child. They are so close now; can you feel the warmth of their kindness; see their dear shapes in the tree-smothered shadows?

Exchange this reality for another. Find what you have lost. Do you agree?

Chandy? Chandy!

Join your dreams. Here is Union.

"Chandy John!"

So many voices. You look up to the bright moon. You count her blemishes: five black scars. You lower your eyes through the ranked stars and galaxies. *Forever and ever, amen.*

You see the branch, edged with pale moonlight, making a delicate filigree against the unfathomably deep and infinite night.

FLOWPOINTS: 3-2

I told Dr C. John, when he and Dr A. Tanaka came to speak to me. Let him go, I said. Let him go. Let there be balance.

Sometimes, when I speak, people do not hear me; or if they hear me, they do not hear what I say.

❖

You stand on tiptoe atop a dead stump and reach up. You grip the branch. The wood is smooth and cold, and your palms hurt with the pressure. The tree shudders slightly, as though with a delicate horror at what may come; but the branch holds. Yes, this will take a man's weight.

Do you agree, Chandy John?
"Chandy John!"
You throw the noosed end over the branch; the loop swings and bounces, seeking always an alignment that corresponds with the exact centre of the Earth. You catch it and make a running bowline. You pull the cord so that the knot travels upwards and tightens, gripping the eucalyptus wood. You tug at it in the traditional way; the branch bends and resists as you would expect.

❖

Oh, Chandy John. In some reality, a lifetime in the past and a cosmos away, you are bent over your schoolwork. *Young's modulus. Hooke's law. Stiffness is not the same as strength.* In this reality, you are overwhelmed by love and pity. *Poor boy – you tried so hard!*
"Chandy John!"
The rope hangs far too low; this will never do. You throw it up and over the branch, once, twice, again, five times. Now, when you stand on the stump, the noose is head-height, inviting superimposition.
The mists have come down again, very heavily; some voices are smothered, some clearer:
Chandy John!
Union: here is union.
Which of my infinite dreams do you desire?
Dawn. Abhishek.
A fleeting thing.
Come now: walk with blue gods under distant stars, where colours breathe.
Exchange this life for another.
Do you agree?
A confusion of calls, a medley of shapes. The mists hug; the moon blurs. The jackal calls: *I am alone.* No longer.
Do you agree?
"Chandy John!"

I beg you: listen. Look. Are our griefs and guilts not infinitely exchangeable? If forgiveness is impossible for one, then how can the other be forgiven? And which is 'you' and which is 'me'?

FLOWPOINTS: 2-0

"Chandy John!"

The mists form dark shapes, stumbling towards him, sobbing, arms out as though in expectation of a fall or an embrace.

"Chandy John!"

"*Aiko?*"

"Chandy, what are you doing?"

But Chandy John is silent; the cold mist slips its fingers into his. *Come away, oh Chandy John, oh Mehbooba, come away.*

"I saw you." Aiko's voice is sharp; it cuts the damp air like a glass shard from a shattered mirror. "I was awake, and saw the lights. On the path. I saw you walking up."

The mists are pushed back, and Aiko shivers in the wind. The unveiled moon picks out the rope, and jewels its hemp crowns in silver and onyx. Chandy John is silent; there is nothing to say. Aiko steps forward.

"Who was with you, Chandy?"

"Nobody. I'm alone." *This night and each dark night.* The jackal's call. *No more.*

"I saw."

"Just shapes in the mist, Aiko." *Blue gods and dead children. Loves broken and loves lost.*

Aiko looks again at the rope; the noose sways in quest of the absolute perpendicular.

"Why?" she asks. "Why?"

"Exactly," says Chandy John.

But Aiko is weeping now, uncontrollably, spasms that come from some core of being that Chandy John had never suspected to exist. It is natural for him to step towards her from beneath the branch, to hug the trembling thing, to share the pain of existence. In her shudders, he feels the exchange of known and unknown griefs, a superposition of realities; the eigenstate that comprises Chandy John and *Union* and the tree and the rope is threaded through by the old universe, the one where Aiko lives and Dawn and Abhishek are dead. One waveform collapses, and another surges upwards.

Union, something whispers from the mist. *Union. Please. Do you agree?* Chandy John looks up: the diffuse air is pearled by a distant paleness, a rumour of what day once was and might be again. Dawn approaches, surely? The mists gather and swirl; they thicken into a suggestion of substance, of interchangeable being. Aiko sees; her grip on him tightens, and her breath quickens.

"It's coming again." Aiko palms at her wet eyes; the rope sways, as though someone had brushed past it.

Do you agree?

To chase the ghosts of dead love? To live in another's reality? To end this one?

Do you agree?

"I do not agree," says Chandy John.

As they watch, the pale wisps rise and dissipate, like dew steamed from meadows in the morning sun; it seems to Chandy John that they follow, at last, an ineluctable flow towards a final, much-sought confluence. High above, blue Chitra glitters, the last star in a lightening sky; basking, it seems, in an effulgence of love. Below, as if in reflection, a glimmer of caerulean, like a sari caught by the wind. All around them, silence: not the emptiness of the void, but the quietness of peace.

"Chandy?"

He can feel her warmth, next to him, like a gift. Companionship envelops him, and sends his vision blurry with its kind union.

"Chandy, do you understand what happened? Because I don't."

"Yes," he says. "Don't worry, Aiko. We're moving on, that's all. We're moving on."

FLOWPOINTS: 00000

Dr A. Tanaka has asked for my help; she is writing a book on the history of Bhabha-Yamada, from its start as the Ooty Cosmic Ray Research Station to the present. I am glad to contribute. She is beautiful. And happy, now that she is married to Dr C. John.

But I will not tell her of grief's shadow, that English soldier, that planter: he wanted only oblivion in this reality, and union in another. There is nothing of him now but his loss, missed by none, forgotten by all. I believe that he too is happy, in some reality. Here, the mists are empty, and that is good.

Nor will I tell her of how I found Dr V. Mulgund. As though his skin had shrunk and his viscera expanded. As though some blue god had said: Burst, melt, and pluck the peeled flesh. By what was once his throat, a stone; it glowed yellow as if lit by the light from another time's sun. It had the weight of zero; as if all the worlds were annulled, all grief void, in its tiny volume.

I am guessing this was necessary for balance, but I do not know the equation.

ACKNOWLEDGEMENTS

Many thanks to Anil Menon and Miranda Miller for invaluable comments on the text. Any remaining faults and flaws are mine alone.

'The Tourist's Story' is a revised version of a story of the same name that was published as 'Another's Place' in Apeiron Review, 2015.

'Seeing John' is a revised version of a story of the same name that was published by the Aesthetica Creative Writing Award, 2017.

'Five Garlands' is a significantly revised and extended version of 'The Speckled God', e-published as a stand-alone story by Unsung Stories in 2017.

'The Dairymen' is a revised version of a story of the same title that made the last 60 of the BBC National Short Story Award, 2018, received a Special Mention in the 2018 Galley Beggar Short Story Prize, and was long-listed in the 2020 Punt Volat Spencer Parker Award for Fiction.

'The Exchange' is a revised version of a story of the same name that was awarded 'Highly Commended' in the 2020 Gatehouse Press New Fiction Prize.

☾

ABOUT THE AUTHOR

Marc Joan, a biomedical scientist, was raised in South India and now lives in England.

marc-joan.com

C

ABOUT DEIXIS PRESS

Deixis Press is an independent publisher of fiction, usually with a darker edge. Our aim is to discover, commission, and curate works of literary art. Every book published by Deixis Press is hand-picked and adored from submission to release and beyond.

www.deixis.press

Lightning Source UK Ltd.
Milton Keynes UK
UKHW010740280722
406510UK00002B/358

9 781739 708108